MARVEL-V

AMERICA CHAVEZ

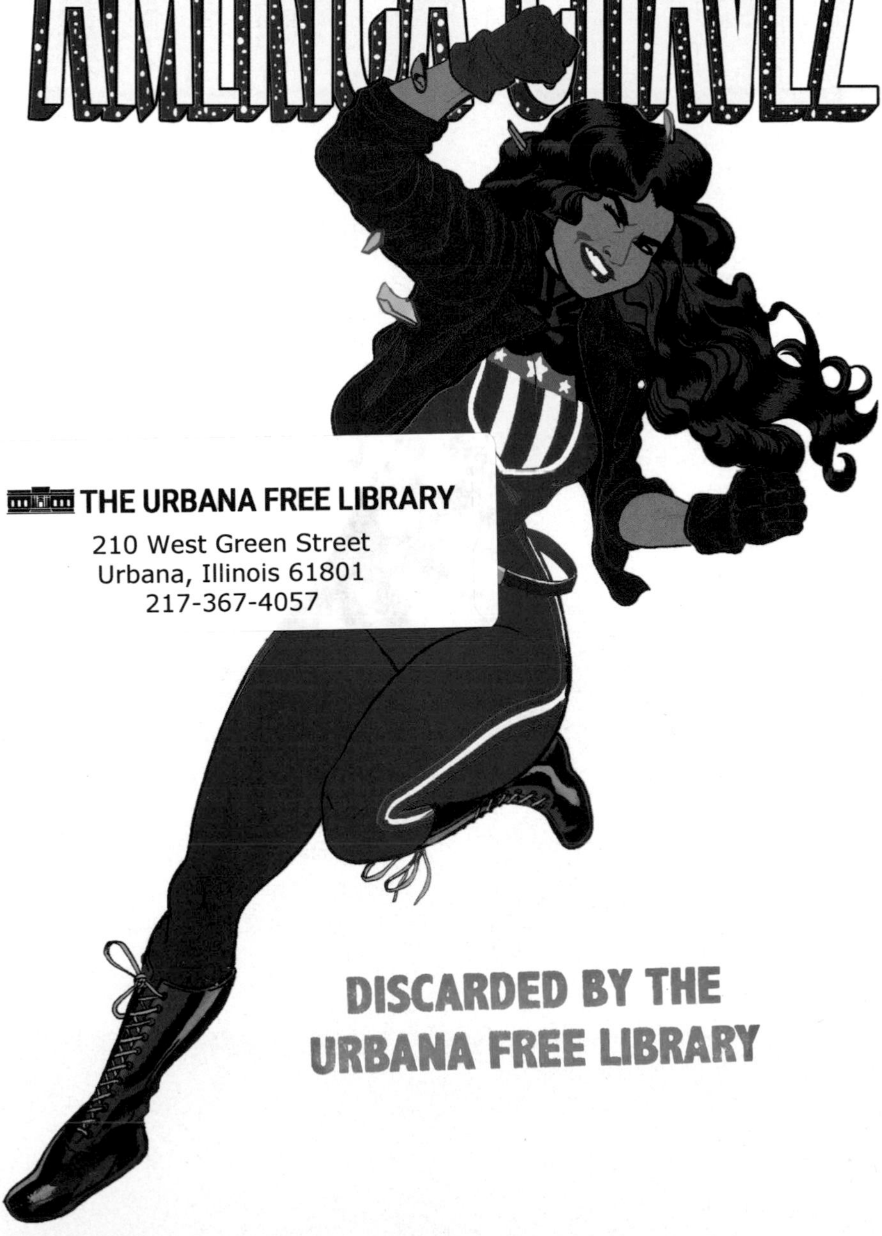

MARVEL-VERSE
AMERICA CHAVEZ

AMERICA CHAVEZ: MARVEL LEGACY PRIMER

WRITER: **ROBBIE THOMPSON**

ARTIST: **DAVID LÓPEZ**

COLORIST: **JOSÉ VILLARRUBIA**

LETTERER: **TRAVIS LANHAM**

ASSISTANT EDITOR: **KATHLEEN WISNESKI**

EDITOR: **DARREN SHAN**

MARVEL NOW! POINT ONE #1

WRITER: **KIERON GILLEN**

ARTISTS: **JAMIE McKELVIE** WITH **MIKE NORTON**

COLORIST: **MATTHEW WILSON**

LETTERER: **VC's CLAYTON COWLES**

COVER ART: **ADI GRANOV**

ASSISTANT EDITOR: **JAKE THOMAS**

EDITOR: **LAUREN SANKOVITCH**

MARVEL-VERSE: AMERICA CHAVEZ. Contains material originally published in magazine form as YOUNG AVENGERS (2013) #3, AMERICA (2017) #1-2 and #11-12, and MARVEL NOW! POINT ONE (2012) #1. First printing 2022. ISBN 978-1-302-93394-4. Published by MARVEL WORLDWIDE, INC., a subsidiary of MARVEL ENTERTAINMENT, LLC. OFFICE OF PUBLICATION: 1290 Avenue of the Americas, New York, NY 10104. © 2022 MARVEL No similarity between any of the names, characters, persons, and/or institutions in this book with those of any living or dead person or institution is intended, and any such similarity which may exist is purely coincidental. **Printed in Canada.** KEVIN FEIGE, Chief Creative Officer; DAN BUCKLEY, President, Marvel Entertainment; JOE QUESADA, EVP & Creative Director; DAVID BOGART, Associate Publisher & SVP of Talent Affairs; TOM BREVOORT, VP, Executive Editor; NICK LOWE, Executive Editor, VP of Content, Digital Publishing; DAVID GABRIEL, VP of Print & Digital Publishing; MARK ANNUNZIATO, VP of Planning & Forecasting; JEFF YOUNGQUIST, VP of Production & Special Projects; ALEX MORALES, Director of Publishing Operations; DAN EDINGTON, Director of Editorial Operations; RICKEY PURDIN, Director of Talent Relations; JENNIFER GRÜNWALD, Director of Production & Special Projects; SUSAN CRESPI, Production Manager; STAN LEE, Chairman Emeritus. For information regarding advertising in Marvel Comics or on Marvel.com, please contact Vit DeBellis, Custom Solutions & Integrated Advertising Manager, at vdebellis@marvel.com. For Marvel subscription inquiries, please call 888-511-5480. **Manufactured between 1/7/2022 and 2/8/2022 by SOLISCO PRINTERS, SCOTT, QC, CANADA.**

10 9 8 7 6 5 4 3 2 1

YOUNG AVENGERS #3

WRITER: **KIERON GILLEN**
ARTISTS: **JAMIE McKELVIE** WITH **MIKE NORTON**
COLORIST: **MATTHEW WILSON**
LETTERER: VC's **CLAYTON COWLES**
COVER ART: **JAMIE McKELVIE & MATTHEW WILSON**
ASSISTANT EDITOR: **JAKE THOMAS**
EDITOR: **LAUREN SANKOVITCH**

AMERICA #1-2

WRITER: **GABBY RIVERA**
PENCILERS: **JOE QUINONES** WITH
MING DOYLE (#2)
INKERS: **JOE RIVERA** WITH **PAOLO RIVERA** (#1)
& **MING DOYLE** (#2)
COLORIST: **JOSÉ VILLARRUBIA**
LETTERER: **TRAVIS LANHAM**
COVER ART: **JOE QUINONES** WITH **JORDAN GIBSON** (#2)
ASSISTANT EDITOR: **CHARLES BEACHAM**
ASSOCIATE EDITOR: **SARAH BRUNSTAD**
EDITOR: **WIL MOSS**
EXECUTIVE EDITOR: **TOM BREVOORT**

AMERICA #11-12

WRITER: **GABBY RIVERA**
ARTISTS: **STACEY LEE & FLAVIANO** WITH **ANNIE WU** (#12)
COLORISTS: **JORDAN GIBSON & CHRIS O'HALLORAN**
LETTERER: **TRAVIS LANHAM**
COVER ART: **JOE QUINONES**
EDITORS: **SARAH BRUNSTAD & WIL MOSS**
EXECUTIVE EDITOR: **TOM BREVOORT**

COLLECTION EDITOR: **JENNIFER GRÜNWALD** ASSISTANT EDITOR: **DANIEL KIRCHHOFFER**
ASSISTANT MANAGING EDITOR: **MAIA LOY** ASSOCIATE MANAGER, TALENT RELATIONS: **LISA MONTALBANO**
ASSOCIATE MANAGER, DIGITAL ASSETS: **JOE HOCHSTEIN** VP PRODUCTION & SPECIAL PROJECTS: **JEFF YOUNGQUIST**
RESEARCH: **JESS HARROLD** BOOK DESIGNERS: **STACIE ZUCKER & ADAM DEL RE** WITH **JAY BOWEN**
SVP PRINT, SALES & MARKETING: **DAVID GABRIEL** EDITOR IN CHIEF: **C.B. CEBULSKI**

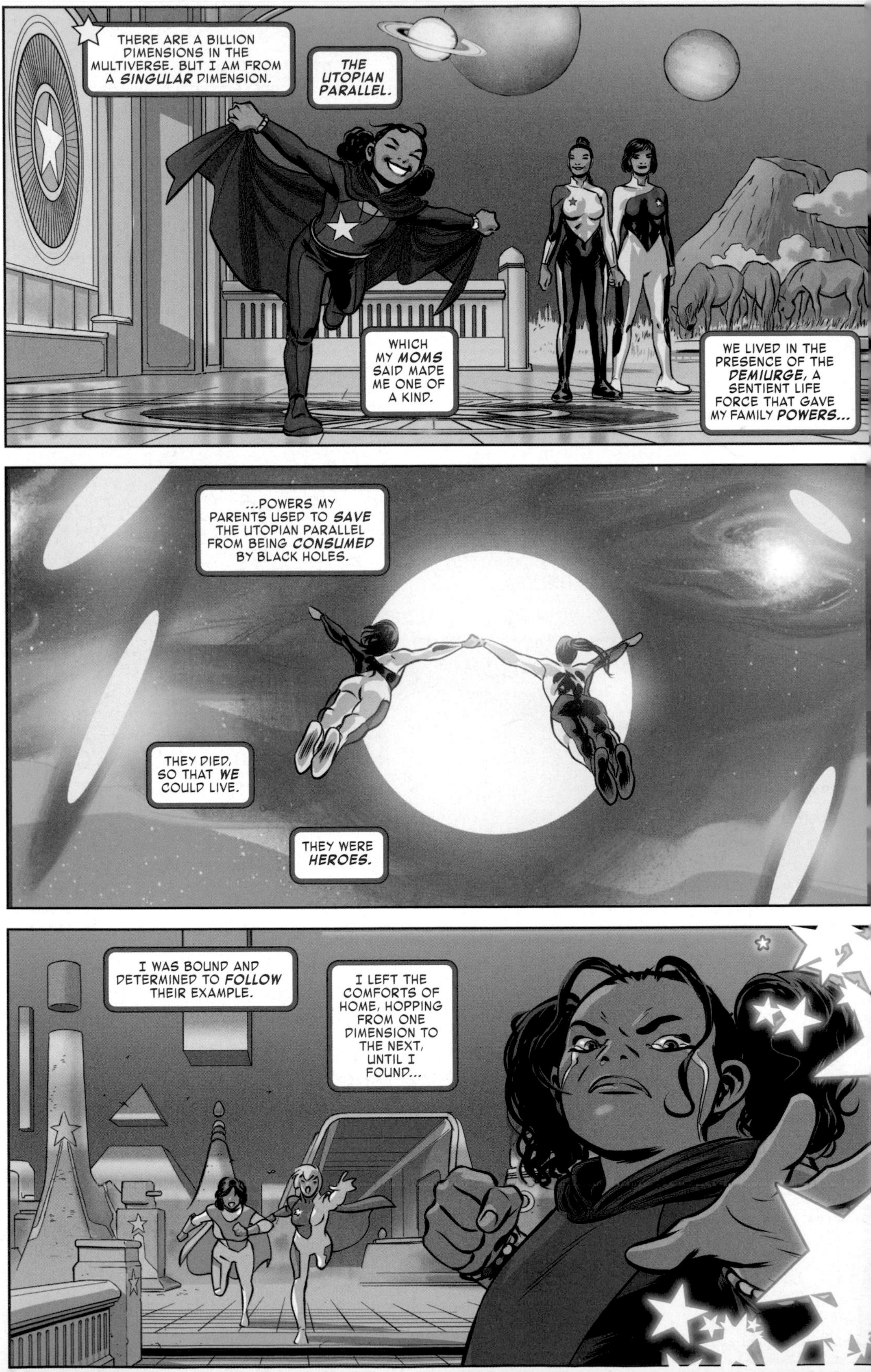
THERE ARE A BILLION DIMENSIONS IN THE MULTIVERSE. BUT I AM FROM A SINGULAR DIMENSION.
THE UTOPIAN PARALLEL.
WHICH MY MOMS SAID MADE ME ONE OF A KIND.
WE LIVED IN THE PRESENCE OF THE DEMIURGE, A SENTIENT LIFE FORCE THAT GAVE MY FAMILY POWERS...
...POWERS MY PARENTS USED TO SAVE THE UTOPIAN PARALLEL FROM BEING CONSUMED BY BLACK HOLES.
THEY DIED, SO THAT WE COULD LIVE.
THEY WERE HEROES.
I WAS BOUND AND DETERMINED TO FOLLOW THEIR EXAMPLE.
I LEFT THE COMFORTS OF HOME, HOPPING FROM ONE DIMENSION TO THE NEXT, UNTIL I FOUND...

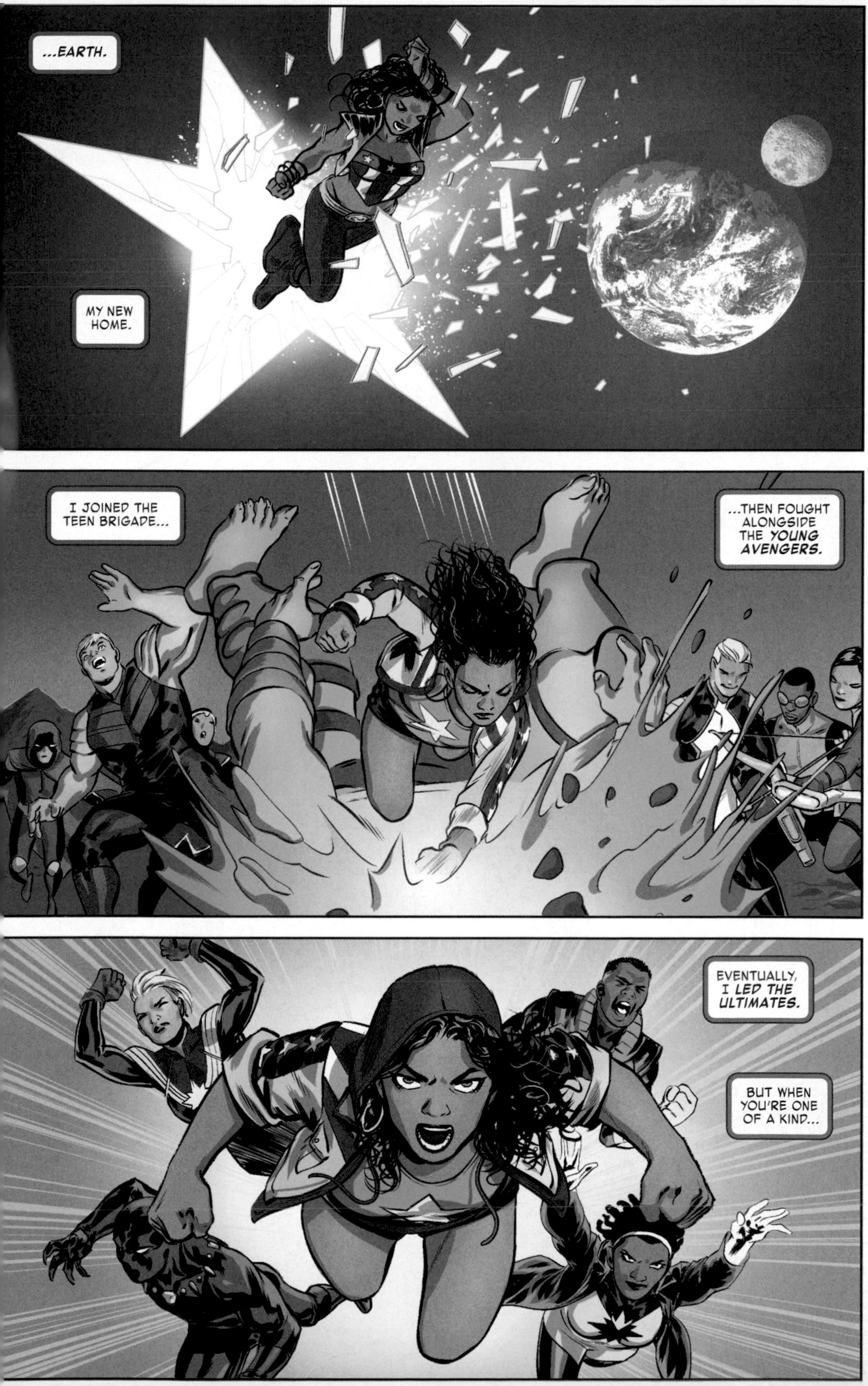
...EARTH.
MY NEW HOME.
I JOINED THE TEEN BRIGADE...
...THEN FOUGHT ALONGSIDE THE *YOUNG AVENGERS.*
EVENTUALLY, *I LED THE ULTIMATES.*
BUT WHEN YOU'RE ONE OF A KIND...

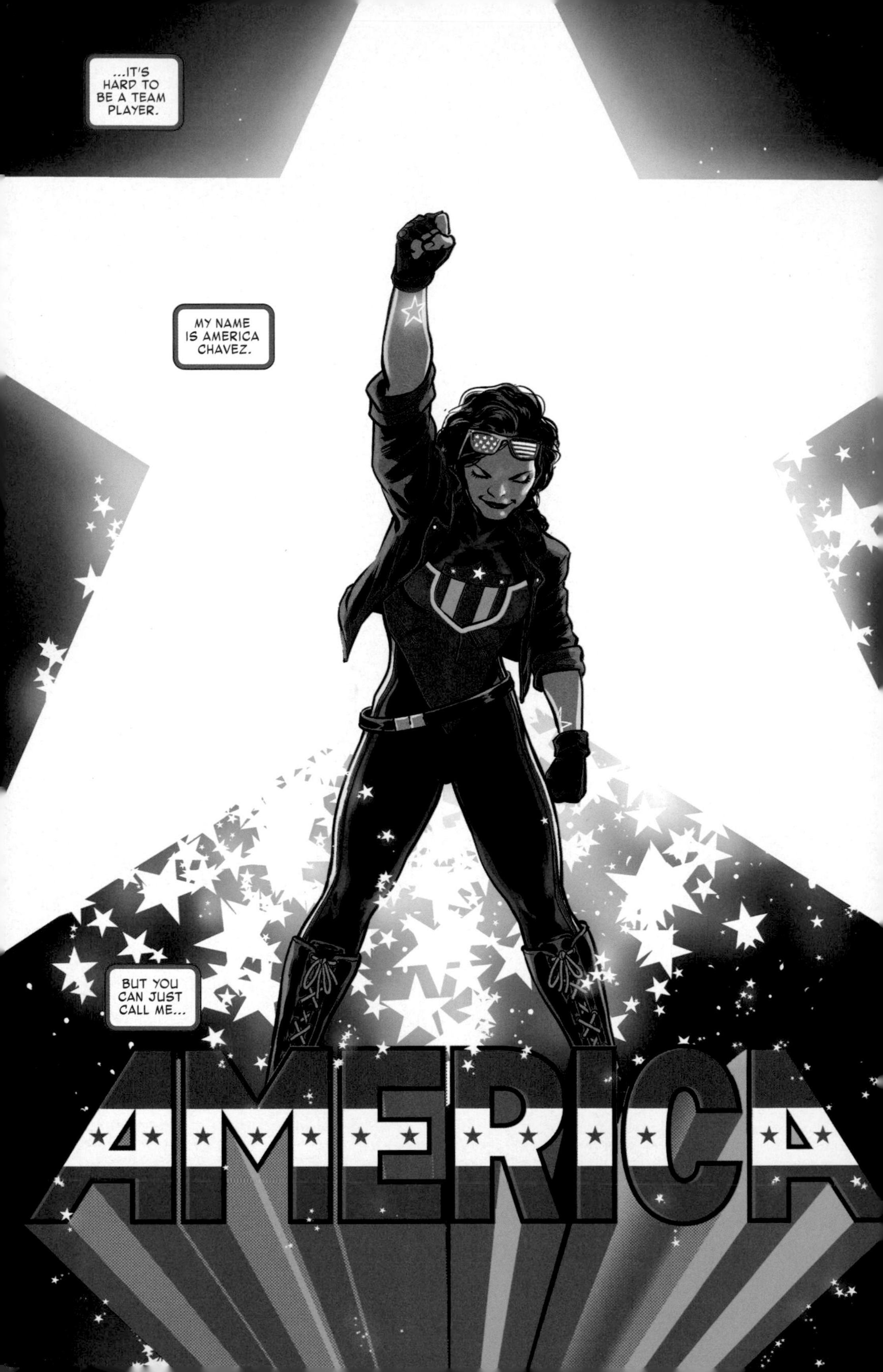
...IT'S HARD TO BE A TEAM PLAYER.
MY NAME IS AMERICA CHAVEZ.
BUT YOU CAN JUST CALL ME...
AMERICA

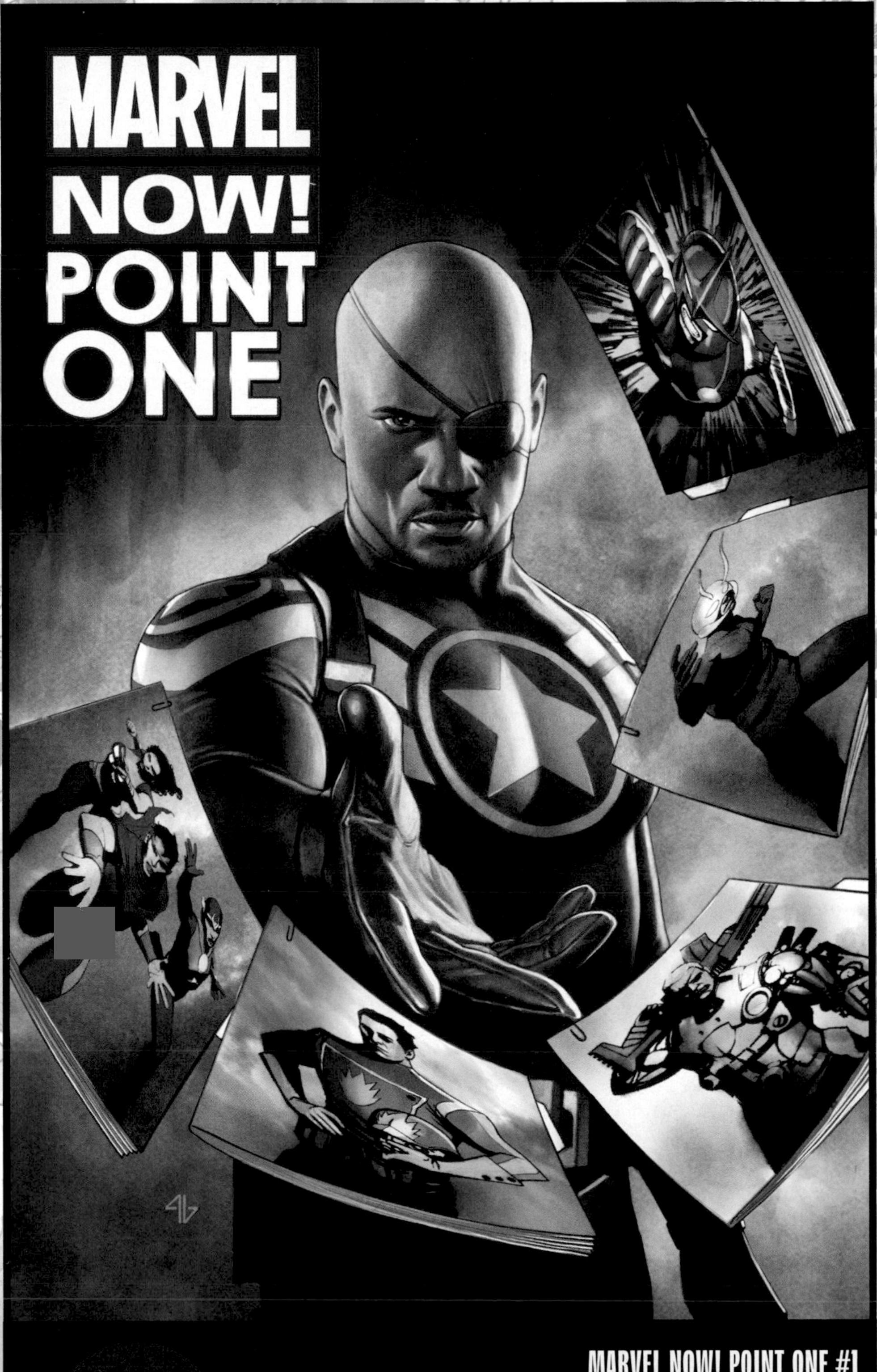
MARVEL
NOW!
POINT
ONE

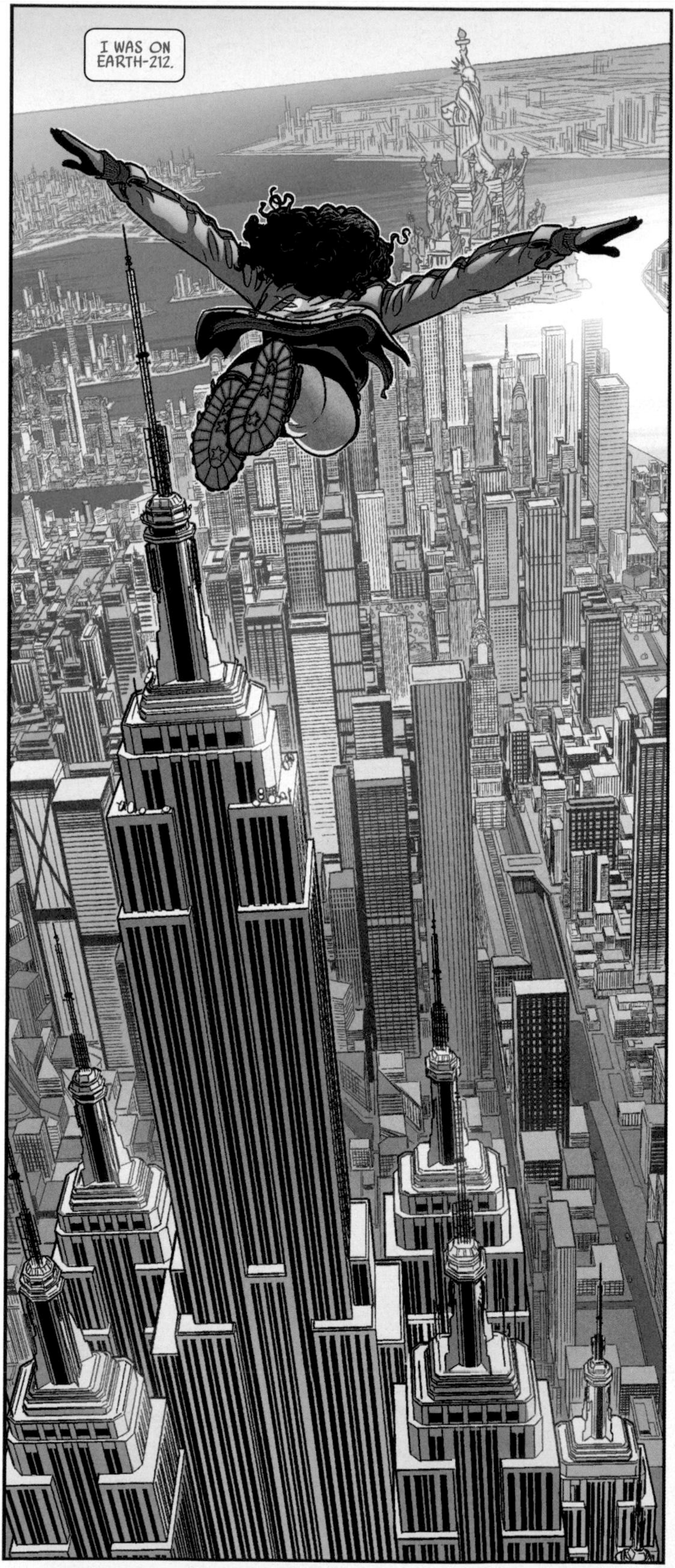
I WAS ON EARTH-212.

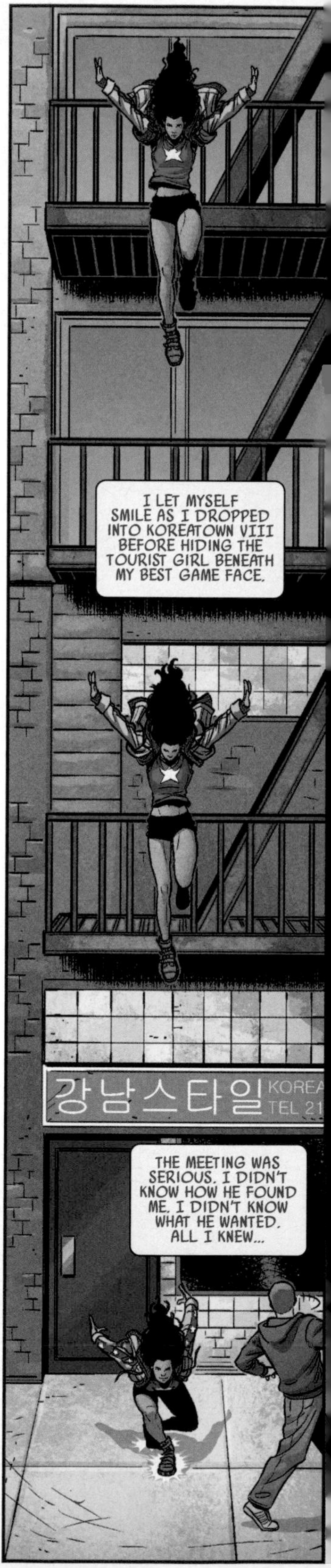
I LET MYSELF SMILE AS I DROPPED INTO KOREATOWN VIII BEFORE HIDING THE TOURIST GIRL BENEATH MY BEST GAME FACE.
강남스타일
THE MEETING WAS SERIOUS. I DIDN'T KNOW HOW HE FOUND ME. I DIDN'T KNOW WHAT HE WANTED. ALL I KNEW...

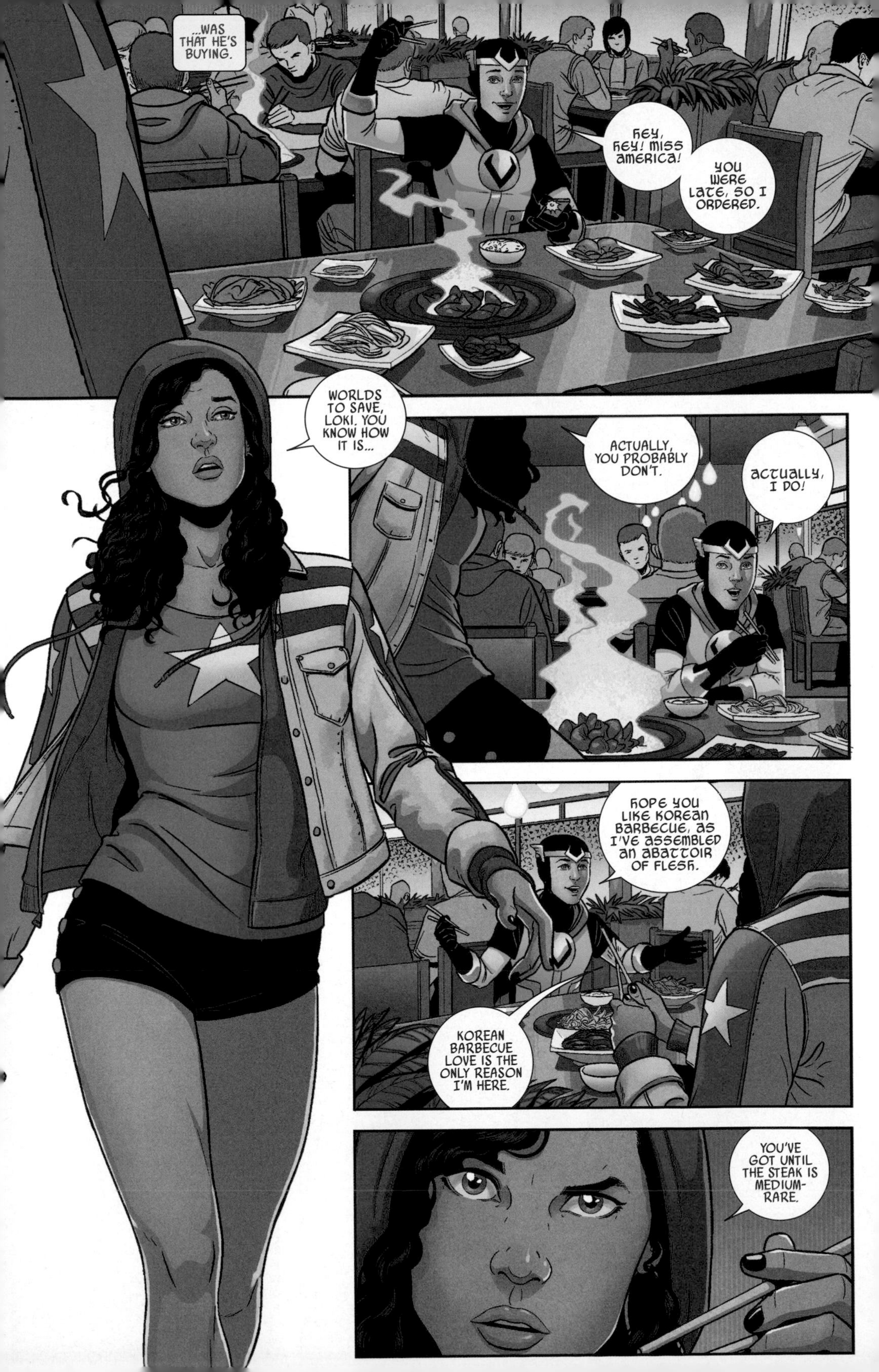
...WAS THAT HE'S BUYING.
HEY, HEY! MISS AMERICA!
YOU WERE LATE, SO I ORDERED.
WORLDS TO SAVE, LOKI. YOU KNOW HOW IT IS...
ACTUALLY, YOU PROBABLY DON'T.
ACTUALLY, I DO!
HOPE YOU LIKE KOREAN BARBECUE, AS I'VE ASSEMBLED AN ABATTOIR OF FLESH.
KOREAN BARBECUE LOVE IS THE ONLY REASON I'M HERE.
YOU'VE GOT UNTIL THE STEAK IS MEDIUM-RARE.

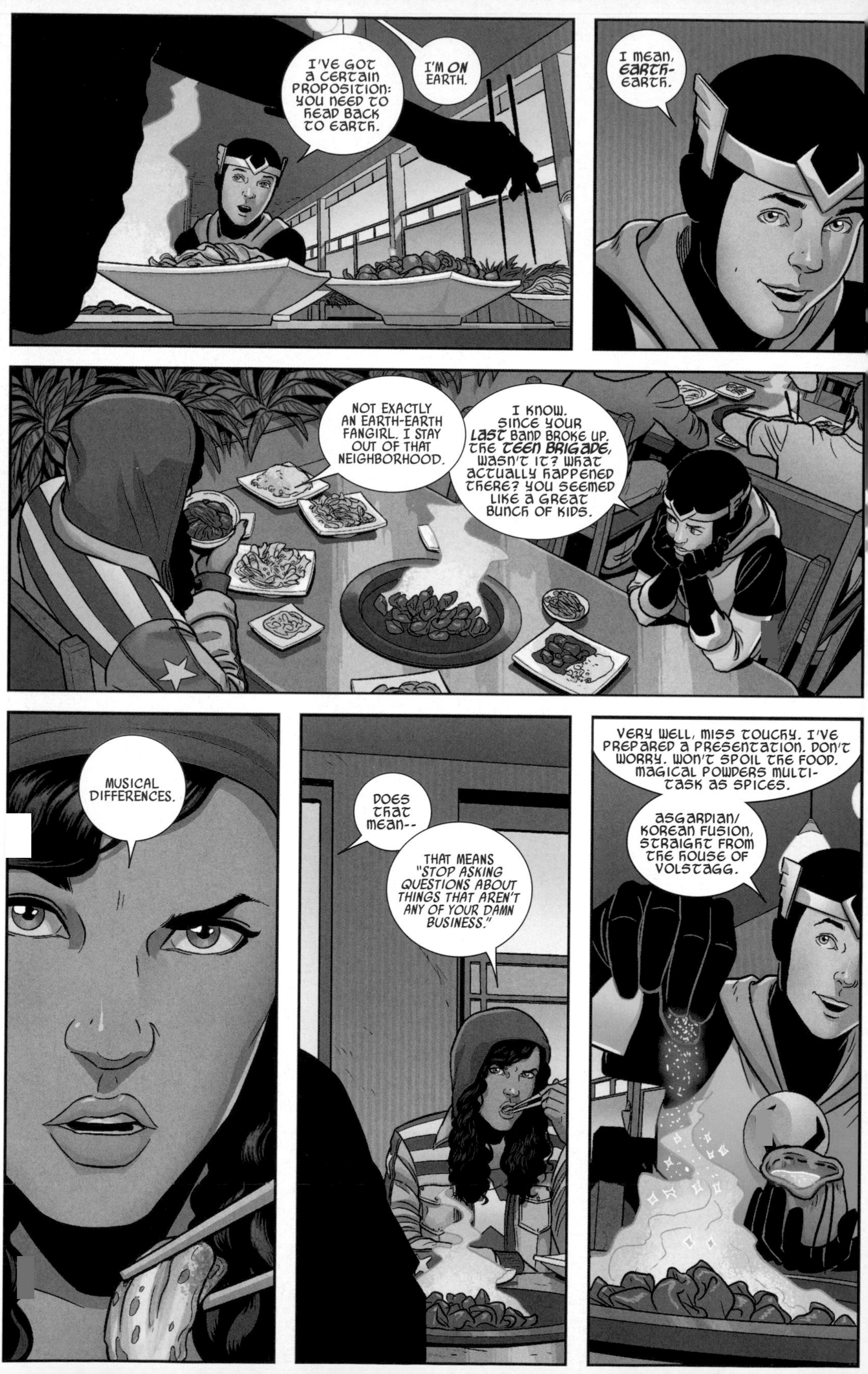
I'VE GOT A CERTAIN PROPOSITION: YOU NEED TO HEAD BACK TO EARTH.
I'M ON EARTH.
I MEAN, EARTH-EARTH.
NOT EXACTLY AN EARTH-EARTH FANGIRL. I STAY OUT OF THAT NEIGHBORHOOD.
I KNOW. SINCE YOUR LAST BAND BROKE UP. THE TEEN BRIGADE, WASN'T IT? WHAT ACTUALLY HAPPENED THERE? YOU SEEMED LIKE A GREAT BUNCH OF KIDS.
MUSICAL DIFFERENCES.
DOES THAT MEAN--
THAT MEANS "STOP ASKING QUESTIONS ABOUT THINGS THAT AREN'T ANY OF YOUR DAMN BUSINESS."
VERY WELL, MISS TOUCHY. I'VE PREPARED A PRESENTATION. DON'T WORRY. WON'T SPOIL THE FOOD. MAGICAL POWDERS MULTI-TASK AS SPICES.
ASGARDIAN/KOREAN FUSION, STRAIGHT FROM THE HOUSE OF VOLSTAGG.

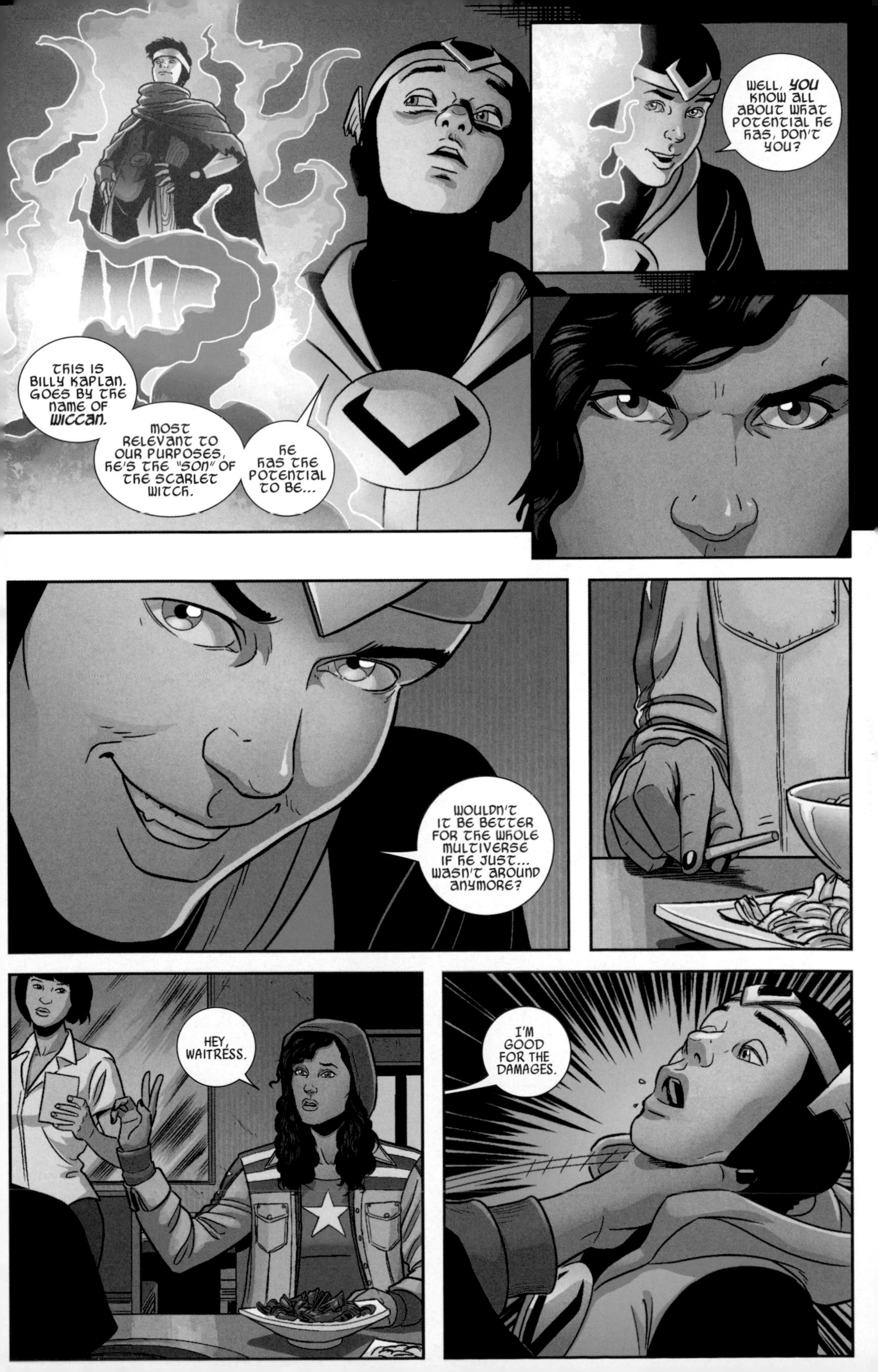
THIS IS BILLY KAPLAN. GOES BY THE NAME OF *WICCAN.*
MOST RELEVANT TO OUR PURPOSES, HE'S THE "SON" OF THE SCARLET WITCH.
HE HAS THE POTENTIAL TO BE...
WELL, *YOU* KNOW ALL ABOUT WHAT POTENTIAL HE HAS, DON'T YOU?
WOULDN'T IT BE BETTER FOR THE WHOLE MULTIVERSE IF HE JUST... WASN'T AROUND ANYMORE?
HEY, WAITRESS.
I'M GOOD FOR THE DAMAGES.

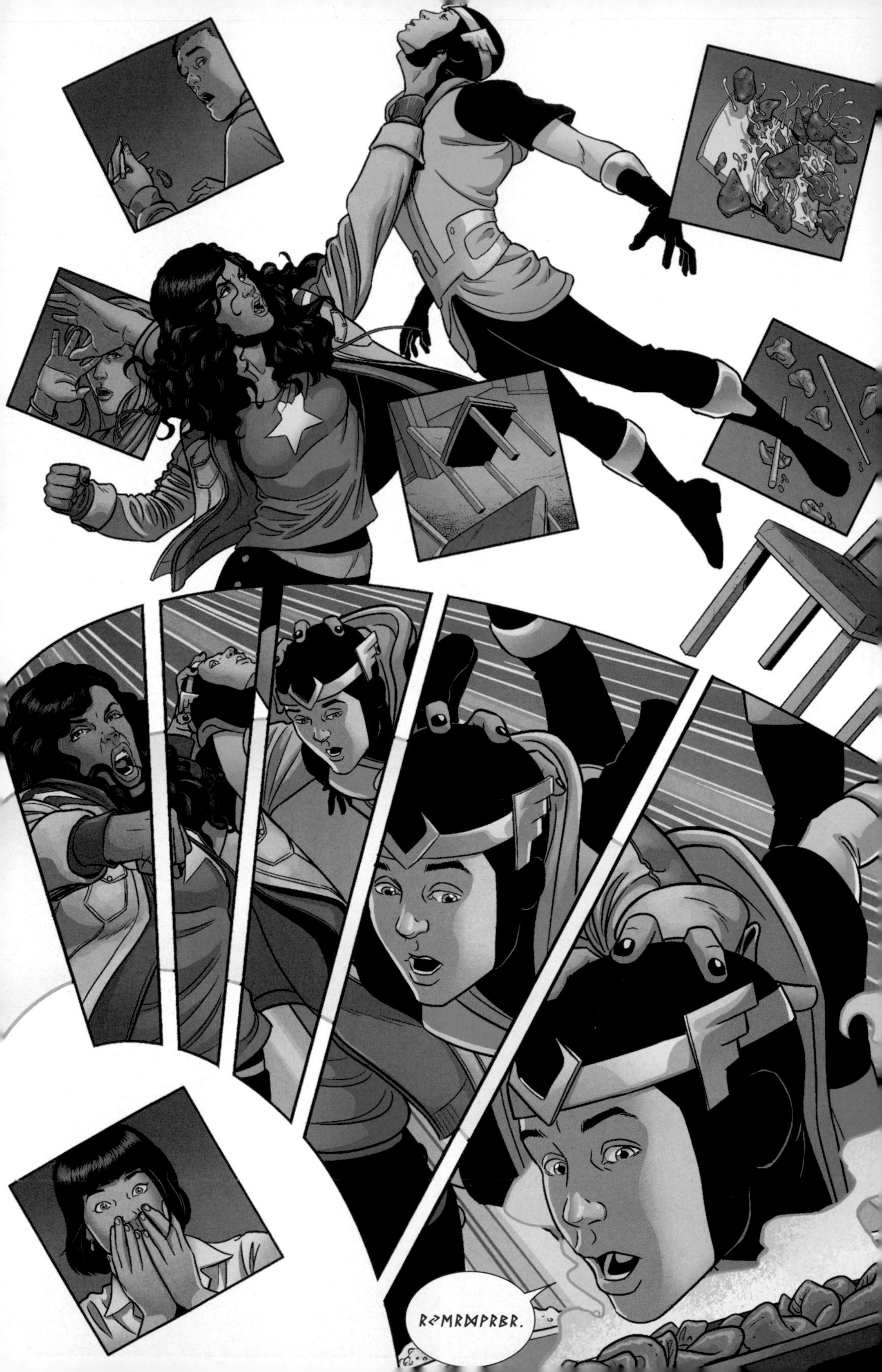
ᚱᛜᛗᚱᛞᚹᚱᛒᚱ.

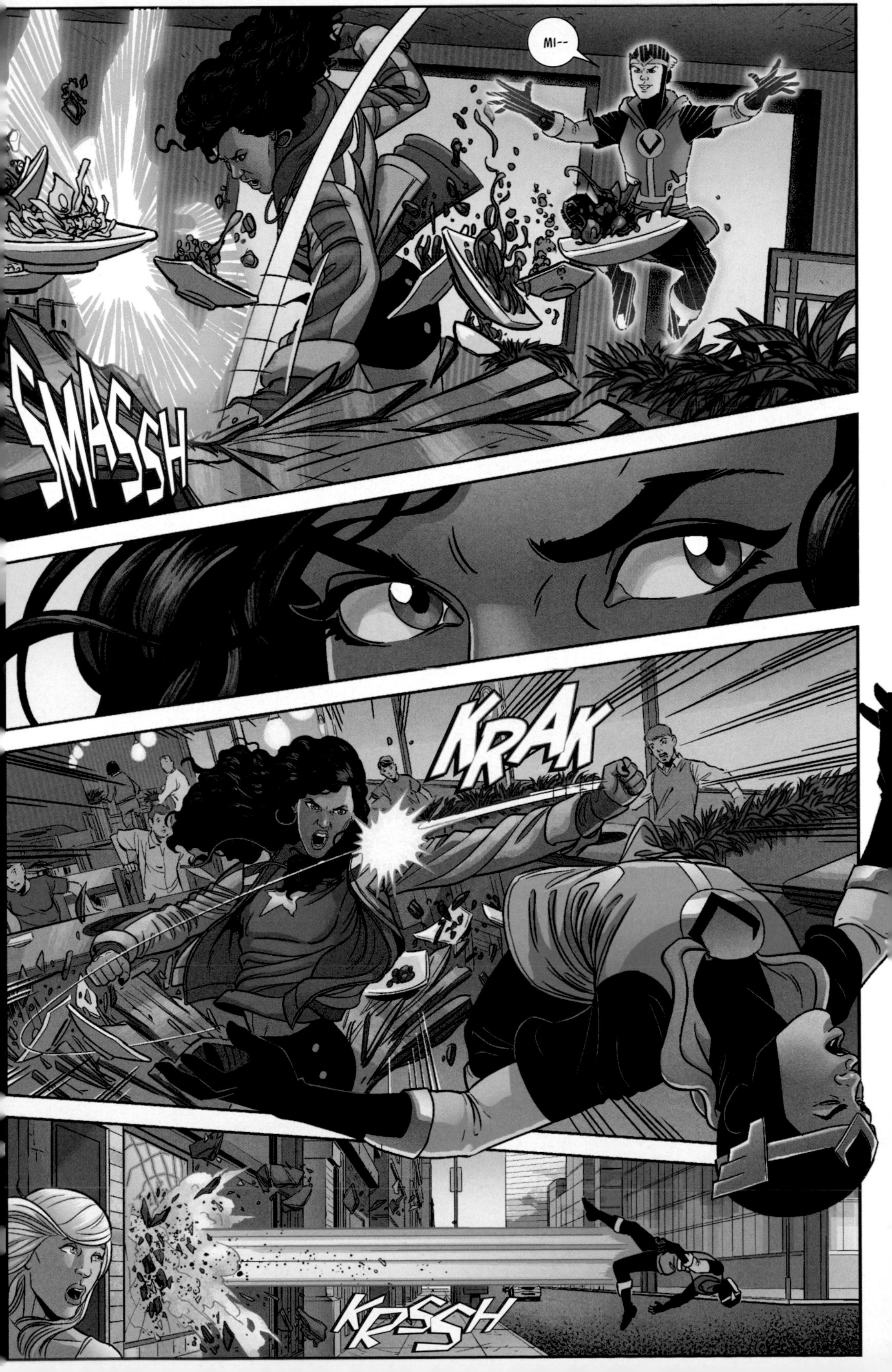
MI--
SMASSH
KRAK
KRSSH

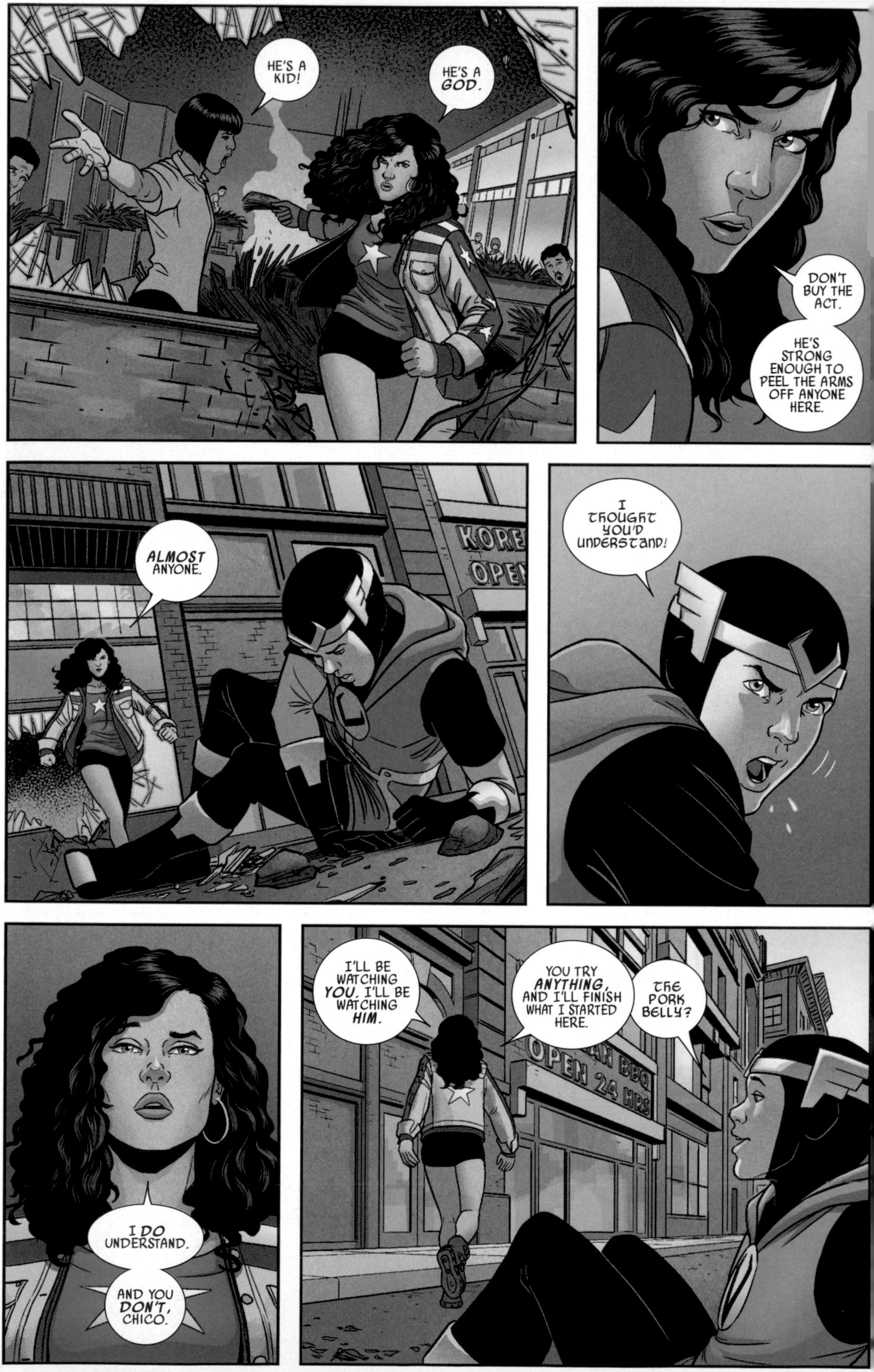
HE'S A KID!
HE'S A GOD.
DON'T BUY THE ACT.
HE'S STRONG ENOUGH TO PEEL THE ARMS OFF ANYONE HERE.
ALMOST ANYONE.
KORE
OPEN
I THOUGHT YOU'D UNDERSTAND!
I DO UNDERSTAND.
AND YOU DON'T, CHICO.
I'LL BE WATCHING YOU. I'LL BE WATCHING HIM.
YOU TRY ANYTHING, AND I'LL FINISH WHAT I STARTED HERE.
THE PORK BELLY?
OPEN 24 HRS

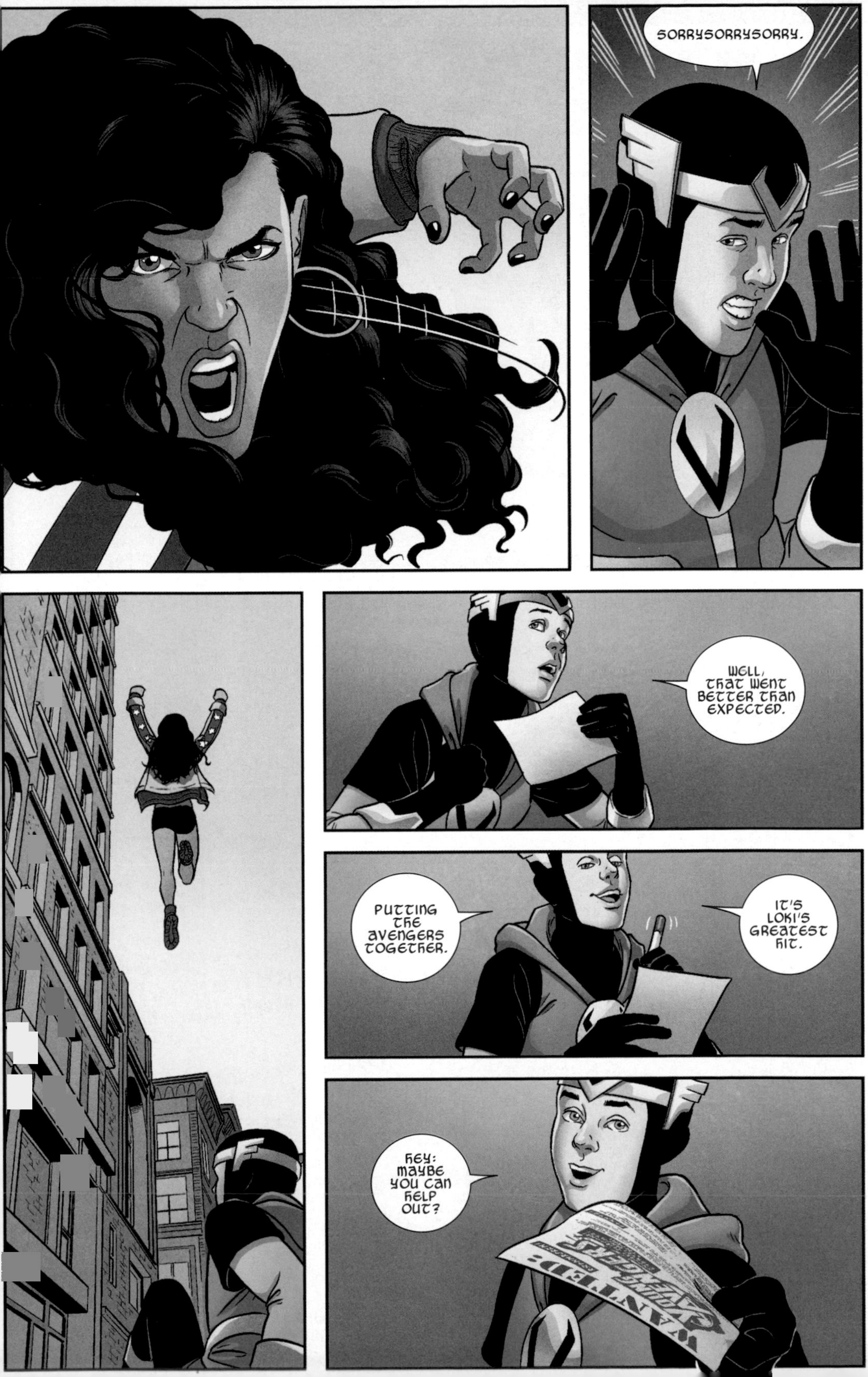
SORRYSORRYSORRY.
WELL, THAT WENT BETTER THAN EXPECTED.
PUTTING THE AVENGERS TOGETHER.
IT'S LOKI'S GREATEST HIT.
HEY: MAYBE YOU CAN HELP OUT?

WANTED

YOUNG AVENGERS

Are you **YOUNG? WILD? FREE?** Only able to buy beer with fake ID? Do your hobbies include saving the world all night then trying to find a place that does a good 5am breakfast? We're looking for **HIP YOUNG BEAMSLINGERS** of every variety.

CAREERISTS NEED NOT APPLY.
If this isn't your vocation, you're in the wrong place.

- [x] One mysterious interdimensional super hero with mysterious background and mysterious anger issues.
- [x] One mischievous and lovable godling who is not **at all** evil and definitely not manipulating everyone.
- [ ] One chaos-magic quasi-messiah/antichrist who thinks he's lost everything in the world except for the love of his life.
- [ ] One shape-changing heir to the Skrull Empire who actually has lost everything in the world except for the love of his life.
- [ ] One banished Kree warrior who's lost everything except his vintage vinyl collection. And his spaceship.
- [ ] One rich girl with no powers whatsoever. And a bow. The bow is important.
- [ ] Whoever else we can pick up along the way who looks interesting. We're big on interesting people. Interesting > boring.
- [ ] Thousands upon thousands of devoted readers, who are beautiful, strong, kind, discerning, and – most of all – numerous.

If you are any of the above, apply to Loki Laufeyson in care of your local comic shop and/or digital comic app. If your application is successful, you will be notified in January 2013.

Be there or be involved in a string of massive corporate crossover events for your entire run.

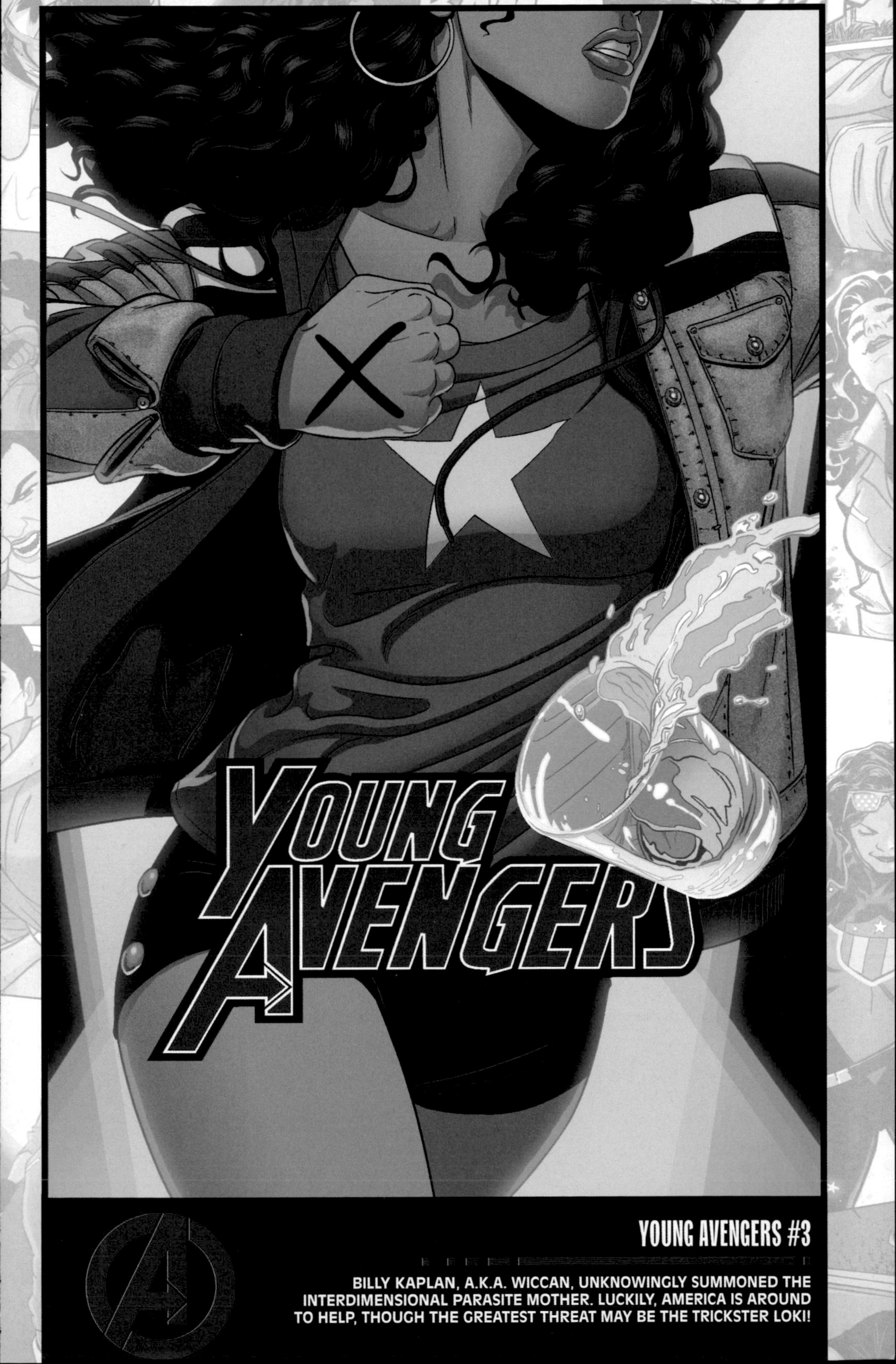
YOUNG
AVENGERS

YOUNG AVENGERS #3

BILLY KAPLAN, A.K.A. WICCAN, UNKNOWINGLY SUMMONED THE INTERDIMENSIONAL PARASITE MOTHER. LUCKILY, AMERICA IS AROUND TO HELP, THOUGH THE GREATEST THREAT MAY BE THE TRICKSTER LOKI!

yamblr.

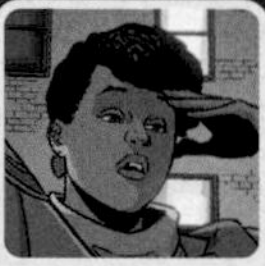

innocentbystander42

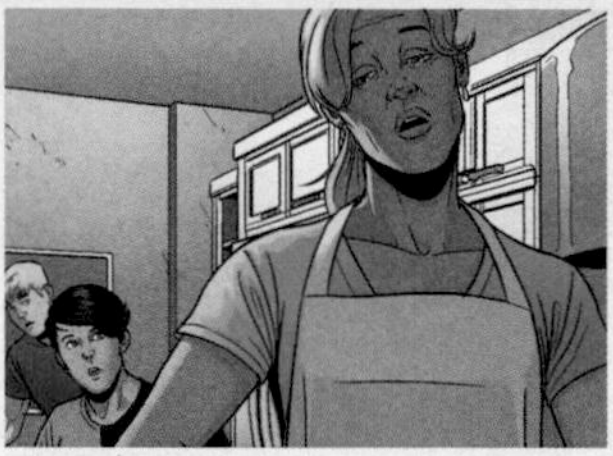

Hoping to make up after a fight, Billy used magic to bring back Teddy's mom. But something seemed…wrong.

#don't moms make kids do the dishes?

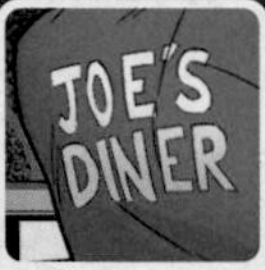
JOE'S DINER

eat@joes

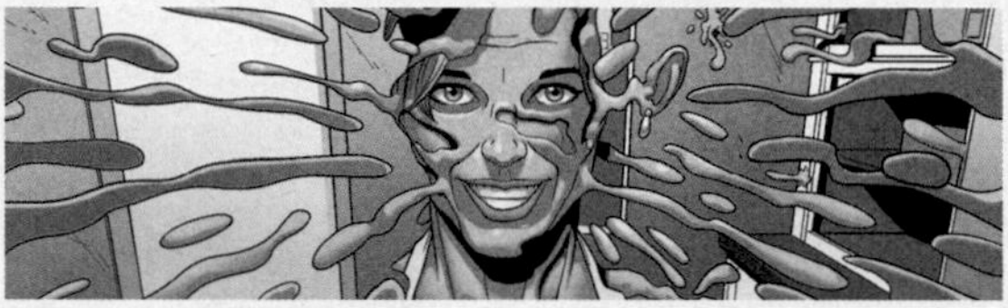

Oh, right. She's actually an evil, interdimensional parasite that has the power of mind-control over adults!

#KNEW IT! #dishes

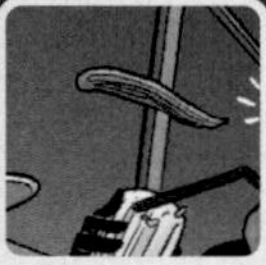

B@C0N_M@G1C

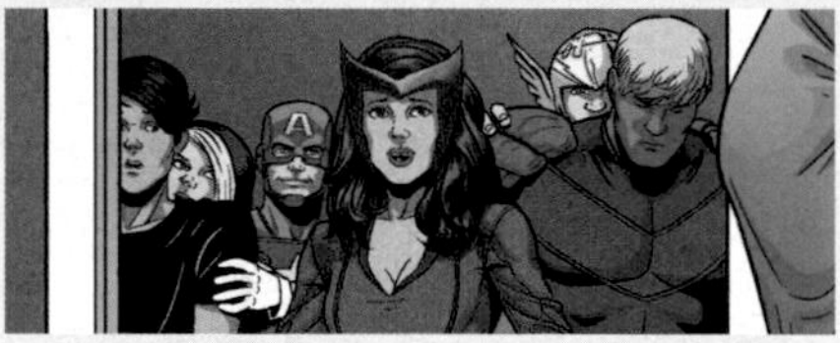

Billy and Teddy escaped her evil clutches, and went to the Avengers for help. Unfortunately, Mother had gotten there first.

#BUSTED! #don't trust anyone over 30!

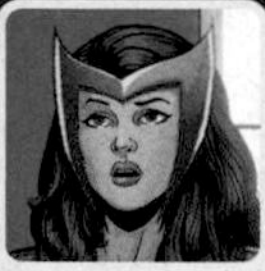

the_scarlet_mom

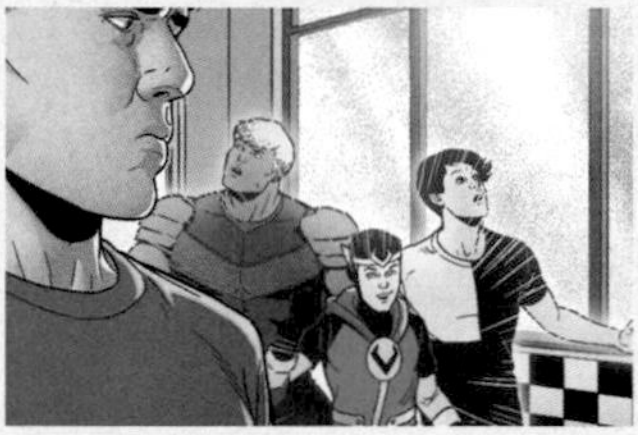

Fortunately, Loki had been keeping an eye on the situation and rescued the boys, transporting them to his fave diner.

#three bacon sandwiches #who brought a wallet?

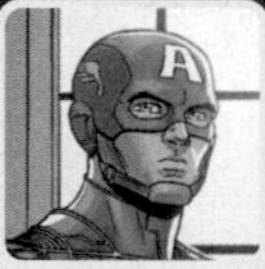

bigpieceofcap

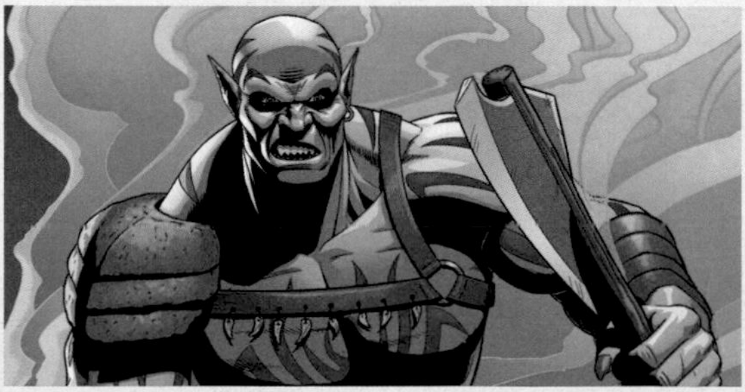

Hoping Asgardian magic might be the solution to their problems, Billy, Teddy and Loki made their way to Asgardia...where Laufey, King of Frost Giants and father of Loki, was waiting for them!

#sometimes parents just don't understand #cool teeth strap, bro

search yamblr

- BUSTED!
- teeth strap
- skull belt
- queen of jackets
- credits page
- Loki's bulging eyes

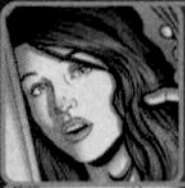

Hawkeye not the hawkguy

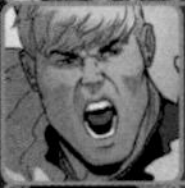

Hulkling shape-shifting alien hybrid guy

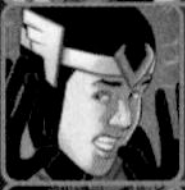

Loki god of mischief

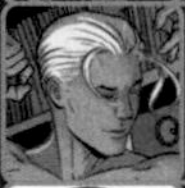

Marvel Boy banished kree music lover

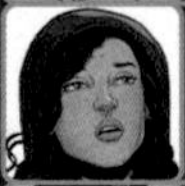

Miss America interdimensional kicker of butt

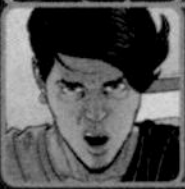

Wiccan angsty chaos-magic user

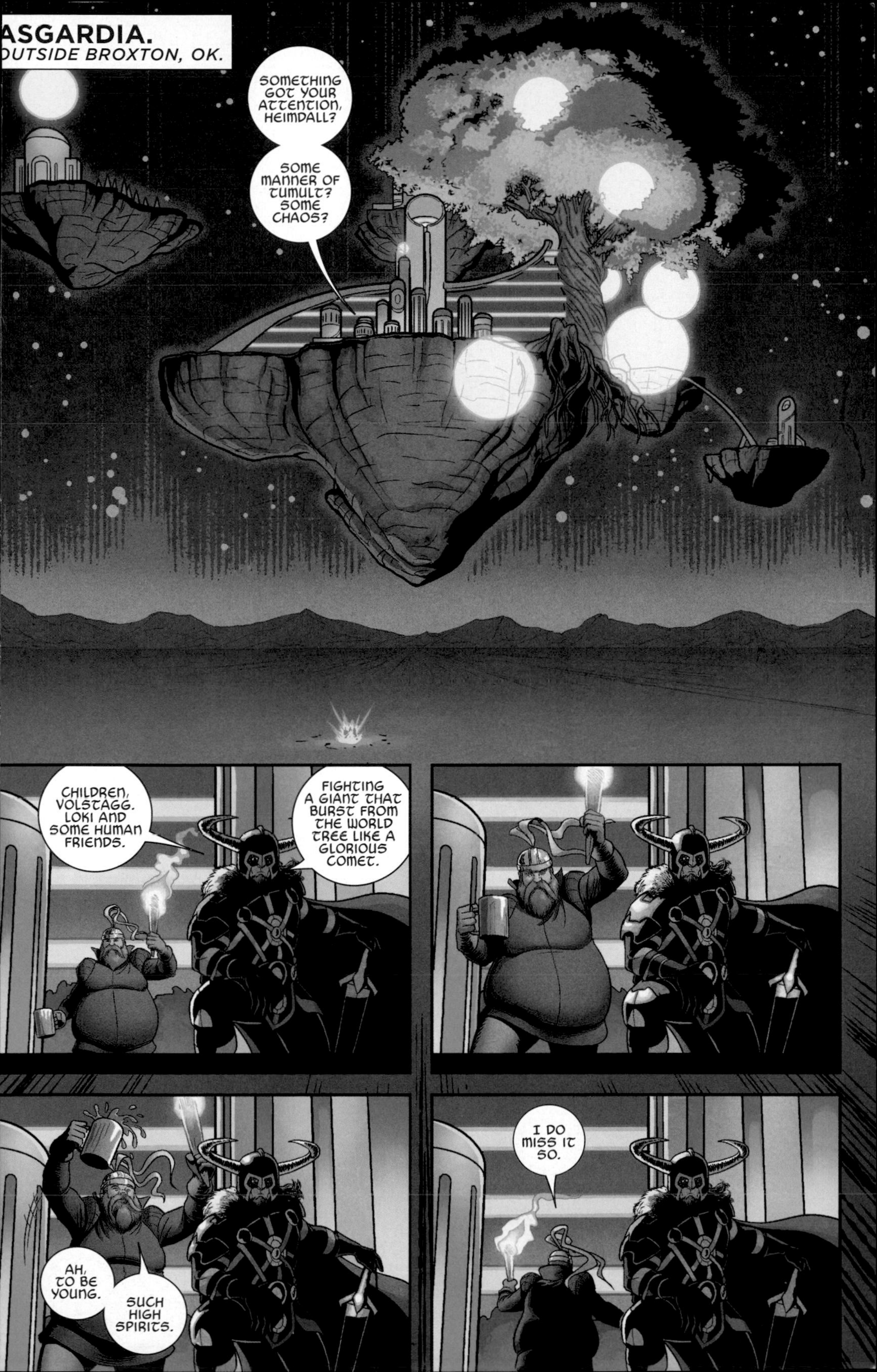
ASGARDIA.
OUTSIDE BROXTON, OK.
SOMETHING GOT YOUR ATTENTION, HEIMDALL?
SOME MANNER OF TUMULT? SOME CHAOS?
CHILDREN, VOLSTAGG. LOKI AND SOME HUMAN FRIENDS.
FIGHTING A GIANT THAT BURST FROM THE WORLD TREE LIKE A GLORIOUS COMET.
AH, TO BE YOUNG.
SUCH HIGH SPIRITS.
I DO MISS IT SO.

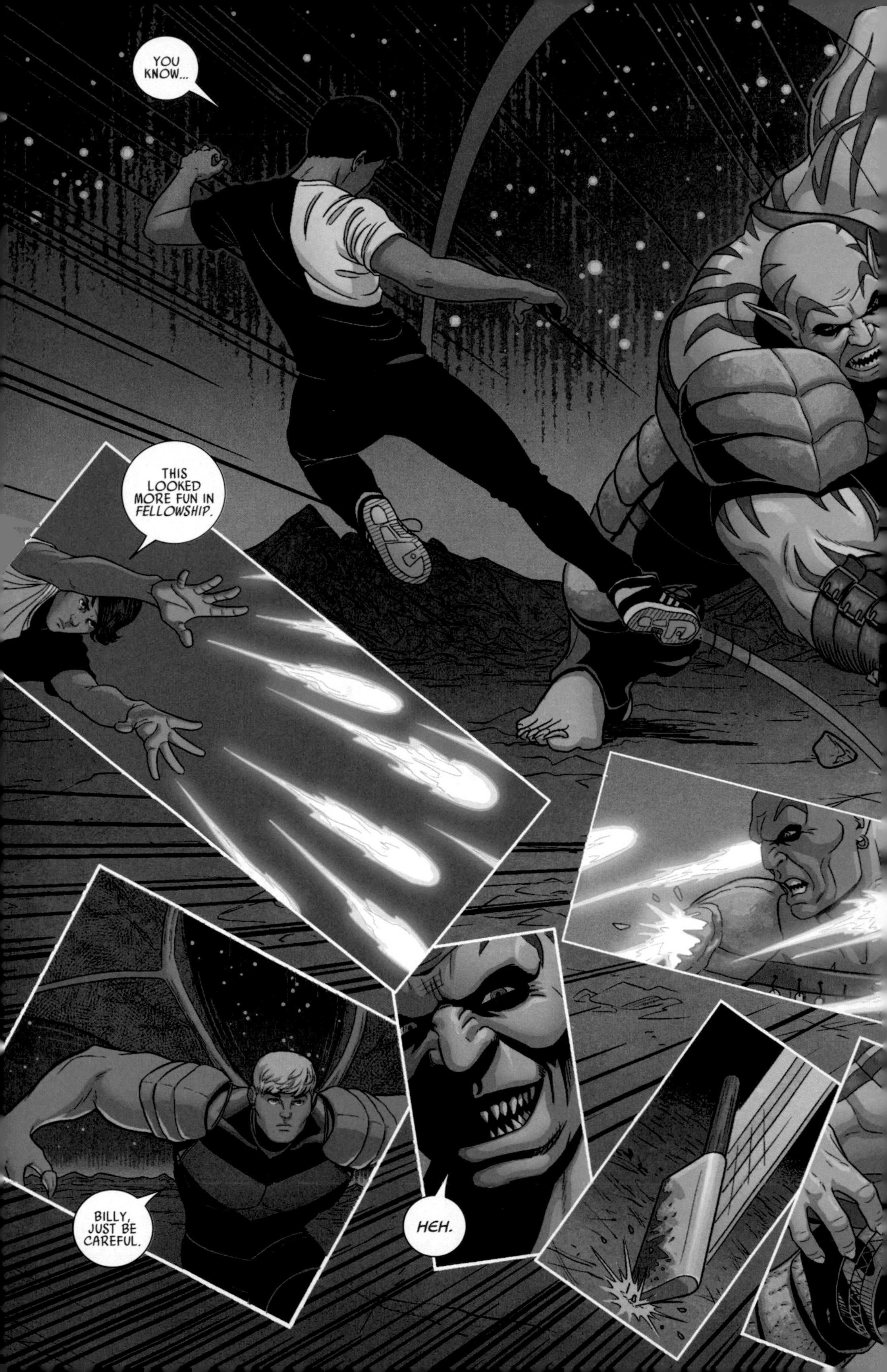
YOU KNOW...
THIS LOOKED MORE FUN IN *FELLOWSHIP.*
BILLY, JUST BE CAREFUL.
HEH.

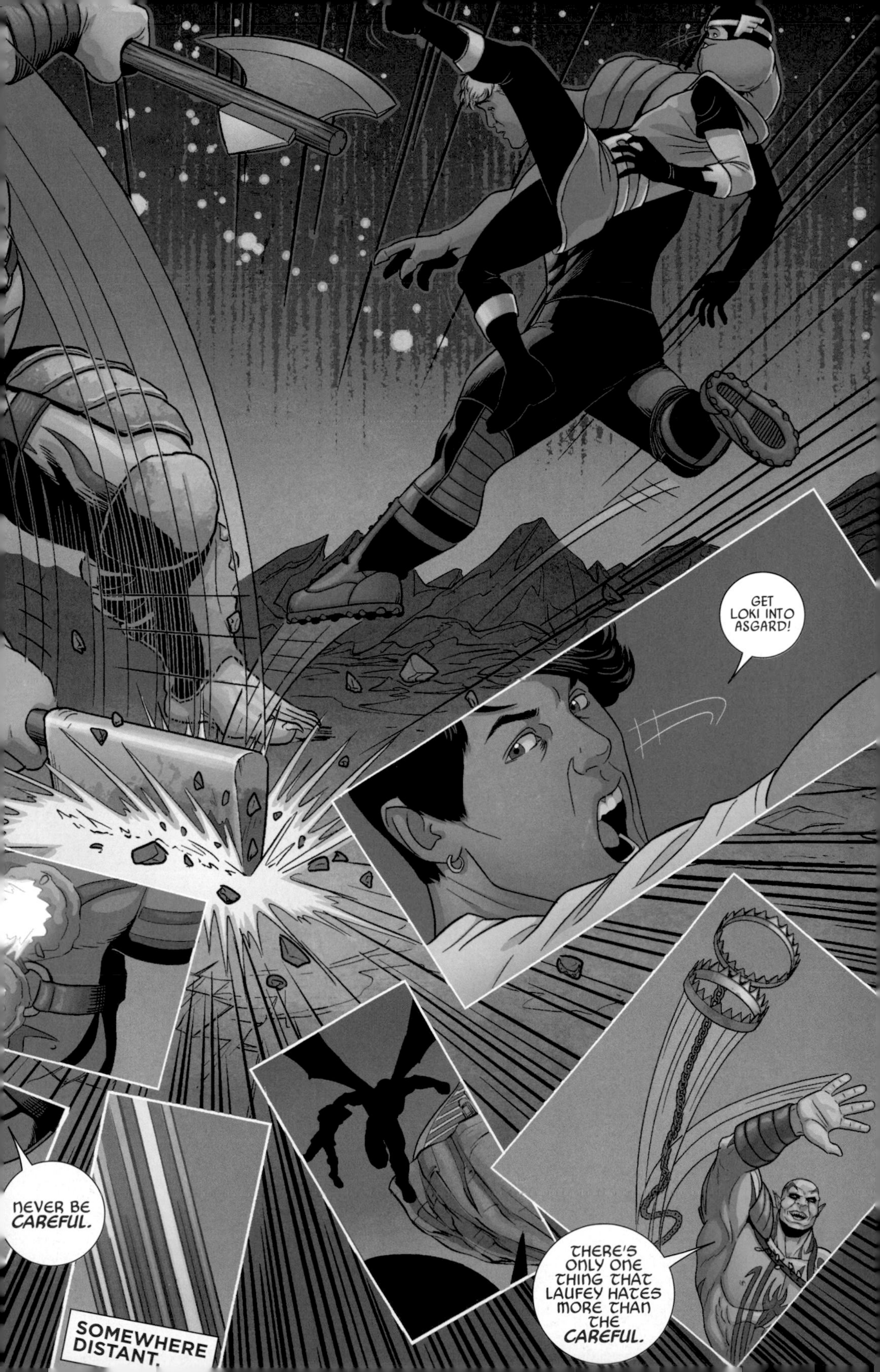
GET LOKI INTO ASGARD!
NEVER BE CAREFUL.
SOMEWHERE DISTANT.
THERE'S ONLY ONE THING THAT LAUFEY HATES MORE THAN THE CAREFUL.

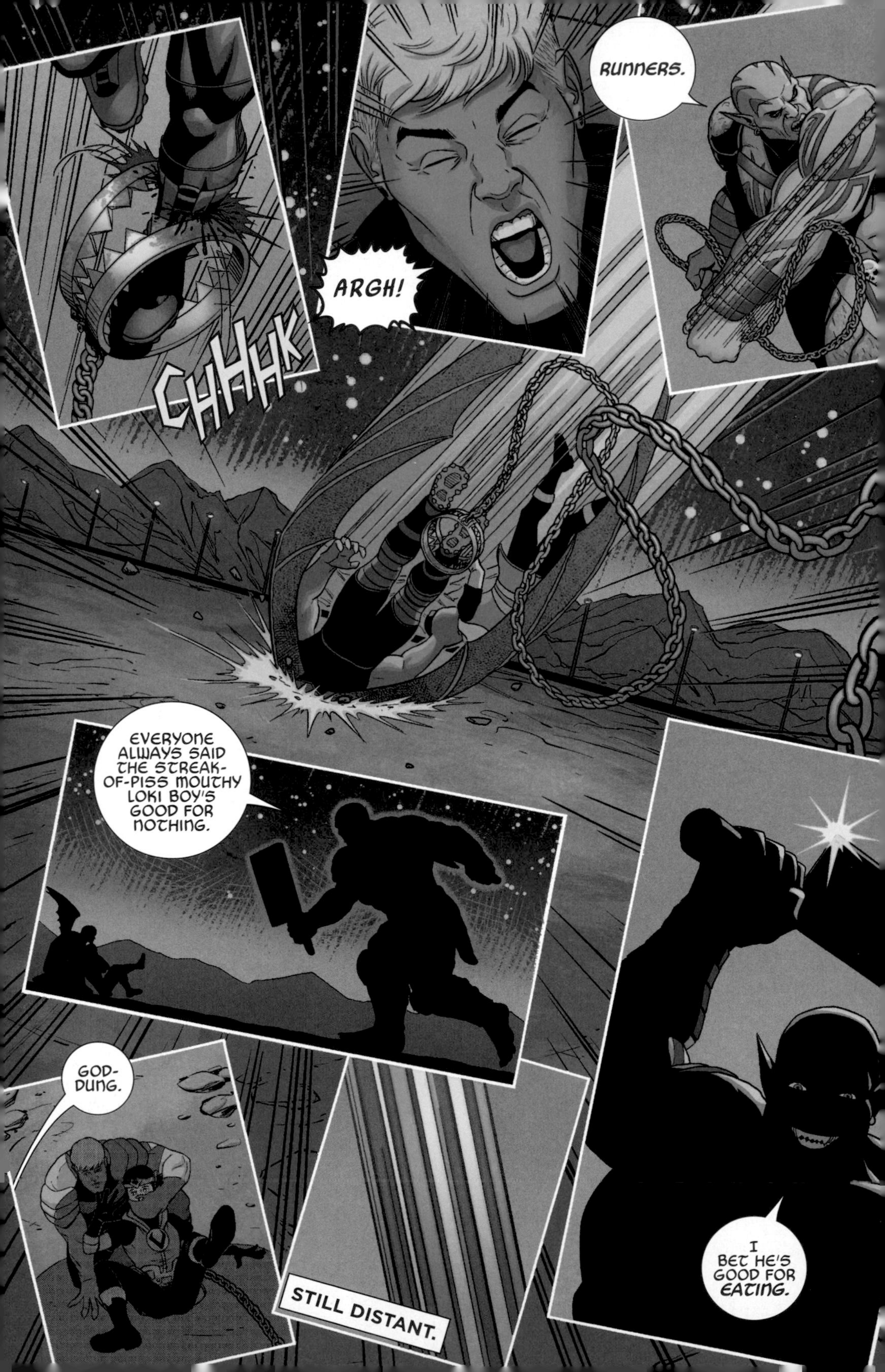
CHHHK
ARGH!
RUNNERS.
EVERYONE ALWAYS SAID THE STREAK-OF-PISS MOUTHY LOKI BOY'S GOOD FOR NOTHING.
I BET HE'S GOOD FOR EATING.
GOD-DUNG.
STILL DISTANT.

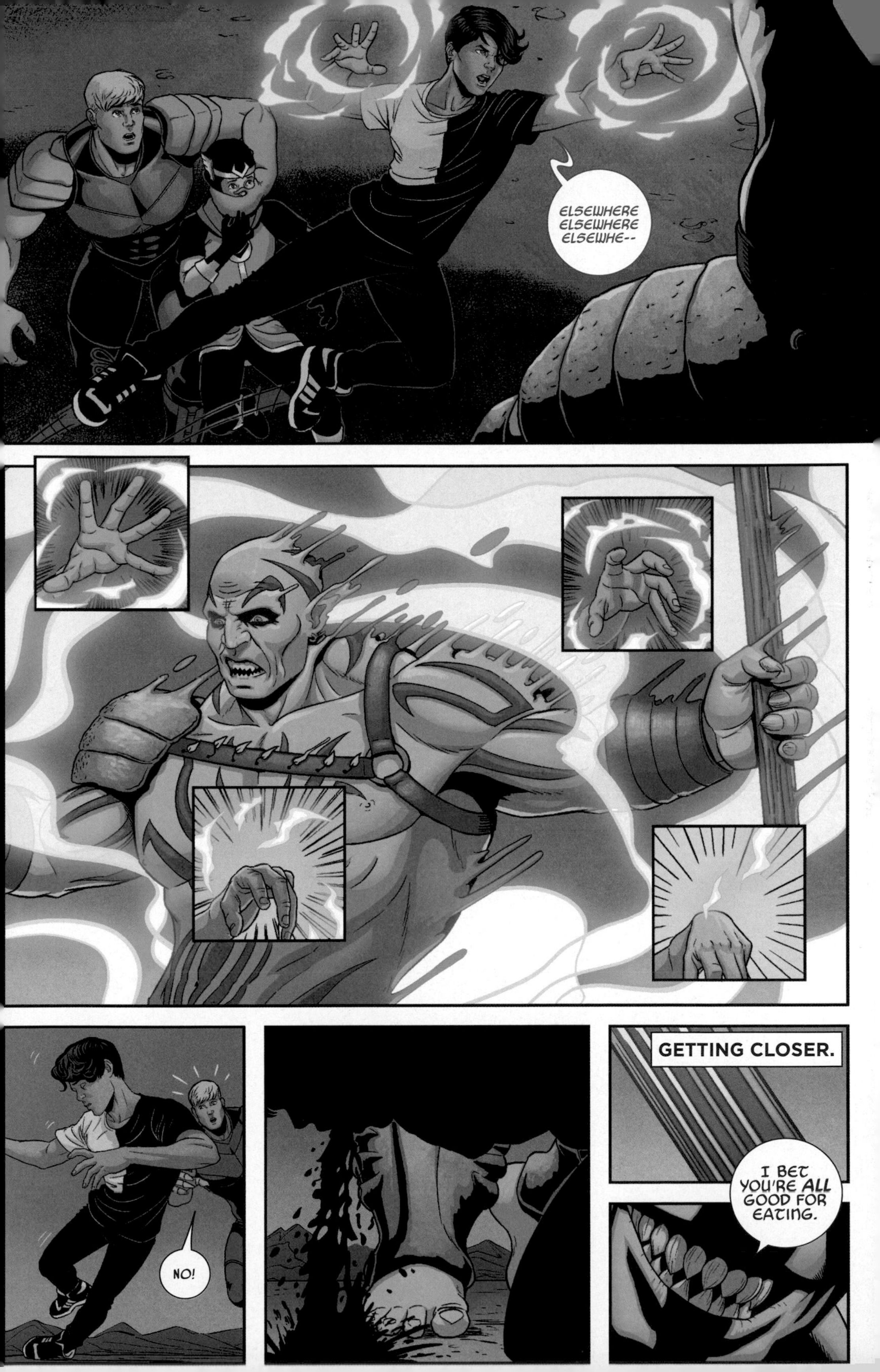
ELSEWHERE
ELSEWHERE
ELSEWHE--
NO!
GETTING CLOSER.
I BET YOU'RE ALL GOOD FOR EATING.

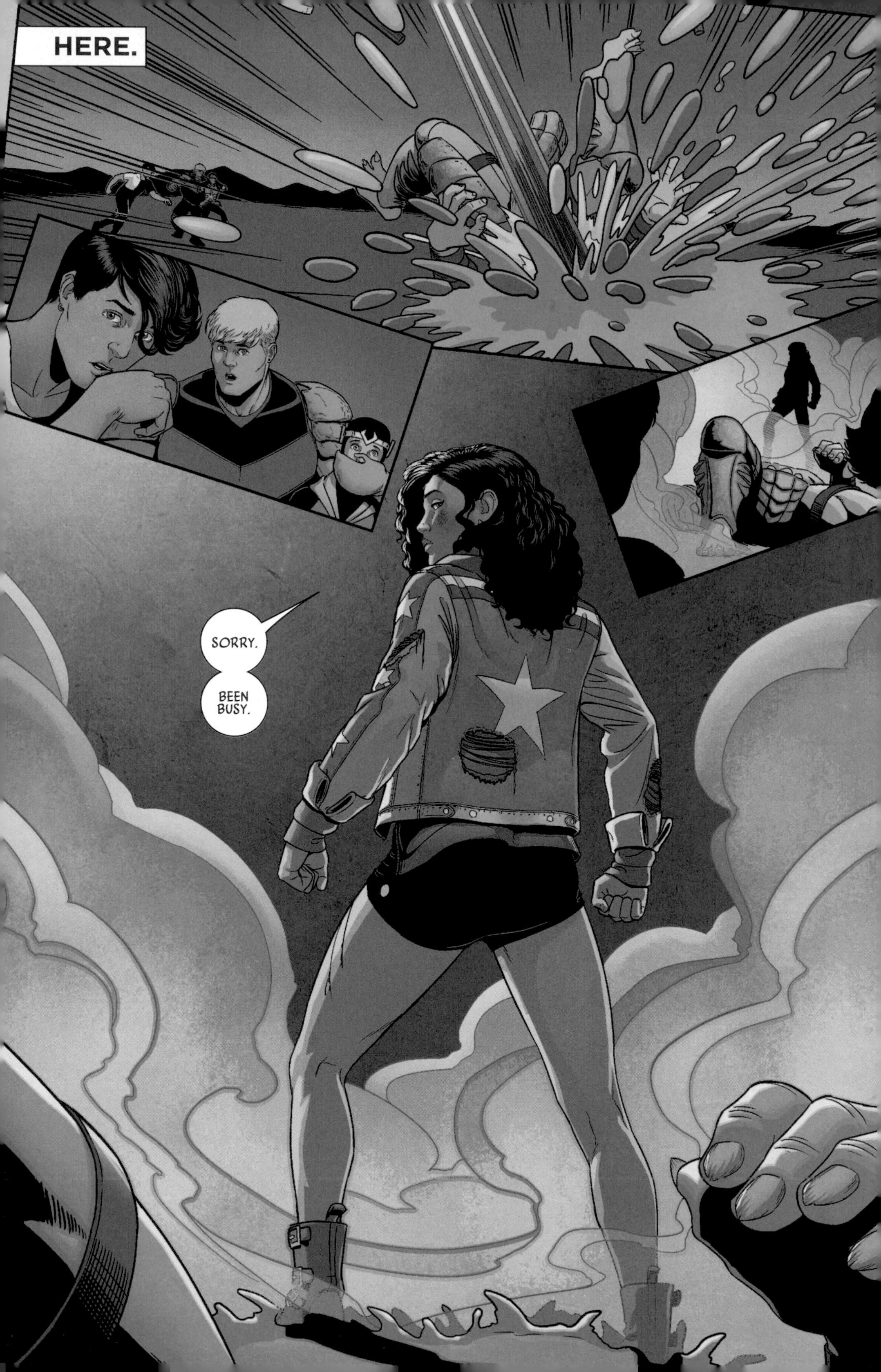
HERE.
SORRY.
BEEN BUSY.

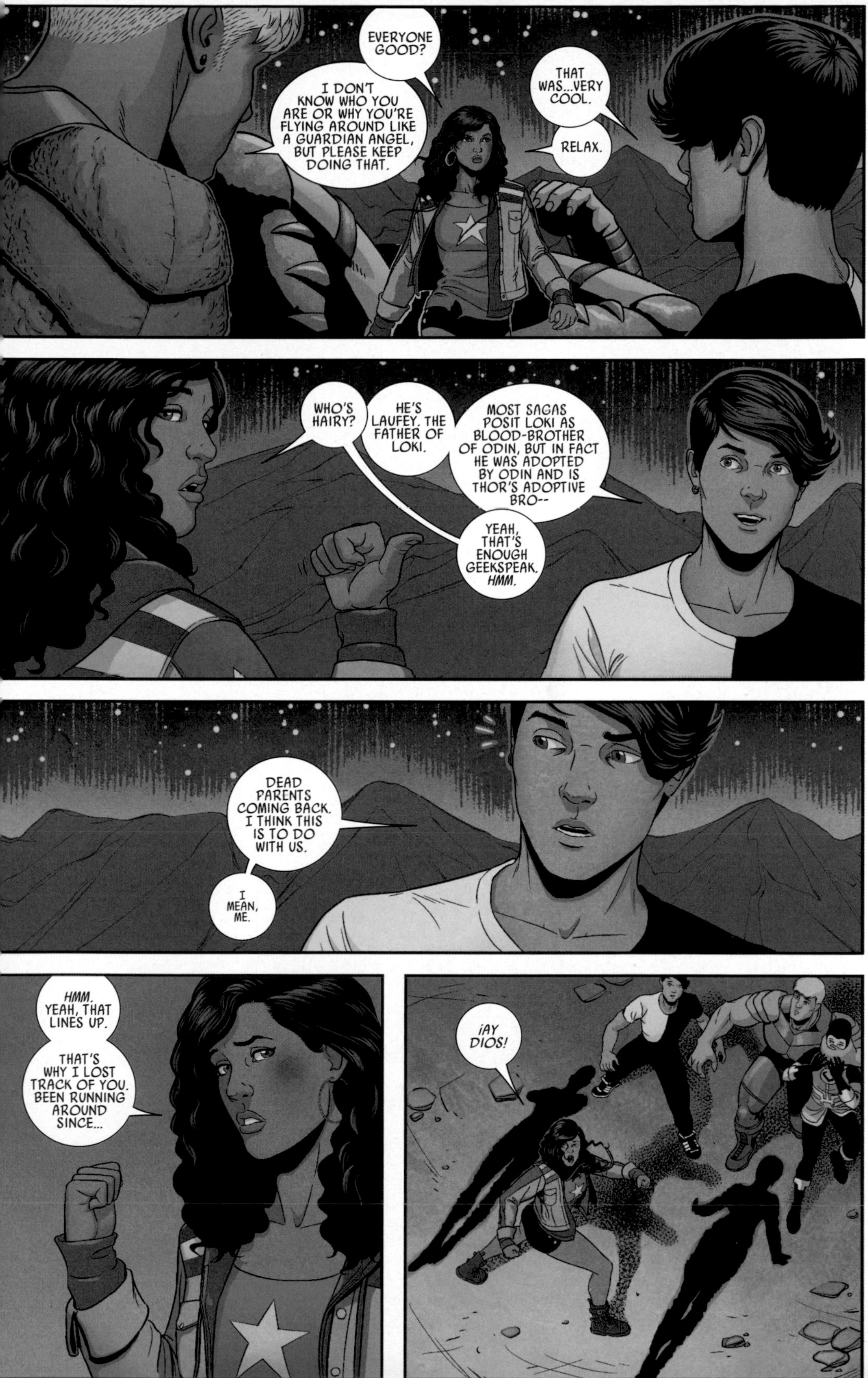
EVERYONE GOOD?
I DON'T KNOW WHO YOU ARE OR WHY YOU'RE FLYING AROUND LIKE A GUARDIAN ANGEL, BUT PLEASE KEEP DOING THAT.
THAT WAS...VERY COOL.
RELAX.
WHO'S HAIRY?
HE'S LAUFEY. THE FATHER OF LOKI.
MOST SAGAS POSIT LOKI AS BLOOD-BROTHER OF ODIN, BUT IN FACT HE WAS ADOPTED BY ODIN AND IS THOR'S ADOPTIVE BRO--
YEAH, THAT'S ENOUGH GEEKSPEAK. HMM.
DEAD PARENTS COMING BACK. I THINK THIS IS TO DO WITH US.
I MEAN, ME.
HMM. YEAH, THAT LINES UP.
THAT'S WHY I LOST TRACK OF YOU. BEEN RUNNING AROUND SINCE...
¡AY DIOS!

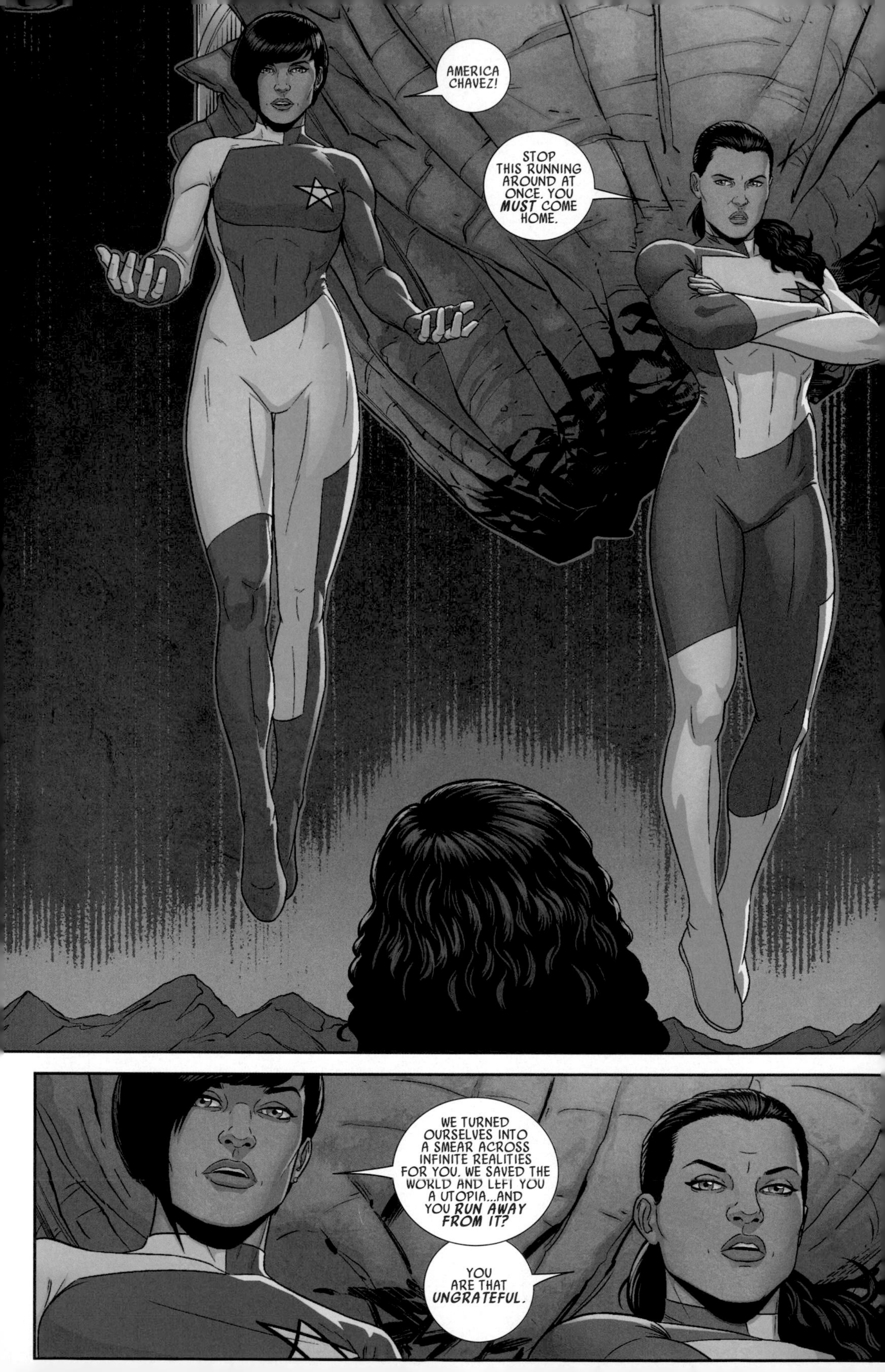
AMERICA CHAVEZ!
STOP THIS RUNNING AROUND AT ONCE. YOU MUST COME HOME.
WE TURNED OURSELVES INTO A SMEAR ACROSS INFINITE REALITIES FOR YOU. WE SAVED THE WORLD AND LEFT YOU A UTOPIA...AND YOU RUN AWAY FROM IT?
YOU ARE THAT UNGRATEFUL.

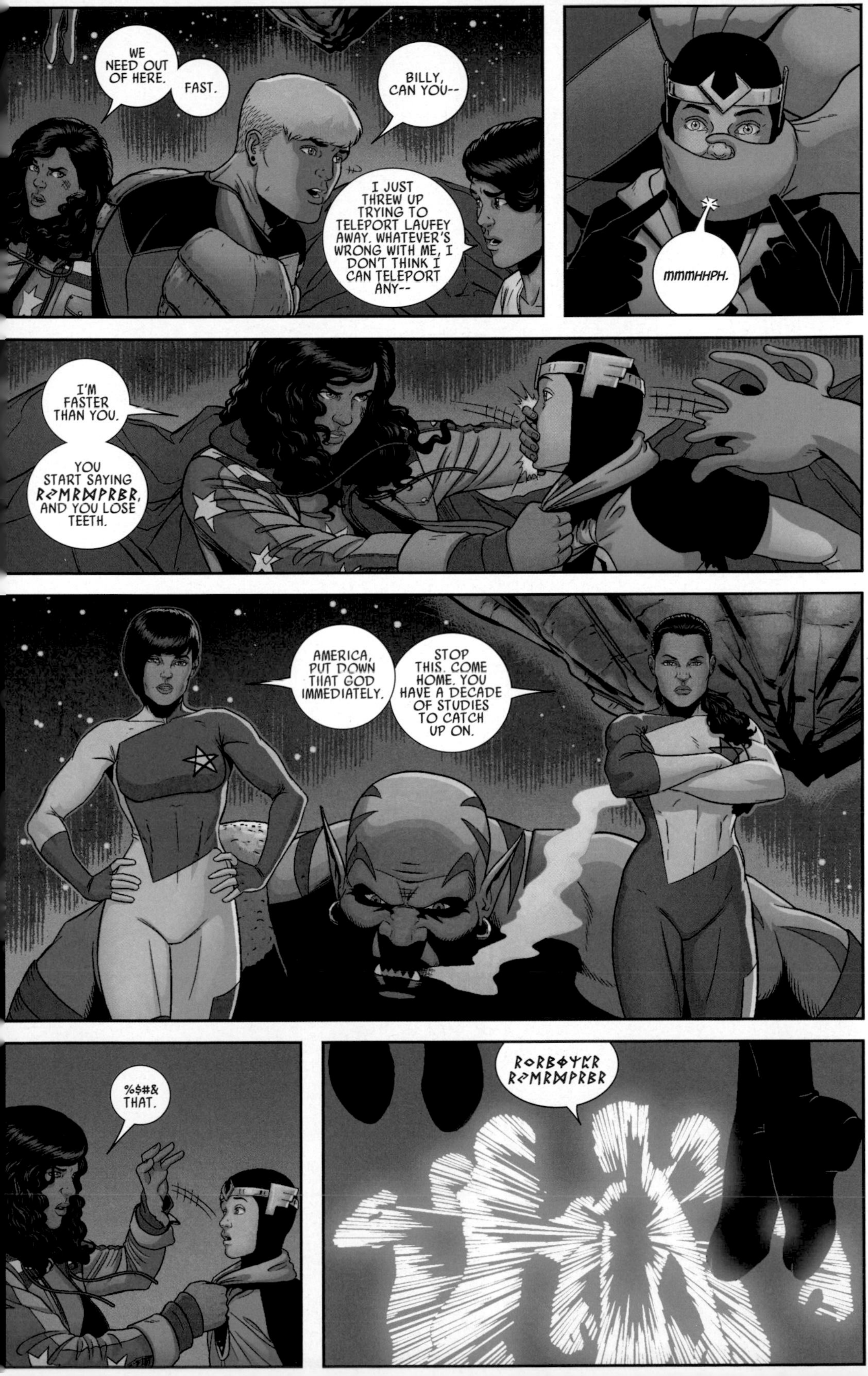
WE NEED OUT OF HERE.
FAST.
BILLY, CAN YOU--
I JUST THREW UP TRYING TO TELEPORT LAUFEY AWAY. WHATEVER'S WRONG WITH ME, I DON'T THINK I CAN TELEPORT ANY--
MMMHHPH.
I'M FASTER THAN YOU.
YOU START SAYING
AND YOU LOSE TEETH.
AMERICA, PUT DOWN THAT GOD IMMEDIATELY.
STOP THIS. COME HOME. YOU HAVE A DECADE OF STUDIES TO CATCH UP ON.
%$#& THAT.

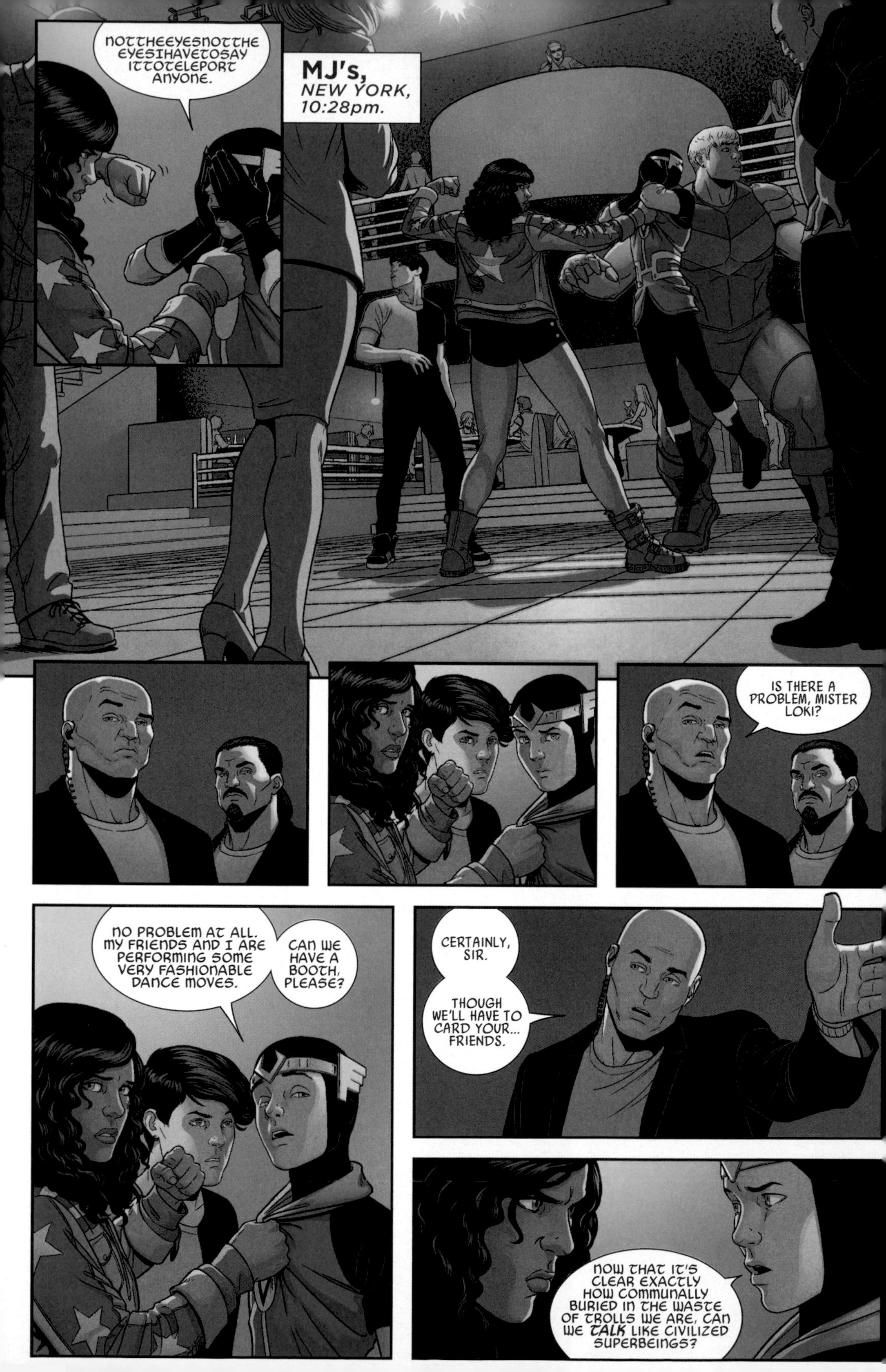
NOTTHEEYESNOTTHE EYESIHAVETOSAY ITTOTELEPORT ANYONE.
MJ's, NEW YORK, 10:28pm.
IS THERE A PROBLEM, MISTER LOKI?
NO PROBLEM AT ALL. MY FRIENDS AND I ARE PERFORMING SOME VERY FASHIONABLE DANCE MOVES.
CAN WE HAVE A BOOTH, PLEASE?
CERTAINLY, SIR.
THOUGH WE'LL HAVE TO CARD YOUR... FRIENDS.
NOW THAT IT'S CLEAR EXACTLY HOW COMMUNALLY BURIED IN THE WASTE OF TROLLS WE ARE, CAN WE TALK LIKE CIVILIZED SUPERBEINGS?

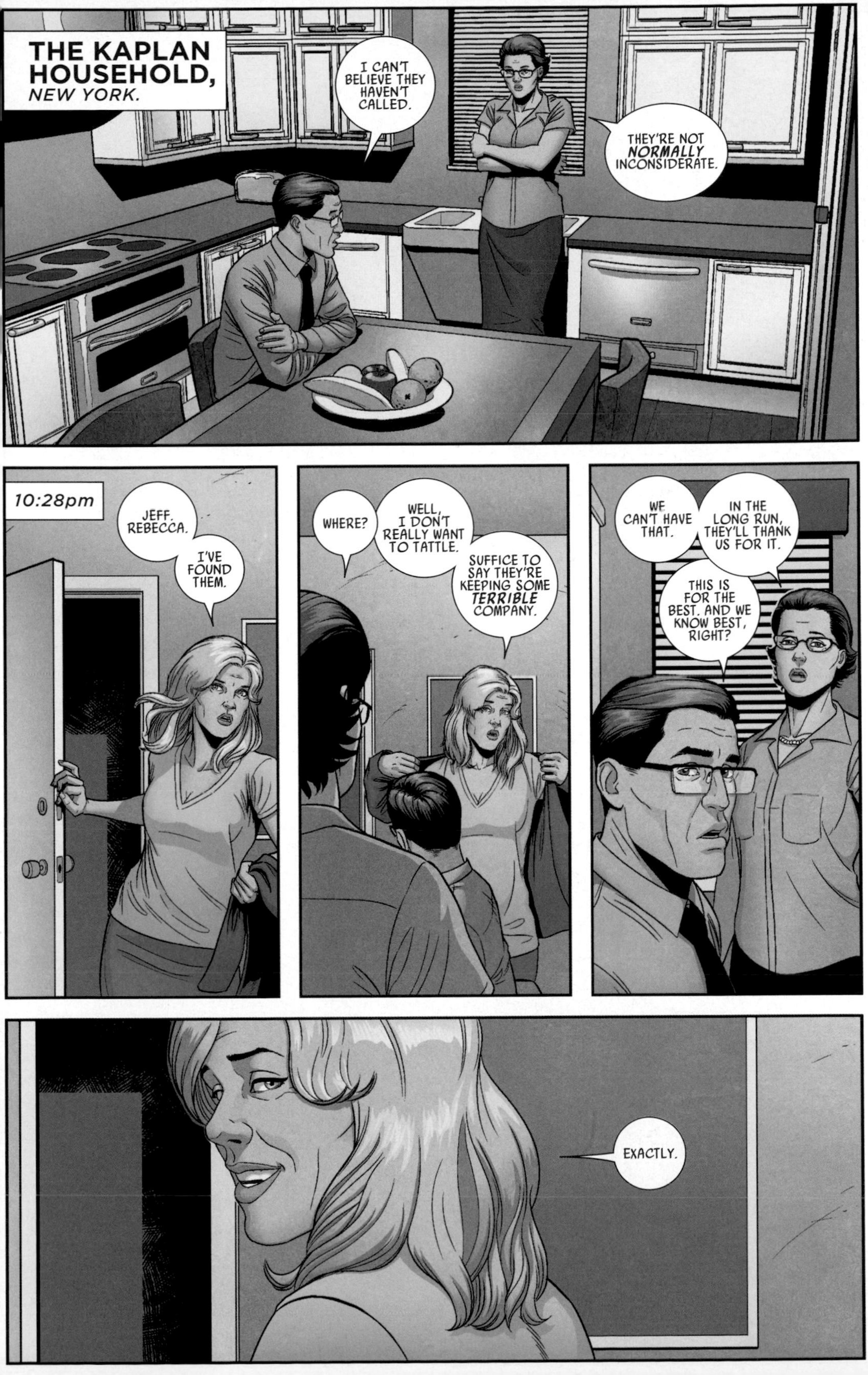
THE KAPLAN HOUSEHOLD, NEW YORK.
I CAN'T BELIEVE THEY HAVEN'T CALLED.
THEY'RE NOT NORMALLY INCONSIDERATE.
10:28pm
JEFF. REBECCA.
I'VE FOUND THEM.
WHERE?
WELL, I DON'T REALLY WANT TO TATTLE.
SUFFICE TO SAY THEY'RE KEEPING SOME TERRIBLE COMPANY.
WE CAN'T HAVE THAT.
IN THE LONG RUN, THEY'LL THANK US FOR IT.
THIS IS FOR THE BEST. AND WE KNOW BEST, RIGHT?
EXACTLY.

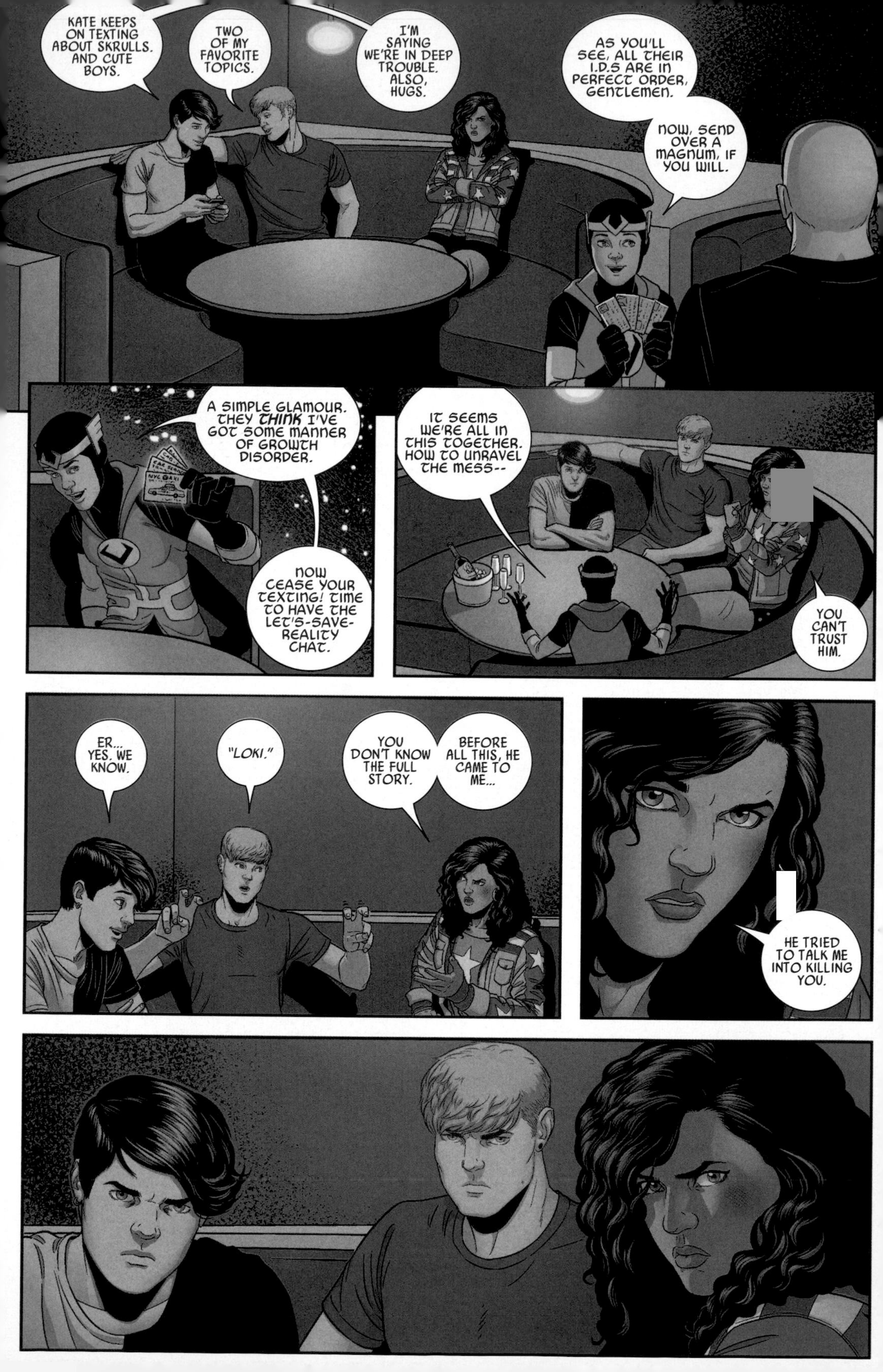
KATE KEEPS ON TEXTING ABOUT SKRULLS. AND CUTE BOYS.
TWO OF MY FAVORITE TOPICS.
I'M SAYING WE'RE IN DEEP TROUBLE. ALSO, HUGS.
AS YOU'LL SEE, ALL THEIR I.D.S ARE IN PERFECT ORDER, GENTLEMEN.
NOW, SEND OVER A MAGNUM, IF YOU WILL.
A SIMPLE GLAMOUR. THEY THINK I'VE GOT SOME MANNER OF GROWTH DISORDER.
NOW CEASE YOUR TEXTING! TIME TO HAVE THE LET'S-SAVE-REALITY CHAT.
IT SEEMS WE'RE ALL IN THIS TOGETHER. HOW TO UNRAVEL THE MESS--
YOU CAN'T TRUST HIM.
ER... YES. WE KNOW.
"LOKI."
YOU DON'T KNOW THE FULL STORY.
BEFORE ALL THIS, HE CAME TO ME...
HE TRIED TO TALK ME INTO KILLING YOU.

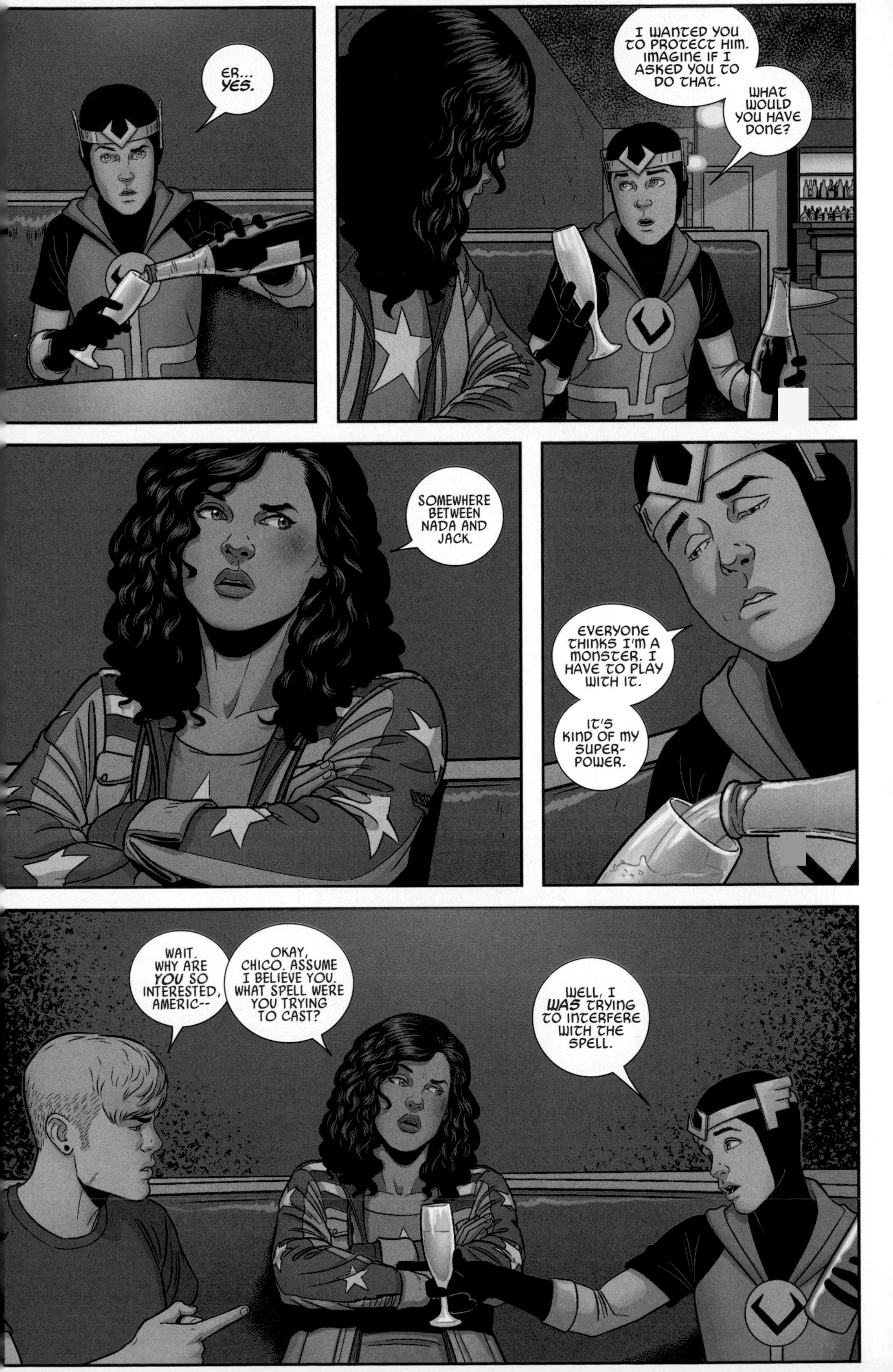
ER... YES.
I WANTED YOU TO PROTECT HIM. IMAGINE IF I ASKED YOU TO DO THAT.
WHAT WOULD YOU HAVE DONE?
SOMEWHERE BETWEEN NADA AND JACK.
EVERYONE THINKS I'M A MONSTER. I HAVE TO PLAY WITH IT.
IT'S KIND OF MY SUPER-POWER.
OKAY, CHICO. ASSUME I BELIEVE YOU. WHAT SPELL WERE YOU TRYING TO CAST?
WELL, I WAS TRYING TO INTERFERE WITH THE SPELL.
WAIT. WHY ARE YOU SO INTERESTED, AMERIC--

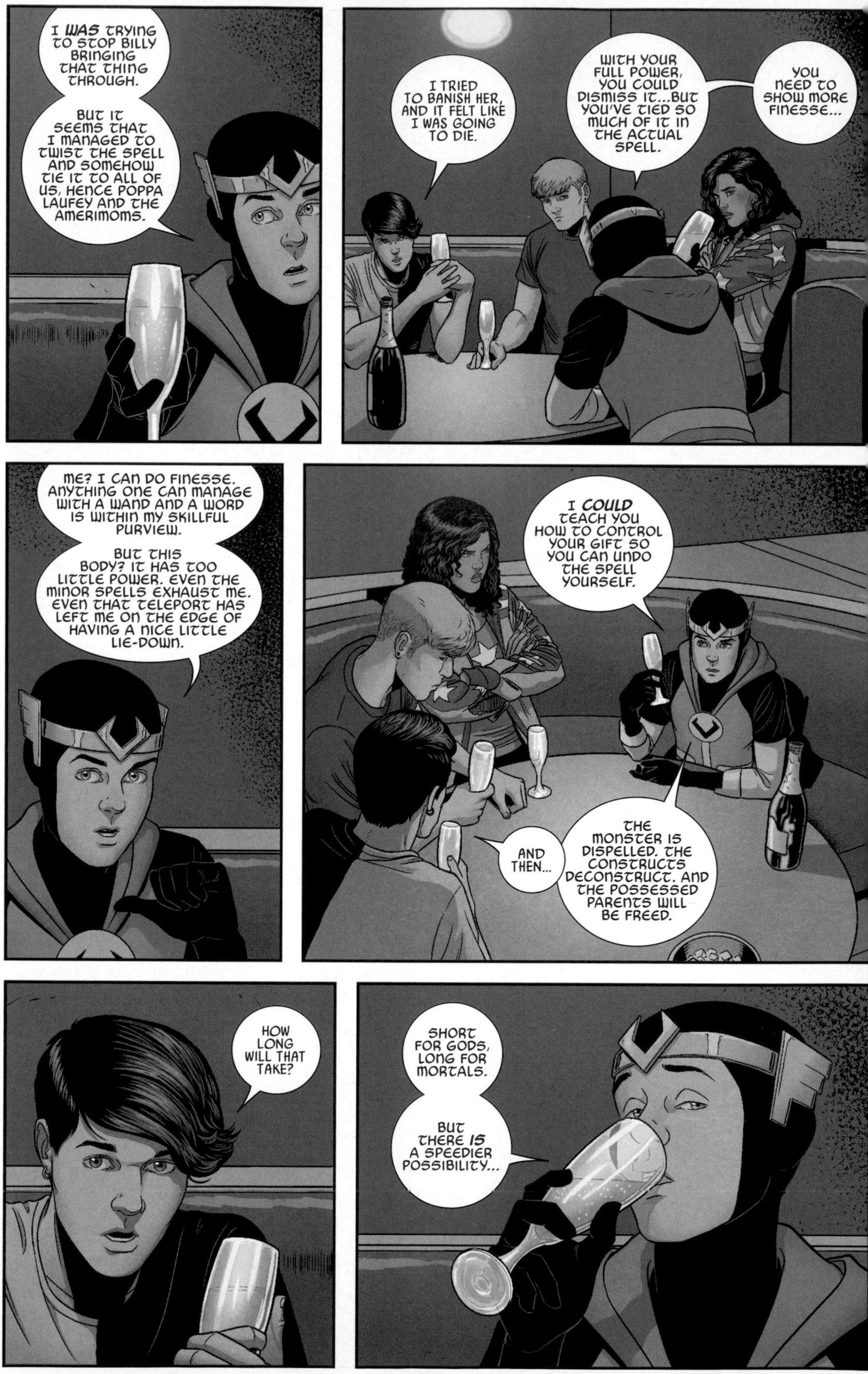
I WAS TRYING TO STOP BILLY BRINGING THAT THING THROUGH.
BUT IT SEEMS THAT I MANAGED TO TWIST THE SPELL AND SOMEHOW TIE IT TO ALL OF US, HENCE POPPA LAUFEY AND THE AMERIMOMS.
I TRIED TO BANISH HER, AND IT FELT LIKE I WAS GOING TO DIE.
WITH YOUR FULL POWER, YOU COULD DISMISS IT...BUT YOU'VE TIED SO MUCH OF IT IN THE ACTUAL SPELL.
YOU NEED TO SHOW MORE FINESSE...
ME? I CAN DO FINESSE. ANYTHING ONE CAN MANAGE WITH A WAND AND A WORD IS WITHIN MY SKILLFUL PURVIEW.
BUT THIS BODY? IT HAS TOO LITTLE POWER. EVEN THE MINOR SPELLS EXHAUST ME. EVEN THAT TELEPORT HAS LEFT ME ON THE EDGE OF HAVING A NICE LITTLE LIE-DOWN.
I COULD TEACH YOU HOW TO CONTROL YOUR GIFT SO YOU CAN UNDO THE SPELL YOURSELF.
AND THEN...
THE MONSTER IS DISPELLED. THE CONSTRUCTS DECONSTRUCT. AND THE POSSESSED PARENTS WILL BE FREED.
HOW LONG WILL THAT TAKE?
SHORT FOR GODS, LONG FOR MORTALS.
BUT THERE IS A SPEEDIER POSSIBILITY...

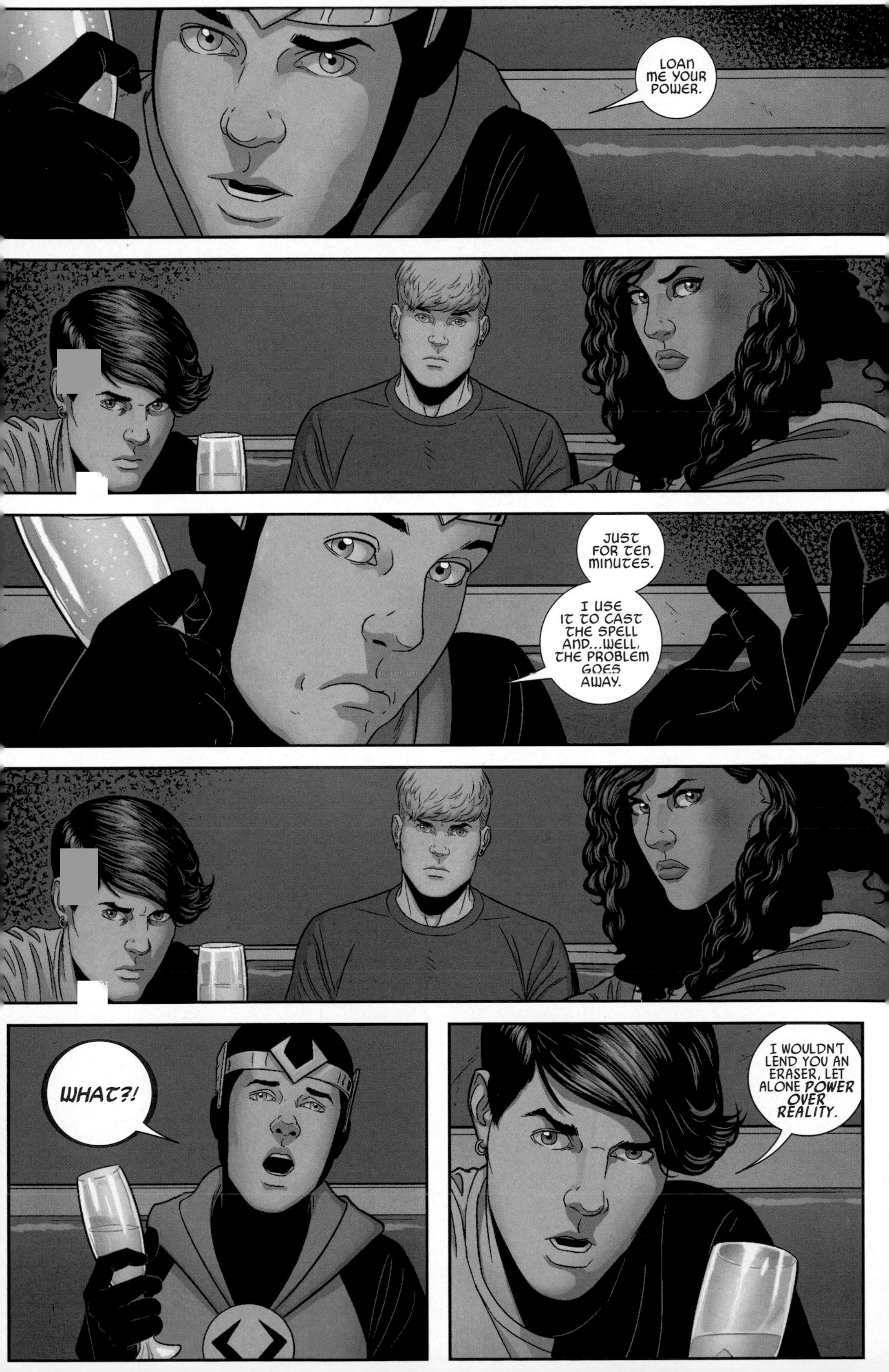
LOAN ME YOUR POWER.
JUST FOR TEN MINUTES.
I USE IT TO CAST THE SPELL AND...WELL, THE PROBLEM GOES AWAY.
WHAT?!
I WOULDN'T LEND YOU AN ERASER, LET ALONE POWER OVER REALITY.

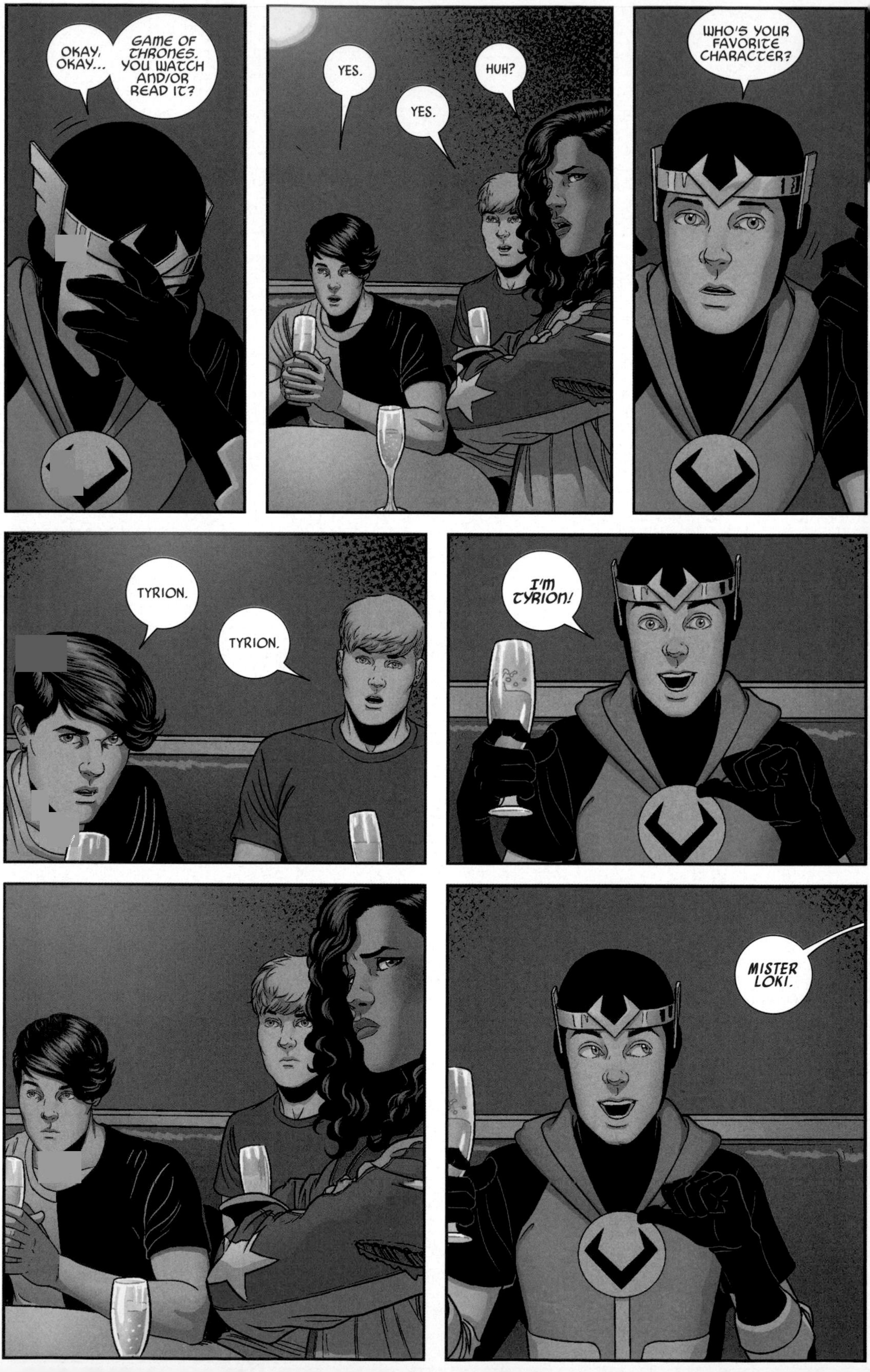

OKAY, OKAY...
GAME OF THRONES. YOU WATCH AND/OR READ IT?
YES.
YES.
HUH?
WHO'S YOUR FAVORITE CHARACTER?
TYRION.
TYRION.
I'M TYRION!
MISTER LOKI.

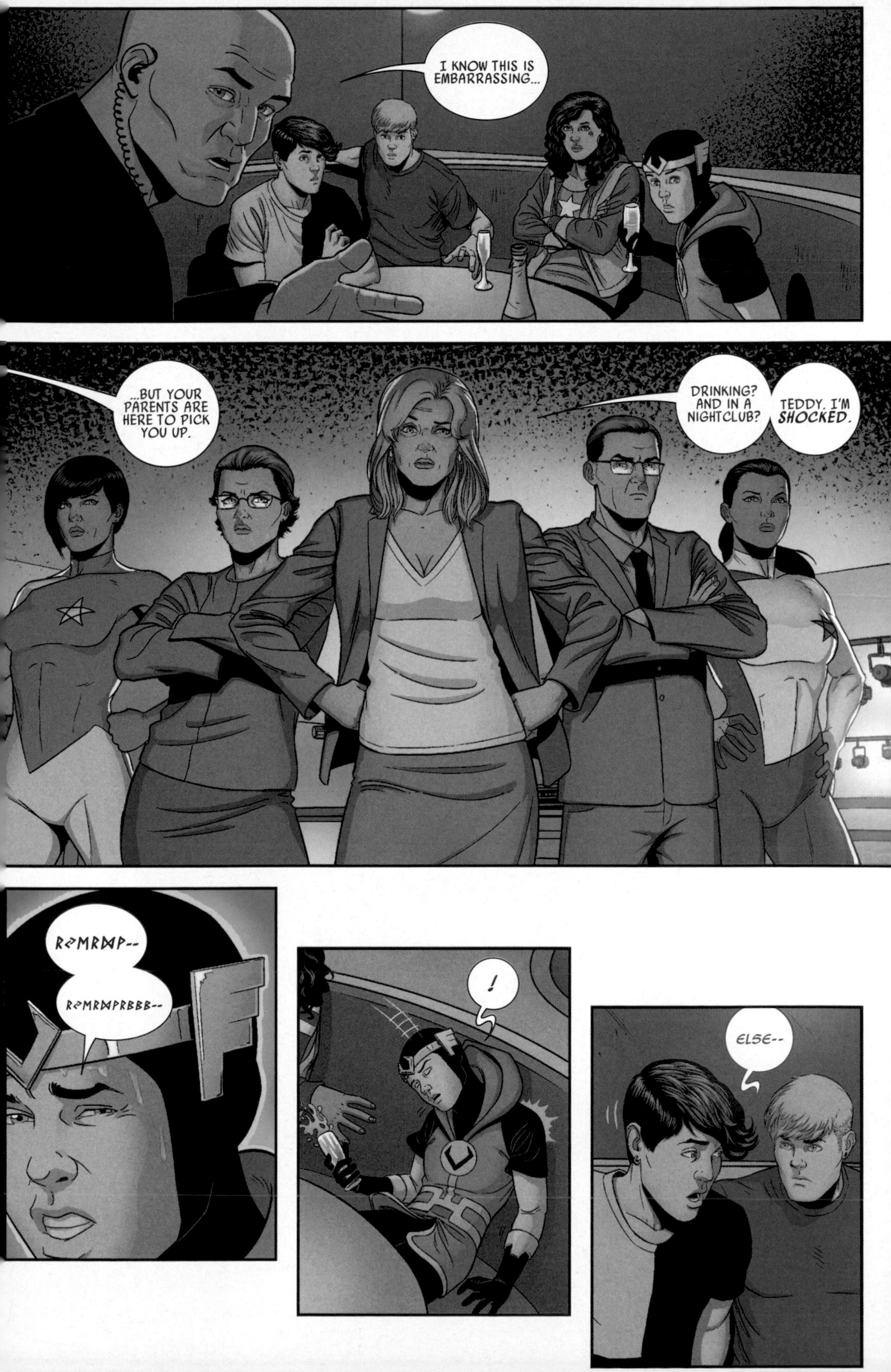
I KNOW THIS IS EMBARRASSING...
...BUT YOUR PARENTS ARE HERE TO PICK YOU UP.
DRINKING? AND IN A NIGHTCLUB?
TEDDY. I'M SHOCKED.
!
ELSE--

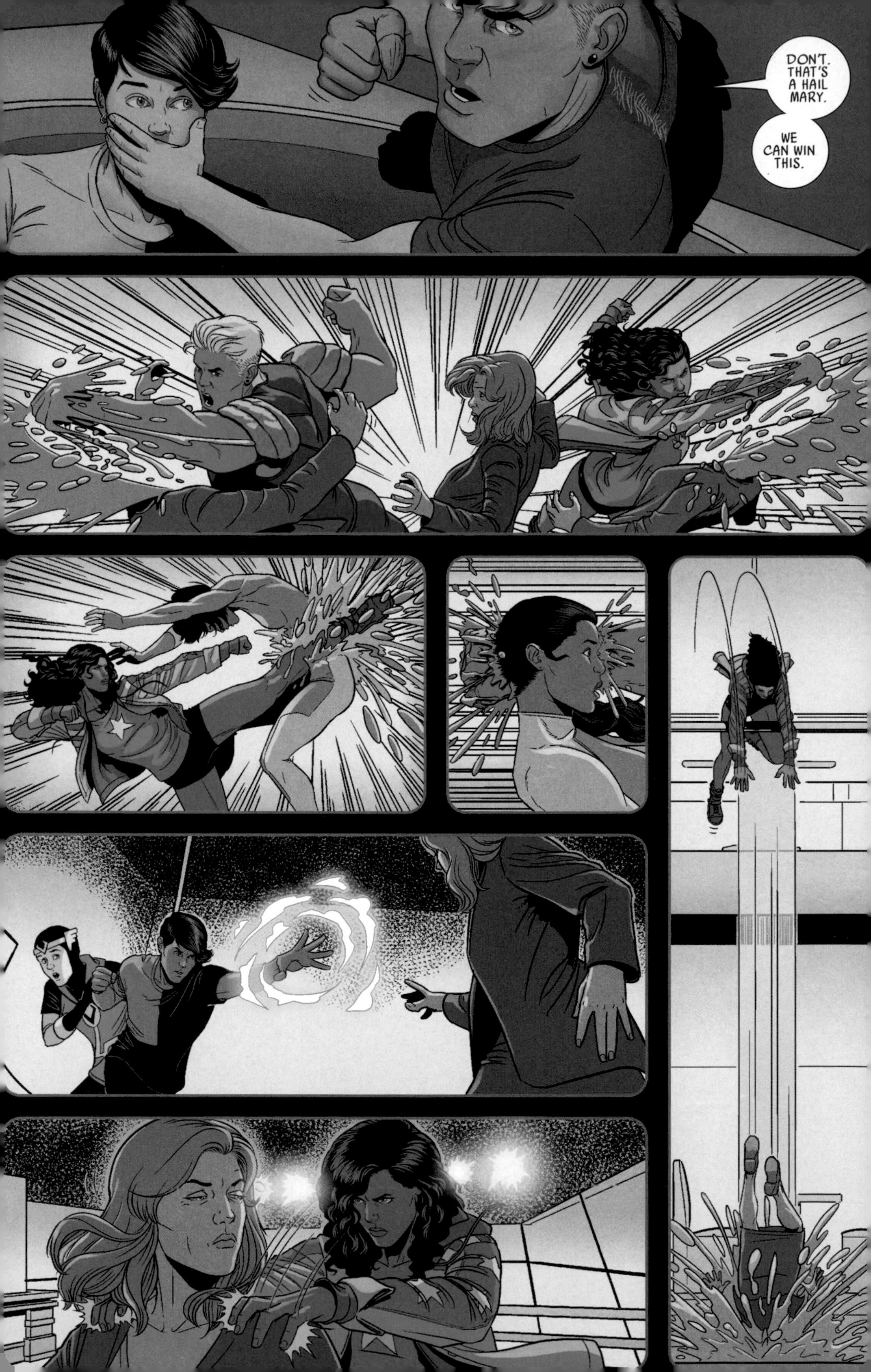
DON'T. THAT'S A HAIL MARY.
WE CAN WIN THIS.

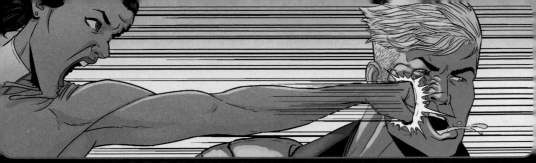

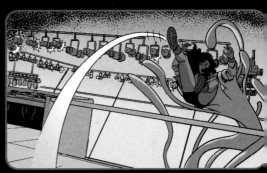

BILLY,
WAKE UP,
BILLY.

FIGHT'S
OVER.

WE ASKED
THE PARENTS
TO STAY AND
EVERYONE ELSE
TO LEAVE.

THEY ALL
DID. THEY ALL
UNDERSTOOD.

GROWN-UPS
ALWAYS
DO.

AND THEN
WE HAD A
LITTLE CHAT
ABOUT YOUR
FUTURE.

AND
WONDERFUL
NEWS!

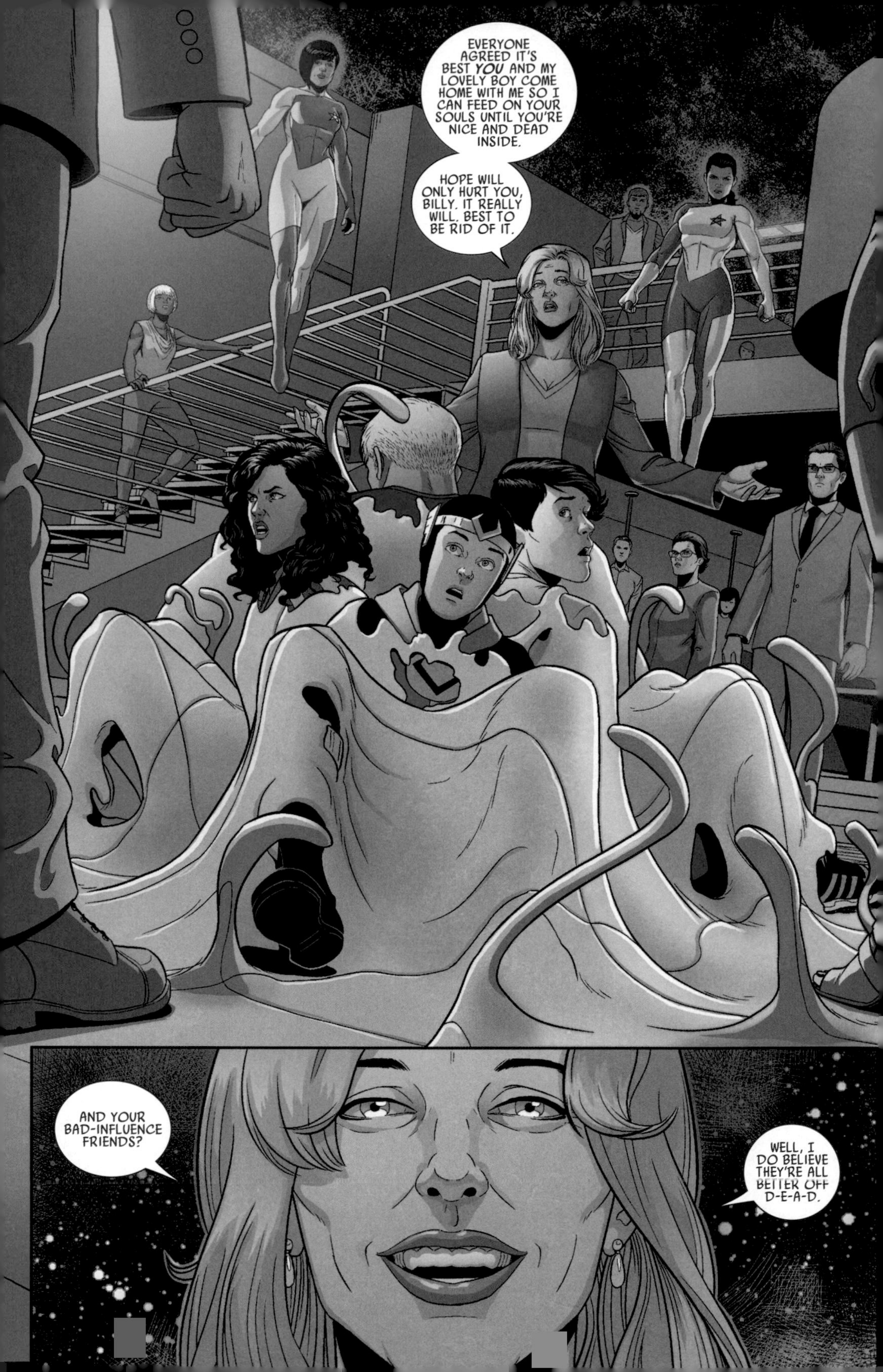
EVERYONE AGREED IT'S BEST YOU AND MY LOVELY BOY COME HOME WITH ME SO I CAN FEED ON YOUR SOULS UNTIL YOU'RE NICE AND DEAD INSIDE.
HOPE WILL ONLY HURT YOU, BILLY. IT REALLY WILL. BEST TO BE RID OF IT.
AND YOUR BAD-INFLUENCE FRIENDS?
WELL, I DO BELIEVE THEY'RE ALL BETTER OFF D-E-A-D.

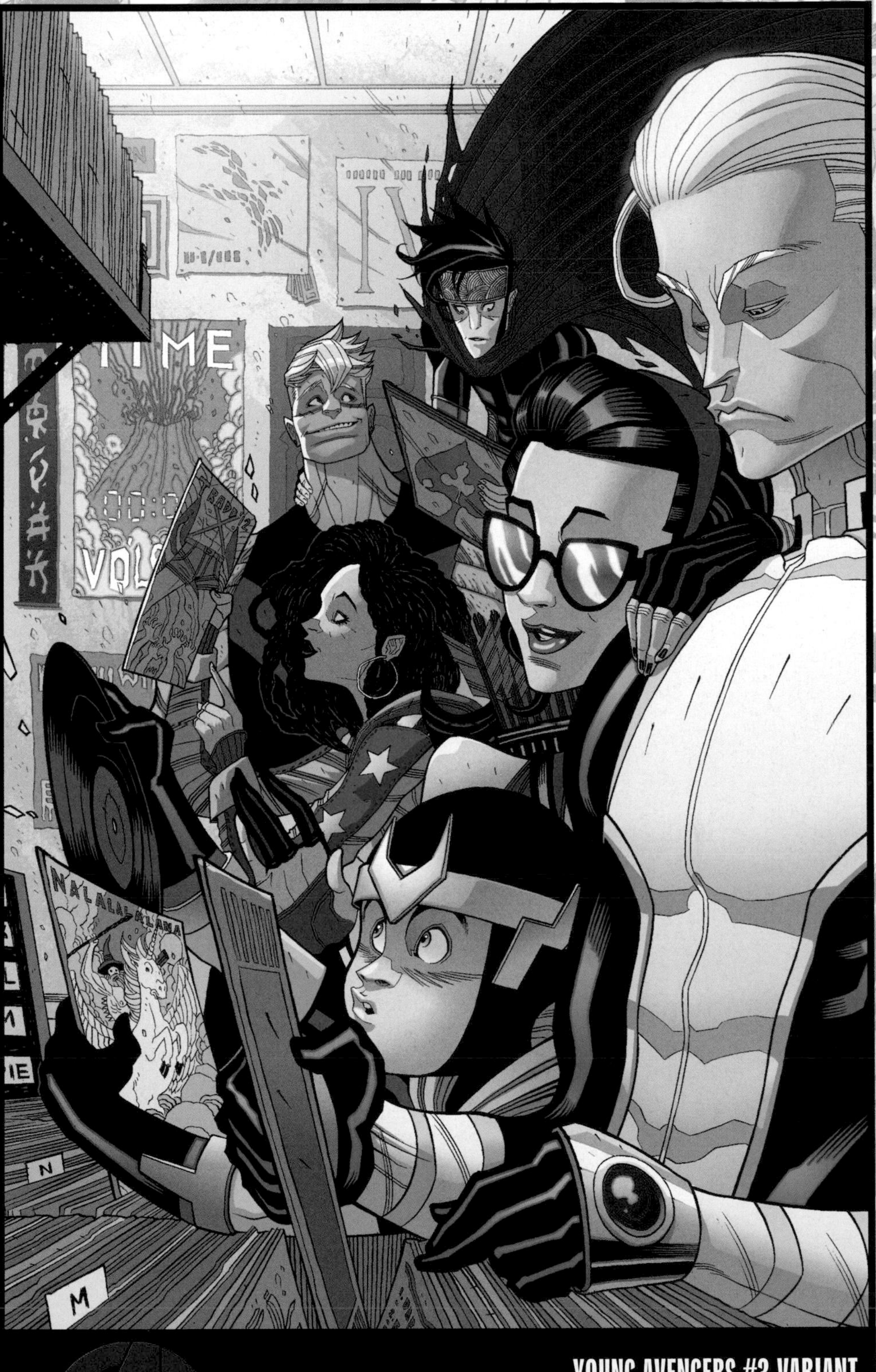
TIME
00:0
VOL
IV
NALALALALANA
N
M

YOUNG AVENGERS #3 VARIANT

BY TRADD MOORE & MATTHEW WILSON

AMERICA #1

AMERICA CHAVEZ STARS IN HER FIRST SOLO SERIES! AND THE FIRST TASK
THIS NO-NONSENSE POWERHOUSE UNDERTAKES? SHE GOES TO COLLEGE!

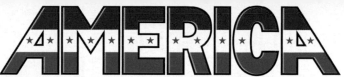

AMERICA

America Chavez is done with the hero scene. She did the Teen Brigade thing. She basically WAS the Young Avengers. And the Ultimates? They're cool, but saving the world every weekend is starting to get old.

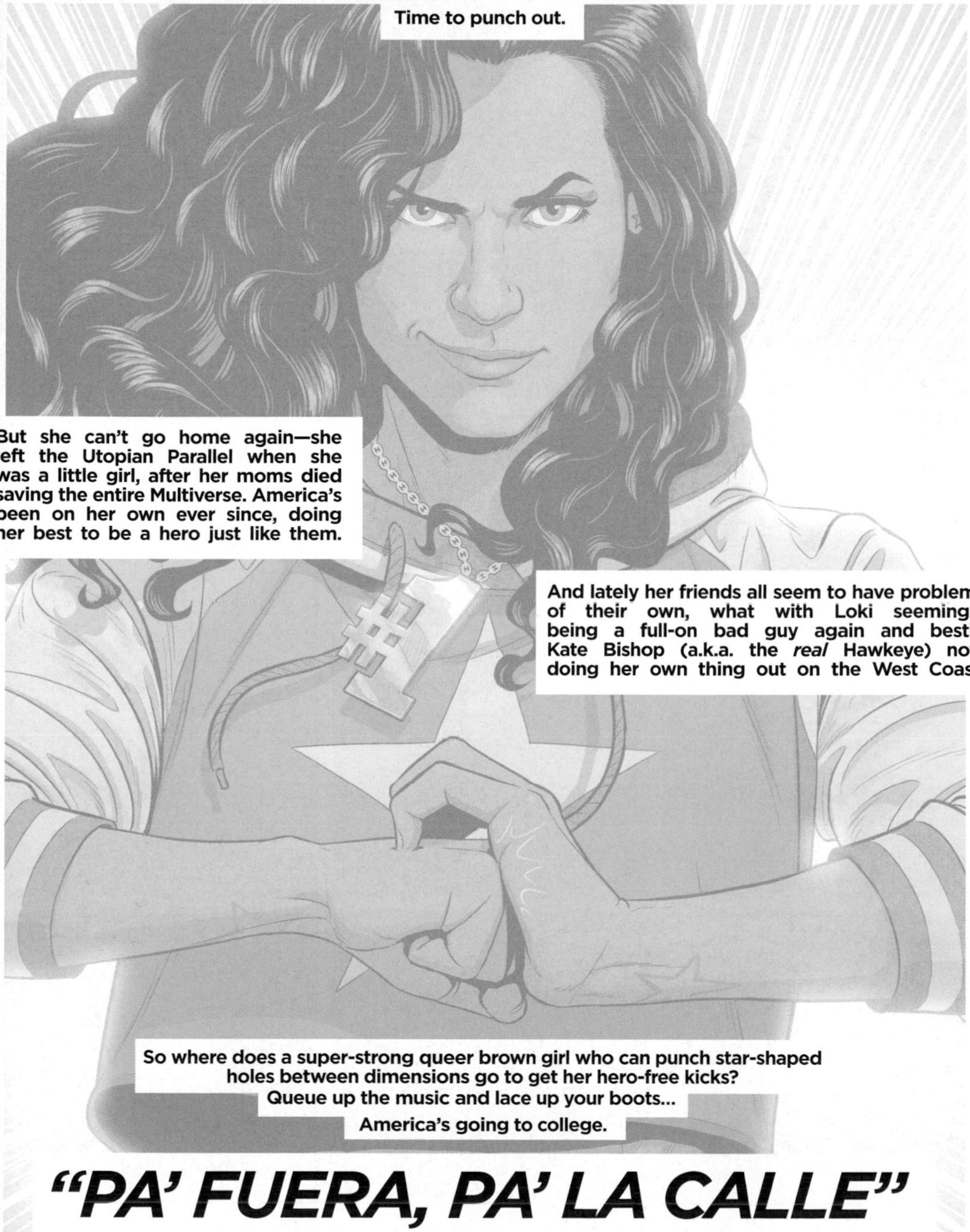
Time to punch out.
But she can't go home again—she left the Utopian Parallel when she was a little girl, after her moms died saving the entire Multiverse. America's been on her own ever since, doing her best to be a hero just like them.
And lately her friends all seem to have problems of their own, what with Loki seemingly being a full-on bad guy again and bestie Kate Bishop (a.k.a. the *real* Hawkeye) now doing her own thing out on the West Coast.
So where does a super-strong queer brown girl who can punch star-shaped holes between dimensions go to get her hero-free kicks?
Queue up the music and lace up your boots...
America's going to college.

"PA' FUERA, PA' LA CALLE"

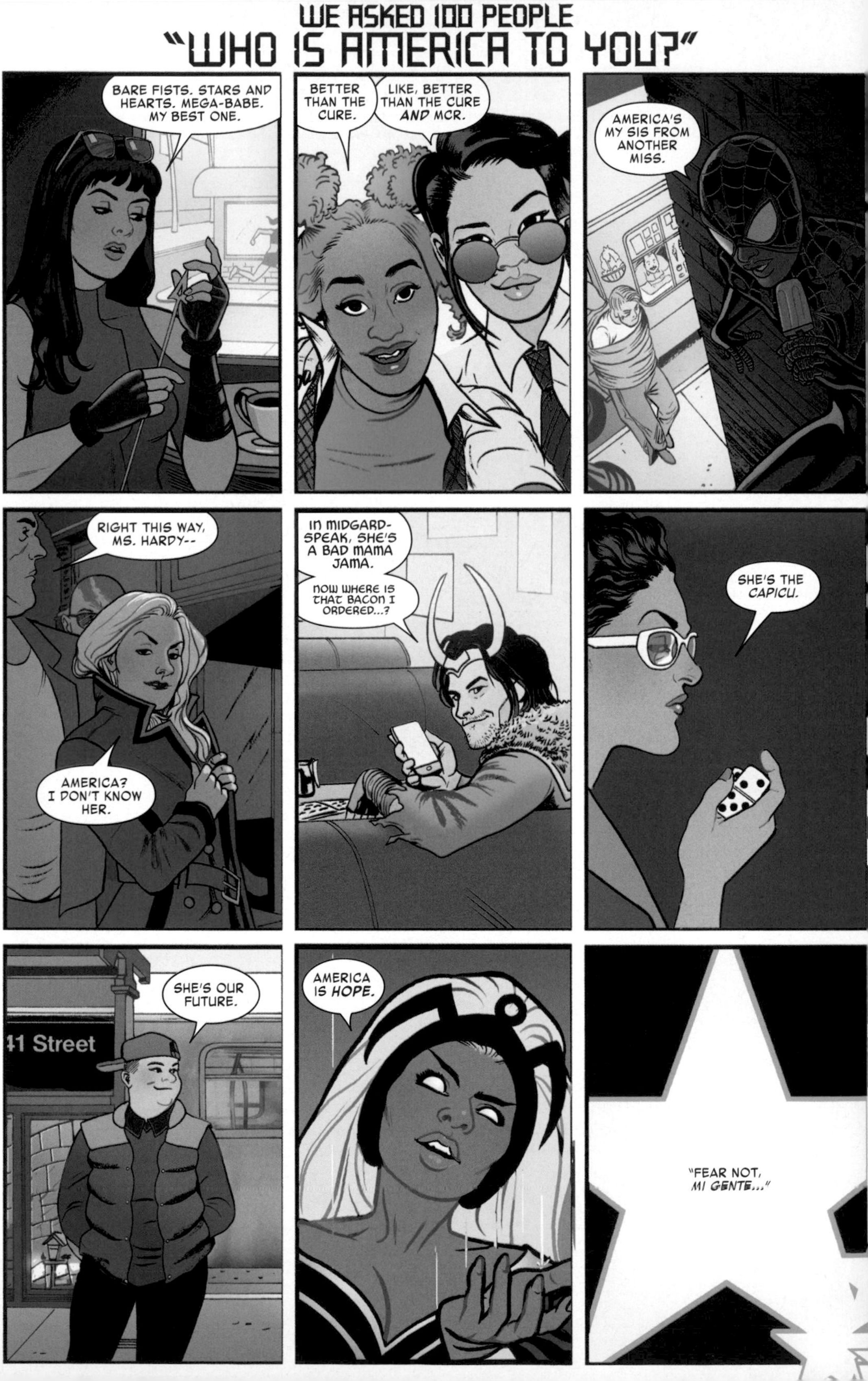
WE ASKED 100 PEOPLE
"WHO IS AMERICA TO YOU?"
BARE FISTS. STARS AND HEARTS. MEGA-BABE. MY BEST ONE.
BETTER THAN THE CURE.
LIKE, BETTER THAN THE CURE AND MCR.
AMERICA'S MY SIS FROM ANOTHER MISS.
RIGHT THIS WAY, MS. HARDY--
AMERICA? I DON'T KNOW HER.
IN MIDGARD-SPEAK, SHE'S A BAD MAMA JAMA.
NOW WHERE IS THAT BACON I ORDERED...?
SHE'S THE CAPICU.
SHE'S OUR FUTURE.
41 Street
AMERICA IS HOPE.
"FEAR NOT, MI GENTE..."

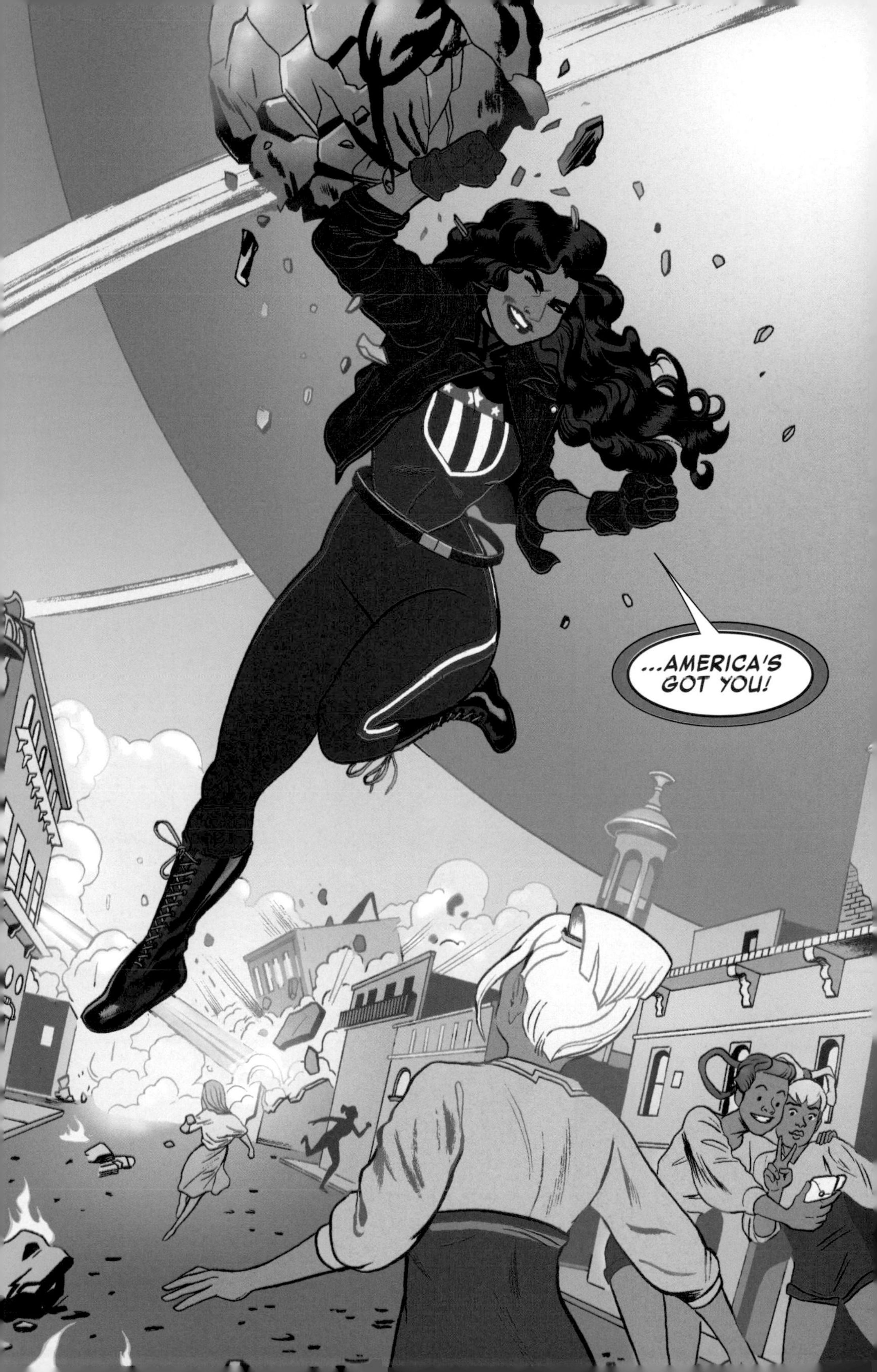
...AMERICA'S GOT YOU!

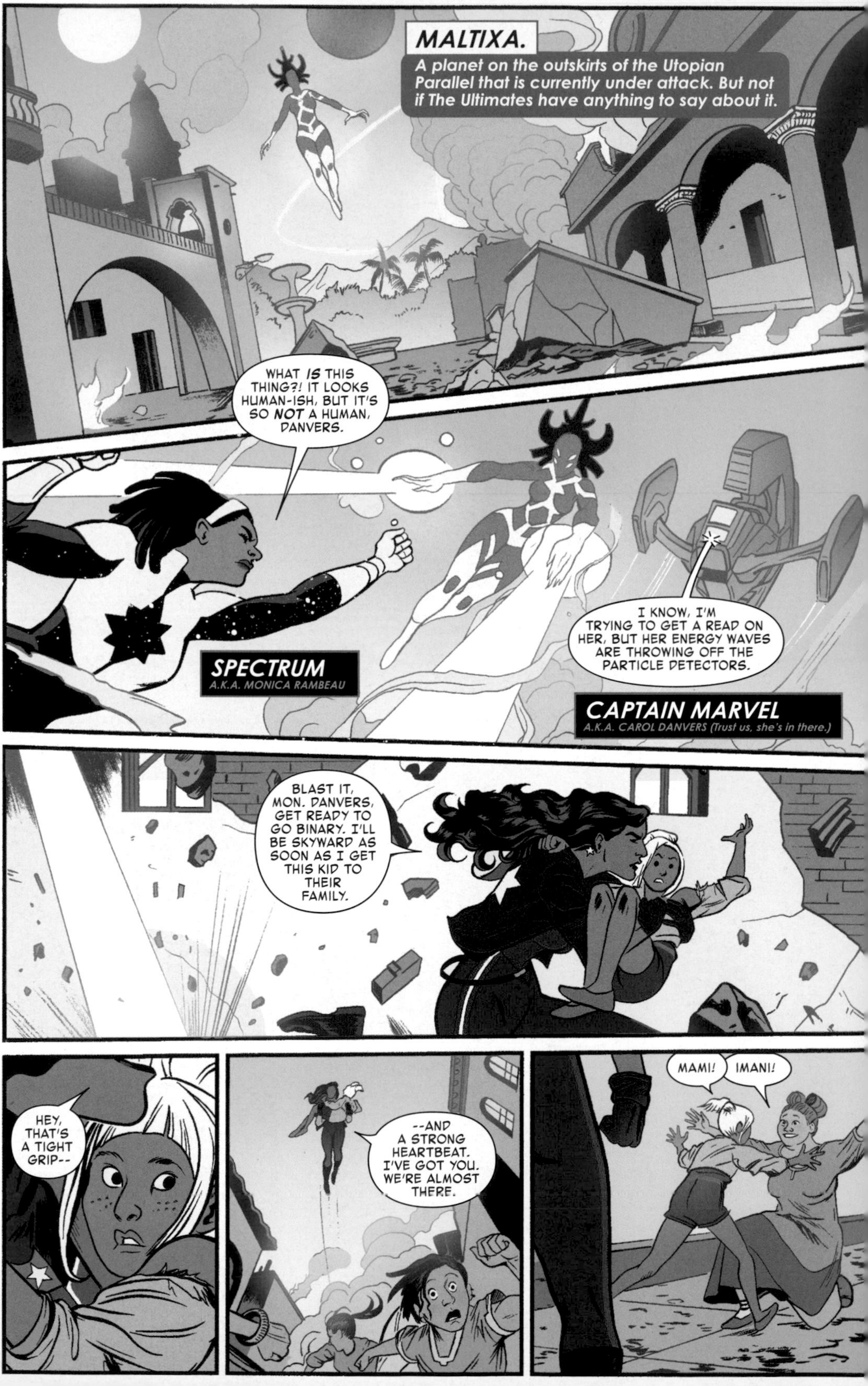

MALTIXA.
A planet on the outskirts of the Utopian Parallel that is currently under attack. But not if The Ultimates have anything to say about it.
WHAT IS THIS THING?! IT LOOKS HUMAN-ISH, BUT IT'S SO NOT A HUMAN, DANVERS.
I KNOW, I'M TRYING TO GET A READ ON HER, BUT HER ENERGY WAVES ARE THROWING OFF THE PARTICLE DETECTORS.
SPECTRUM
A.K.A. MONICA RAMBEAU
CAPTAIN MARVEL
A.K.A. CAROL DANVERS (Trust us, she's in there.)
BLAST IT, MON. DANVERS, GET READY TO GO BINARY. I'LL BE SKYWARD AS SOON AS I GET THIS KID TO THEIR FAMILY.
HEY, THAT'S A TIGHT GRIP--
--AND A STRONG HEARTBEAT. I'VE GOT YOU. WE'RE ALMOST THERE.
MAMI!
IMANI!

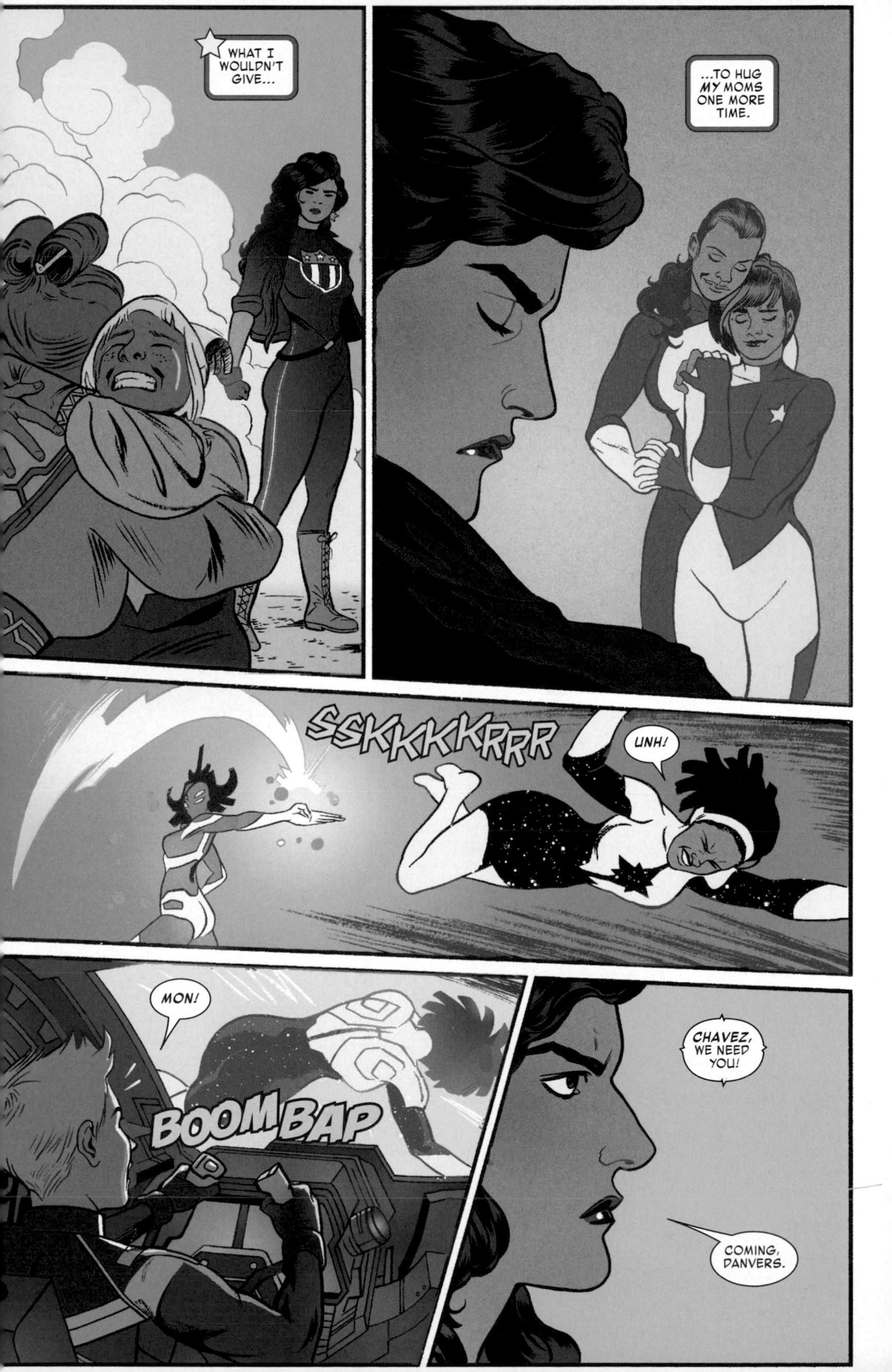
WHAT I WOULDN'T GIVE...
...TO HUG MY MOMS ONE MORE TIME.
SSKKKKRRR
UNH!
MON!
BOOM BAP
CHAVEZ, WE NEED YOU!
COMING, DANVERS.

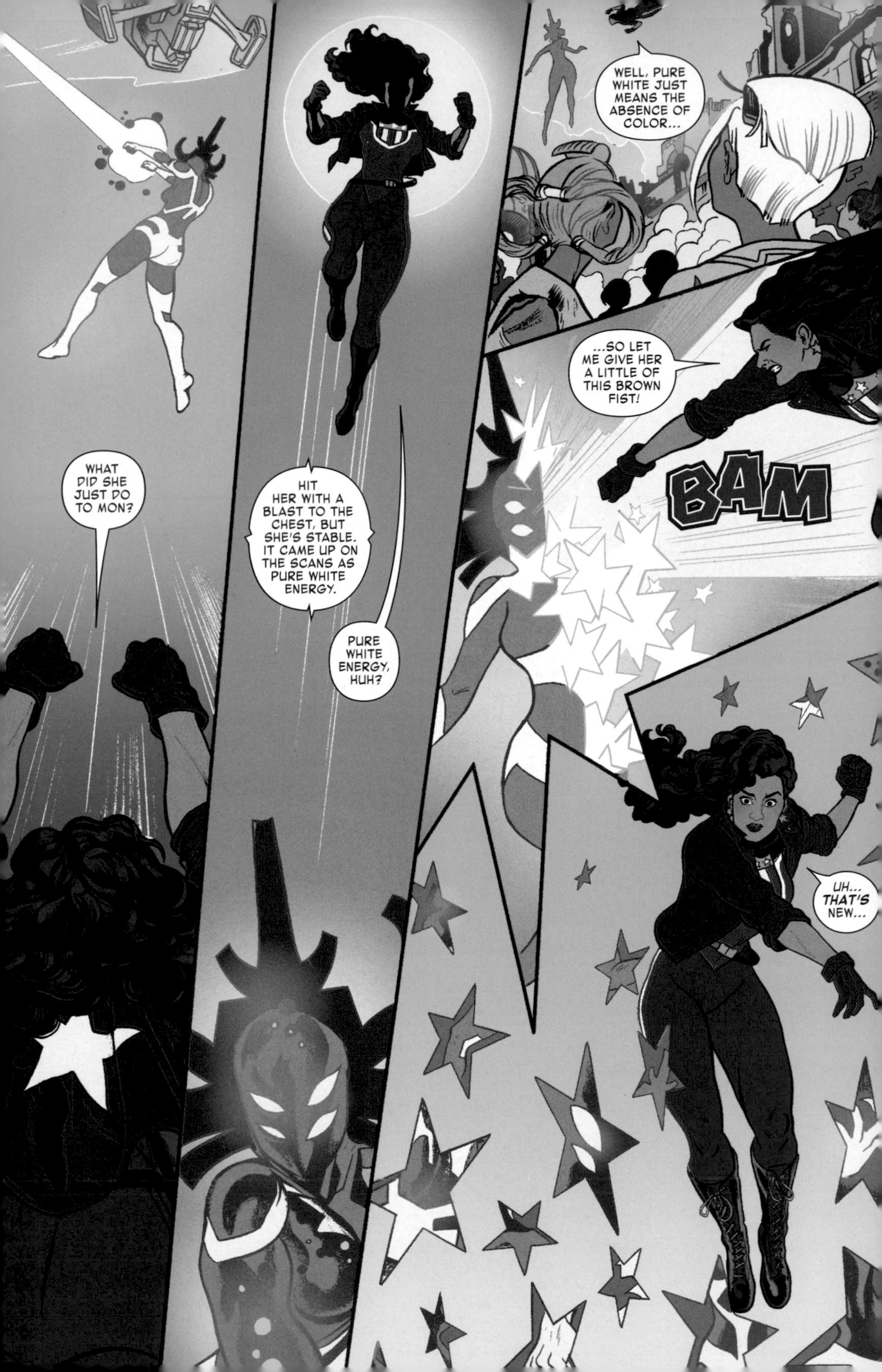
WHAT DID SHE JUST DO TO MON?
HIT HER WITH A BLAST TO THE CHEST, BUT SHE'S STABLE. IT CAME UP ON THE SCANS AS PURE WHITE ENERGY.
PURE WHITE ENERGY, HUH?
WELL, PURE WHITE JUST MEANS THE ABSENCE OF COLOR...
...SO LET ME GIVE HER A LITTLE OF THIS BROWN FIST!
BAM
UH... THAT'S NEW...

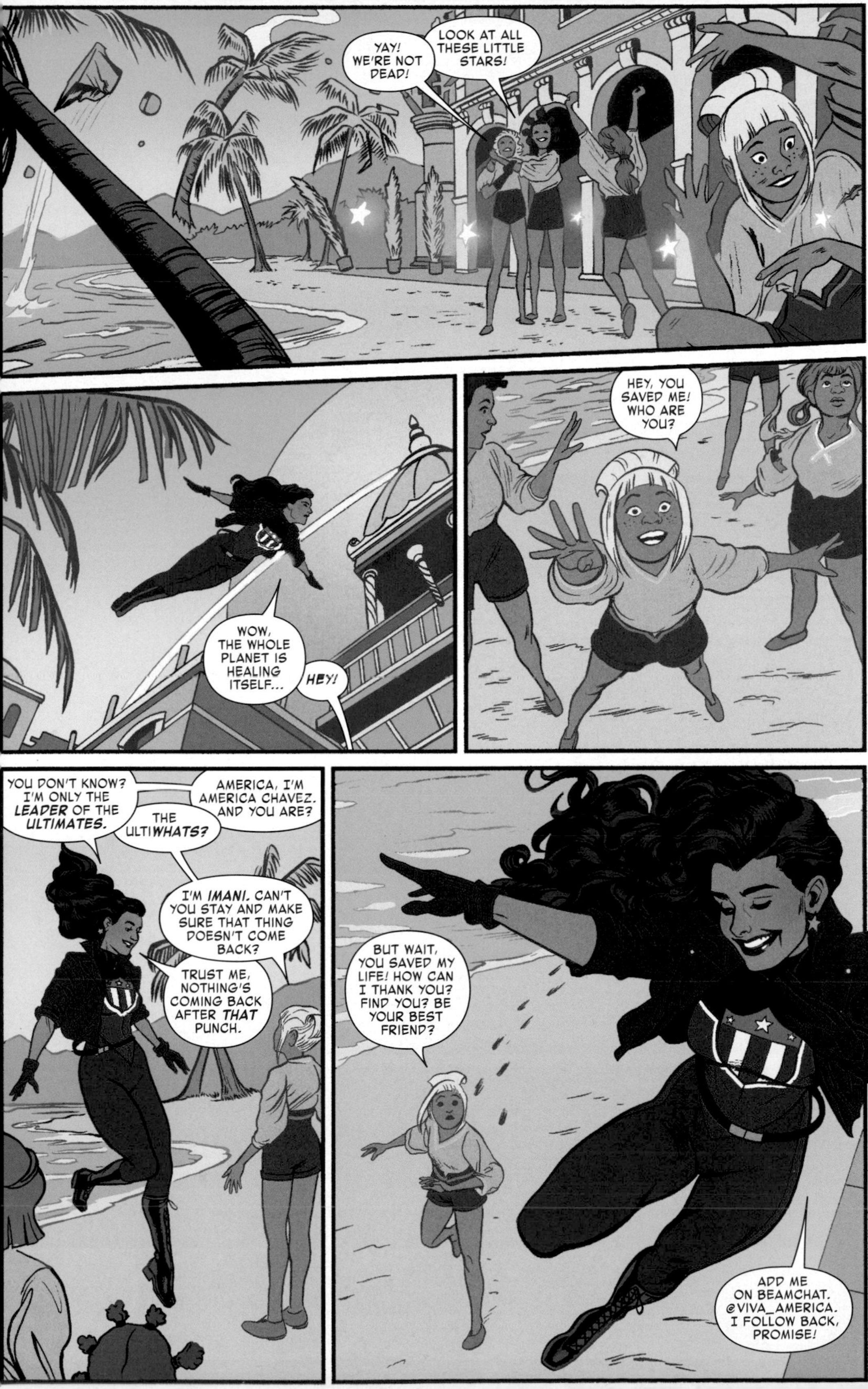
YAY! WE'RE NOT DEAD!
LOOK AT ALL THESE LITTLE STARS!
WOW, THE WHOLE PLANET IS HEALING ITSELF...
HEY!
HEY, YOU SAVED ME! WHO ARE YOU?
AMERICA, I'M AMERICA CHAVEZ. AND YOU ARE?
YOU DON'T KNOW? I'M ONLY THE LEADER OF THE ULTIMATES.
THE ULTIWHATS?
I'M IMANI. CAN'T YOU STAY AND MAKE SURE THAT THING DOESN'T COME BACK?
TRUST ME, NOTHING'S COMING BACK AFTER THAT PUNCH.
BUT WAIT, YOU SAVED MY LIFE! HOW CAN I THANK YOU? FIND YOU? BE YOUR BEST FRIEND?
ADD ME ON BEAMCHAT. @VIVA_AMERICA. I FOLLOW BACK, PROMISE!

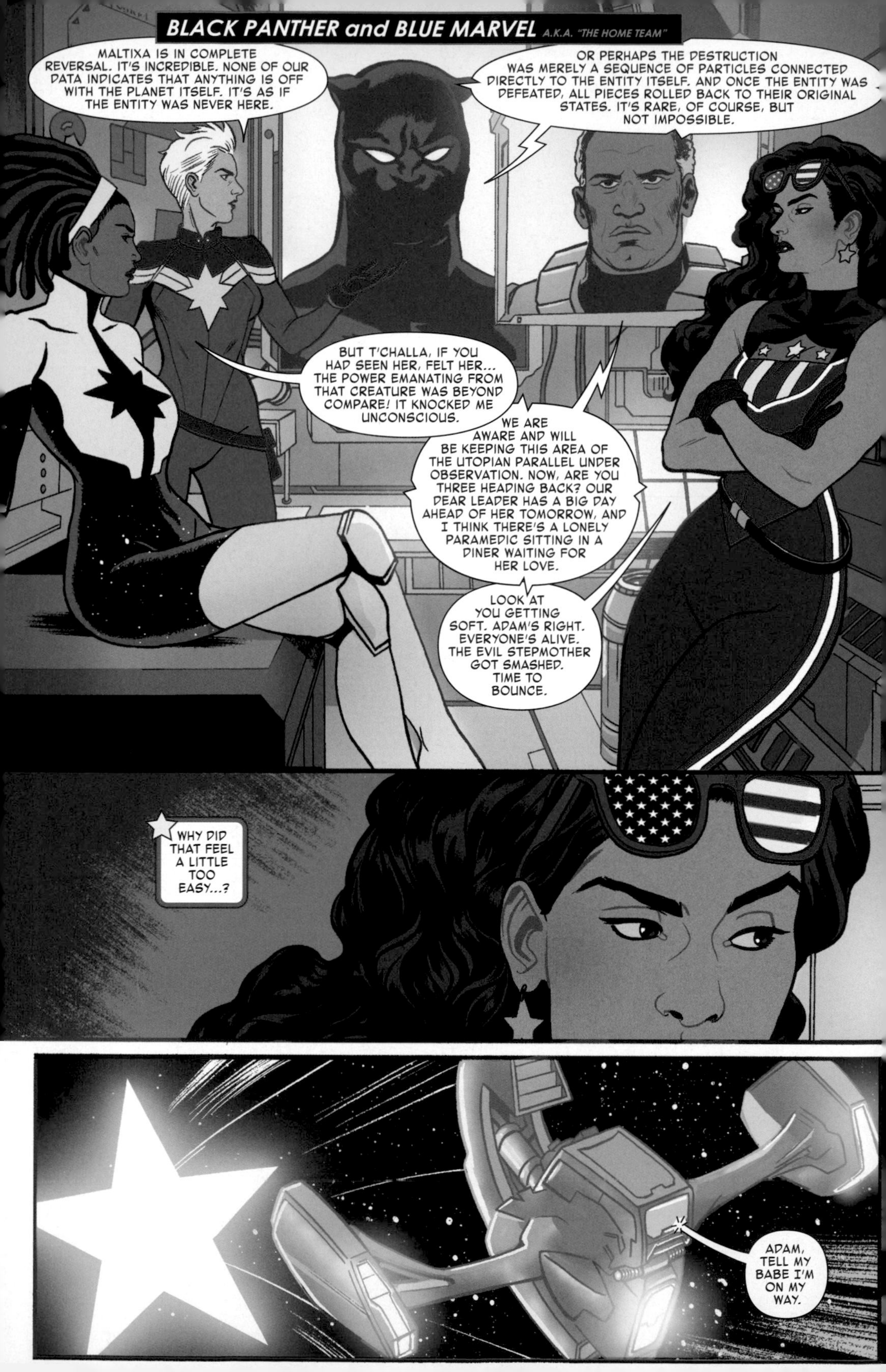
BLACK PANTHER and BLUE MARVEL A.K.A. "THE HOME TEAM"
MALTIXA IS IN COMPLETE REVERSAL. IT'S INCREDIBLE. NONE OF OUR DATA INDICATES THAT ANYTHING IS OFF WITH THE PLANET ITSELF. IT'S AS IF THE ENTITY WAS NEVER HERE.
OR PERHAPS THE DESTRUCTION WAS MERELY A SEQUENCE OF PARTICLES CONNECTED DIRECTLY TO THE ENTITY ITSELF. AND ONCE THE ENTITY WAS DEFEATED, ALL PIECES ROLLED BACK TO THEIR ORIGINAL STATES. IT'S RARE, OF COURSE, BUT NOT IMPOSSIBLE.
BUT T'CHALLA, IF YOU HAD SEEN HER, FELT HER... THE POWER EMANATING FROM THAT CREATURE WAS BEYOND COMPARE! IT KNOCKED ME UNCONSCIOUS.
WE ARE AWARE AND WILL BE KEEPING THIS AREA OF THE UTOPIAN PARALLEL UNDER OBSERVATION. NOW, ARE YOU THREE HEADING BACK? OUR DEAR LEADER HAS A BIG DAY AHEAD OF HER TOMORROW, AND I THINK THERE'S A LONELY PARAMEDIC SITTING IN A DINER WAITING FOR HER LOVE.
LOOK AT YOU GETTING SOFT. ADAM'S RIGHT. EVERYONE'S ALIVE. THE EVIL STEPMOTHER GOT SMASHED. TIME TO BOUNCE.
WHY DID THAT FEEL A LITTLE TOO EASY...?
ADAM, TELL MY BABE I'M ON MY WAY.

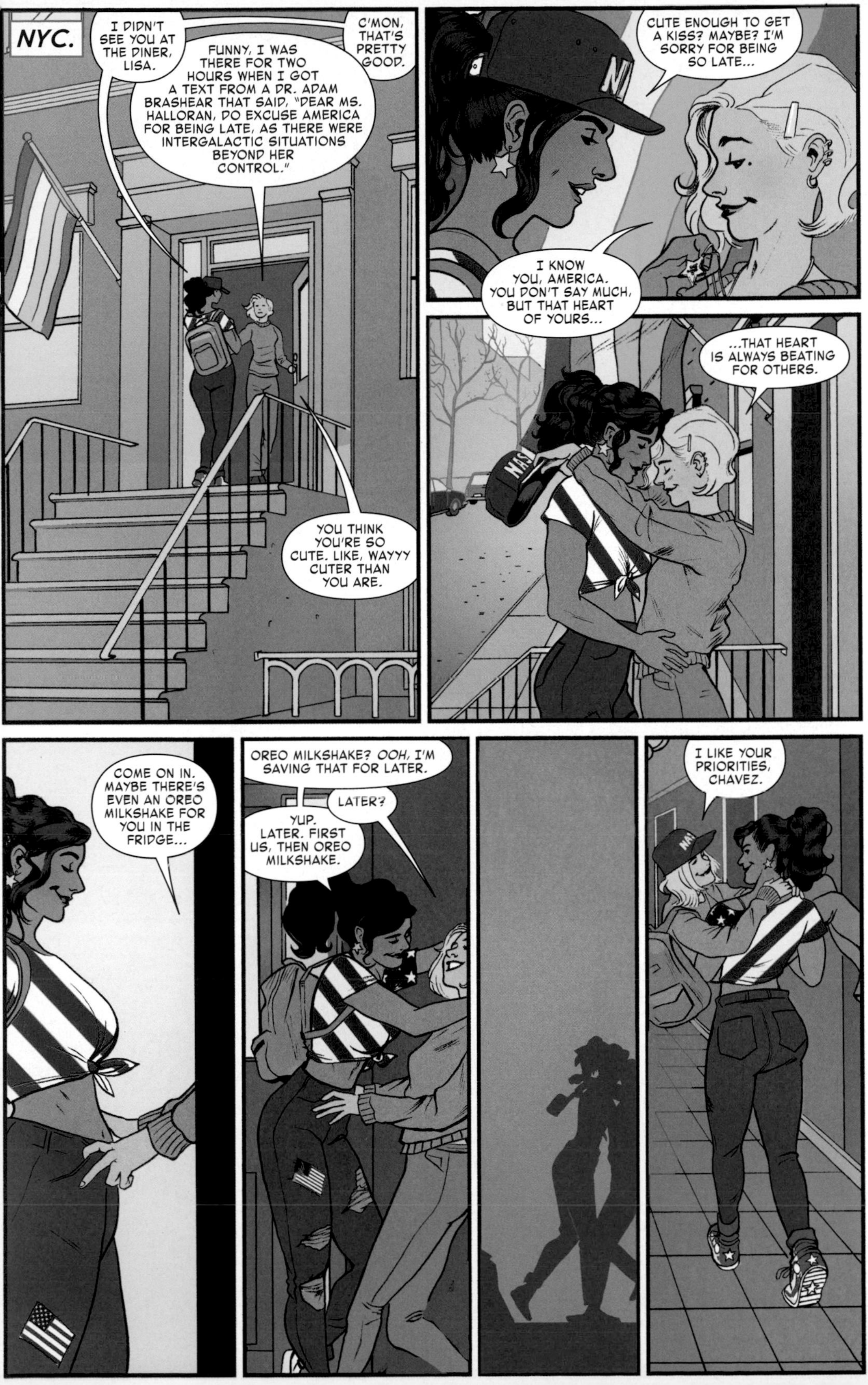
NYC.
I DIDN'T SEE YOU AT THE DINER, LISA.
FUNNY, I WAS THERE FOR TWO HOURS WHEN I GOT A TEXT FROM A DR. ADAM BRASHEAR THAT SAID, "DEAR MS. HALLORAN, DO EXCUSE AMERICA FOR BEING LATE, AS THERE WERE INTERGALACTIC SITUATIONS BEYOND HER CONTROL."
C'MON, THAT'S PRETTY GOOD.
YOU THINK YOU'RE SO CUTE. LIKE, WAYYY CUTER THAN YOU ARE.
CUTE ENOUGH TO GET A KISS? MAYBE? I'M SORRY FOR BEING SO LATE...
I KNOW YOU, AMERICA. YOU DON'T SAY MUCH, BUT THAT HEART OF YOURS...
...THAT HEART IS ALWAYS BEATING FOR OTHERS.
COME ON IN. MAYBE THERE'S EVEN AN OREO MILKSHAKE FOR YOU IN THE FRIDGE...
OREO MILKSHAKE? *OOH*, I'M SAVING THAT FOR LATER.
LATER?
YUP. LATER. FIRST US, THEN OREO MILKSHAKE.
I LIKE YOUR PRIORITIES, CHAVEZ.

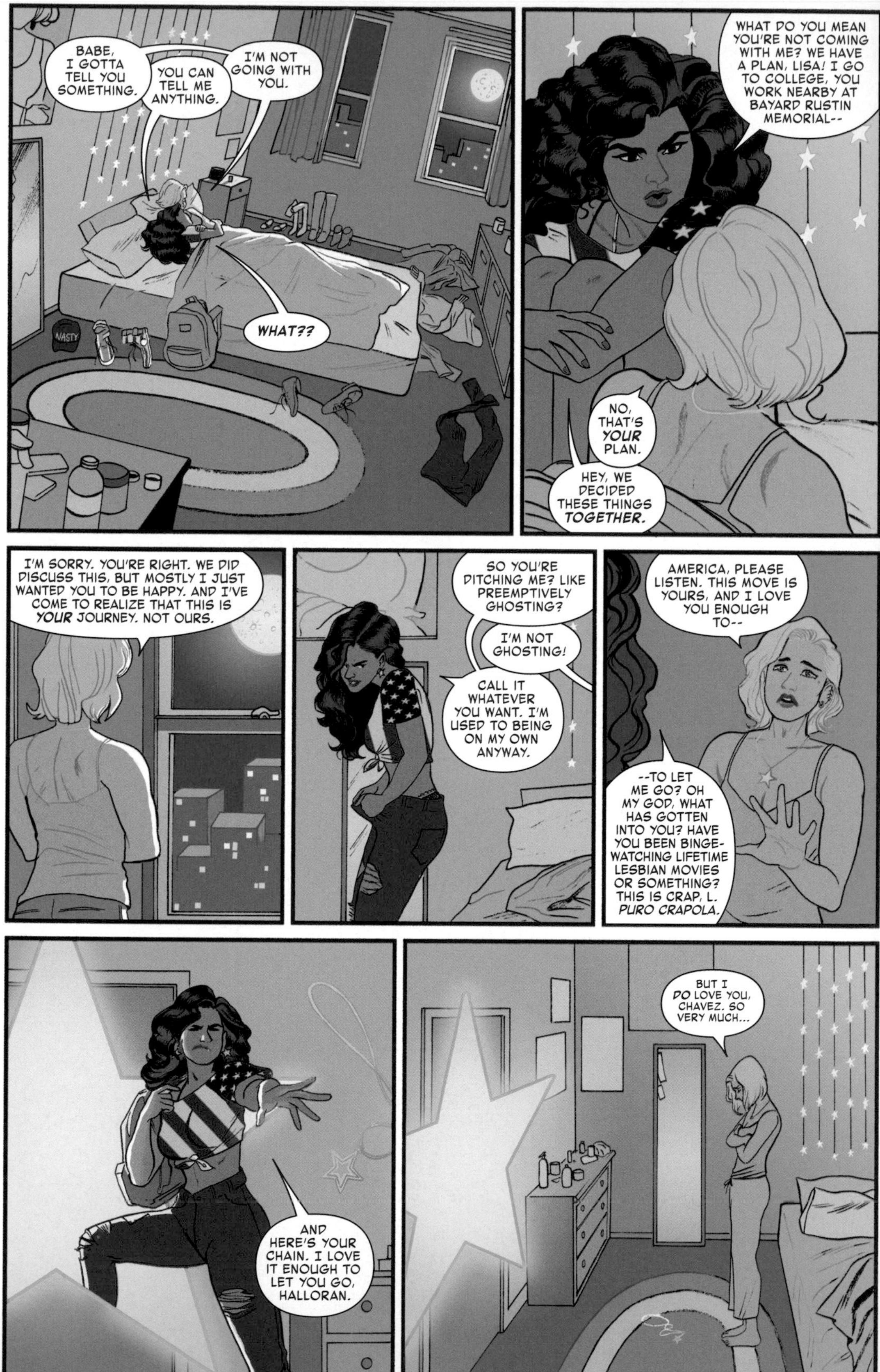
BABE, I GOTTA TELL YOU SOMETHING.
YOU CAN TELL ME ANYTHING.
I'M NOT GOING WITH YOU.
WHAT??
WHAT DO YOU MEAN YOU'RE NOT COMING WITH ME? WE HAVE A PLAN, LISA! I GO TO COLLEGE, YOU WORK NEARBY AT BAYARD RUSTIN MEMORIAL--
NO, THAT'S YOUR PLAN.
HEY, WE DECIDED THESE THINGS TOGETHER.
I'M SORRY. YOU'RE RIGHT. WE DID DISCUSS THIS, BUT MOSTLY I JUST WANTED YOU TO BE HAPPY. AND I'VE COME TO REALIZE THAT THIS IS YOUR JOURNEY. NOT OURS.
SO YOU'RE DITCHING ME? LIKE PREEMPTIVELY GHOSTING?
I'M NOT GHOSTING!
CALL IT WHATEVER YOU WANT. I'M USED TO BEING ON MY OWN ANYWAY.
AMERICA, PLEASE LISTEN. THIS MOVE IS YOURS, AND I LOVE YOU ENOUGH TO--
--TO LET ME GO? OH MY GOD, WHAT HAS GOTTEN INTO YOU? HAVE YOU BEEN BINGE-WATCHING LIFETIME LESBIAN MOVIES OR SOMETHING? THIS IS CRAP, L. PURO CRAPOLA.
AND HERE'S YOUR CHAIN. I LOVE IT ENOUGH TO LET YOU GO, HALLORAN.
BUT I DO LOVE YOU, CHAVEZ. SO VERY MUCH...

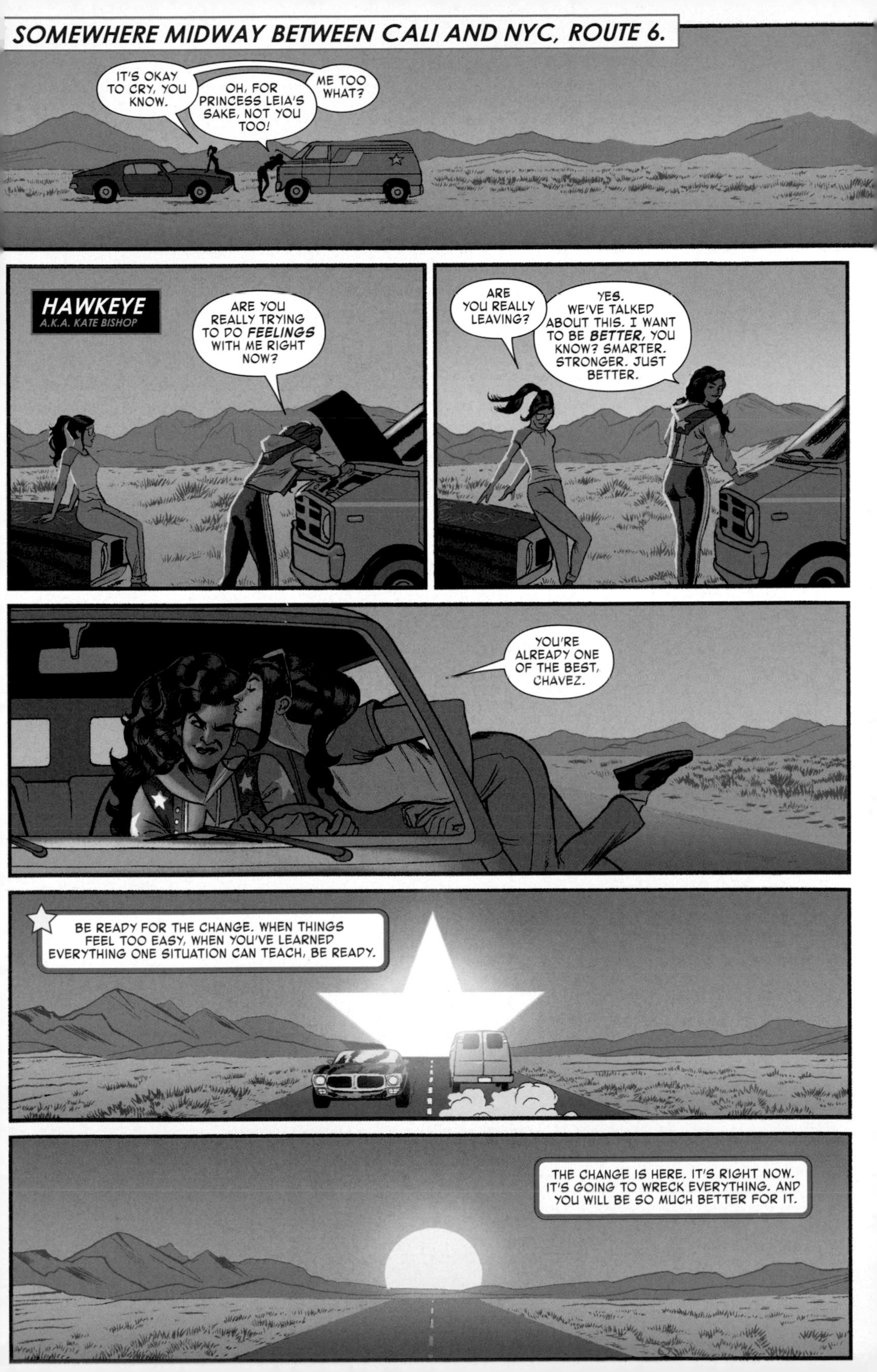
SOMEWHERE MIDWAY BETWEEN CALI AND NYC, ROUTE 6.
IT'S OKAY TO CRY, YOU KNOW.
OH, FOR PRINCESS LEIA'S SAKE, NOT YOU TOO!
ME TOO WHAT?
HAWKEYE
A.K.A. KATE BISHOP
ARE YOU REALLY TRYING TO DO FEELINGS WITH ME RIGHT NOW?
ARE YOU REALLY LEAVING?
YES. WE'VE TALKED ABOUT THIS. I WANT TO BE BETTER, YOU KNOW? SMARTER. STRONGER. JUST BETTER.
YOU'RE ALREADY ONE OF THE BEST, CHAVEZ.
BE READY FOR THE CHANGE. WHEN THINGS FEEL TOO EASY, WHEN YOU'VE LEARNED EVERYTHING ONE SITUATION CAN TEACH, BE READY.
THE CHANGE IS HERE. IT'S RIGHT NOW. IT'S GOING TO WRECK EVERYTHING. AND YOU WILL BE SO MUCH BETTER FOR IT.

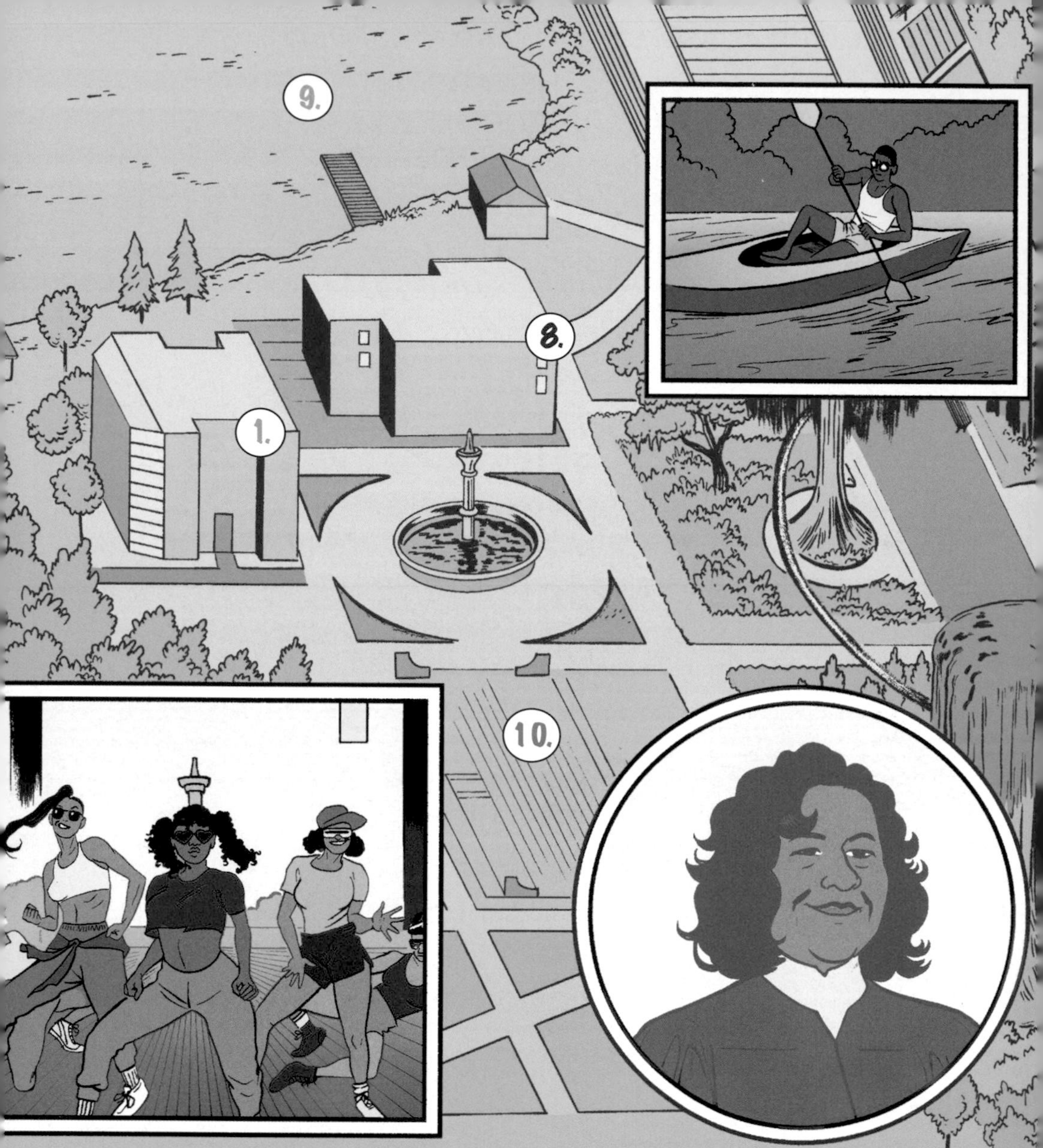
9.
8.
1.
10.

SOTOMAYOR UNIVERSITY

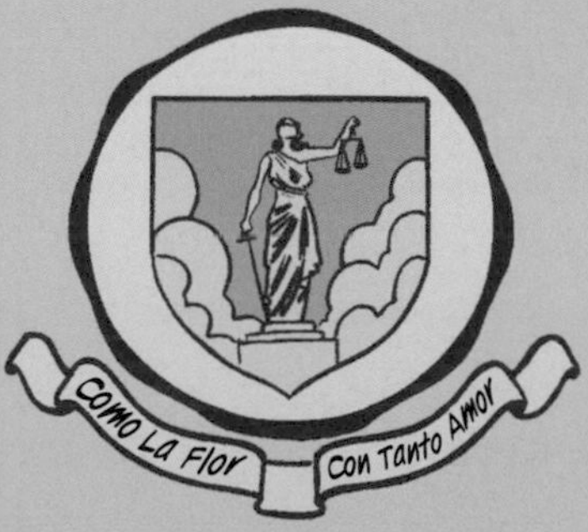
Como La Flor
Con Tanto Amor

MAP KEY

1. HOUSING
2. ACADEMIC AFFAIRS
3. LABS
4. SPORTS/REC
5. FOOD COURT
PERFORMING ARTS
7. MAGIC/MUTANT POWER TEST ZONES
8. THE DEPARTMENT OF RADICAL WOMEN & INTERGALACTIC INDIGENOUS PEOPLES
9. ROWING LAKE
10. OUTDOOR DANCE FIELD
11. SONIA SOTOMAYOR HOLOGRAM GREETER
12. THE MAJESTIC GARDENS

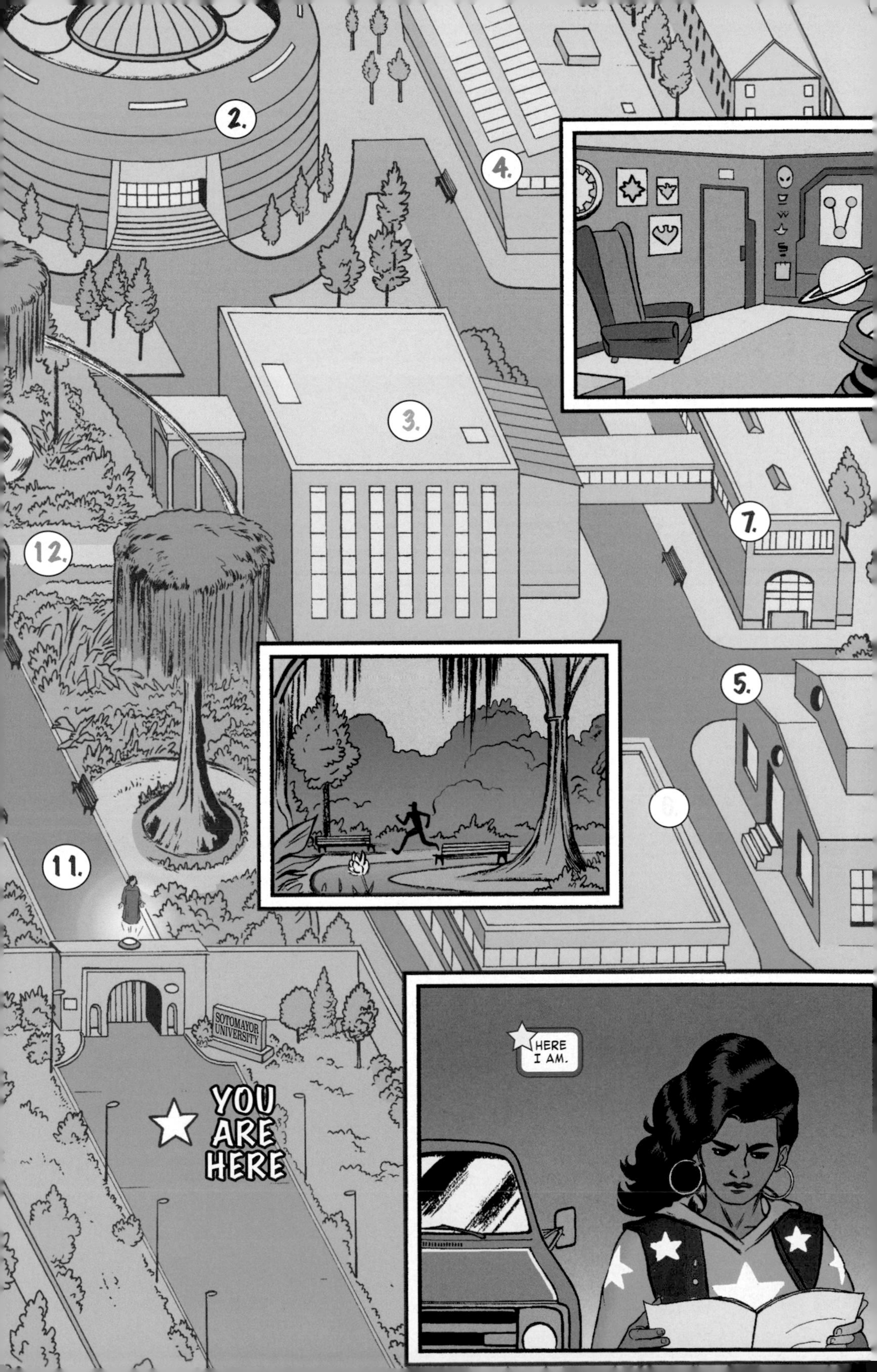
2.
4.
3.
7.
12.
5.
11.
SOTOMAYOR UNIVERSITY
YOU ARE HERE
HERE I AM.

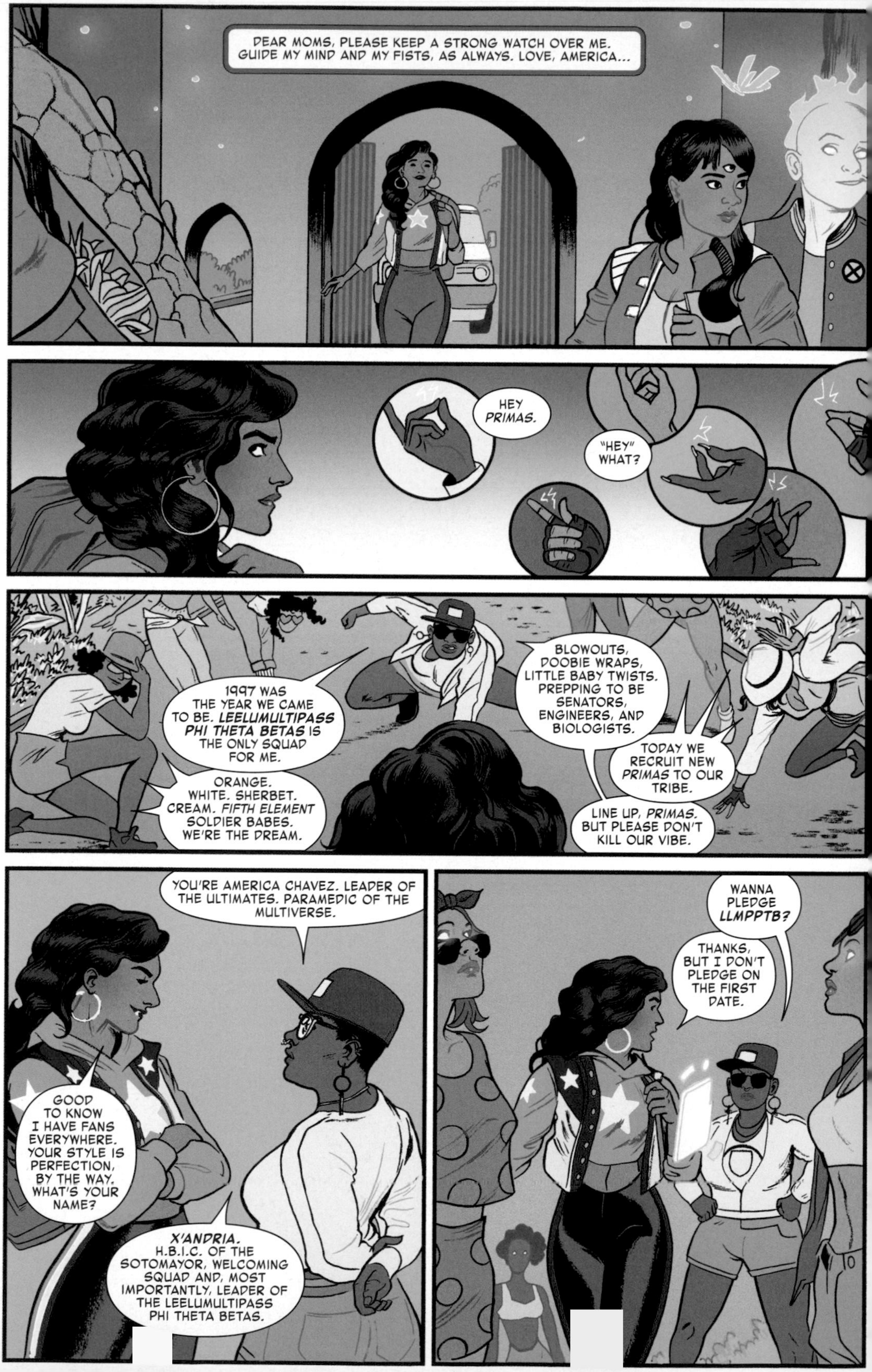

DEAR MOMS, PLEASE KEEP A STRONG WATCH OVER ME. GUIDE MY MIND AND MY FISTS, AS ALWAYS. LOVE, AMERICA...
HEY *PRIMAS.*
"HEY" WHAT?
1997 WAS THE YEAR WE CAME TO BE. ***LEELUMULTIPASS PHI THETA BETAS*** IS THE ONLY SQUAD FOR ME.
ORANGE. WHITE. SHERBET. CREAM. *FIFTH ELEMENT* SOLDIER BABES. WE'RE THE DREAM.
BLOWOUTS, DOOBIE WRAPS, LITTLE BABY TWISTS. PREPPING TO BE SENATORS, ENGINEERS, AND BIOLOGISTS.
TODAY WE RECRUIT NEW *PRIMAS* TO OUR TRIBE.
LINE UP, *PRIMAS.* BUT PLEASE DON'T KILL OUR VIBE.
YOU'RE AMERICA CHAVEZ. LEADER OF THE ULTIMATES. PARAMEDIC OF THE MULTIVERSE.
GOOD TO KNOW I HAVE FANS EVERYWHERE. YOUR STYLE IS PERFECTION, BY THE WAY. WHAT'S YOUR NAME?
X'ANDRIA. H.B.I.C. OF THE SOTOMAYOR, WELCOMING SQUAD AND, MOST IMPORTANTLY, LEADER OF THE LEELUMULTIPASS PHI THETA BETAS.
WANNA PLEDGE ***LLMPPTB?***
THANKS, BUT I DON'T PLEDGE ON THE FIRST DATE.

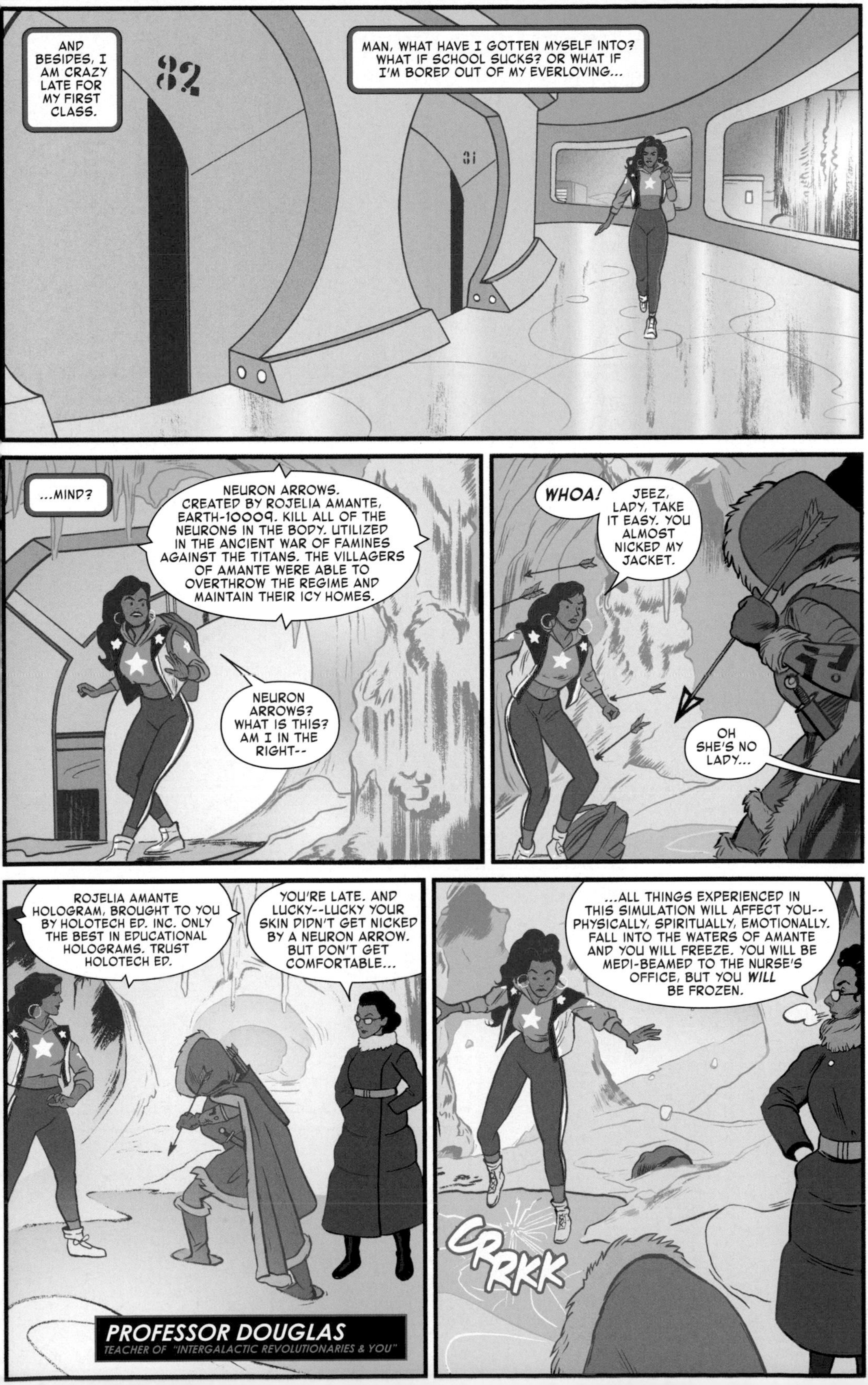
AND BESIDES, I AM CRAZY LATE FOR MY FIRST CLASS.
MAN, WHAT HAVE I GOTTEN MYSELF INTO? WHAT IF SCHOOL SUCKS? OR WHAT IF I'M BORED OUT OF MY EVERLOVING...
82
31
...MIND?
NEURON ARROWS. CREATED BY ROJELIA AMANTE, EARTH-10009. KILL ALL OF THE NEURONS IN THE BODY. UTILIZED IN THE ANCIENT WAR OF FAMINES AGAINST THE TITANS. THE VILLAGERS OF AMANTE WERE ABLE TO OVERTHROW THE REGIME AND MAINTAIN THEIR ICY HOMES.
NEURON ARROWS? WHAT IS THIS? AM I IN THE RIGHT--
WHOA!
JEEZ, LADY, TAKE IT EASY. YOU ALMOST NICKED MY JACKET.
OH SHE'S NO LADY...
ROJELIA AMANTE HOLOGRAM, BROUGHT TO YOU BY HOLOTECH ED. INC. ONLY THE BEST IN EDUCATIONAL HOLOGRAMS. TRUST HOLOTECH ED.
YOU'RE LATE. AND LUCKY--LUCKY YOUR SKIN DIDN'T GET NICKED BY A NEURON ARROW. BUT DON'T GET COMFORTABLE...
PROFESSOR DOUGLAS
TEACHER OF "INTERGALACTIC REVOLUTIONARIES & YOU"
...ALL THINGS EXPERIENCED IN THIS SIMULATION WILL AFFECT YOU--PHYSICALLY, SPIRITUALLY, EMOTIONALLY. FALL INTO THE WATERS OF AMANTE AND YOU WILL FREEZE. YOU WILL BE MEDI-BEAMED TO THE NURSE'S OFFICE, BUT YOU WILL BE FROZEN.
CRRKK

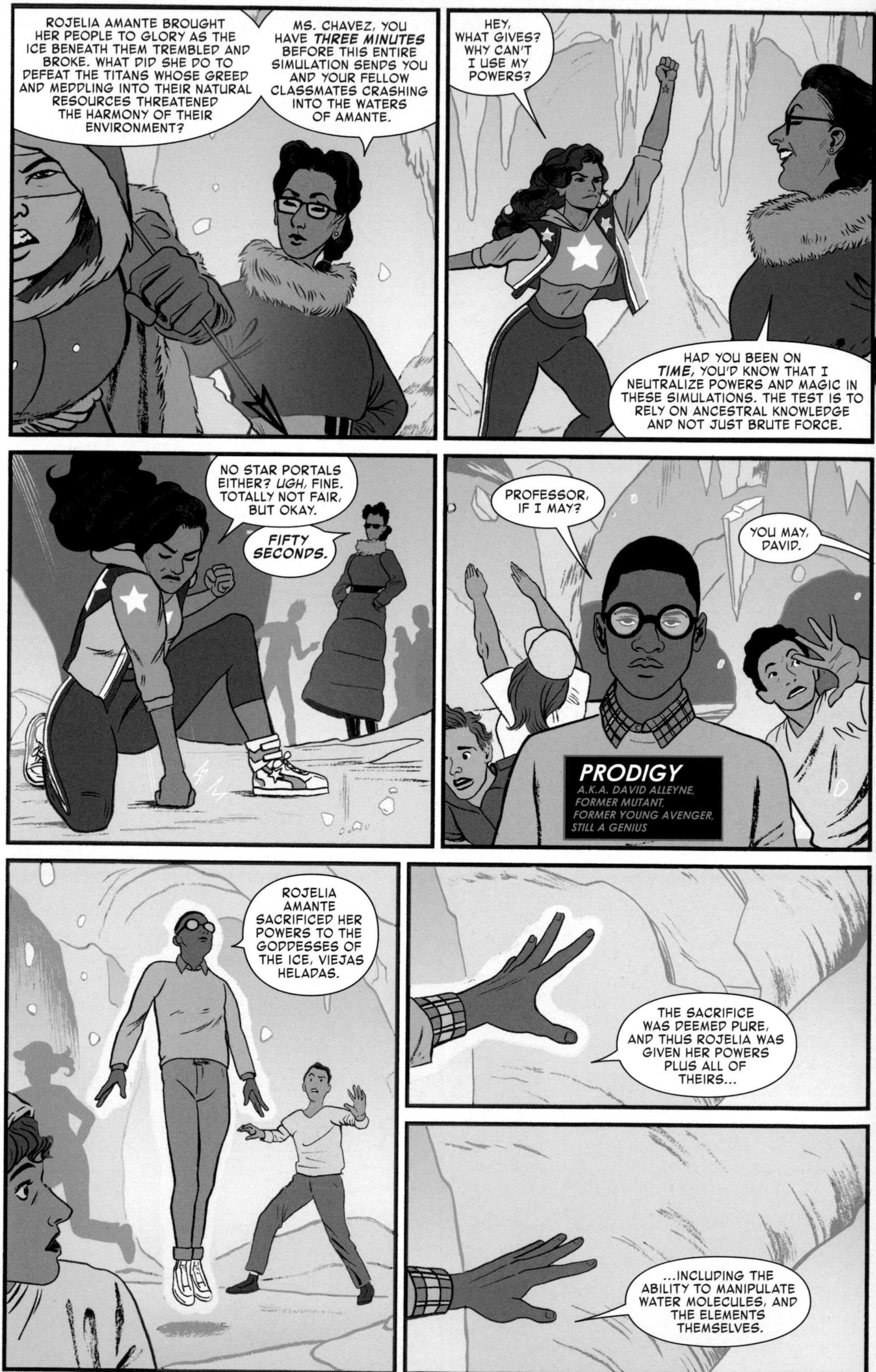
ROJELIA AMANTE BROUGHT HER PEOPLE TO GLORY AS THE ICE BENEATH THEM TREMBLED AND BROKE. WHAT DID SHE DO TO DEFEAT THE TITANS WHOSE GREED AND MEDDLING INTO THEIR NATURAL RESOURCES THREATENED THE HARMONY OF THEIR ENVIRONMENT?
MS. CHAVEZ, YOU HAVE THREE MINUTES BEFORE THIS ENTIRE SIMULATION SENDS YOU AND YOUR FELLOW CLASSMATES CRASHING INTO THE WATERS OF AMANTE.
HEY, WHAT GIVES? WHY CAN'T I USE MY POWERS?
HAD YOU BEEN ON TIME, YOU'D KNOW THAT I NEUTRALIZE POWERS AND MAGIC IN THESE SIMULATIONS. THE TEST IS TO RELY ON ANCESTRAL KNOWLEDGE AND NOT JUST BRUTE FORCE.
NO STAR PORTALS EITHER? UGH, FINE. TOTALLY NOT FAIR, BUT OKAY.
FIFTY SECONDS.
PROFESSOR, IF I MAY?
YOU MAY, DAVID.
PRODIGY
A.K.A. DAVID ALLEYNE, FORMER MUTANT, FORMER YOUNG AVENGER, STILL A GENIUS
ROJELIA AMANTE SACRIFICED HER POWERS TO THE GODDESSES OF THE ICE, VIEJAS HELADAS.
THE SACRIFICE WAS DEEMED PURE, AND THUS ROJELIA WAS GIVEN HER POWERS PLUS ALL OF THEIRS...
...INCLUDING THE ABILITY TO MANIPULATE WATER MOLECULES, AND THE ELEMENTS THEMSELVES.

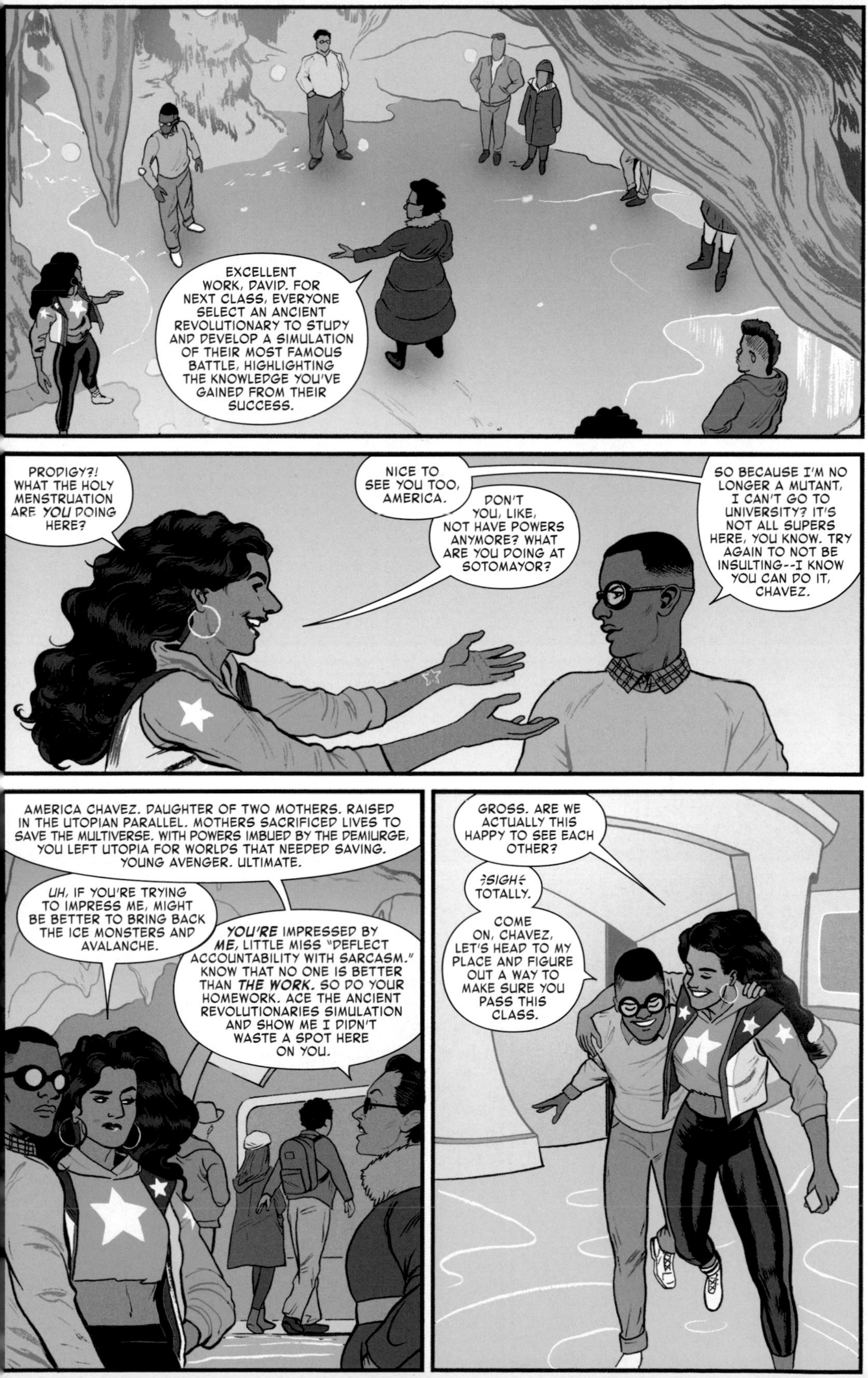
EXCELLENT WORK, DAVID. FOR NEXT CLASS, EVERYONE SELECT AN ANCIENT REVOLUTIONARY TO STUDY AND DEVELOP A SIMULATION OF THEIR MOST FAMOUS BATTLE, HIGHLIGHTING THE KNOWLEDGE YOU'VE GAINED FROM THEIR SUCCESS.
PRODIGY?! WHAT THE HOLY MENSTRUATION ARE *YOU* DOING HERE?
NICE TO SEE YOU TOO, AMERICA.
DON'T YOU, LIKE, NOT HAVE POWERS ANYMORE? WHAT ARE YOU DOING AT SOTOMAYOR?
SO BECAUSE I'M NO LONGER A MUTANT, I CAN'T GO TO UNIVERSITY? IT'S NOT ALL SUPERS HERE, YOU KNOW. TRY AGAIN TO NOT BE INSULTING--I KNOW YOU CAN DO IT, CHAVEZ.
AMERICA CHAVEZ. DAUGHTER OF TWO MOTHERS. RAISED IN THE UTOPIAN PARALLEL. MOTHERS SACRIFICED LIVES TO SAVE THE MULTIVERSE. WITH POWERS IMBUED BY THE DEMIURGE, YOU LEFT UTOPIA FOR WORLDS THAT NEEDED SAVING. YOUNG AVENGER. ULTIMATE.
UH, IF YOU'RE TRYING TO IMPRESS ME, MIGHT BE BETTER TO BRING BACK THE ICE MONSTERS AND AVALANCHE.
YOU'RE IMPRESSED BY ***ME,*** LITTLE MISS "DEFLECT ACCOUNTABILITY WITH SARCASM." KNOW THAT NO ONE IS BETTER THAN ***THE WORK.*** SO DO YOUR HOMEWORK. ACE THE ANCIENT REVOLUTIONARIES SIMULATION AND SHOW ME I DIDN'T WASTE A SPOT HERE ON YOU.
GROSS. ARE WE ACTUALLY THIS HAPPY TO SEE EACH OTHER?
SIGH TOTALLY.
COME ON, CHAVEZ, LET'S HEAD TO MY PLACE AND FIGURE OUT A WAY TO MAKE SURE YOU PASS THIS CLASS.

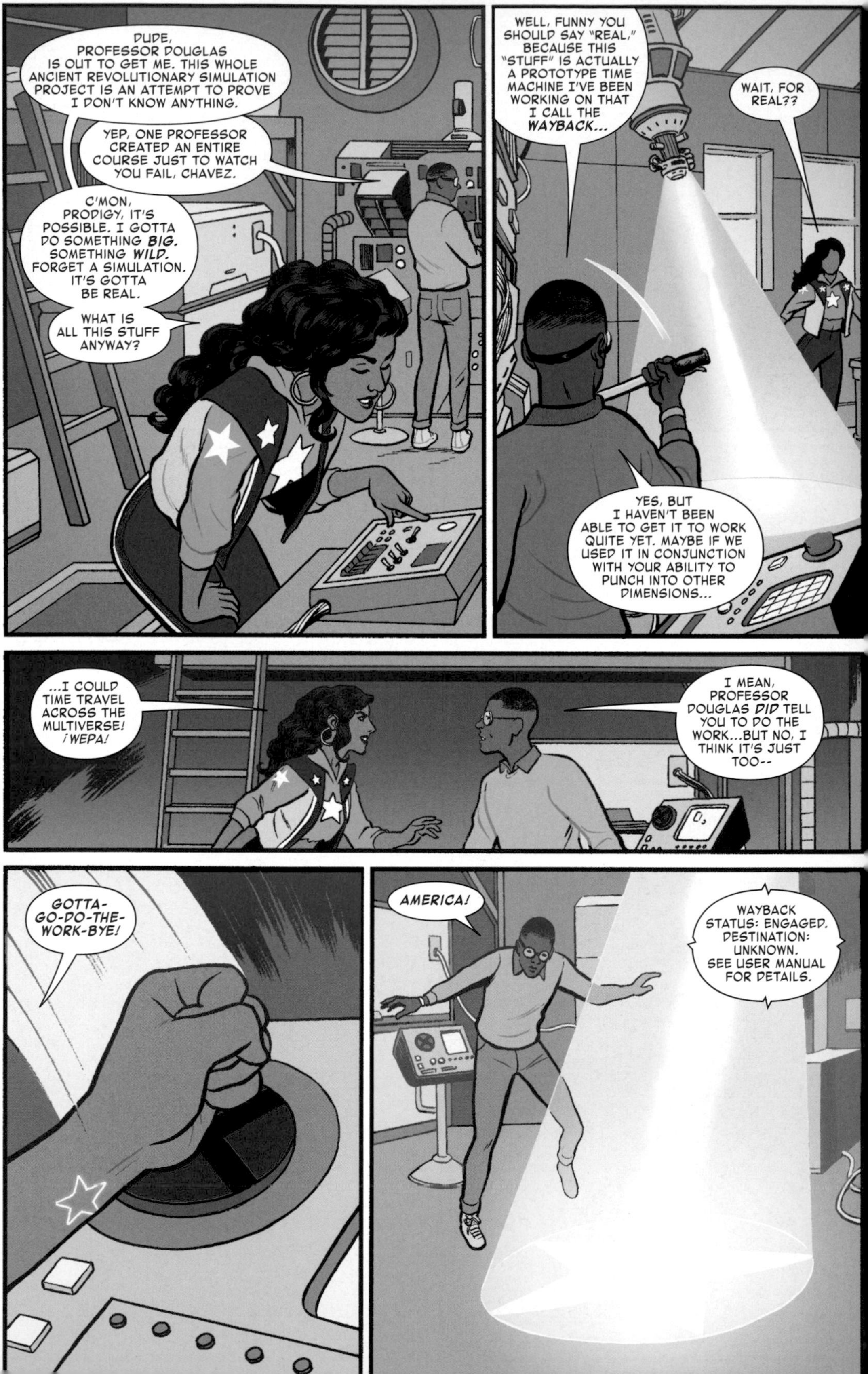
DUDE, PROFESSOR DOUGLAS IS OUT TO GET ME. THIS WHOLE ANCIENT REVOLUTIONARY SIMULATION PROJECT IS AN ATTEMPT TO PROVE I DON'T KNOW ANYTHING.
YEP, ONE PROFESSOR CREATED AN ENTIRE COURSE JUST TO WATCH YOU FAIL, CHAVEZ.
C'MON, PRODIGY, IT'S POSSIBLE. I GOTTA DO SOMETHING *BIG.* SOMETHING *WILD.* FORGET A SIMULATION. IT'S GOTTA BE REAL.
WHAT IS ALL THIS STUFF ANYWAY?
WELL, FUNNY YOU SHOULD SAY "REAL," BECAUSE THIS "STUFF" IS ACTUALLY A PROTOTYPE TIME MACHINE I'VE BEEN WORKING ON THAT I CALL THE ***WAYBACK...***
WAIT, FOR REAL??
YES, BUT I HAVEN'T BEEN ABLE TO GET IT TO WORK QUITE YET. MAYBE IF WE USED IT IN CONJUNCTION WITH YOUR ABILITY TO PUNCH INTO OTHER DIMENSIONS...
...I COULD TIME TRAVEL ACROSS THE MULTIVERSE! *¡WEPA!*
I MEAN, PROFESSOR DOUGLAS *DID* TELL YOU TO DO THE WORK...BUT NO, I THINK IT'S JUST TOO--
GOTTA-GO-DO-THE-WORK-BYE!
AMERICA!
WAYBACK STATUS: ENGAGED. DESTINATION: UNKNOWN. SEE USER MANUAL FOR DETAILS.

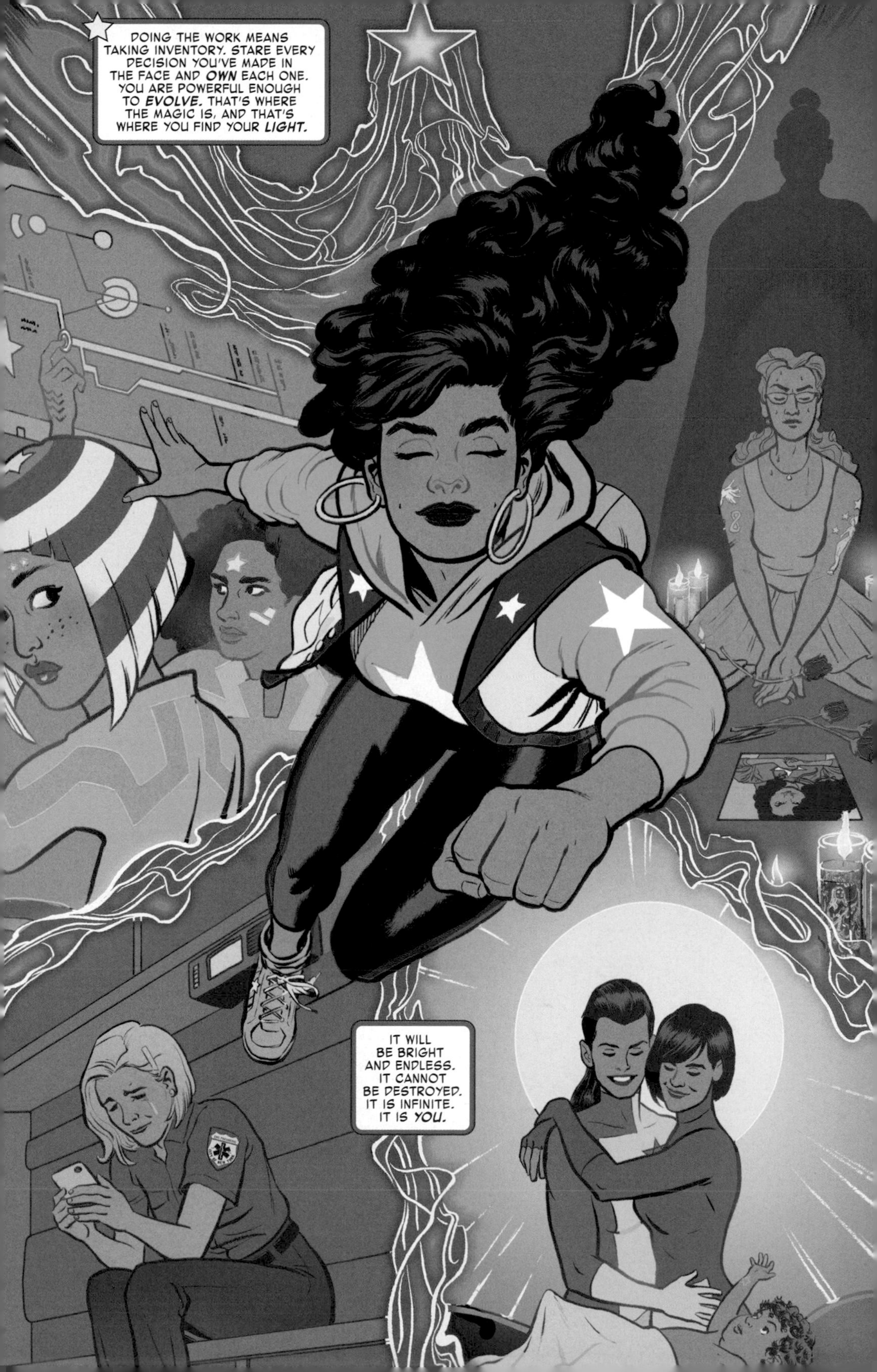
DOING THE WORK MEANS TAKING INVENTORY. STARE EVERY DECISION YOU'VE MADE IN THE FACE AND OWN EACH ONE. YOU ARE POWERFUL ENOUGH TO EVOLVE. THAT'S WHERE THE MAGIC IS, AND THAT'S WHERE YOU FIND YOUR LIGHT.
IT WILL BE BRIGHT AND ENDLESS. IT CANNOT BE DESTROYED. IT IS INFINITE. IT IS YOU.

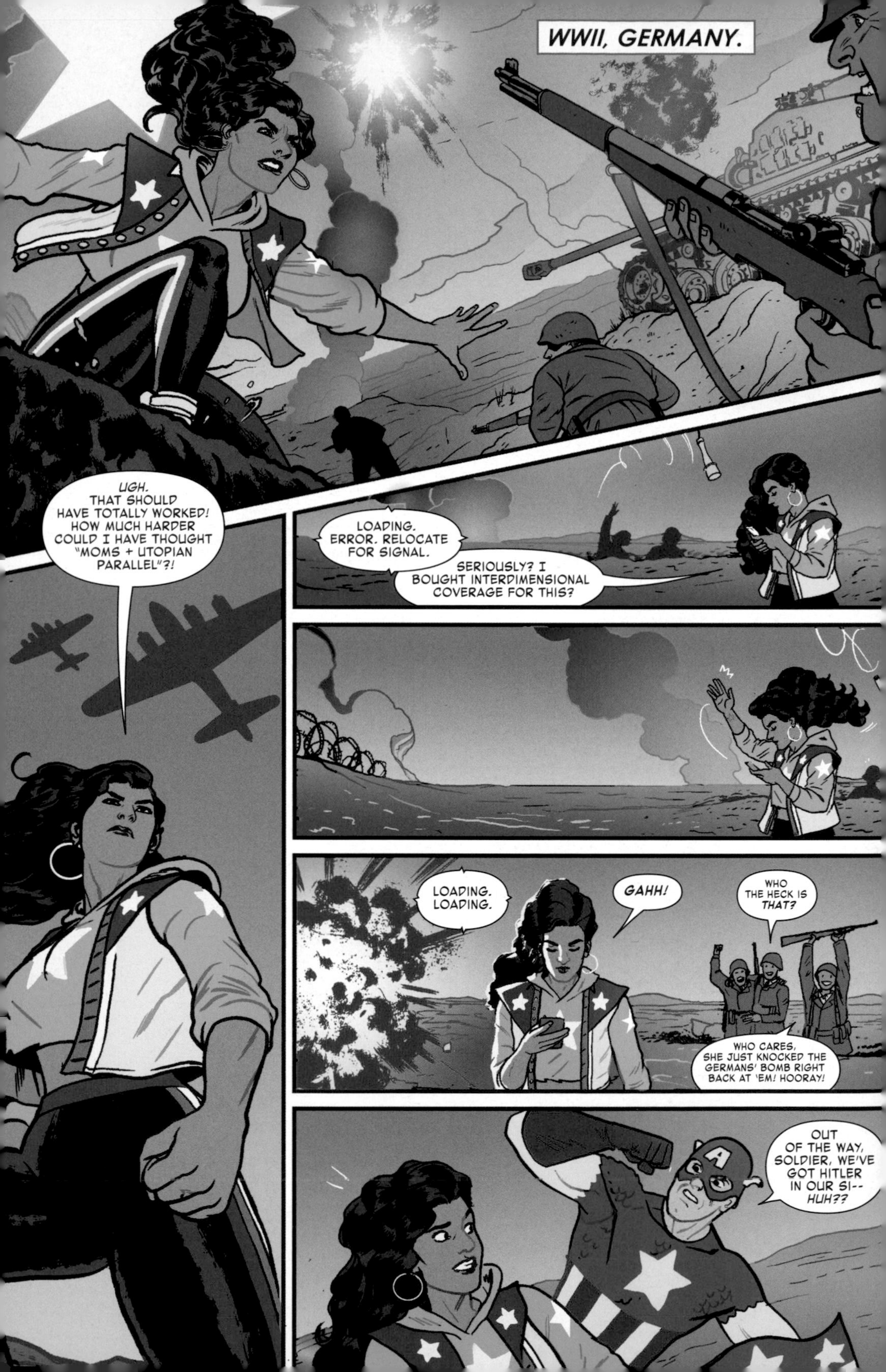

WWII, GERMANY.
UGH. THAT SHOULD HAVE TOTALLY WORKED! HOW MUCH HARDER COULD I HAVE THOUGHT "MOMS + UTOPIAN PARALLEL"?!
LOADING. ERROR. RELOCATE FOR SIGNAL.
SERIOUSLY? I BOUGHT INTERDIMENSIONAL COVERAGE FOR THIS?
LOADING. LOADING.
GAHH!
WHO THE HECK IS THAT?
WHO CARES, SHE JUST KNOCKED THE GERMANS' BOMB RIGHT BACK AT 'EM! HOORAY!
OUT OF THE WAY, SOLDIER, WE'VE GOT HITLER IN OUR SI-- HUH??

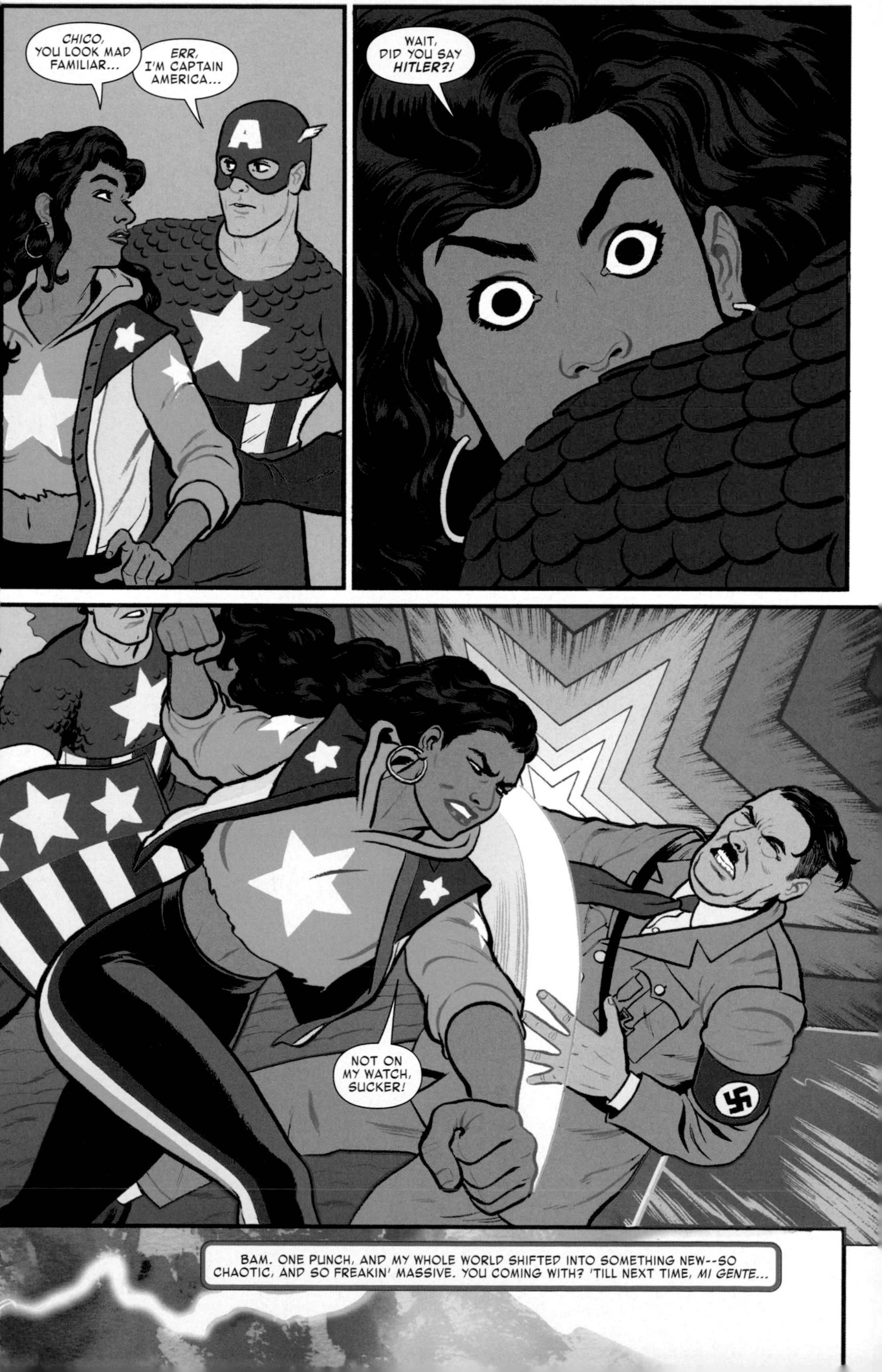
CHICO, YOU LOOK MAD FAMILIAR...
ERR, I'M CAPTAIN AMERICA...
WAIT, DID YOU SAY *HITLER?!*
NOT ON MY WATCH, SUCKER!
BAM. ONE PUNCH, AND MY WHOLE WORLD SHIFTED INTO SOMETHING NEW--SO CHAOTIC, AND SO FREAKIN' MASSIVE. YOU COMING WITH? 'TILL NEXT TIME, *MI GENTE...*

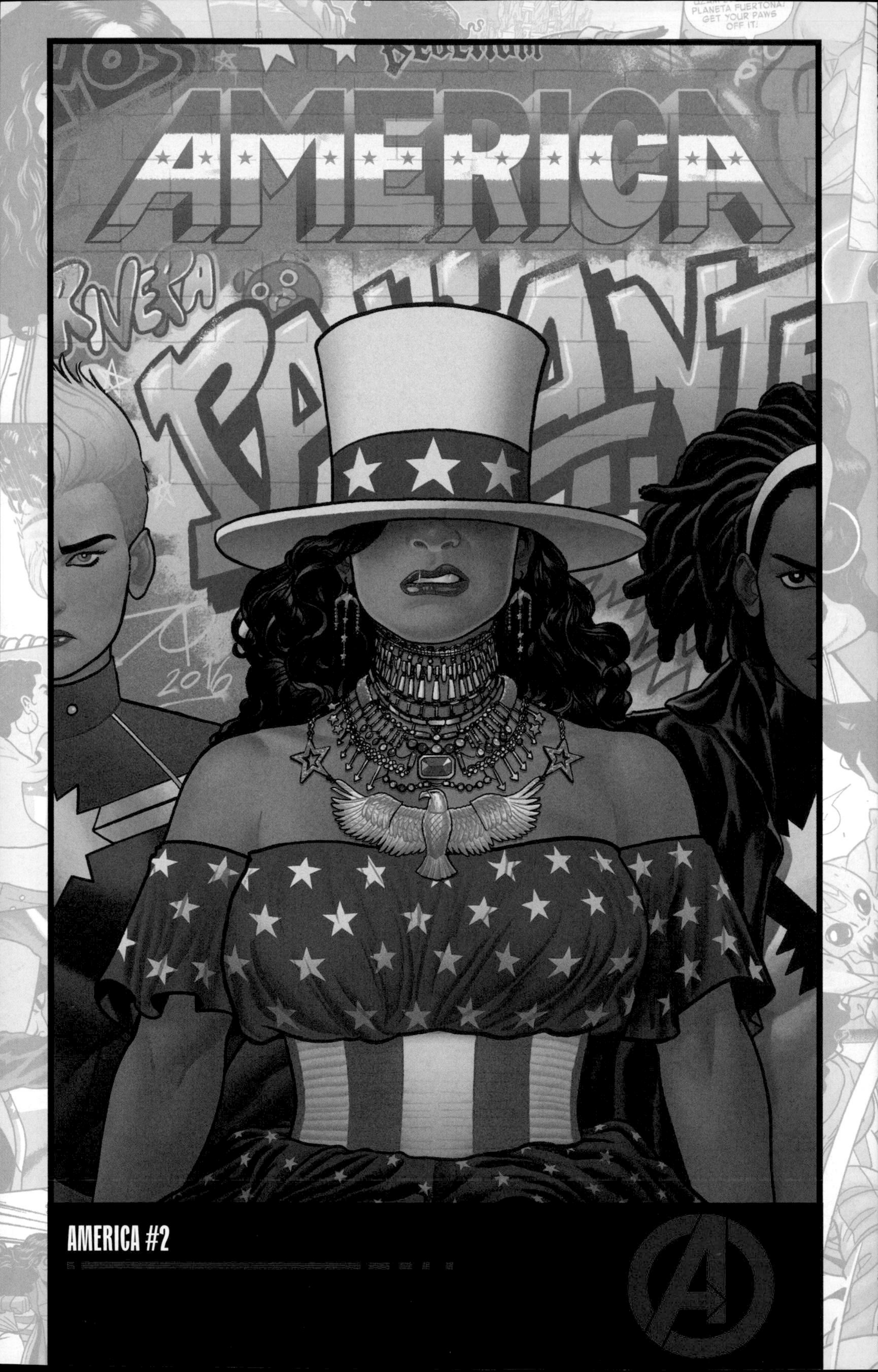
PLANETA FUERTONA! GET YOUR PAWS OFF IT!
AMERICA

AMERICA #2

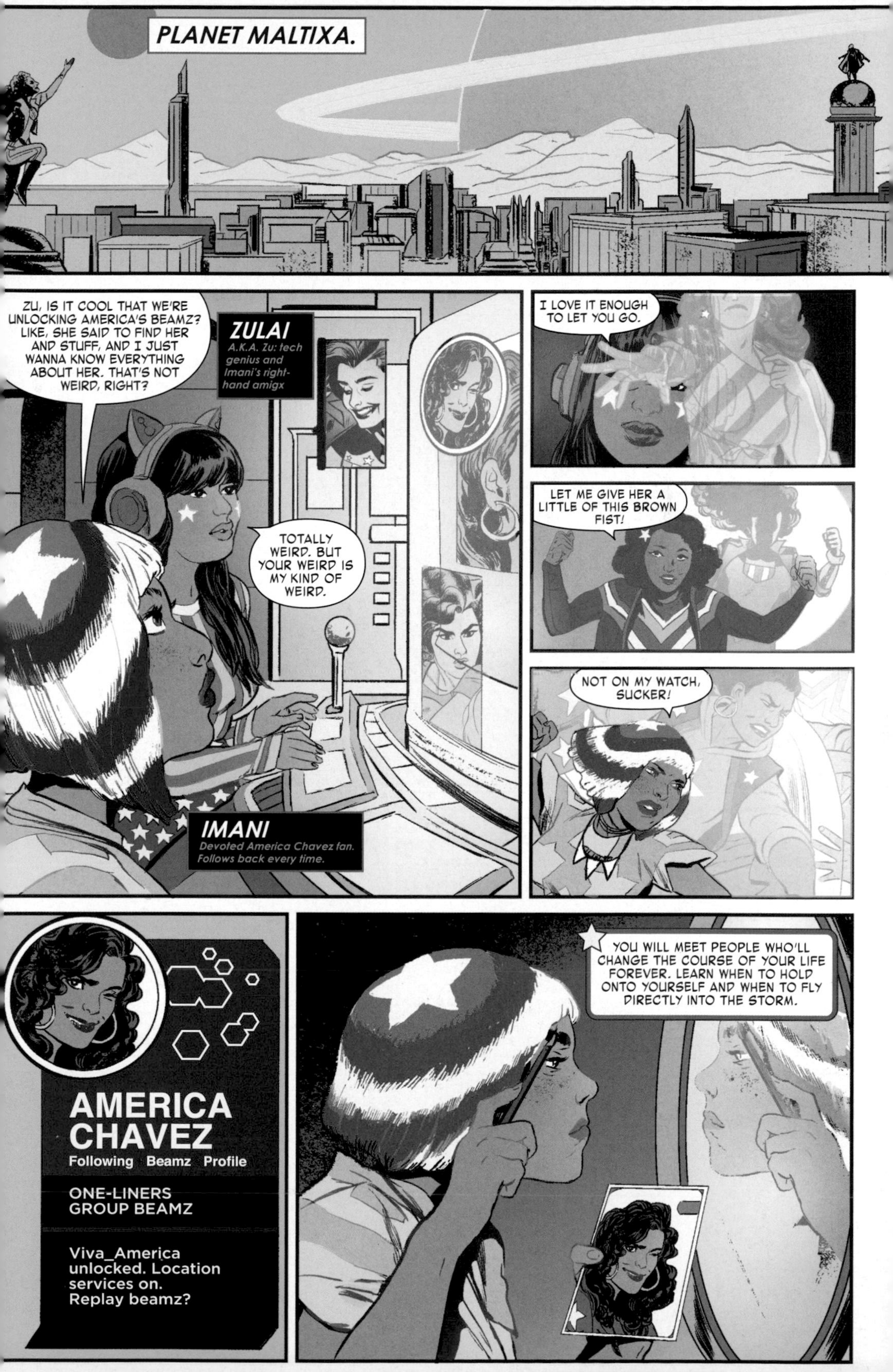
PLANET MALTIXA.
ZU, IS IT COOL THAT WE'RE UNLOCKING AMERICA'S BEAMZ? LIKE, SHE SAID TO FIND HER AND STUFF, AND I JUST WANNA KNOW EVERYTHING ABOUT HER. THAT'S NOT WEIRD, RIGHT?
ZULAI
A.K.A. Zu: tech genius and Imani's right-hand amigx
TOTALLY WEIRD. BUT YOUR WEIRD IS MY KIND OF WEIRD.
IMANI
Devoted America Chavez fan. Follows back every time.
I LOVE IT ENOUGH TO LET YOU GO.
LET ME GIVE HER A LITTLE OF THIS BROWN FIST!
NOT ON MY WATCH, SUCKER!
AMERICA CHAVEZ
Following Beamz Profile
ONE-LINERS
GROUP BEAMZ
Viva_America unlocked. Location services on. Replay beamz?
YOU WILL MEET PEOPLE WHO'LL CHANGE THE COURSE OF YOUR LIFE FOREVER. LEARN WHEN TO HOLD ONTO YOURSELF AND WHEN TO FLY DIRECTLY INTO THE STORM.

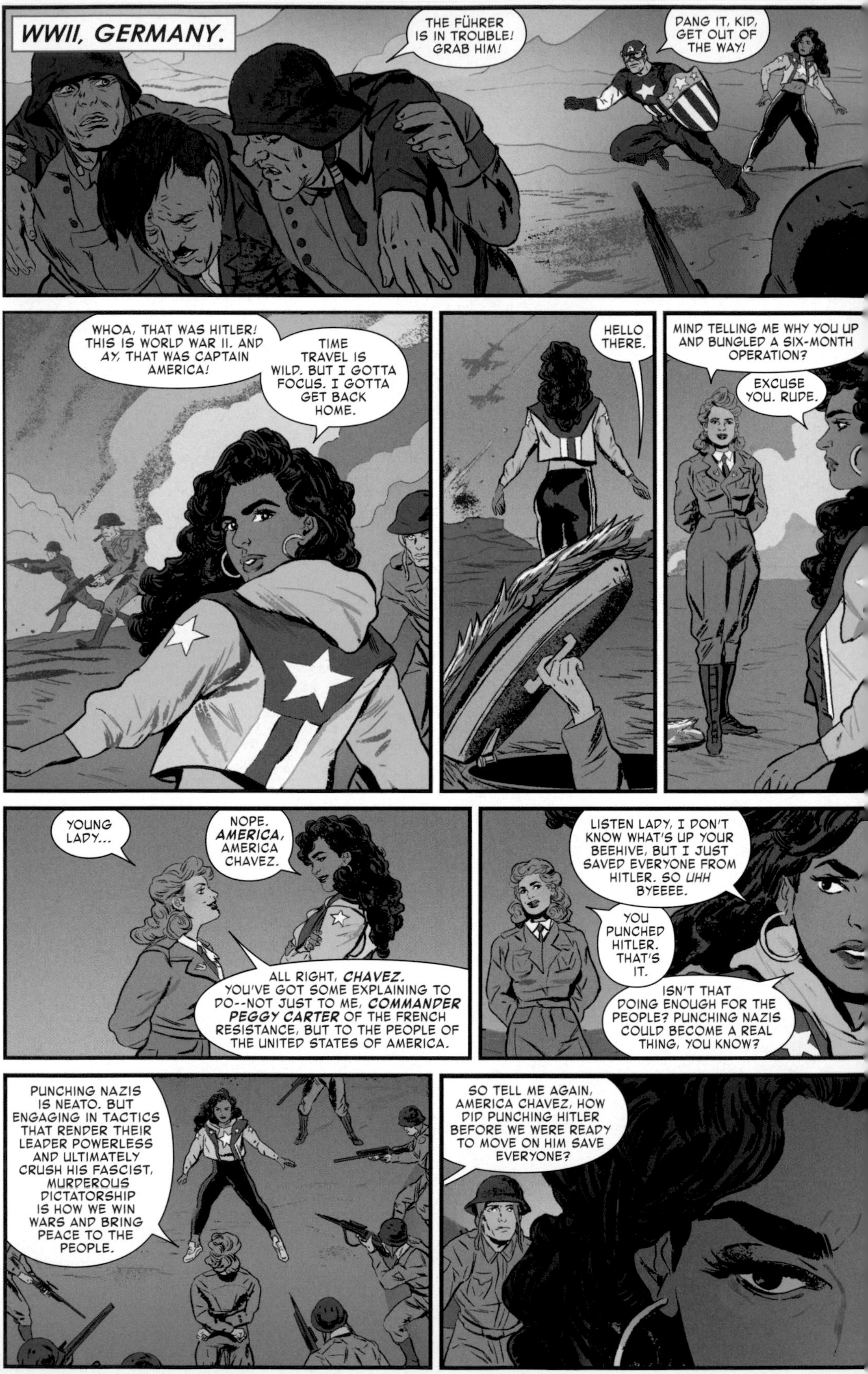
WWII, GERMANY.
THE FÜHRER IS IN TROUBLE! GRAB HIM!
DANG IT, KID, GET OUT OF THE WAY!
WHOA, THAT WAS HITLER! THIS IS WORLD WAR II. AND AY, THAT WAS CAPTAIN AMERICA!
TIME TRAVEL IS WILD. BUT I GOTTA FOCUS. I GOTTA GET BACK HOME.
HELLO THERE.
MIND TELLING ME WHY YOU UP AND BUNGLED A SIX-MONTH OPERATION?
EXCUSE YOU. RUDE.
YOUNG LADY...
NOPE. AMERICA, AMERICA CHAVEZ.
ALL RIGHT, CHAVEZ. YOU'VE GOT SOME EXPLAINING TO DO--NOT JUST TO ME, COMMANDER PEGGY CARTER OF THE FRENCH RESISTANCE, BUT TO THE PEOPLE OF THE UNITED STATES OF AMERICA.
LISTEN LADY, I DON'T KNOW WHAT'S UP YOUR BEEHIVE, BUT I JUST SAVED EVERYONE FROM HITLER. SO UHH BYEEEE.
YOU PUNCHED HITLER. THAT'S IT.
ISN'T THAT DOING ENOUGH FOR THE PEOPLE? PUNCHING NAZIS COULD BECOME A REAL THING, YOU KNOW?
PUNCHING NAZIS IS NEATO. BUT ENGAGING IN TACTICS THAT RENDER THEIR LEADER POWERLESS AND ULTIMATELY CRUSH HIS FASCIST, MURDEROUS DICTATORSHIP IS HOW WE WIN WARS AND BRING PEACE TO THE PEOPLE.
SO TELL ME AGAIN, AMERICA CHAVEZ, HOW DID PUNCHING HITLER BEFORE WE WERE READY TO MOVE ON HIM SAVE EVERYONE?

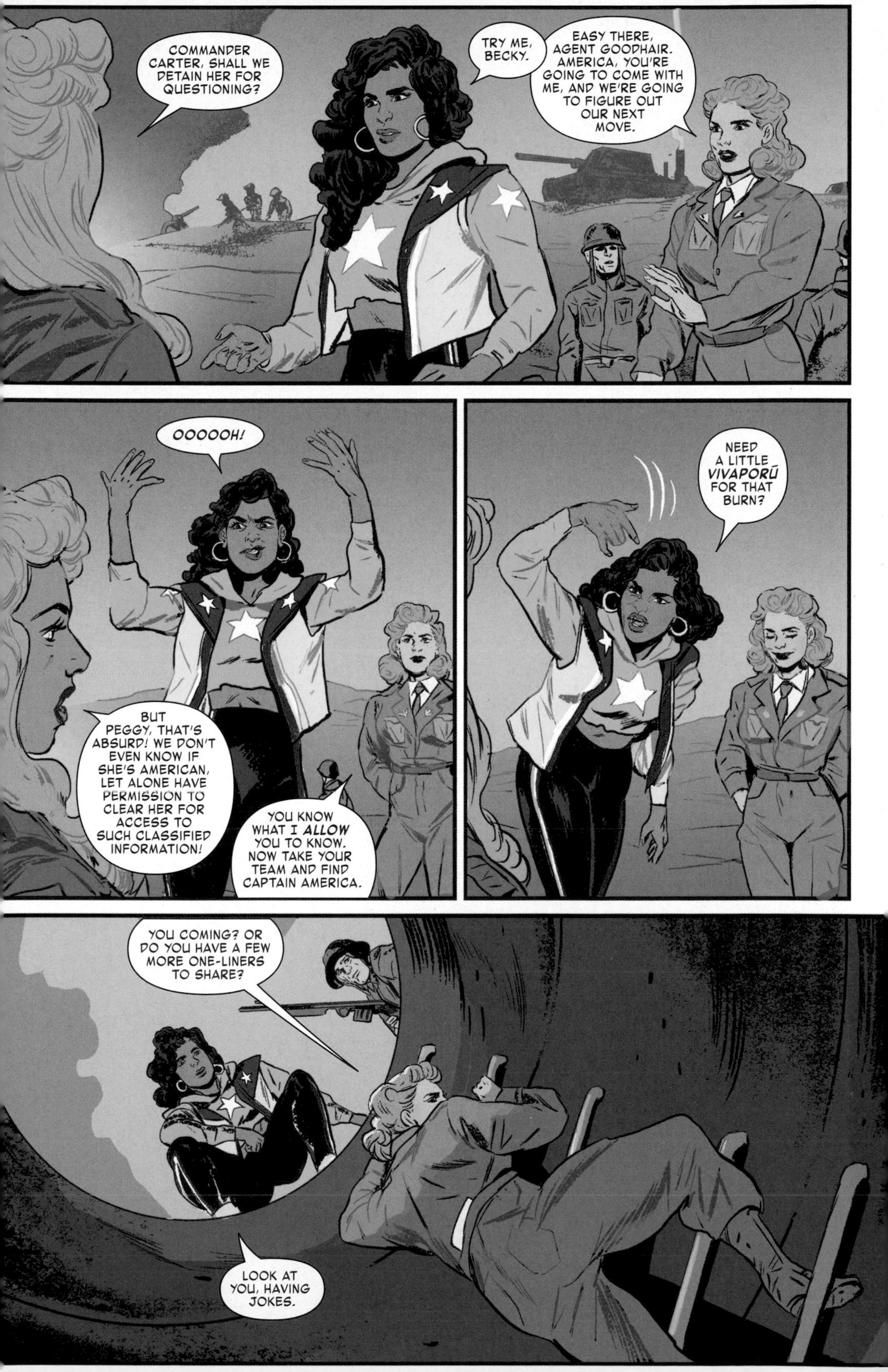
COMMANDER CARTER, SHALL WE DETAIN HER FOR QUESTIONING?
TRY ME, BECKY.
EASY THERE, AGENT GOODHAIR. AMERICA, YOU'RE GOING TO COME WITH ME, AND WE'RE GOING TO FIGURE OUT OUR NEXT MOVE.
OOOOOH!
BUT PEGGY, THAT'S ABSURD! WE DON'T EVEN KNOW IF SHE'S AMERICAN, LET ALONE HAVE PERMISSION TO CLEAR HER FOR ACCESS TO SUCH CLASSIFIED INFORMATION!
YOU KNOW WHAT I *ALLOW* YOU TO KNOW. NOW TAKE YOUR TEAM AND FIND CAPTAIN AMERICA.
NEED A LITTLE *VIVAPORŪ* FOR THAT BURN?
YOU COMING? OR DO YOU HAVE A FEW MORE ONE-LINERS TO SHARE?
LOOK AT YOU, HAVING JOKES.

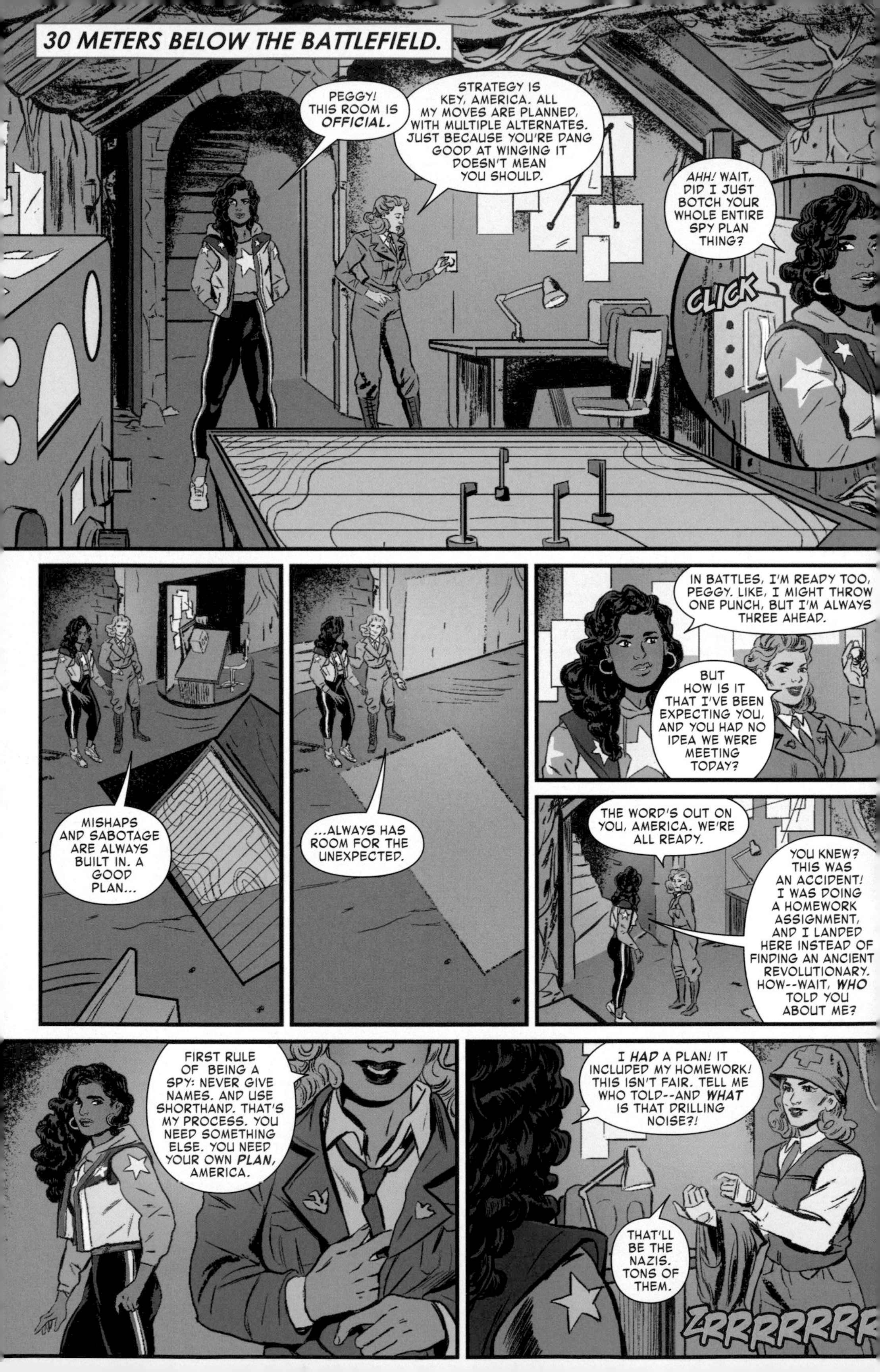
30 METERS BELOW THE BATTLEFIELD.
PEGGY! THIS ROOM IS *OFFICIAL.*
STRATEGY IS KEY, AMERICA. ALL MY MOVES ARE PLANNED, WITH MULTIPLE ALTERNATES. JUST BECAUSE YOU'RE DANG GOOD AT WINGING IT DOESN'T MEAN YOU SHOULD.
AHH! WAIT, DID I JUST BOTCH YOUR WHOLE ENTIRE SPY PLAN THING?
CLICK
MISHAPS AND SABOTAGE ARE ALWAYS BUILT IN. A GOOD PLAN...
...ALWAYS HAS ROOM FOR THE UNEXPECTED.
IN BATTLES, I'M READY TOO, PEGGY. LIKE, I MIGHT THROW ONE PUNCH, BUT I'M ALWAYS THREE AHEAD.
BUT HOW IS IT THAT I'VE BEEN EXPECTING YOU, AND YOU HAD NO IDEA WE WERE MEETING TODAY?
THE WORD'S OUT ON YOU, AMERICA. WE'RE ALL READY.
YOU KNEW? THIS WAS AN ACCIDENT! I WAS DOING A HOMEWORK ASSIGNMENT, AND I LANDED HERE INSTEAD OF FINDING AN ANCIENT REVOLUTIONARY. HOW--WAIT, *WHO* TOLD YOU ABOUT ME?
FIRST RULE OF BEING A SPY: NEVER GIVE NAMES. AND USE SHORTHAND. THAT'S MY PROCESS. YOU NEED SOMETHING ELSE. YOU NEED YOUR OWN *PLAN,* AMERICA.
I *HAD* A PLAN! IT INCLUDED MY HOMEWORK! THIS ISN'T FAIR. TELL ME WHO TOLD--AND *WHAT* IS THAT DRILLING NOISE?!
THAT'LL BE THE NAZIS. TONS OF THEM.
ZRRRRRRR

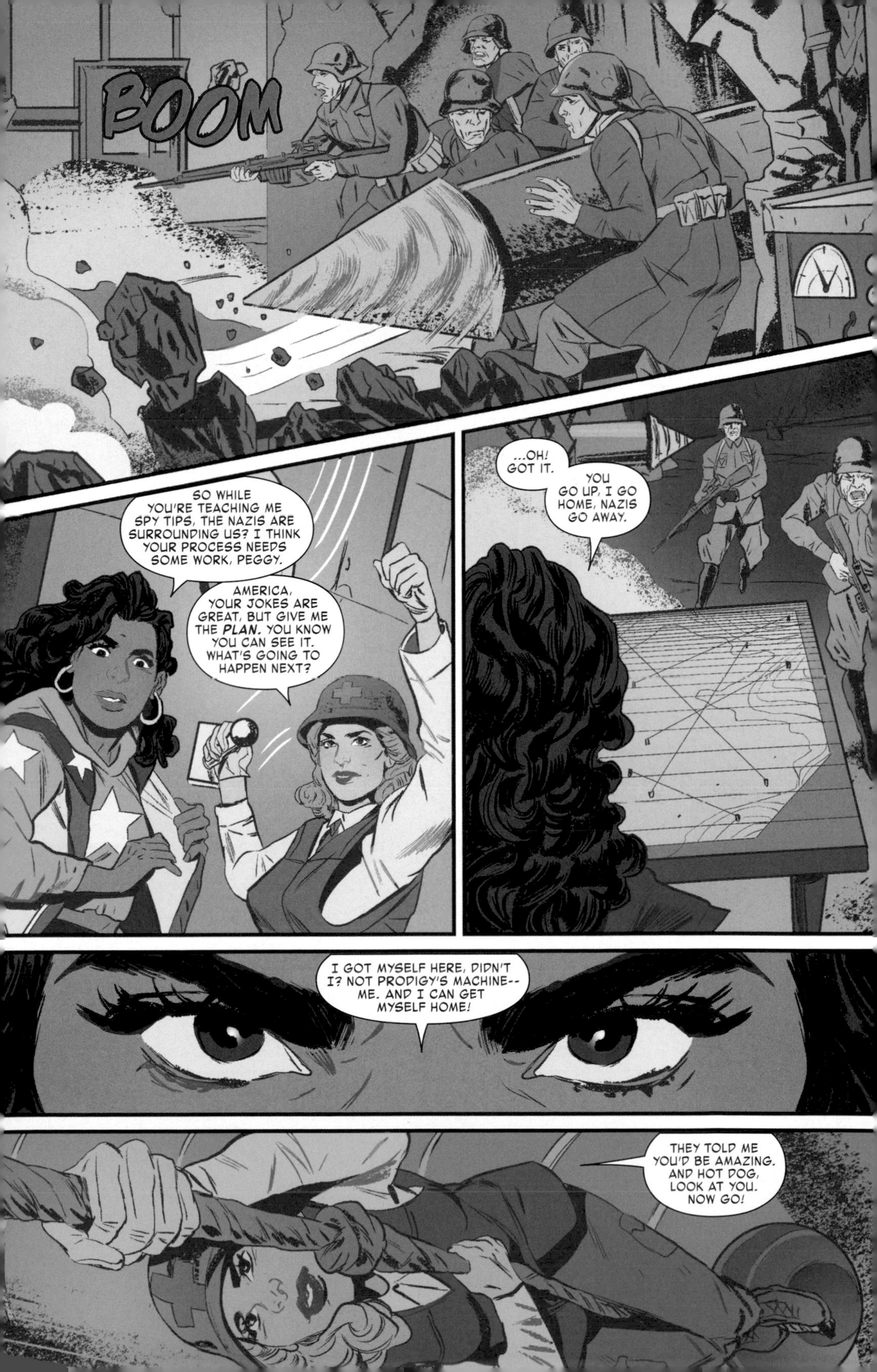
BOOM
SO WHILE YOU'RE TEACHING ME SPY TIPS, THE NAZIS ARE SURROUNDING US? I THINK YOUR PROCESS NEEDS SOME WORK, PEGGY.
AMERICA, YOUR JOKES ARE GREAT, BUT GIVE ME THE ***PLAN.*** YOU KNOW YOU CAN SEE IT. WHAT'S GOING TO HAPPEN NEXT?
...OH! GOT IT.
YOU GO UP, I GO HOME, NAZIS GO AWAY.
I GOT MYSELF HERE, DIDN'T I? NOT PRODIGY'S MACHINE-- ME. AND I CAN GET MYSELF HOME*!*
THEY TOLD ME YOU'D BE AMAZING. AND HOT DOG, LOOK AT YOU. NOW GO*!*

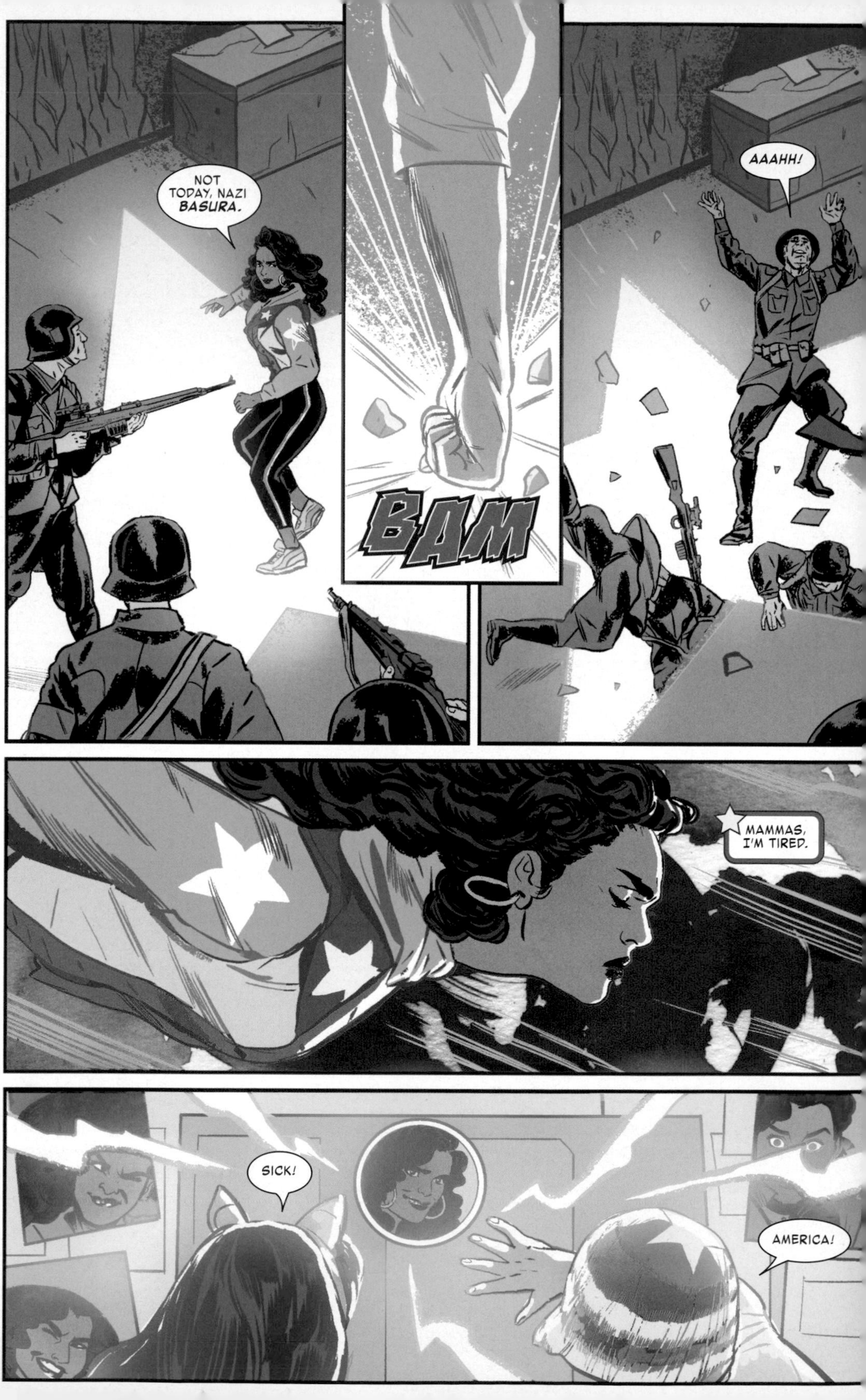
NOT TODAY, NAZI BASURA.
BAM
AAAHH!
MAMMAS, I'M TIRED.
SICK!
AMERICA!

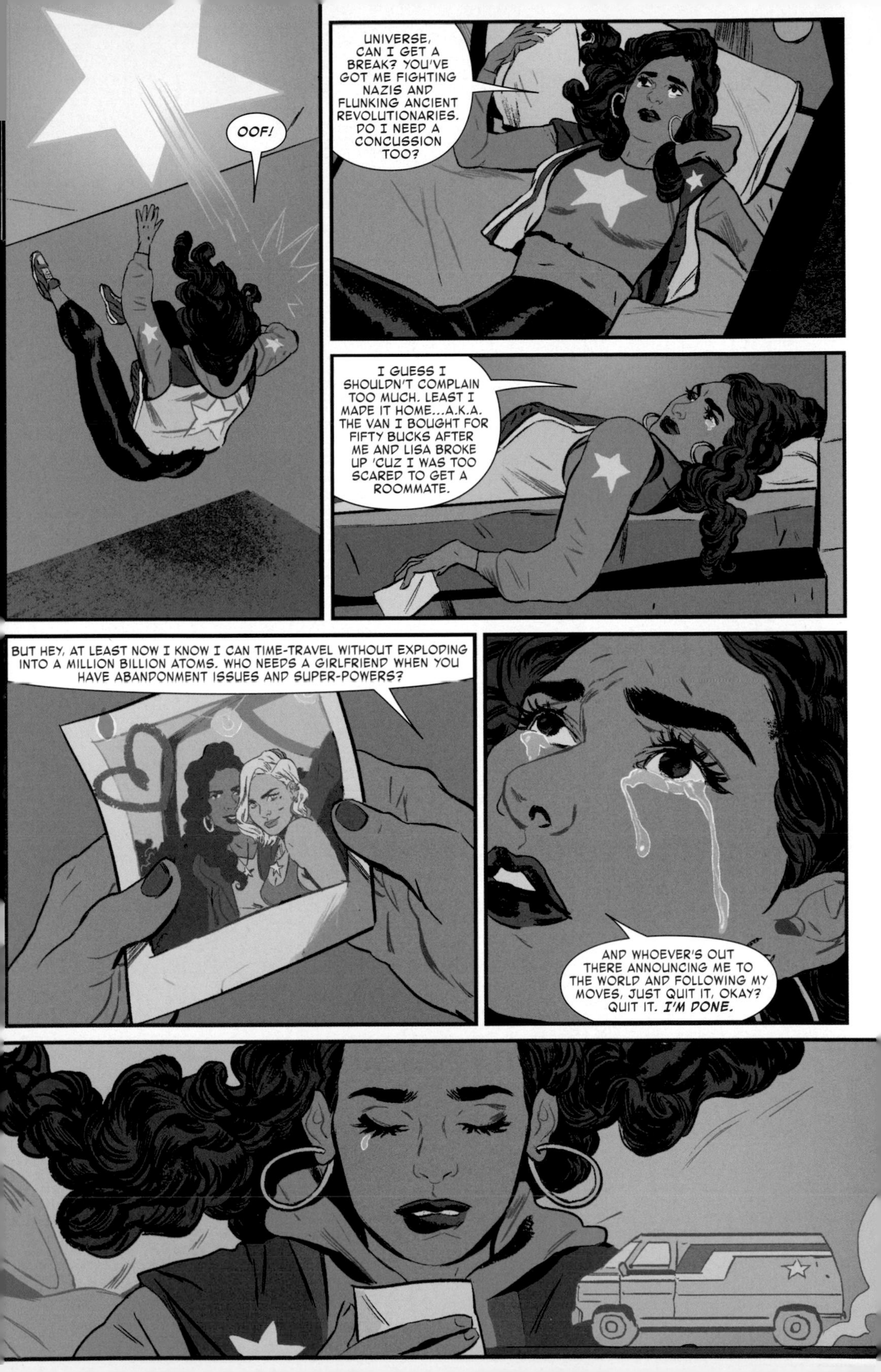
OOF!
UNIVERSE, CAN I GET A BREAK? YOU'VE GOT ME FIGHTING NAZIS AND FLUNKING ANCIENT REVOLUTIONARIES. DO I NEED A CONCUSSION TOO?
I GUESS I SHOULDN'T COMPLAIN TOO MUCH. LEAST I MADE IT HOME...A.K.A. THE VAN I BOUGHT FOR FIFTY BUCKS AFTER ME AND LISA BROKE UP 'CUZ I WAS TOO SCARED TO GET A ROOMMATE.
BUT HEY, AT LEAST NOW I KNOW I CAN TIME-TRAVEL WITHOUT EXPLODING INTO A MILLION BILLION ATOMS. WHO NEEDS A GIRLFRIEND WHEN YOU HAVE ABANDONMENT ISSUES AND SUPER-POWERS?
AND WHOEVER'S OUT THERE ANNOUNCING ME TO THE WORLD AND FOLLOWING MY MOVES, JUST QUIT IT, OKAY? QUIT IT. *I'M DONE.*

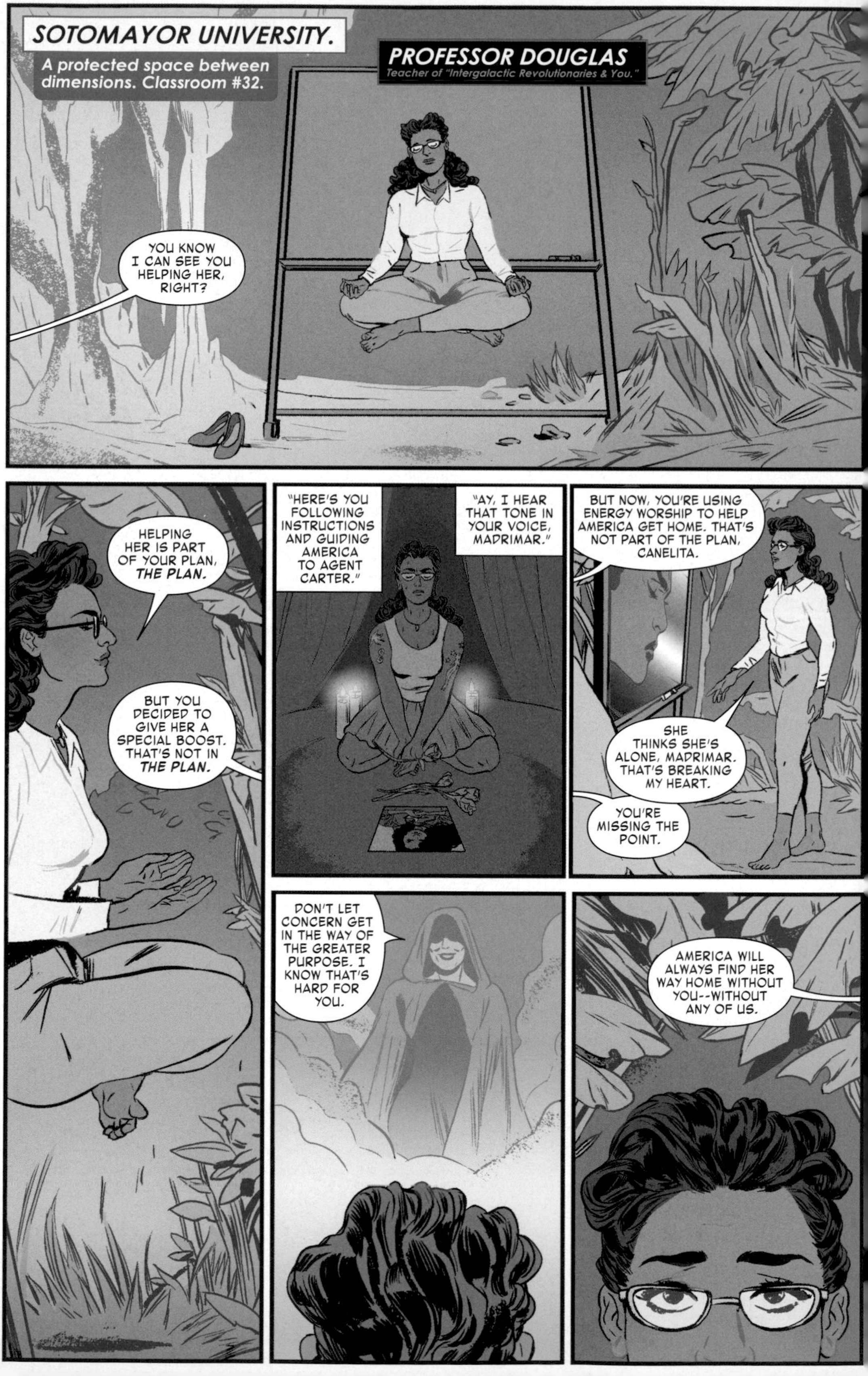
SOTOMAYOR UNIVERSITY.
A protected space between dimensions. Classroom #32.
PROFESSOR DOUGLAS
Teacher of "Intergalactic Revolutionaries & You."
YOU KNOW I CAN SEE YOU HELPING HER, RIGHT?
HELPING HER IS PART OF YOUR PLAN, THE PLAN.
BUT YOU DECIDED TO GIVE HER A SPECIAL BOOST. THAT'S NOT IN THE PLAN.
"HERE'S YOU FOLLOWING INSTRUCTIONS AND GUIDING AMERICA TO AGENT CARTER."
"AY, I HEAR THAT TONE IN YOUR VOICE, MADRIMAR."
BUT NOW, YOU'RE USING ENERGY WORSHIP TO HELP AMERICA GET HOME. THAT'S NOT PART OF THE PLAN, CANELITA.
SHE THINKS SHE'S ALONE, MADRIMAR. THAT'S BREAKING MY HEART.
YOU'RE MISSING THE POINT.
DON'T LET CONCERN GET IN THE WAY OF THE GREATER PURPOSE. I KNOW THAT'S HARD FOR YOU.
AMERICA WILL ALWAYS FIND HER WAY HOME WITHOUT YOU--WITHOUT ANY OF US.

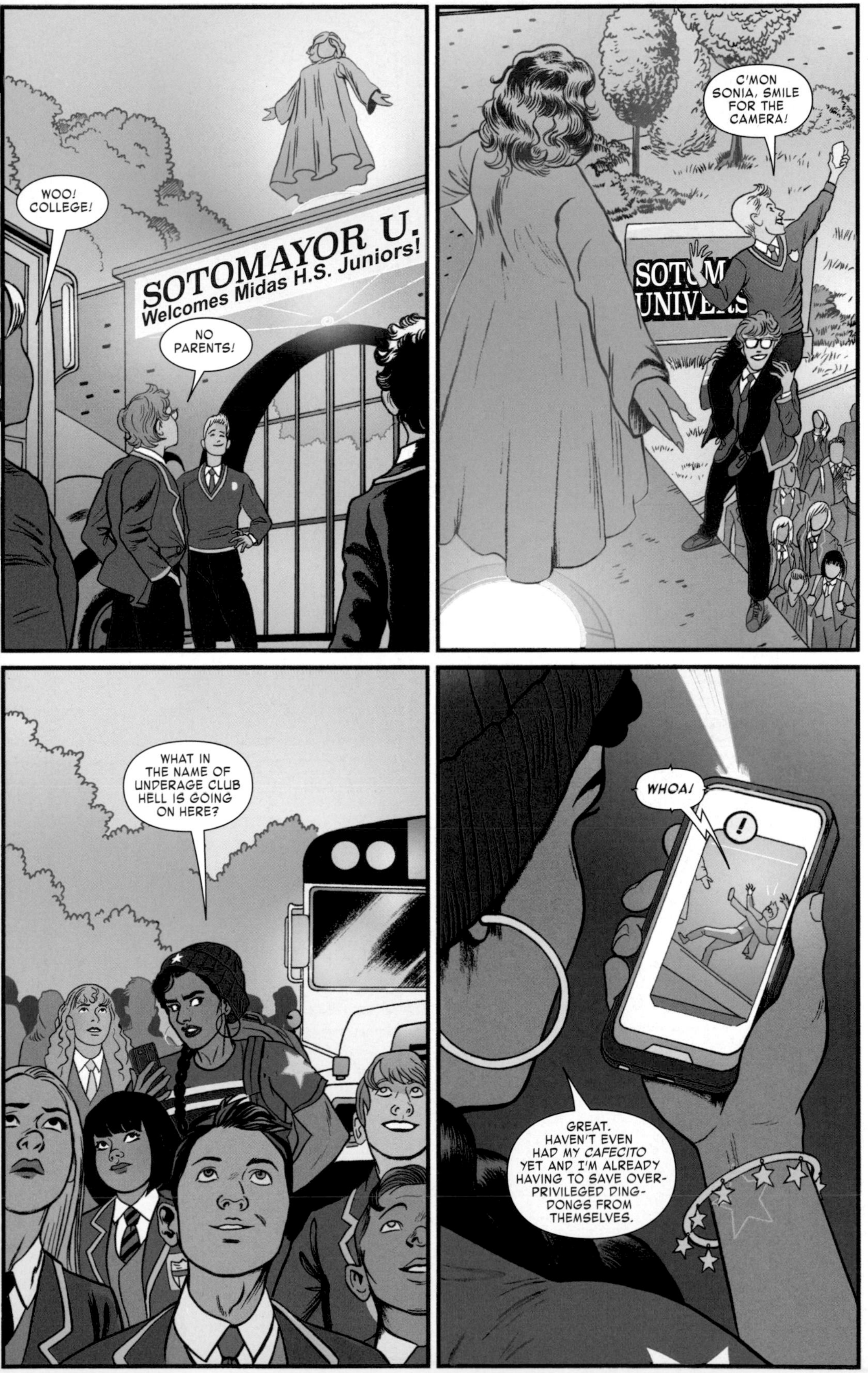
WOO! COLLEGE!
SOTOMAYOR U.
Welcomes Midas H.S. Juniors!
NO PARENTS!
C'MON SONIA, SMILE FOR THE CAMERA!
SOTOM
UNIVE
WHAT IN THE NAME OF UNDERAGE CLUB HELL IS GOING ON HERE?
WHOA!
!
GREAT. HAVEN'T EVEN HAD MY *CAFECITO* YET AND I'M ALREADY HAVING TO SAVE OVER-PRIVILEGED DING-DONGS FROM THEMSELVES.

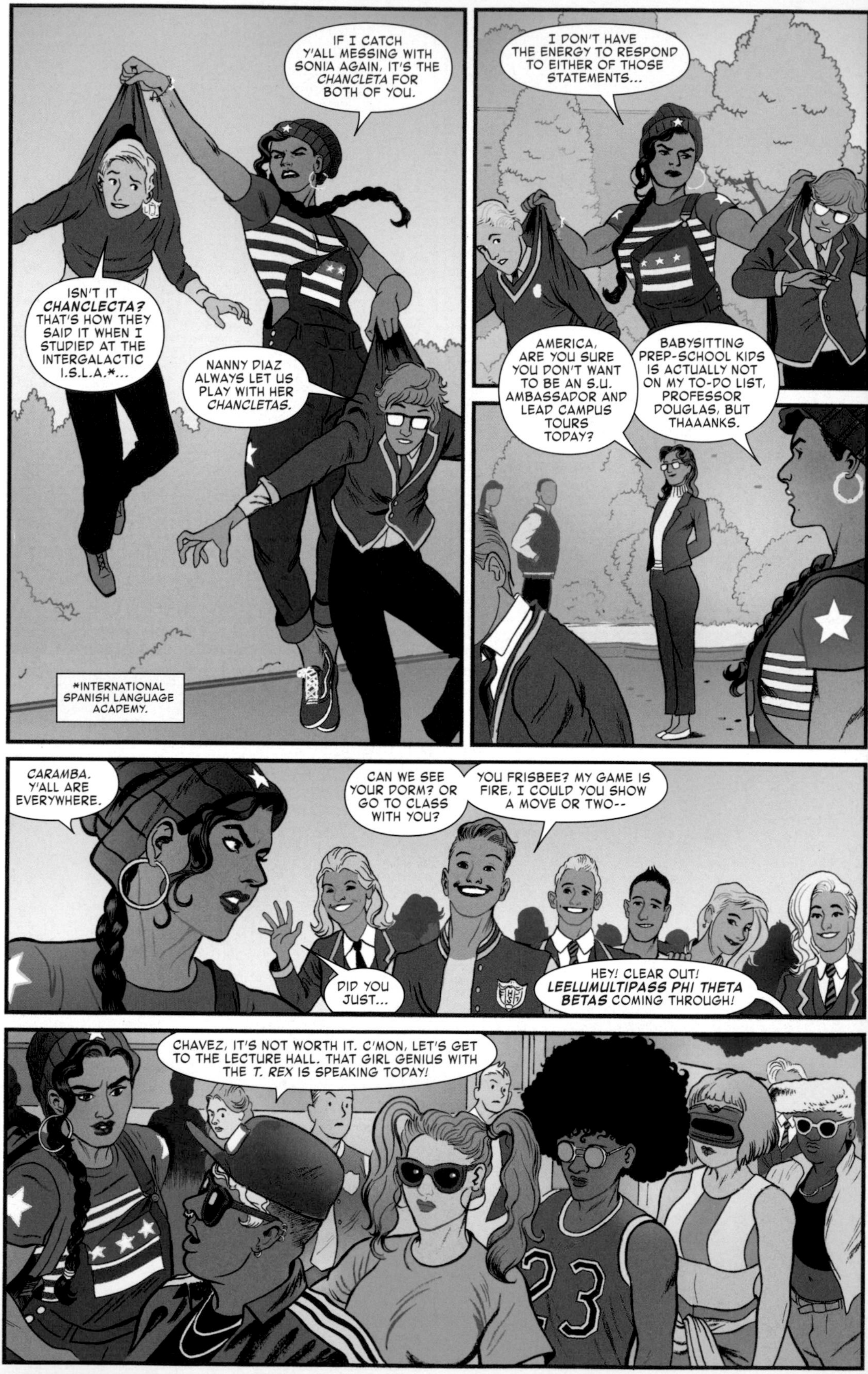
IF I CATCH Y'ALL MESSING WITH SONIA AGAIN, IT'S THE CHANCLETA FOR BOTH OF YOU.
ISN'T IT CHANCLECTA? THAT'S HOW THEY SAID IT WHEN I STUDIED AT THE INTERGALACTIC I.S.L.A.*...
NANNY DIAZ ALWAYS LET US PLAY WITH HER CHANCLETAS.
*INTERNATIONAL SPANISH LANGUAGE ACADEMY.
I DON'T HAVE THE ENERGY TO RESPOND TO EITHER OF THOSE STATEMENTS...
AMERICA, ARE YOU SURE YOU DON'T WANT TO BE AN S.U. AMBASSADOR AND LEAD CAMPUS TOURS TODAY?
BABYSITTING PREP-SCHOOL KIDS IS ACTUALLY NOT ON MY TO-DO LIST, PROFESSOR DOUGLAS, BUT THAAANKS.
CARAMBA. Y'ALL ARE EVERYWHERE.
CAN WE SEE YOUR DORM? OR GO TO CLASS WITH YOU?
YOU FRISBEE? MY GAME IS FIRE, I COULD YOU SHOW A MOVE OR TWO--
DID YOU JUST...
HEY! CLEAR OUT! LEELUMULTIPASS PHI THETA BETAS COMING THROUGH!
CHAVEZ, IT'S NOT WORTH IT. C'MON, LET'S GET TO THE LECTURE HALL. THAT GIRL GENIUS WITH THE T. REX IS SPEAKING TODAY!

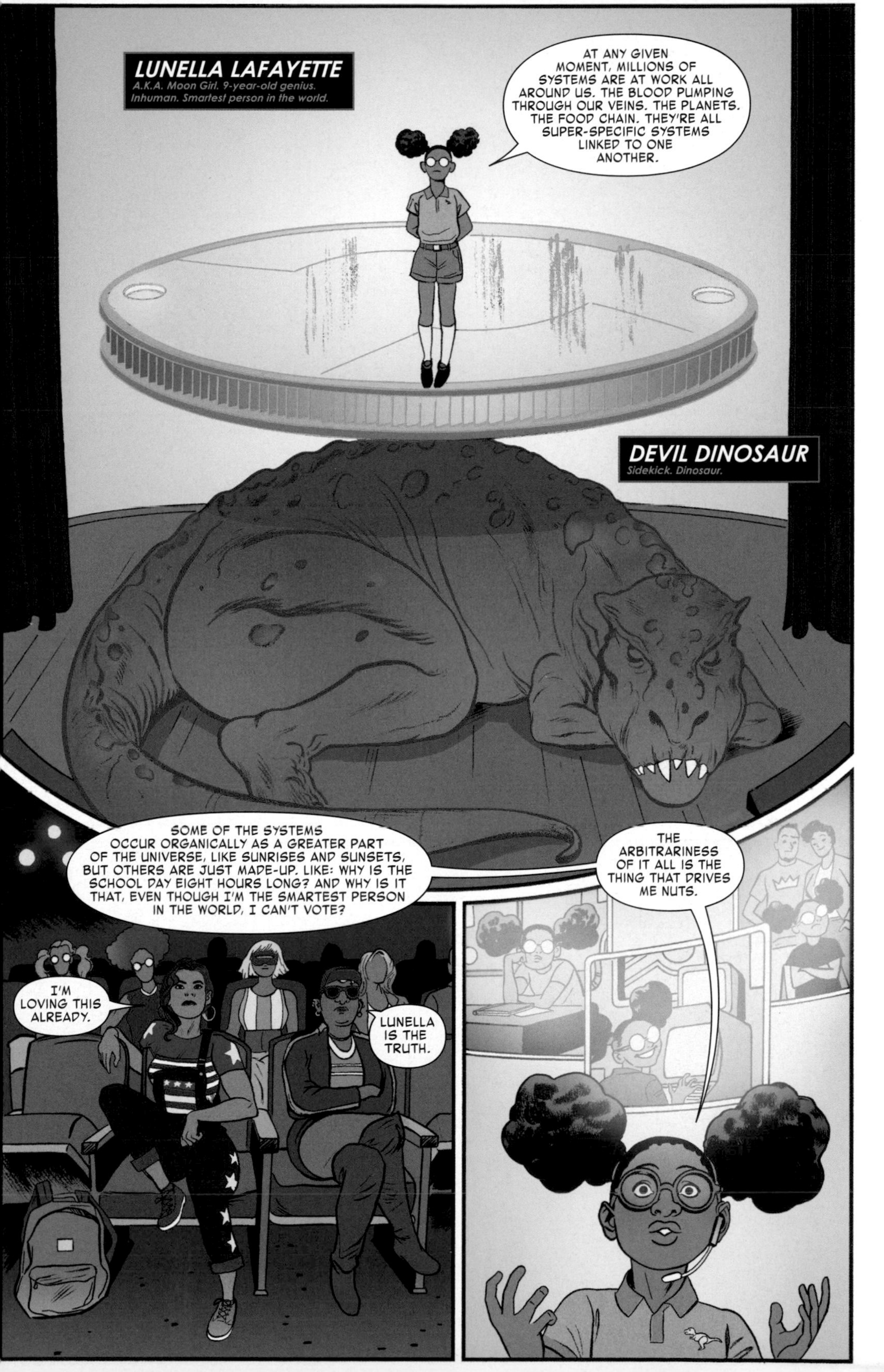
LUNELLA LAFAYETTE
A.K.A. Moon Girl. 9-year-old genius. Inhuman. Smartest person in the world.
AT ANY GIVEN MOMENT, MILLIONS OF SYSTEMS ARE AT WORK ALL AROUND US. THE BLOOD PUMPING THROUGH OUR VEINS. THE PLANETS. THE FOOD CHAIN. THEY'RE ALL SUPER-SPECIFIC SYSTEMS LINKED TO ONE ANOTHER.
DEVIL DINOSAUR
Sidekick. Dinosaur.
SOME OF THE SYSTEMS OCCUR ORGANICALLY AS A GREATER PART OF THE UNIVERSE, LIKE SUNRISES AND SUNSETS, BUT OTHERS ARE JUST MADE-UP. LIKE: WHY IS THE SCHOOL DAY EIGHT HOURS LONG? AND WHY IS IT THAT, EVEN THOUGH I'M THE SMARTEST PERSON IN THE WORLD, I CAN'T VOTE?
I'M LOVING THIS ALREADY.
LUNELLA IS THE TRUTH.
THE ARBITRARINESS OF IT ALL IS THE THING THAT DRIVES ME NUTS.

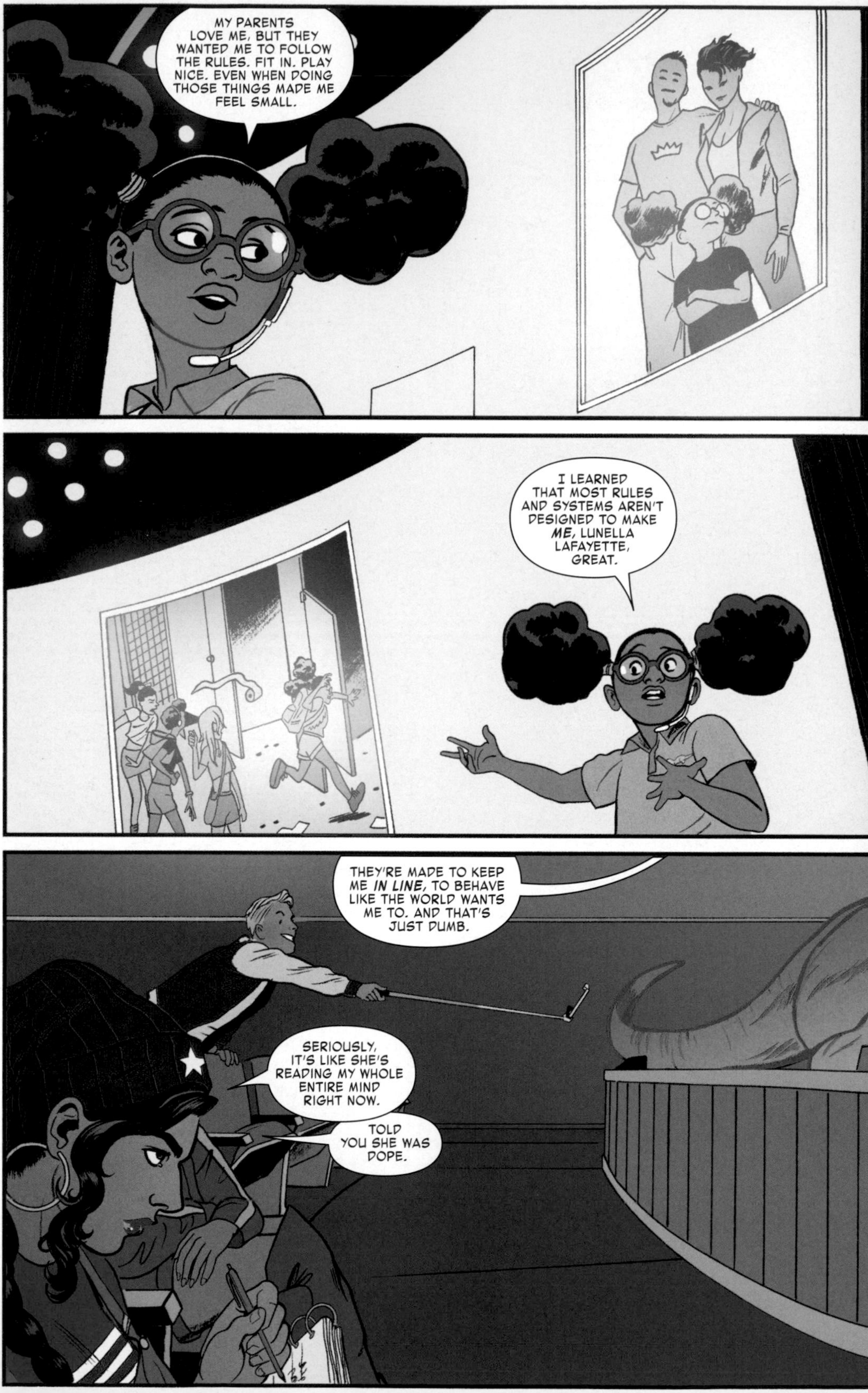
MY PARENTS LOVE ME, BUT THEY WANTED ME TO FOLLOW THE RULES. FIT IN. PLAY NICE. EVEN WHEN DOING THOSE THINGS MADE ME FEEL SMALL.
I LEARNED THAT MOST RULES AND SYSTEMS AREN'T DESIGNED TO MAKE *ME,* LUNELLA LAFAYETTE, GREAT.
THEY'RE MADE TO KEEP ME *IN LINE,* TO BEHAVE LIKE THE WORLD WANTS ME TO. AND THAT'S JUST DUMB.
SERIOUSLY, IT'S LIKE SHE'S READING MY WHOLE ENTIRE MIND RIGHT NOW.
TOLD YOU SHE WAS DOPE.

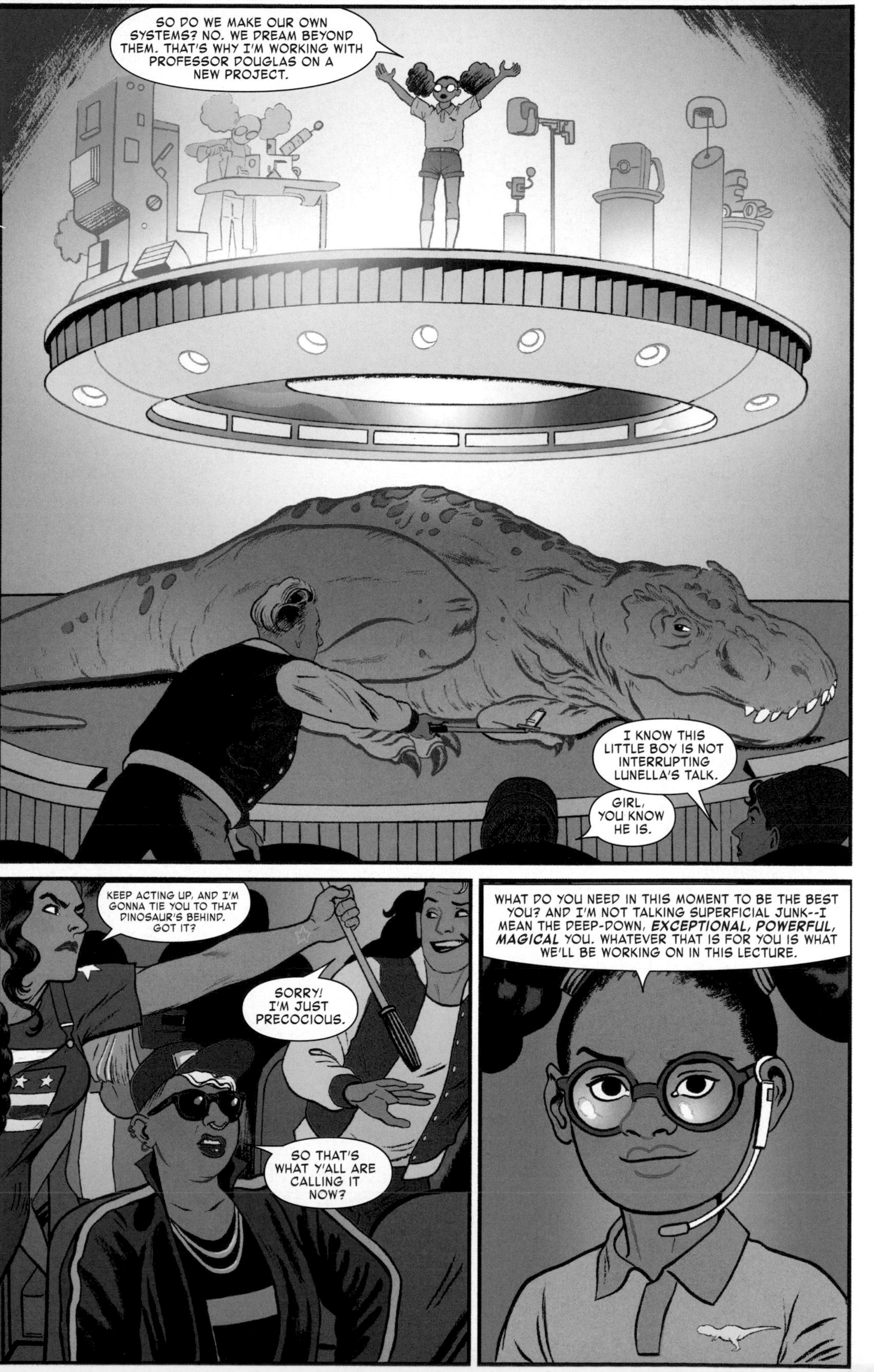
SO DO WE MAKE OUR OWN SYSTEMS? NO. WE DREAM BEYOND THEM. THAT'S WHY I'M WORKING WITH PROFESSOR DOUGLAS ON A NEW PROJECT.
I KNOW THIS LITTLE BOY IS NOT INTERRUPTING LUNELLA'S TALK.
GIRL, YOU KNOW HE IS.
KEEP ACTING UP, AND I'M GONNA TIE YOU TO THAT DINOSAUR'S BEHIND. GOT IT?
SORRY! I'M JUST PRECOCIOUS.
SO THAT'S WHAT Y'ALL ARE CALLING IT NOW?
WHAT DO YOU NEED IN THIS MOMENT TO BE THE BEST YOU? AND I'M NOT TALKING SUPERFICIAL JUNK--I MEAN THE DEEP-DOWN, ***EXCEPTIONAL, POWERFUL, MAGICAL*** YOU. WHATEVER THAT IS FOR YOU IS WHAT WE'LL BE WORKING ON IN THIS LECTURE.

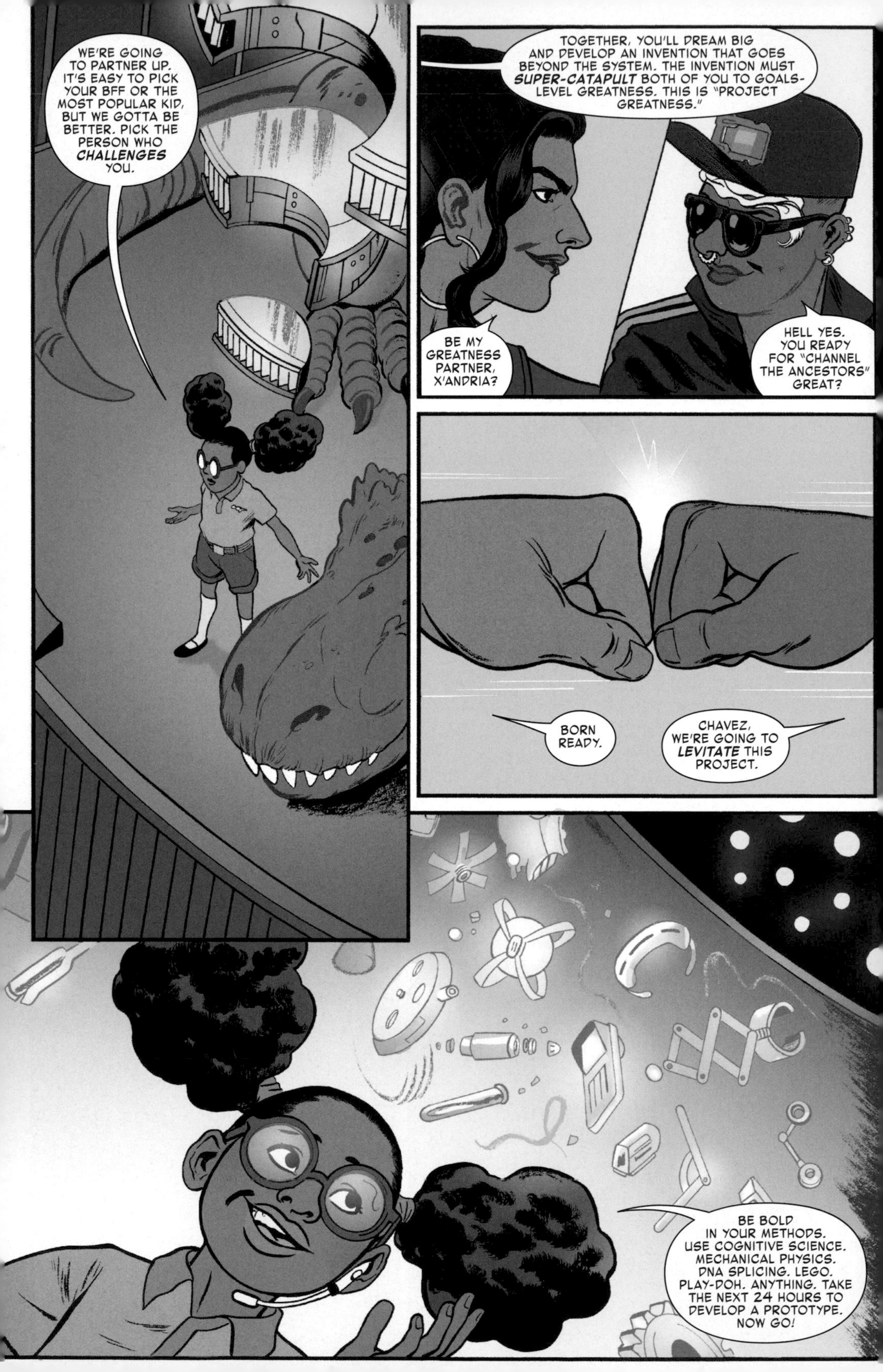
WE'RE GOING TO PARTNER UP. IT'S EASY TO PICK YOUR BFF OR THE MOST POPULAR KID, BUT WE GOTTA BE BETTER. PICK THE PERSON WHO *CHALLENGES* YOU.
TOGETHER, YOU'LL DREAM BIG AND DEVELOP AN INVENTION THAT GOES BEYOND THE SYSTEM. THE INVENTION MUST *SUPER-CATAPULT* BOTH OF YOU TO GOALS-LEVEL GREATNESS. THIS IS "PROJECT GREATNESS."
BE MY GREATNESS PARTNER, X'ANDRIA?
HELL YES. YOU READY FOR "CHANNEL THE ANCESTORS" GREAT?
BORN READY.
CHAVEZ, WE'RE GOING TO *LEVITATE* THIS PROJECT.
BE BOLD IN YOUR METHODS. USE COGNITIVE SCIENCE. MECHANICAL PHYSICS. DNA SPLICING. LEGO. PLAY-DOH. ANYTHING. TAKE THE NEXT 24 HOURS TO DEVELOP A PROTOTYPE. NOW GO!

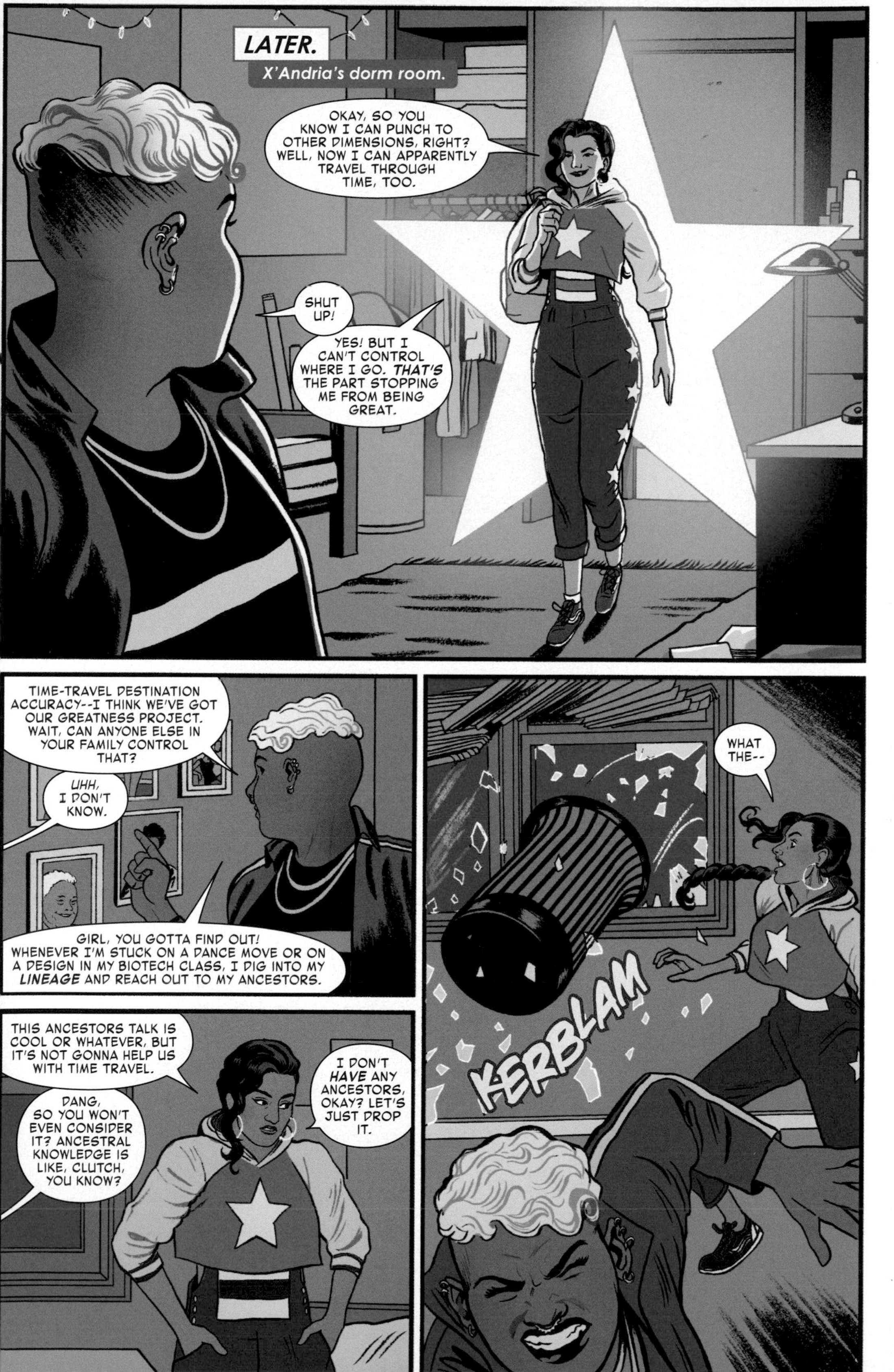
LATER.
X'Andria's dorm room.
OKAY, SO YOU KNOW I CAN PUNCH TO OTHER DIMENSIONS, RIGHT? WELL, NOW I CAN APPARENTLY TRAVEL THROUGH TIME, TOO.
SHUT UP!
YES! BUT I CAN'T CONTROL WHERE I GO. *THAT'S* THE PART STOPPING ME FROM BEING GREAT.
TIME-TRAVEL DESTINATION ACCURACY--I THINK WE'VE GOT OUR GREATNESS PROJECT. WAIT, CAN ANYONE ELSE IN YOUR FAMILY CONTROL THAT?
UHH, I DON'T KNOW.
GIRL, YOU GOTTA FIND OUT! WHENEVER I'M STUCK ON A DANCE MOVE OR ON A DESIGN IN MY BIOTECH CLASS, I DIG INTO MY *LINEAGE* AND REACH OUT TO MY ANCESTORS.
THIS ANCESTORS TALK IS COOL OR WHATEVER, BUT IT'S NOT GONNA HELP US WITH TIME TRAVEL.
DANG, SO YOU WON'T EVEN CONSIDER IT? ANCESTRAL KNOWLEDGE IS LIKE, CLUTCH, YOU KNOW?
I DON'T *HAVE* ANY ANCESTORS, OKAY? LET'S JUST DROP IT.
WHAT THE--
KERBLAM

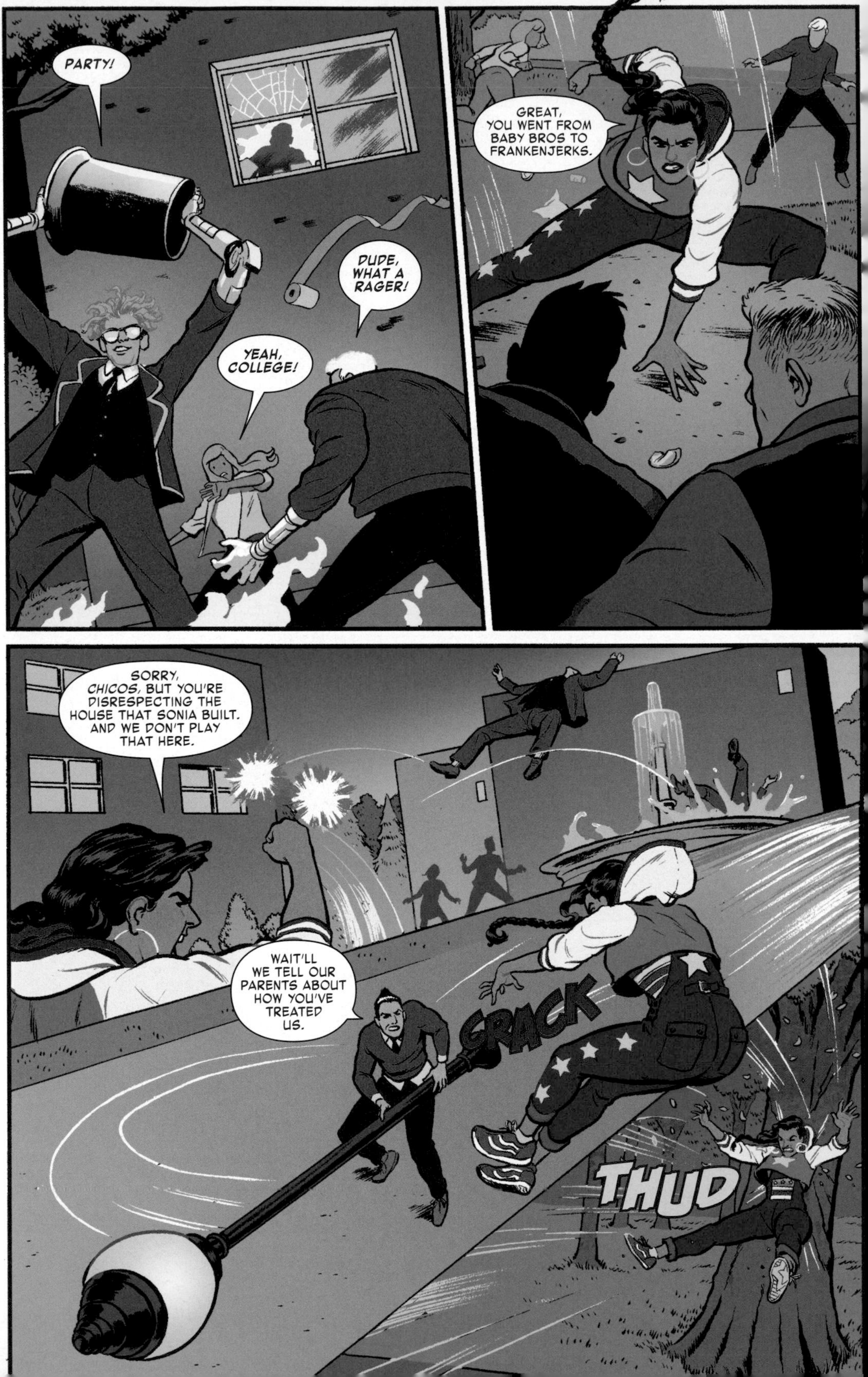
PARTY!
DUDE, WHAT A RAGER!
YEAH, COLLEGE!
GREAT, YOU WENT FROM BABY BROS TO FRANKENJERKS.
SORRY, CHICOS, BUT YOU'RE DISRESPECTING THE HOUSE THAT SONIA BUILT. AND WE DON'T PLAY THAT HERE.
WAIT'LL WE TELL OUR PARENTS ABOUT HOW YOU'VE TREATED US.
CRACK
THUD

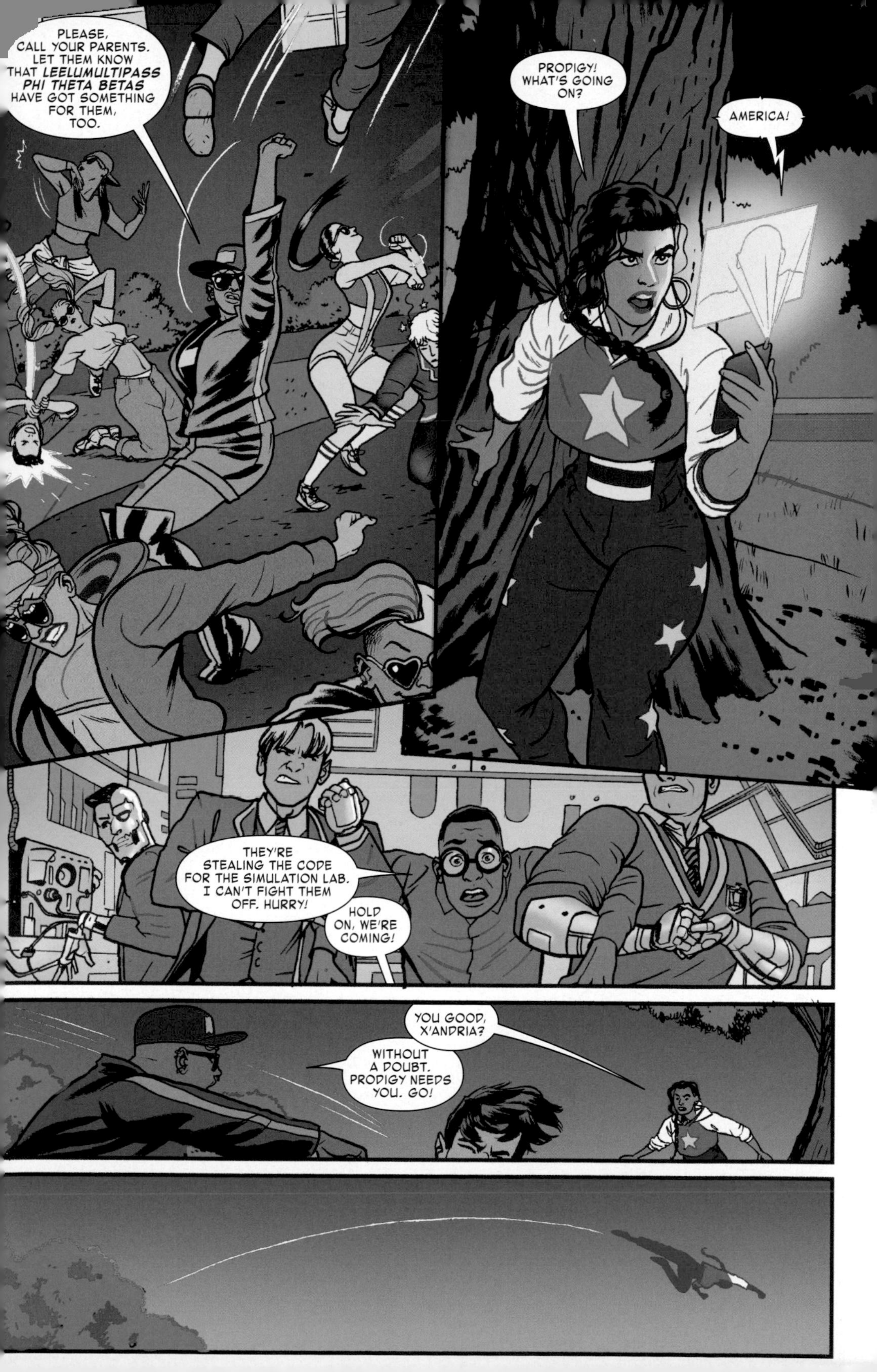
PLEASE, CALL YOUR PARENTS. LET THEM KNOW THAT *LEELUMULTIPASS PHI THETA BETAS* HAVE GOT SOMETHING FOR THEM, TOO.
PRODIGY! WHAT'S GOING ON?
AMERICA!
THEY'RE STEALING THE CODE FOR THE SIMULATION LAB. I CAN'T FIGHT THEM OFF. HURRY!
HOLD ON, WE'RE COMING!
YOU GOOD, X'ANDRIA?
WITHOUT A DOUBT. PRODIGY NEEDS YOU. GO!

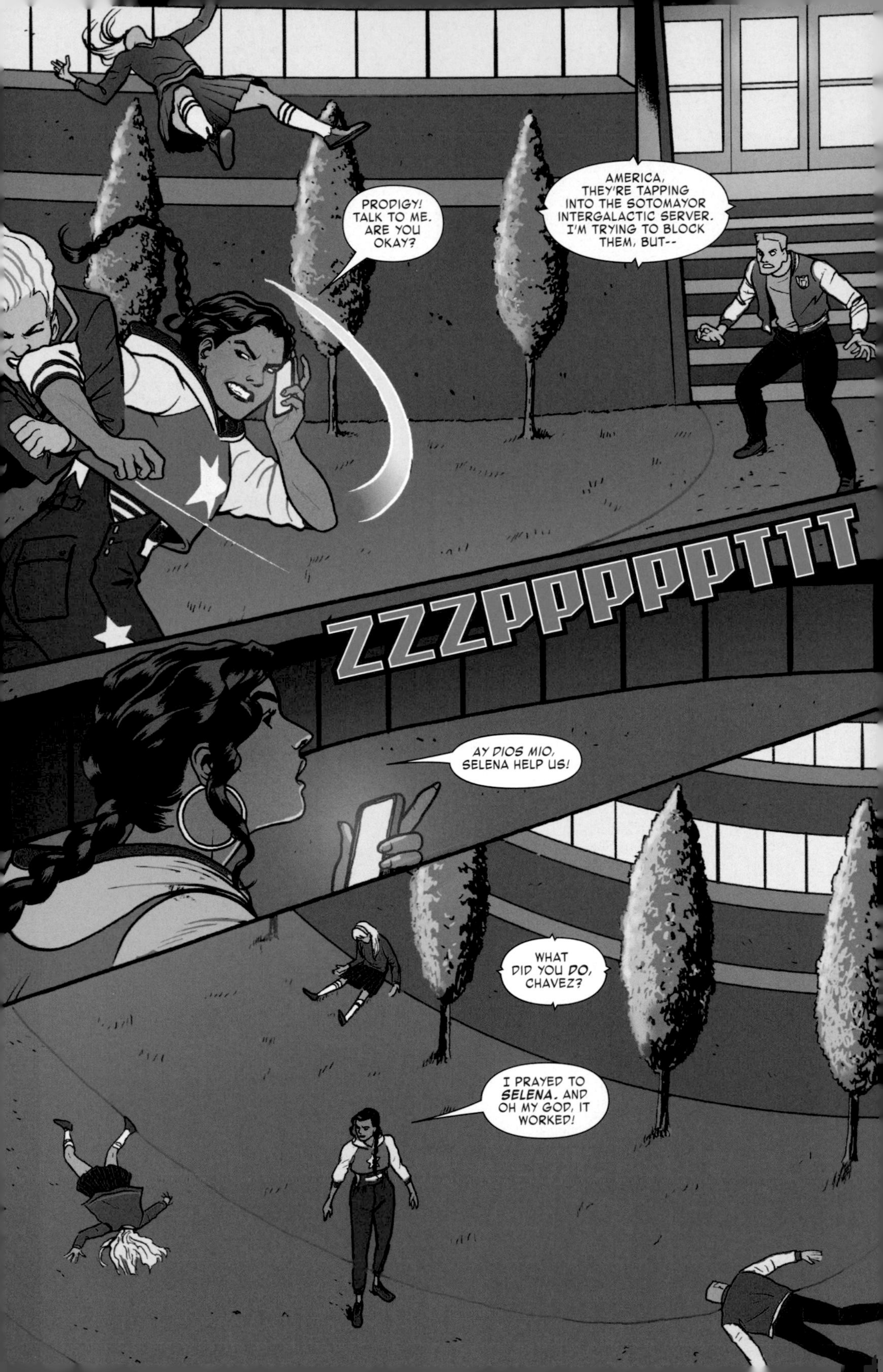
PRODIGY! TALK TO ME. ARE YOU OKAY?
AMERICA, THEY'RE TAPPING INTO THE SOTOMAYOR INTERGALACTIC SERVER. I'M TRYING TO BLOCK THEM, BUT--
ZZZPPPPPTTT
AY DIOS MIO, SELENA HELP US!
WHAT DID YOU DO, CHAVEZ?
I PRAYED TO SELENA. AND OH MY GOD, IT WORKED!

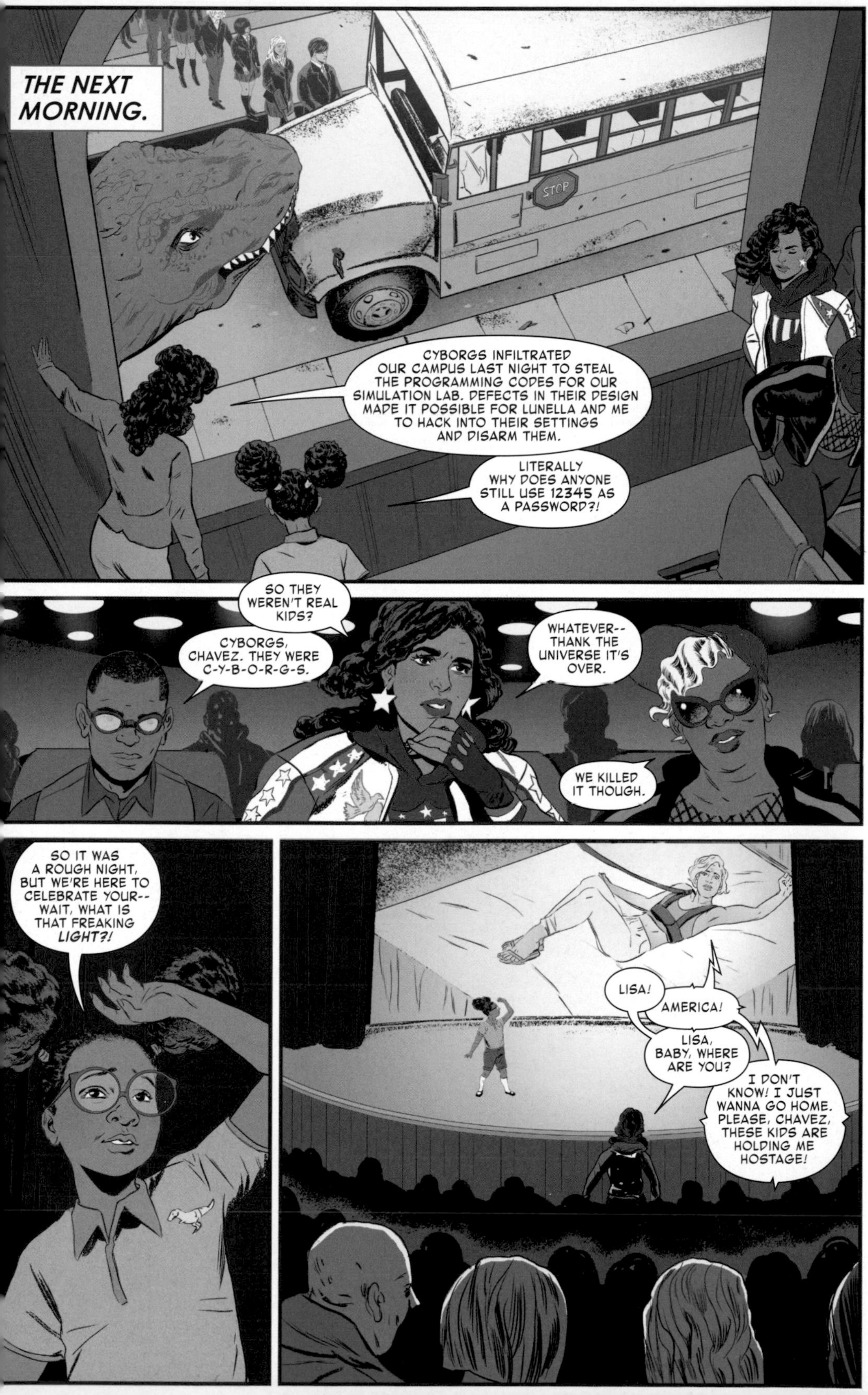
THE NEXT MORNING.
CYBORGS INFILTRATED OUR CAMPUS LAST NIGHT TO STEAL THE PROGRAMMING CODES FOR OUR SIMULATION LAB. DEFECTS IN THEIR DESIGN MADE IT POSSIBLE FOR LUNELLA AND ME TO HACK INTO THEIR SETTINGS AND DISARM THEM.
LITERALLY WHY DOES ANYONE STILL USE 12345 AS A PASSWORD?!
SO THEY WEREN'T REAL KIDS?
CYBORGS, CHAVEZ. THEY WERE C-Y-B-O-R-G-S.
WHATEVER-- THANK THE UNIVERSE IT'S OVER.
WE KILLED IT THOUGH.
SO IT WAS A ROUGH NIGHT, BUT WE'RE HERE TO CELEBRATE YOUR-- WAIT, WHAT IS THAT FREAKING *LIGHT?!*
LISA!
AMERICA!
LISA, BABY, WHERE ARE YOU?
I DON'T KNOW! I JUST WANNA GO HOME. PLEASE, CHAVEZ, THESE KIDS ARE HOLDING ME HOSTAGE!
STOP

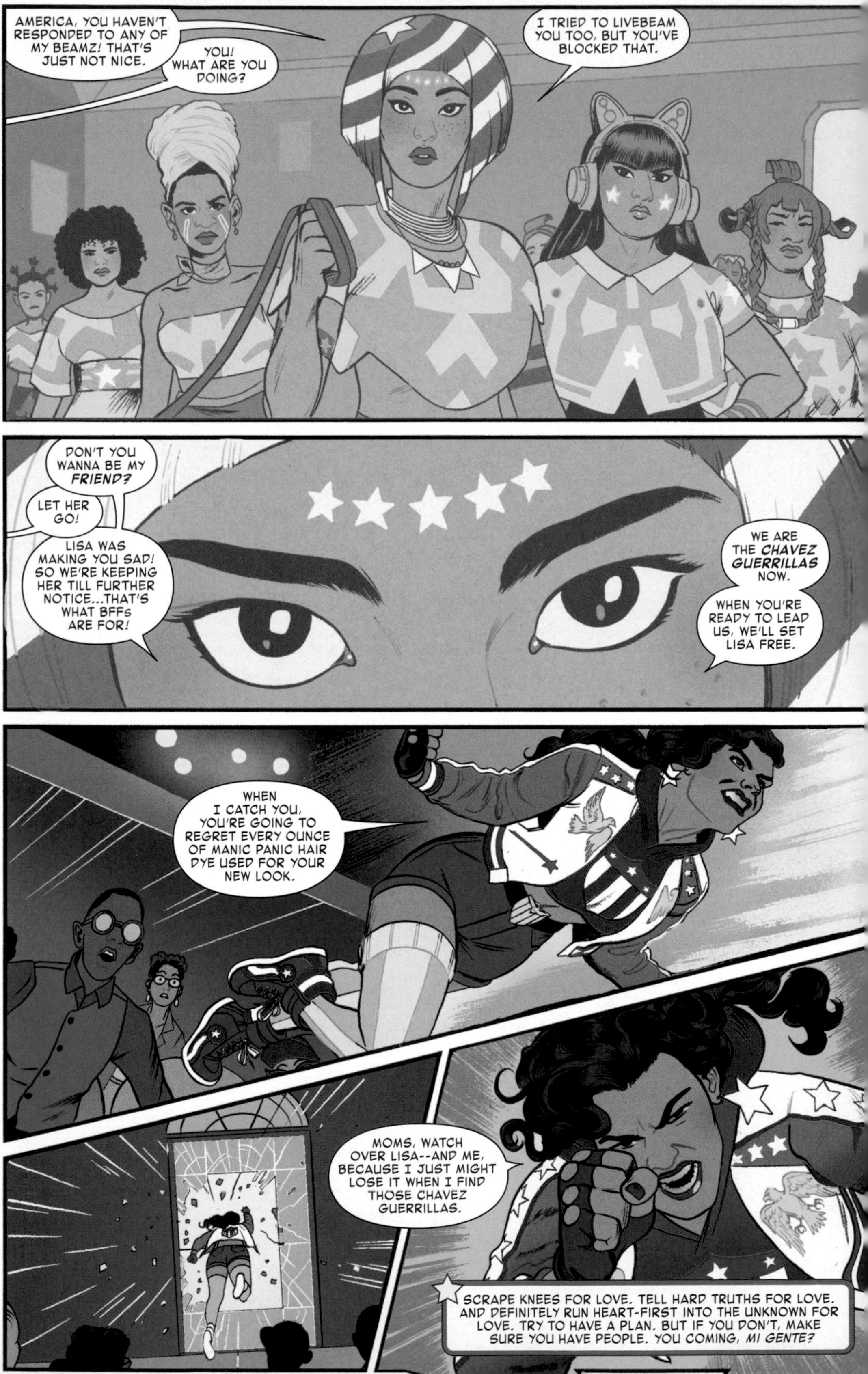
AMERICA, YOU HAVEN'T RESPONDED TO ANY OF MY BEAMZ! THAT'S JUST NOT NICE.
YOU! WHAT ARE YOU DOING?
I TRIED TO LIVEBEAM YOU TOO, BUT YOU'VE BLOCKED THAT.
DON'T YOU WANNA BE MY *FRIEND?*
LET HER GO!
LISA WAS MAKING YOU SAD! SO WE'RE KEEPING HER TILL FURTHER NOTICE...THAT'S WHAT BFFs ARE FOR!
WE ARE THE *CHAVEZ GUERRILLAS* NOW.
WHEN YOU'RE READY TO LEAD US, WE'LL SET LISA FREE.
WHEN I CATCH YOU, YOU'RE GOING TO REGRET EVERY OUNCE OF MANIC PANIC HAIR DYE USED FOR YOUR NEW LOOK.
MOMS, WATCH OVER LISA--AND ME, BECAUSE I JUST MIGHT LOSE IT WHEN I FIND THOSE CHAVEZ GUERRILLAS.
SCRAPE KNEES FOR LOVE. TELL HARD TRUTHS FOR LOVE. AND DEFINITELY RUN HEART-FIRST INTO THE UNKNOWN FOR LOVE. TRY TO HAVE A PLAN. BUT IF YOU DON'T, MAKE SURE YOU HAVE PEOPLE. YOU COMING, *MI GENTE?*

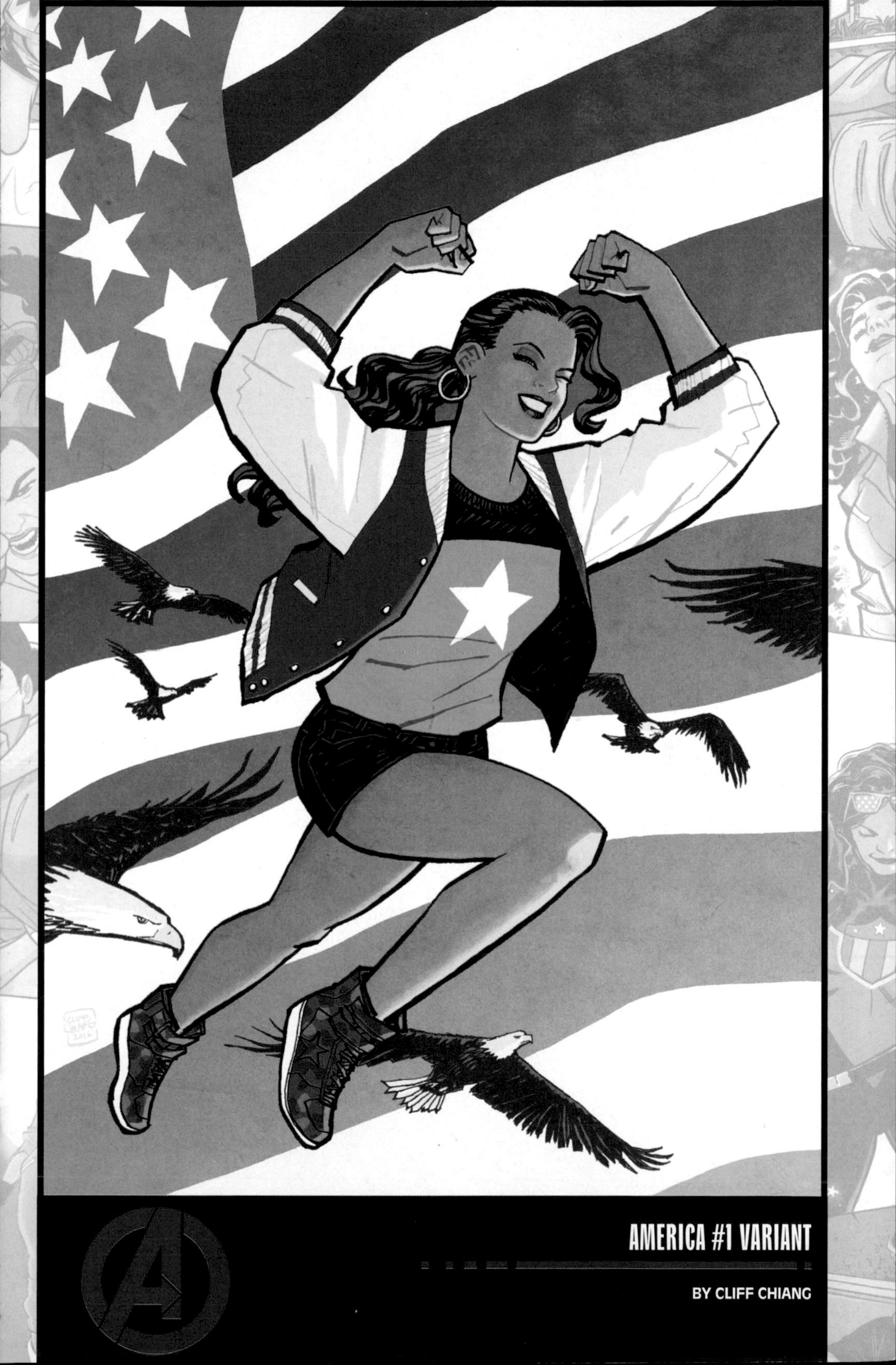

AMERICA #1 VARIANT

BY CLIFF CHIANG

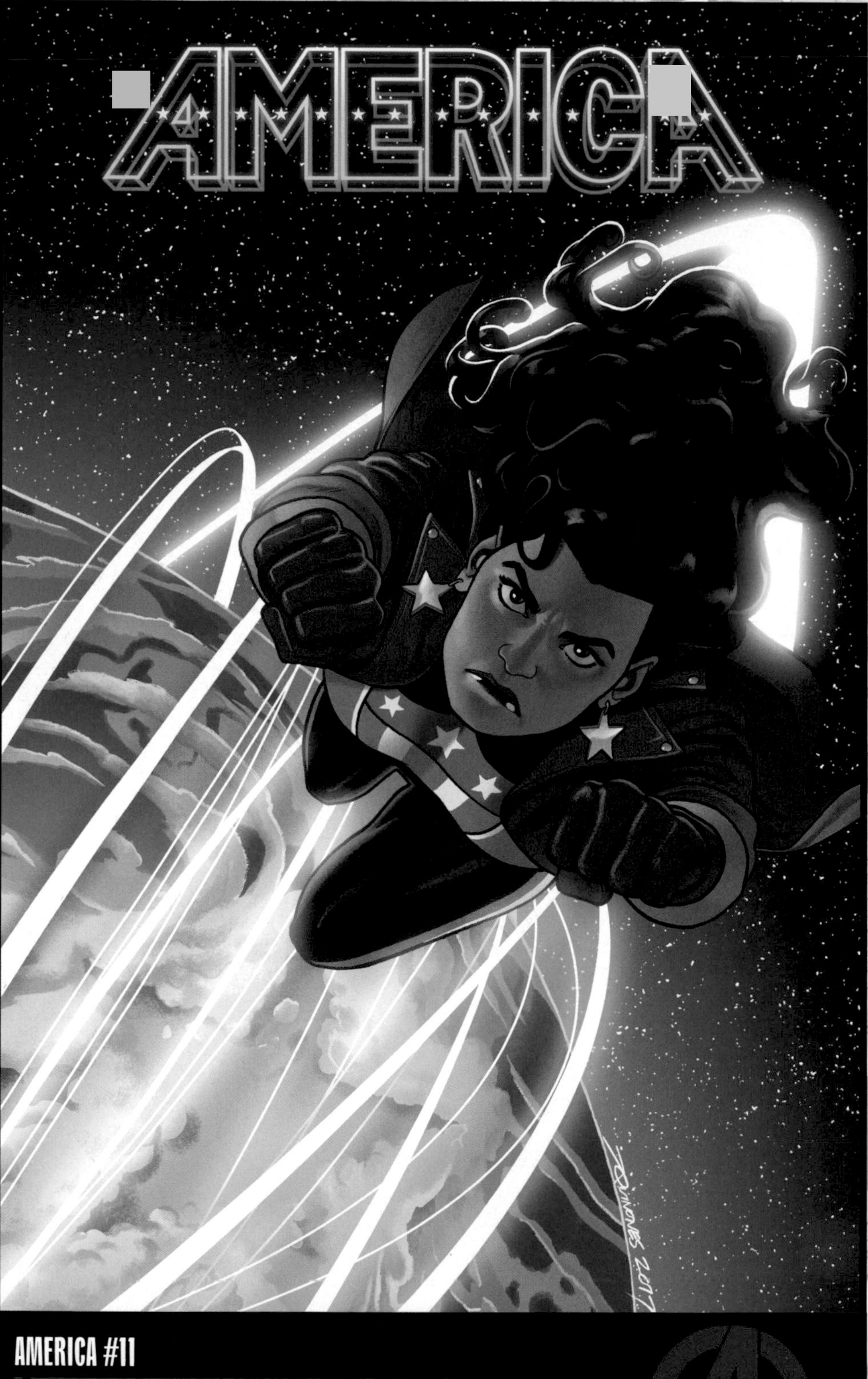
AMERICA

AMERICA #11

AMERICA HAS FINALLY FOUND THE FAMILY SHE'S BEEN SEARCHING FOR. BUT WHEN A DECADES-OLD THREAT AWAKENS, EVERYTHING AMERICA HAS FOUGHT FOR IS PUT IN DANGER!

VIVA_AMERICA

That's right, it's me: America Chavez, exile of the Utopian Parallel and student at Sotomayor U. And I'm not new. I'm Teen Brigade, Young Avengers and the Ultimates certified. You don't need to see I.D. I've got my own solo series now, *oíste?*

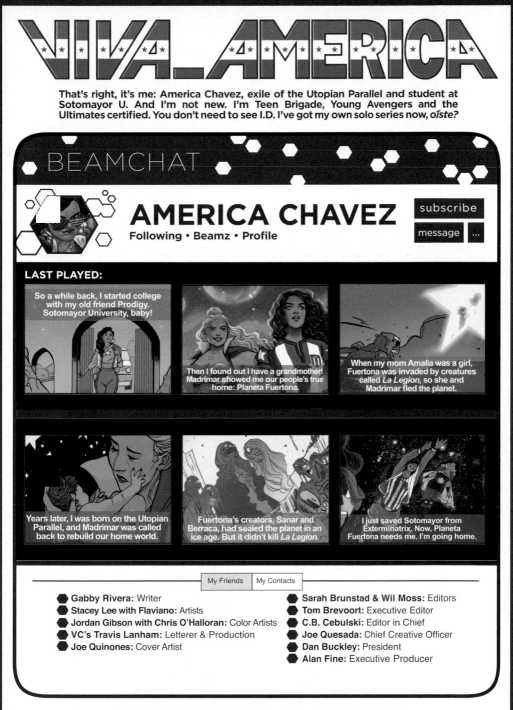

BEAMCHAT

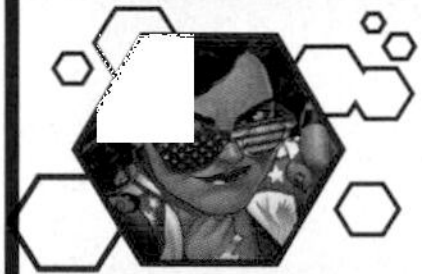

AMERICA CHAVEZ

Following • Beamz • Profile

subscribe

message ...

LAST PLAYED:

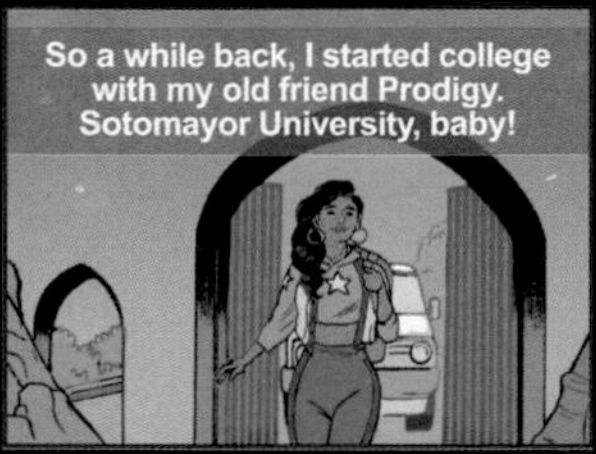
So a while back, I started college with my old friend Prodigy. Sotomayor University, baby!

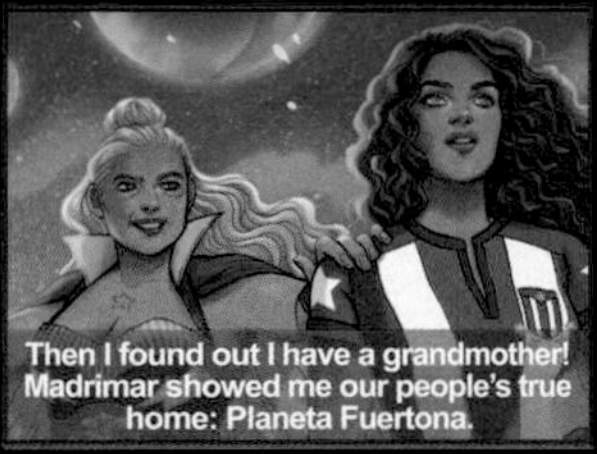
Then I found out I have a grandmother! Madrimar showed me our people's true home: Planeta Fuertona.

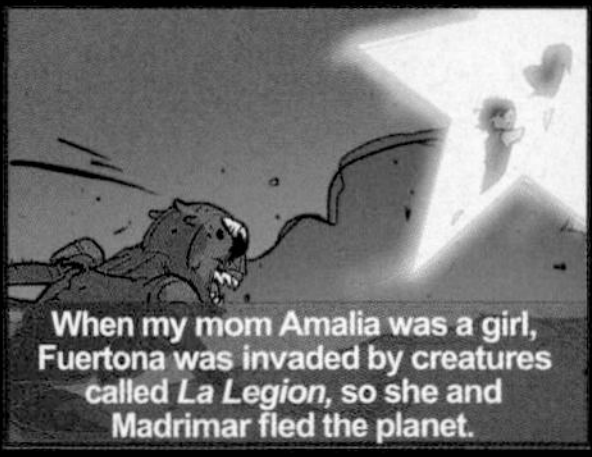
When my mom Amalia was a girl, Fuertona was invaded by creatures called La Legion, so she and Madrimar fled the planet.

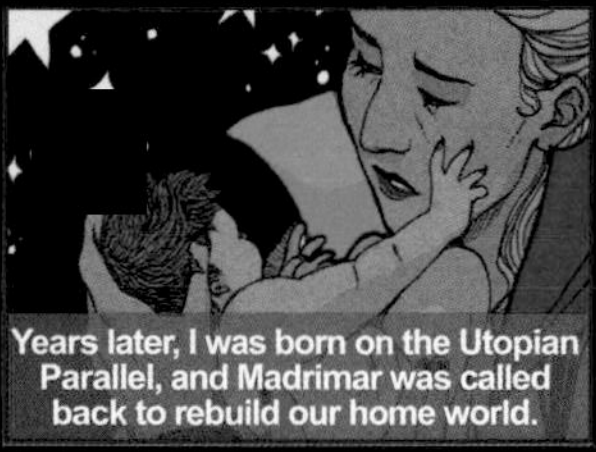
Years later, I was born on the Utopian Parallel, and Madrimar was called back to rebuild our home world.

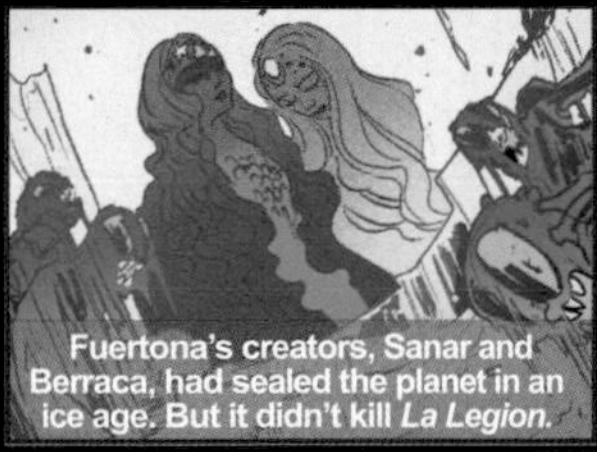
Fuertona's creators, Sanar and Berraca, had sealed the planet in an ice age. But it didn't kill La Legion.

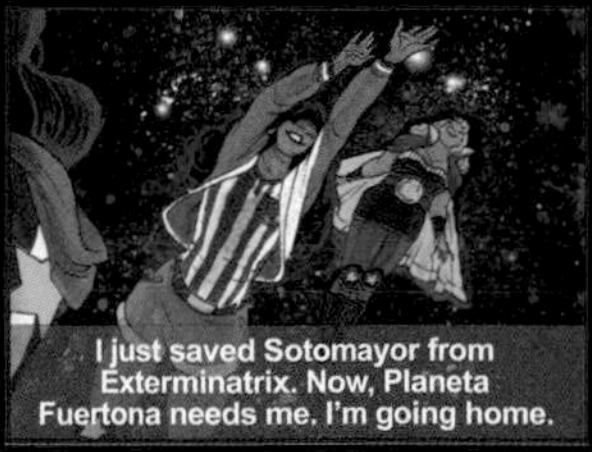
I just saved Sotomayor from Exterminatrix. Now, Planeta Fuertona needs me. I'm going home.

My Friends | My Contacts

- **Gabby Rivera:** Writer
- **Stacey Lee with Flaviano:** Artists
- **Jordan Gibson with Chris O'Halloran:** Color Artists
- **VC's Travis Lanham:** Letterer & Production
- **Joe Quinones:** Cover Artist
- **Sarah Brunstad & Wil Moss:** Editors
- **Tom Brevoort:** Executive Editor
- **C.B. Cebulski:** Editor in Chief
- **Joe Quesada:** Chief Creative Officer
- **Dan Buckley:** President
- **Alan Fine:** Executive Producer

"ULTRALIGHT BEAM"

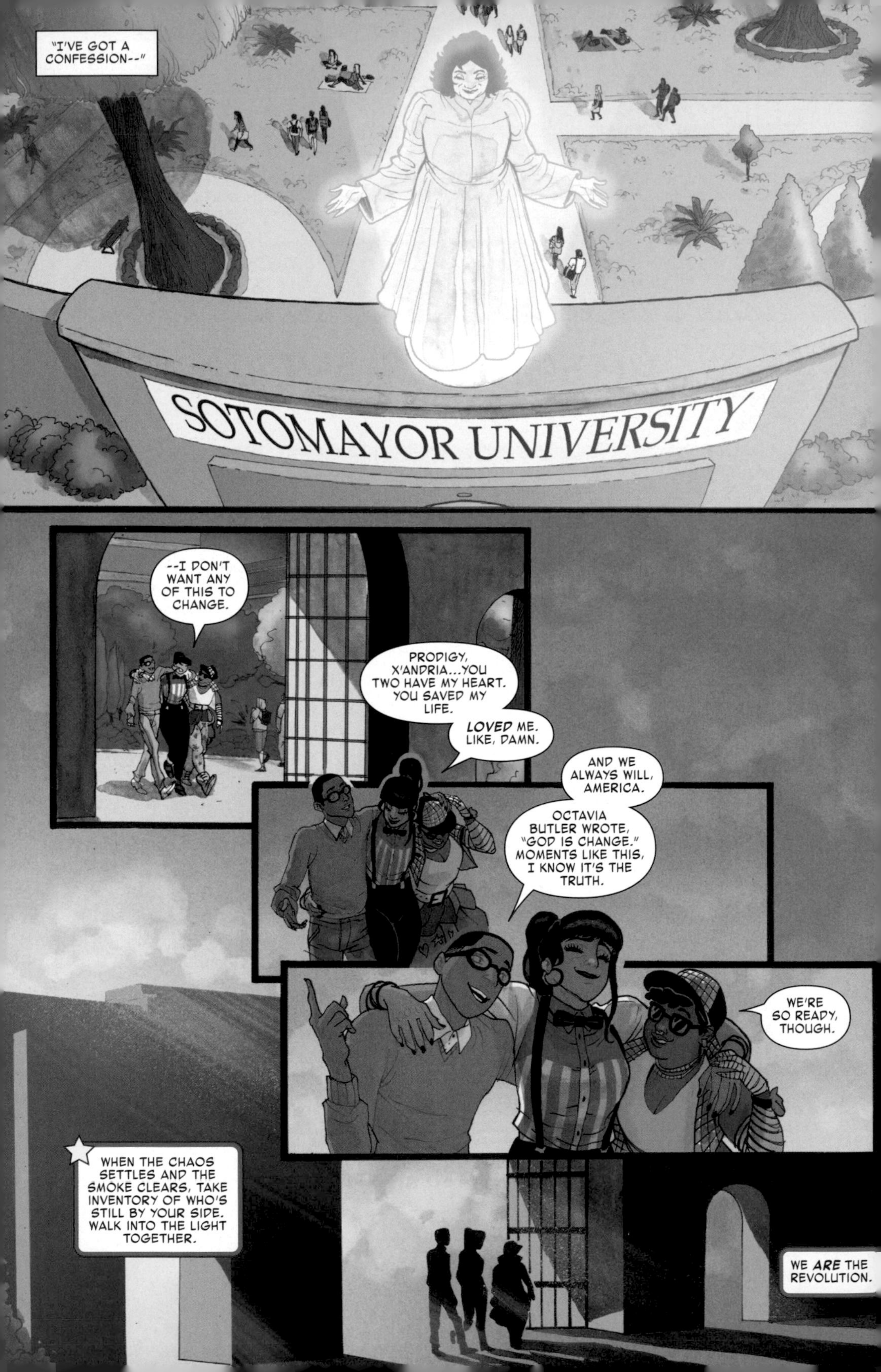
"I'VE GOT A CONFESSION--"
SOTOMAYOR UNIVERSITY
--I DON'T WANT ANY OF THIS TO CHANGE.
PRODIGY, X'ANDRIA...YOU TWO HAVE MY HEART. YOU SAVED MY LIFE.
LOVED ME. LIKE, DAMN.
AND WE ALWAYS WILL, AMERICA.
OCTAVIA BUTLER WROTE, "GOD IS CHANGE." MOMENTS LIKE THIS, I KNOW IT'S THE TRUTH.
WE'RE SO READY, THOUGH.
WHEN THE CHAOS SETTLES AND THE SMOKE CLEARS, TAKE INVENTORY OF WHO'S STILL BY YOUR SIDE. WALK INTO THE LIGHT TOGETHER.
WE ARE THE REVOLUTION.

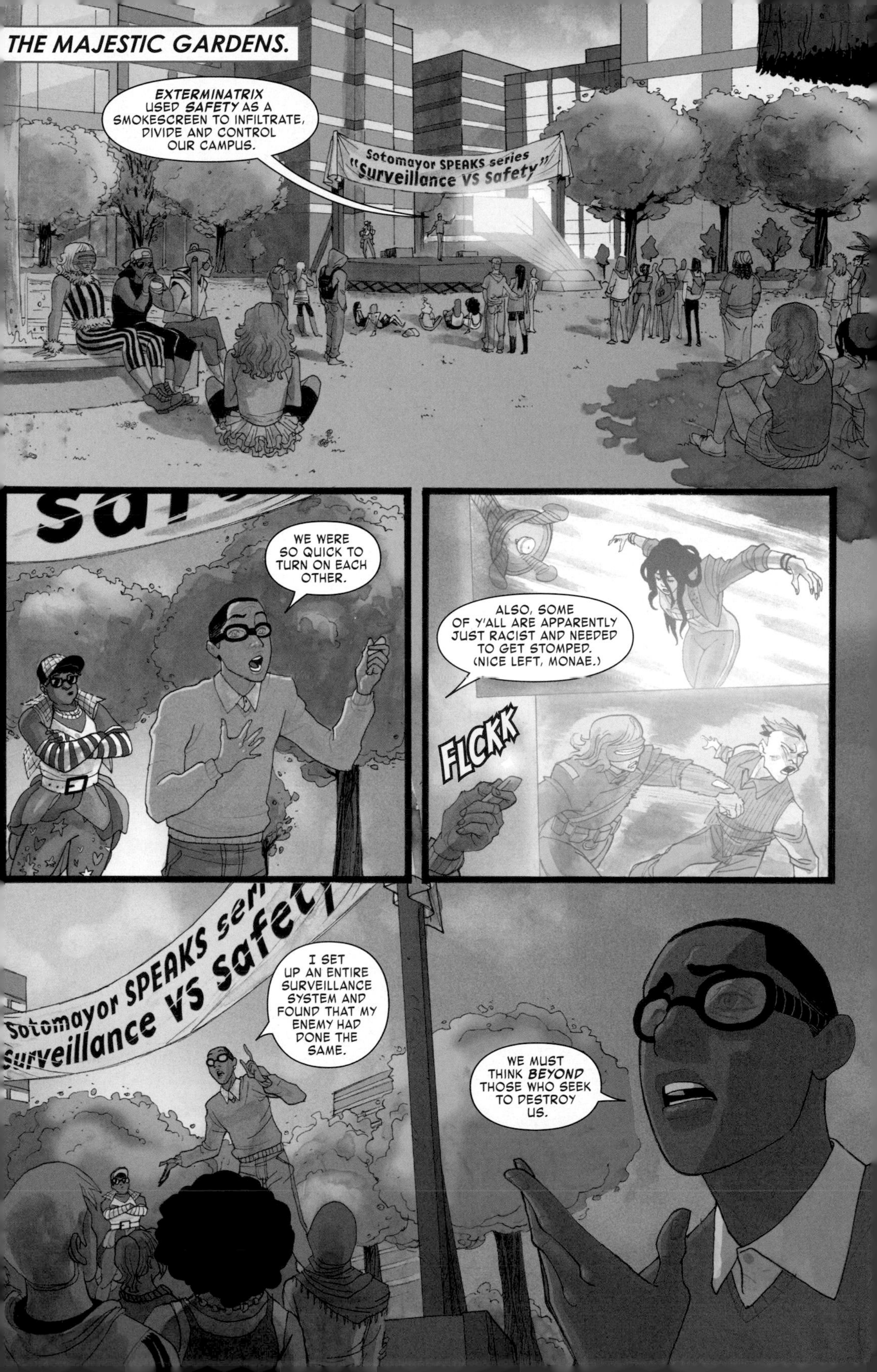

THE MAJESTIC GARDENS.
EXTERMINATRIX USED SAFETY AS A SMOKESCREEN TO INFILTRATE, DIVIDE AND CONTROL OUR CAMPUS.
Sotomayor SPEAKS series "Surveillance VS Safety"
WE WERE SO QUICK TO TURN ON EACH OTHER.
ALSO, SOME OF Y'ALL ARE APPARENTLY JUST RACIST AND NEEDED TO GET STOMPED. (NICE LEFT, MONAE.)
FLCKK
I SET UP AN ENTIRE SURVEILLANCE SYSTEM AND FOUND THAT MY ENEMY HAD DONE THE SAME.
WE MUST THINK BEYOND THOSE WHO SEEK TO DESTROY US.

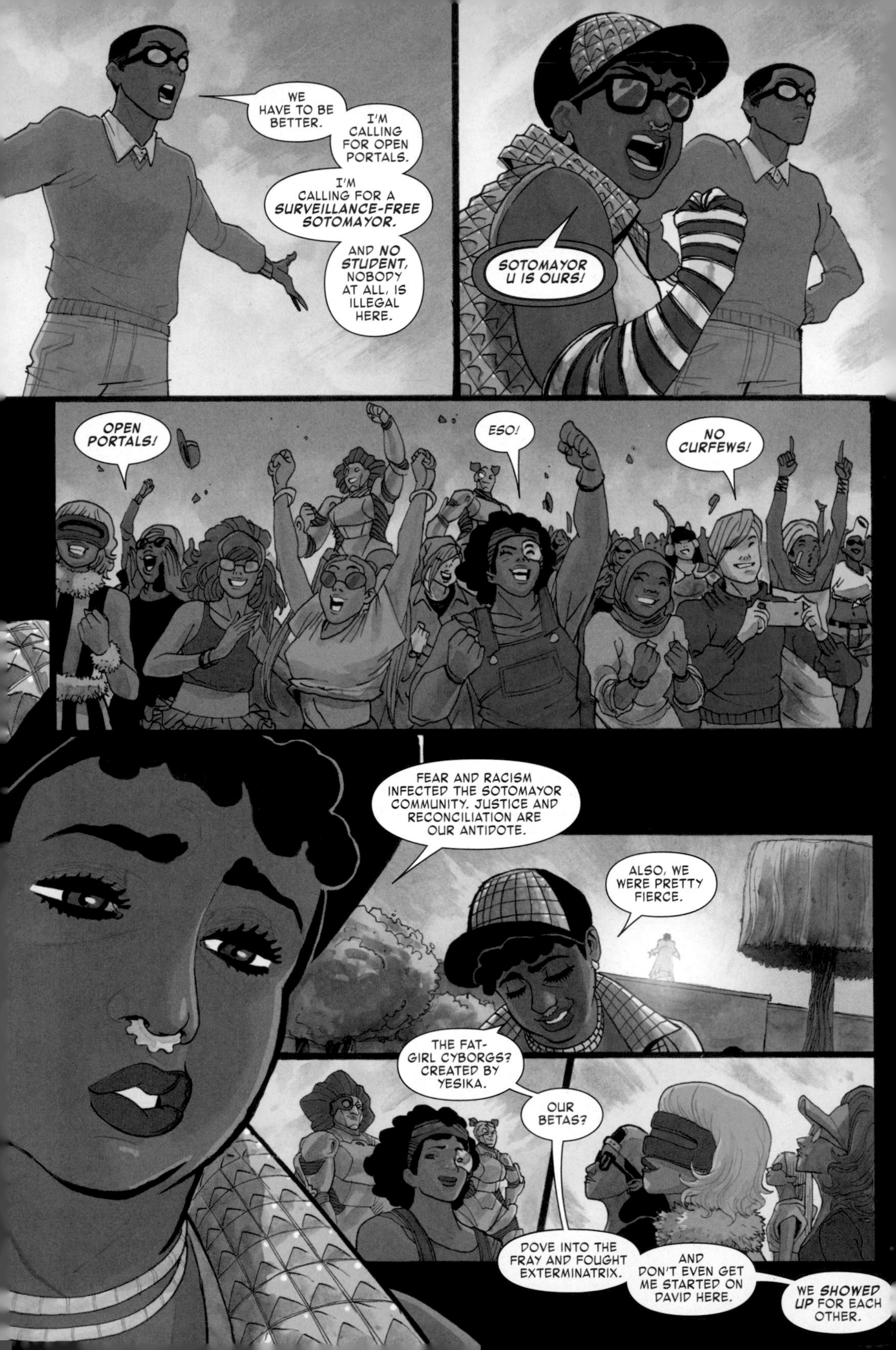

WE HAVE TO BE BETTER.
I'M CALLING FOR OPEN PORTALS.
I'M CALLING FOR A SURVEILLANCE-FREE SOTOMAYOR.
AND NO STUDENT, NOBODY AT ALL, IS ILLEGAL HERE.
SOTOMAYOR U IS OURS!
OPEN PORTALS!
ESO!
NO CURFEWS!
FEAR AND RACISM INFECTED THE SOTOMAYOR COMMUNITY. JUSTICE AND RECONCILIATION ARE OUR ANTIDOTE.
ALSO, WE WERE PRETTY FIERCE.
THE FAT-GIRL CYBORGS? CREATED BY YESIKA.
OUR BETAS?
DOVE INTO THE FRAY AND FOUGHT EXTERMINATRIX.
AND DON'T EVEN GET ME STARTED ON DAVID HERE.
WE SHOWED UP FOR EACH OTHER.

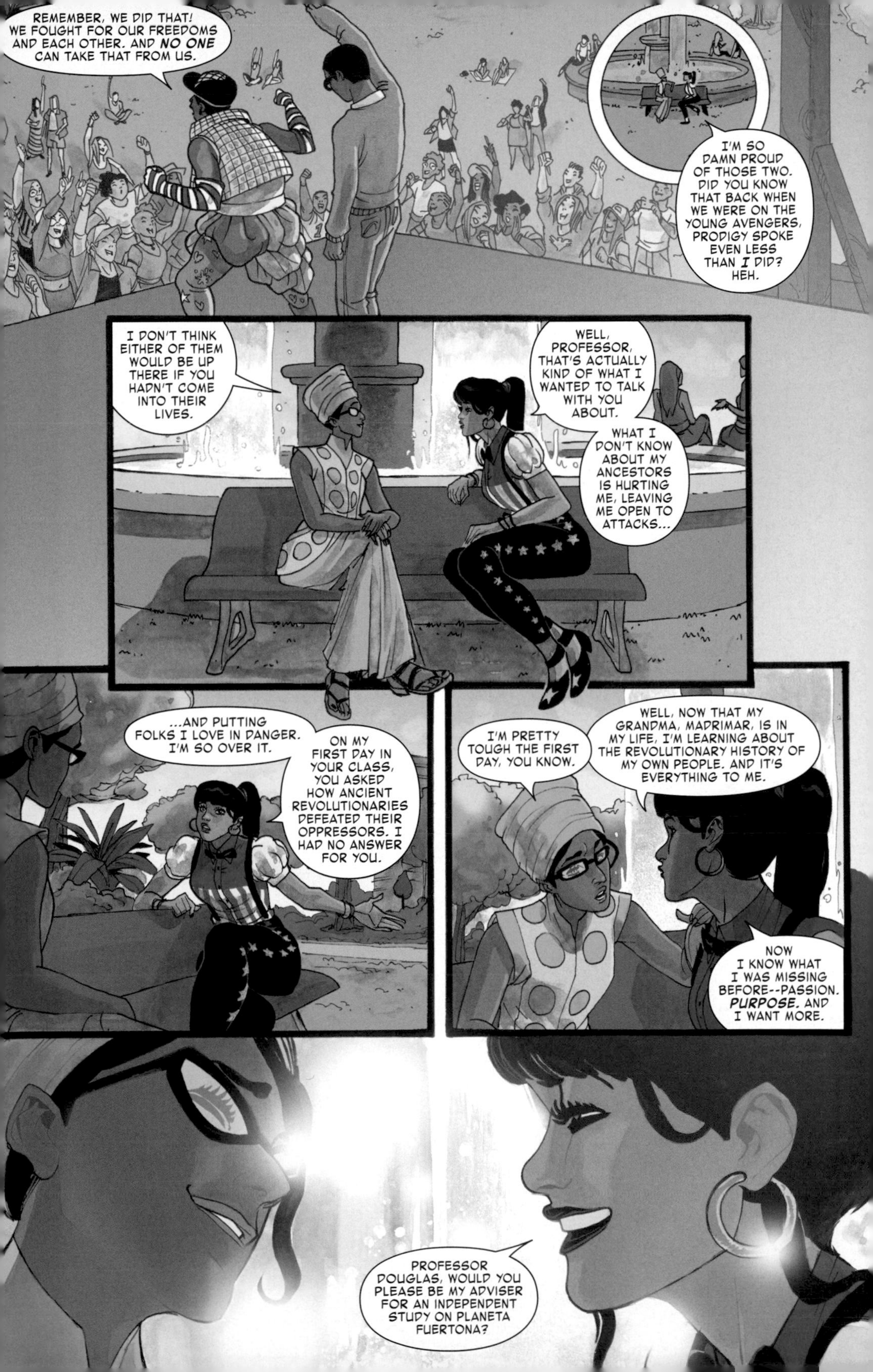
REMEMBER, WE DID THAT! WE FOUGHT FOR OUR FREEDOMS AND EACH OTHER. AND *NO ONE* CAN TAKE THAT FROM US.
I'M SO DAMN PROUD OF THOSE TWO. DID YOU KNOW THAT BACK WHEN WE WERE ON THE YOUNG AVENGERS, PRODIGY SPOKE EVEN LESS THAN *I* DID? HEH.
I DON'T THINK EITHER OF THEM WOULD BE UP THERE IF YOU HADN'T COME INTO THEIR LIVES.
WELL, PROFESSOR, THAT'S ACTUALLY KIND OF WHAT I WANTED TO TALK WITH YOU ABOUT.
WHAT I DON'T KNOW ABOUT MY ANCESTORS IS HURTING ME, LEAVING ME OPEN TO ATTACKS...
...AND PUTTING FOLKS I LOVE IN DANGER. I'M SO OVER IT.
ON MY FIRST DAY IN YOUR CLASS, YOU ASKED HOW ANCIENT REVOLUTIONARIES DEFEATED THEIR OPPRESSORS. I HAD NO ANSWER FOR YOU.
I'M PRETTY TOUGH THE FIRST DAY, YOU KNOW.
WELL, NOW THAT MY GRANDMA, MADRIMAR, IS IN MY LIFE, I'M LEARNING ABOUT THE REVOLUTIONARY HISTORY OF MY OWN PEOPLE. AND IT'S EVERYTHING TO ME.
NOW I KNOW WHAT I WAS MISSING BEFORE--PASSION. ***PURPOSE.*** AND I WANT MORE.
PROFESSOR DOUGLAS, WOULD YOU PLEASE BE MY ADVISER FOR AN INDEPENDENT STUDY ON PLANETA FUERTONA?

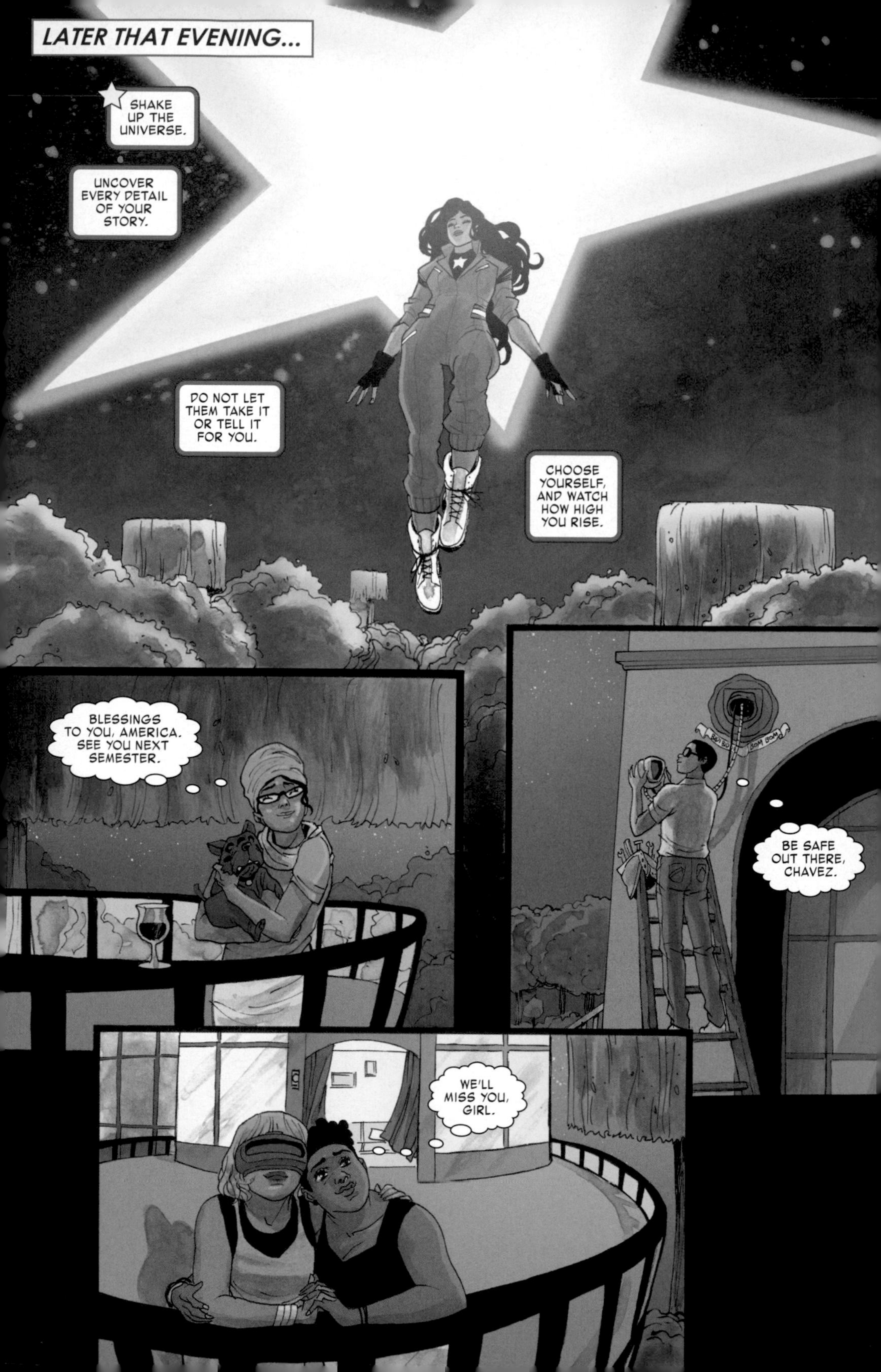
LATER THAT EVENING...
SHAKE UP THE UNIVERSE.
UNCOVER EVERY DETAIL OF YOUR STORY.
DO NOT LET THEM TAKE IT OR TELL IT FOR YOU.
CHOOSE YOURSELF, AND WATCH HOW HIGH YOU RISE.
BLESSINGS TO YOU, AMERICA. SEE YOU NEXT SEMESTER.
BE SAFE OUT THERE, CHAVEZ.
WE'LL MISS YOU, GIRL.

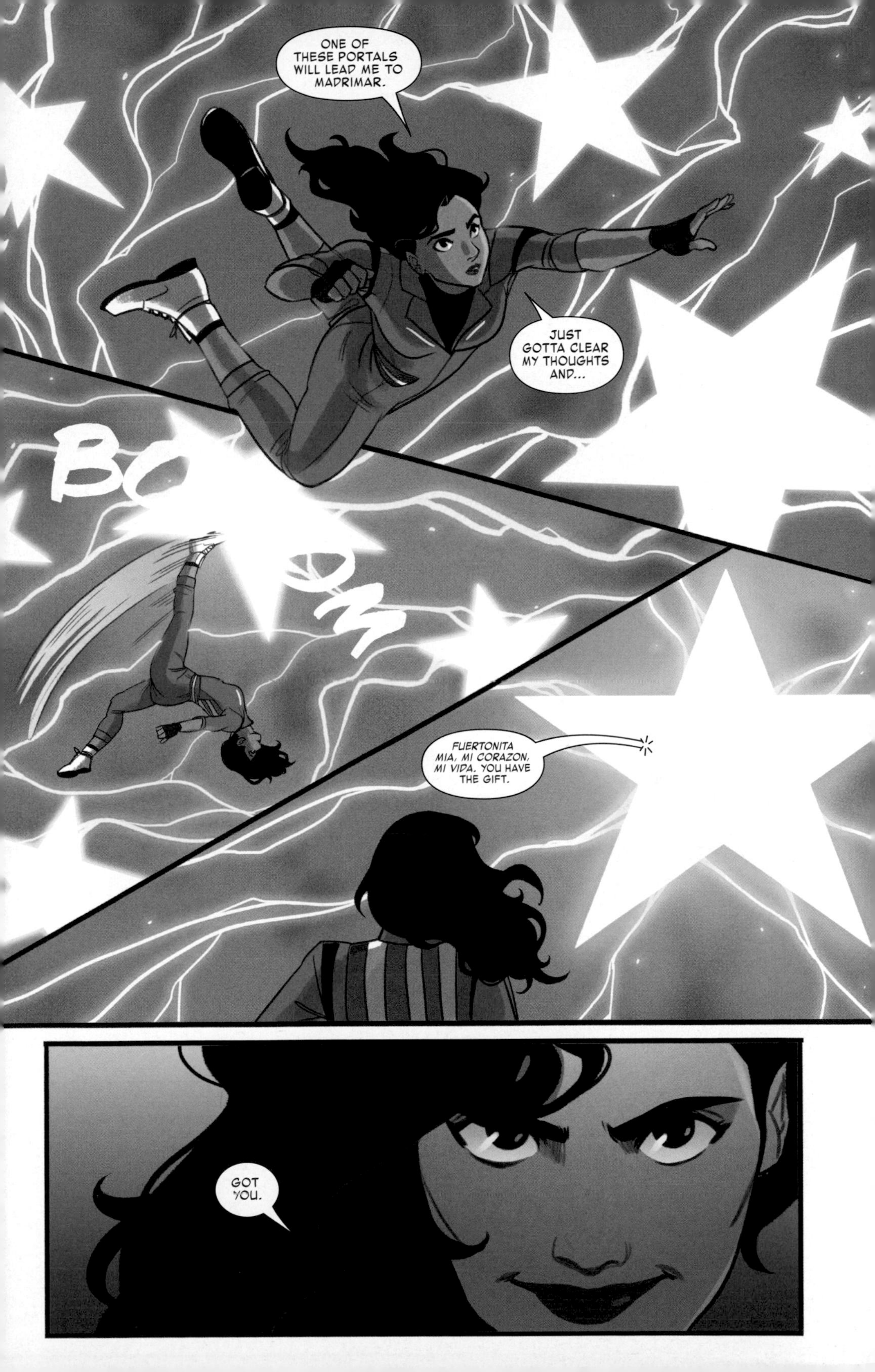
ONE OF THESE PORTALS WILL LEAD ME TO MADRIMAR.
JUST GOTTA CLEAR MY THOUGHTS AND...
FUERTONITA MIA, MI CORAZON, MI VIDA. YOU HAVE THE GIFT.
GOT YOU.

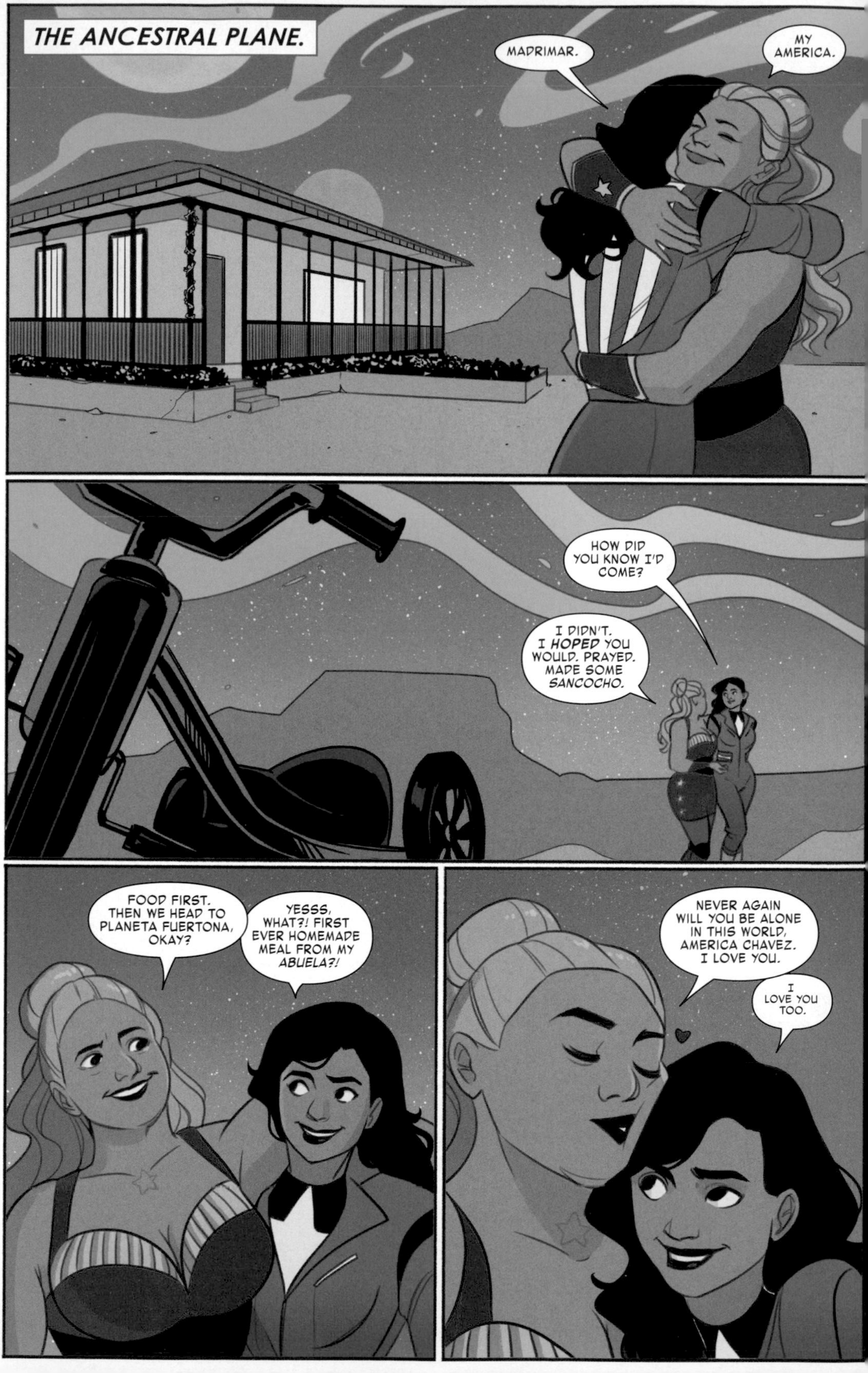

THE ANCESTRAL PLANE.
MADRIMAR.
MY AMERICA.
HOW DID YOU KNOW I'D COME?
I DIDN'T. I HOPED YOU WOULD. PRAYED. MADE SOME SANCOCHO.
FOOD FIRST. THEN WE HEAD TO PLANETA FUERTONA, OKAY?
YESSS, WHAT?! FIRST EVER HOMEMADE MEAL FROM MY ABUELA?!
NEVER AGAIN WILL YOU BE ALONE IN THIS WORLD, AMERICA CHAVEZ. I LOVE YOU.
I LOVE YOU TOO.

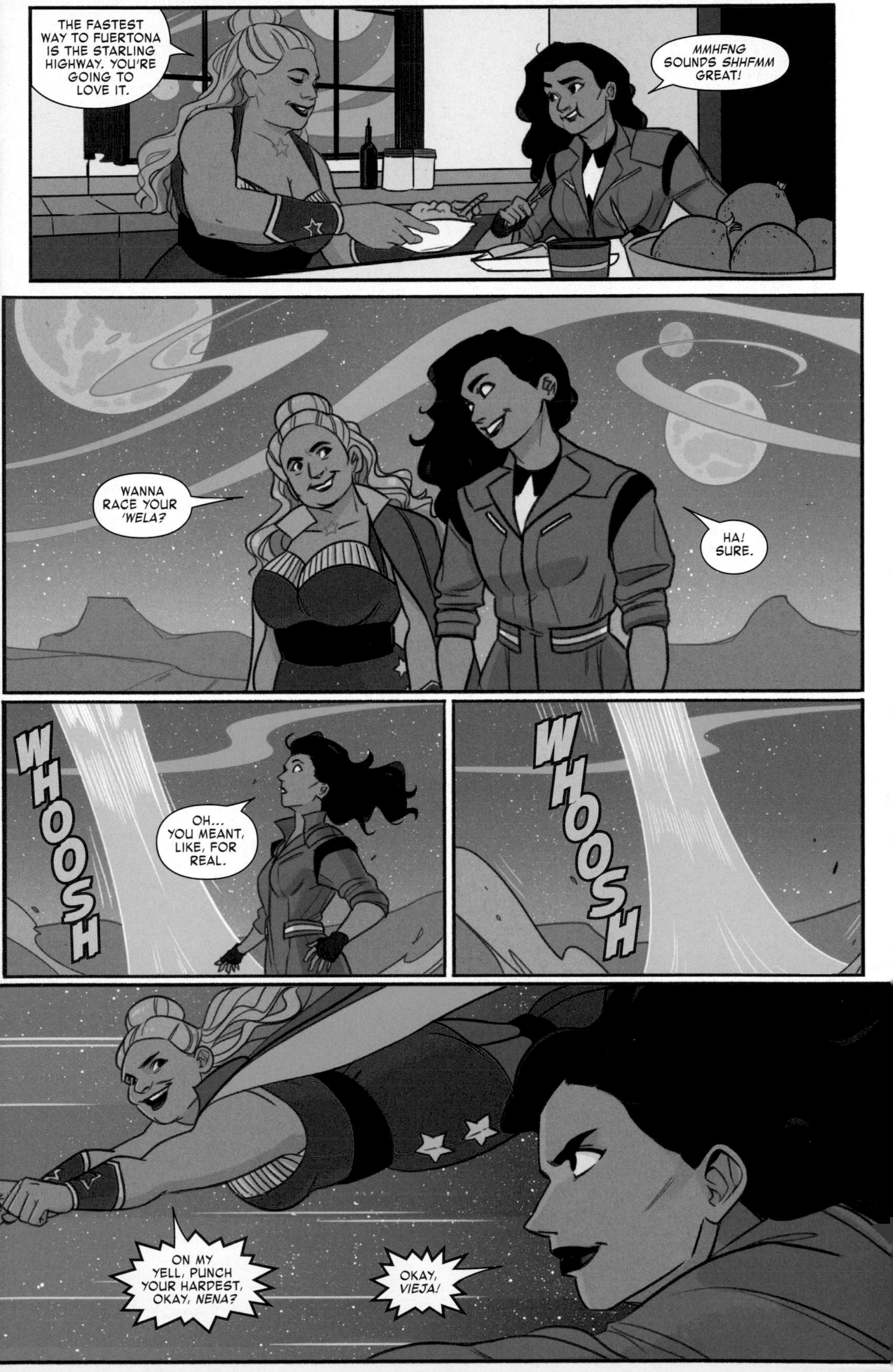

THE FASTEST WAY TO FUERTONA IS THE STARLING HIGHWAY. YOU'RE GOING TO LOVE IT.
MMHFNG SOUNDS *SHHFMM* GREAT!
WANNA RACE YOUR *'WELA?*
HA! SURE.
WHOOSH
OH... YOU MEANT, LIKE, FOR REAL.
WHOOSH
ON MY YELL, PUNCH YOUR HARDEST, OKAY, *NENA?*
OKAY, *VIEJA!*

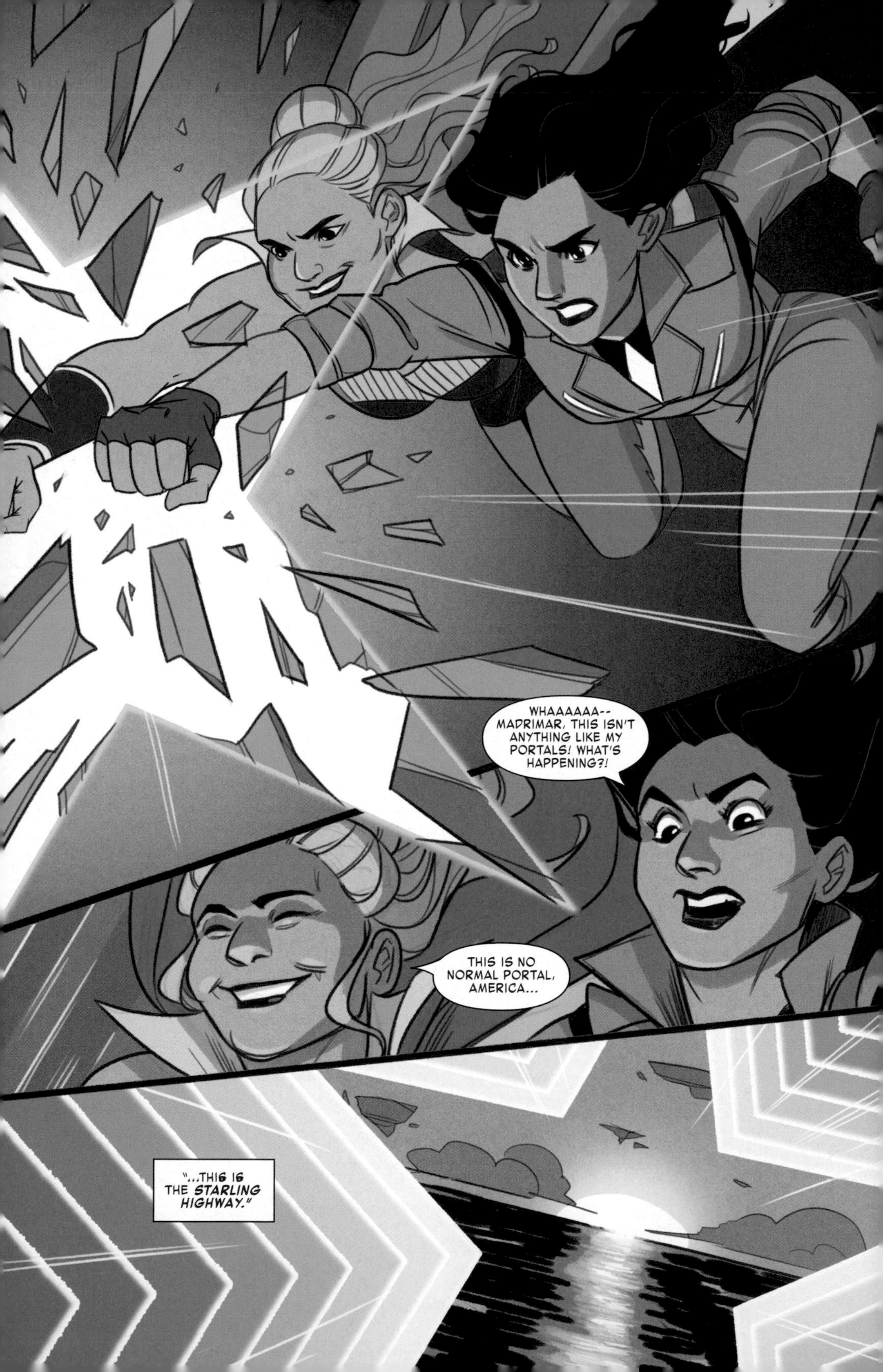
WHAAAAAA-- MADRIMAR, THIS ISN'T ANYTHING LIKE MY PORTALS! WHAT'S HAPPENING?!
THIS IS NO NORMAL PORTAL, AMERICA...
"...THIS IS THE STARLING HIGHWAY."

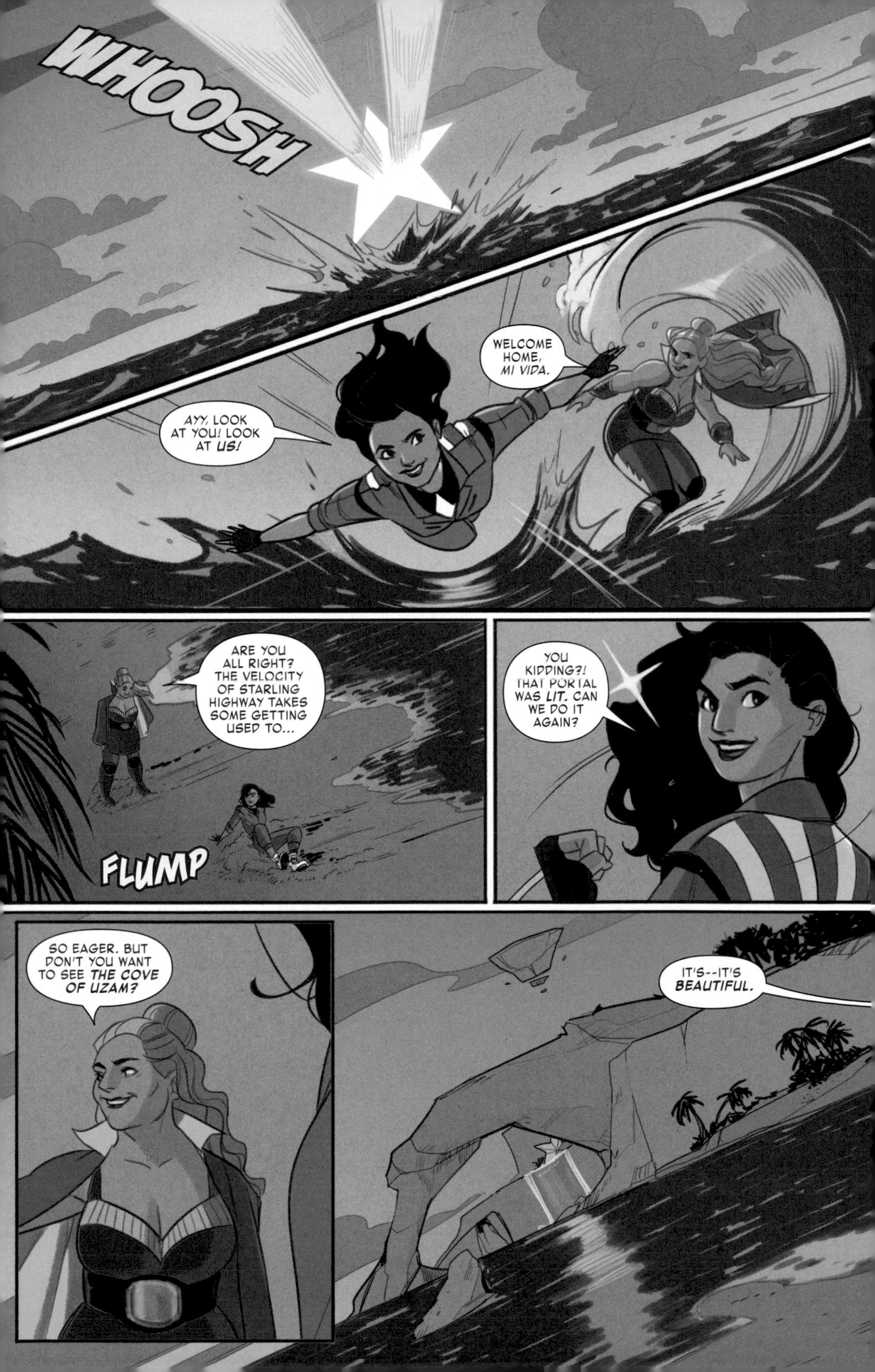
WHOOSH
WELCOME HOME, MI VIDA.
AYY, LOOK AT YOU! LOOK AT US!
ARE YOU ALL RIGHT? THE VELOCITY OF STARLING HIGHWAY TAKES SOME GETTING USED TO...
FLUMP
YOU KIDDING?! THAT PORTAL WAS LIT. CAN WE DO IT AGAIN?
SO EAGER. BUT DON'T YOU WANT TO SEE THE COVE OF UZAM?
IT'S--IT'S BEAUTIFUL.

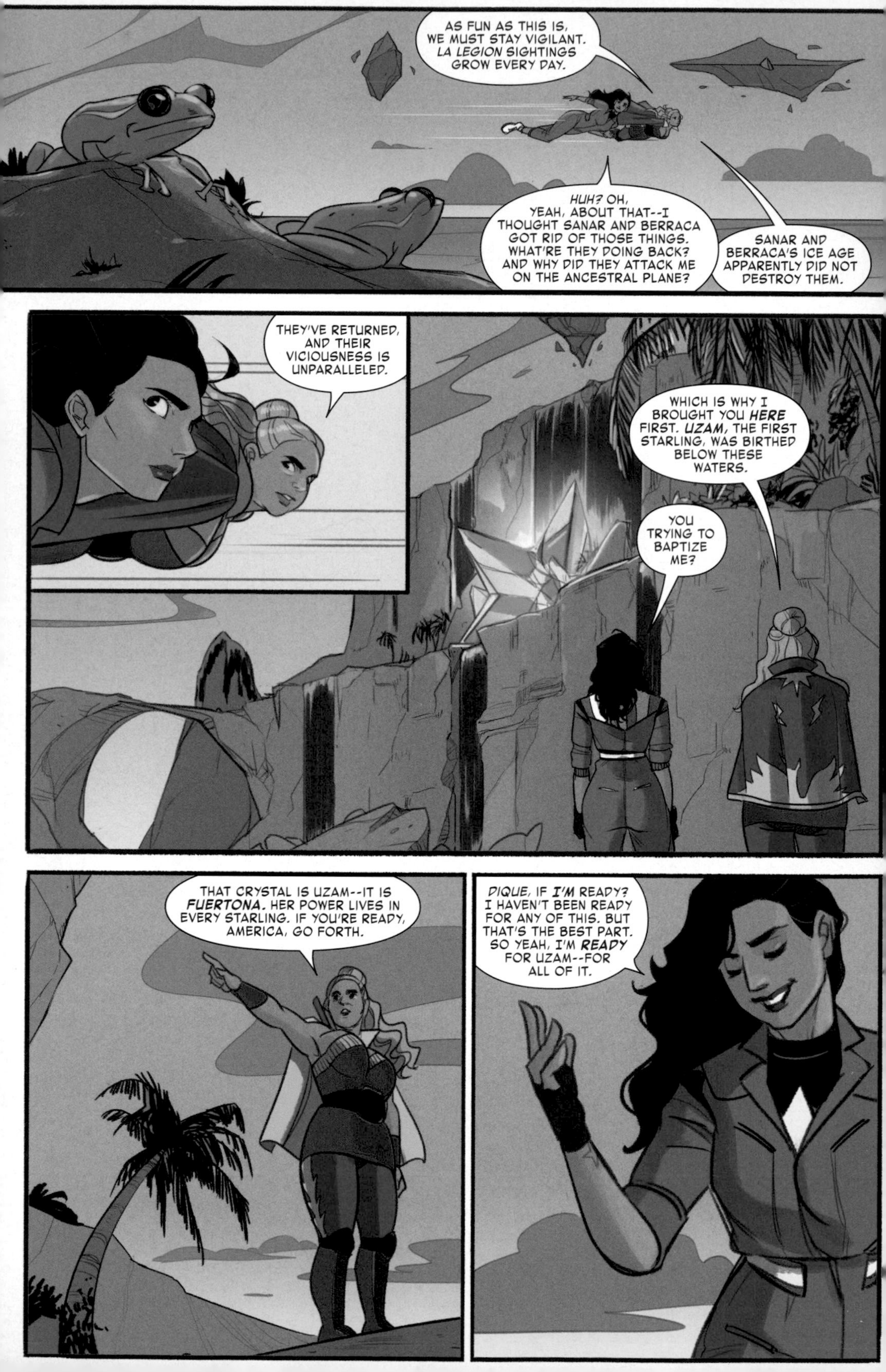
AS FUN AS THIS IS, WE MUST STAY VIGILANT. *LA LEGION* SIGHTINGS GROW EVERY DAY.
HUH? OH, YEAH, ABOUT THAT--I THOUGHT SANAR AND BERRACA GOT RID OF THOSE THINGS. WHAT'RE THEY DOING BACK? AND WHY DID THEY ATTACK ME ON THE ANCESTRAL PLANE?
SANAR AND BERRACA'S ICE AGE APPARENTLY DID NOT DESTROY THEM.
THEY'VE RETURNED, AND THEIR VICIOUSNESS IS UNPARALLELED.
WHICH IS WHY I BROUGHT YOU ***HERE*** FIRST. ***UZAM,*** THE FIRST STARLING, WAS BIRTHED BELOW THESE WATERS.
YOU TRYING TO BAPTIZE ME?
THAT CRYSTAL IS UZAM--IT IS ***FUERTONA.*** HER POWER LIVES IN EVERY STARLING. IF YOU'RE READY, AMERICA, GO FORTH.
DIQUE, IF ***I'M*** READY? I HAVEN'T BEEN READY FOR ANY OF THIS. BUT THAT'S THE BEST PART. SO YEAH, I'M ***READY*** FOR UZAM--FOR ALL OF IT.

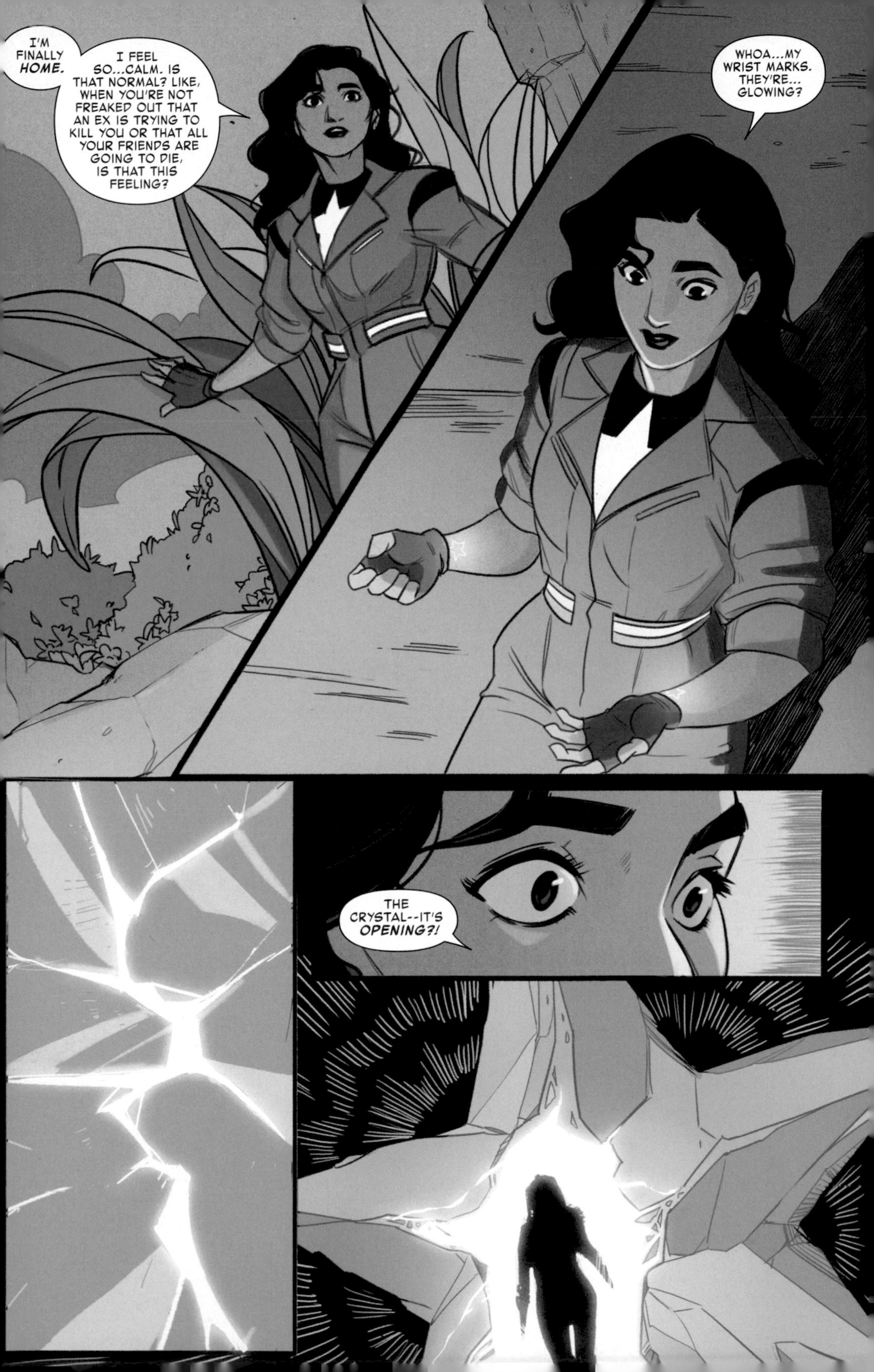
I'M FINALLY *HOME.*
I FEEL SO...CALM. IS THAT NORMAL? LIKE, WHEN YOU'RE NOT FREAKED OUT THAT AN EX IS TRYING TO KILL YOU OR THAT ALL YOUR FRIENDS ARE GOING TO DIE, IS THAT THIS FEELING?
WHOA...MY WRIST MARKS. THEY'RE... GLOWING?
THE CRYSTAL--IT'S *OPENING?!*

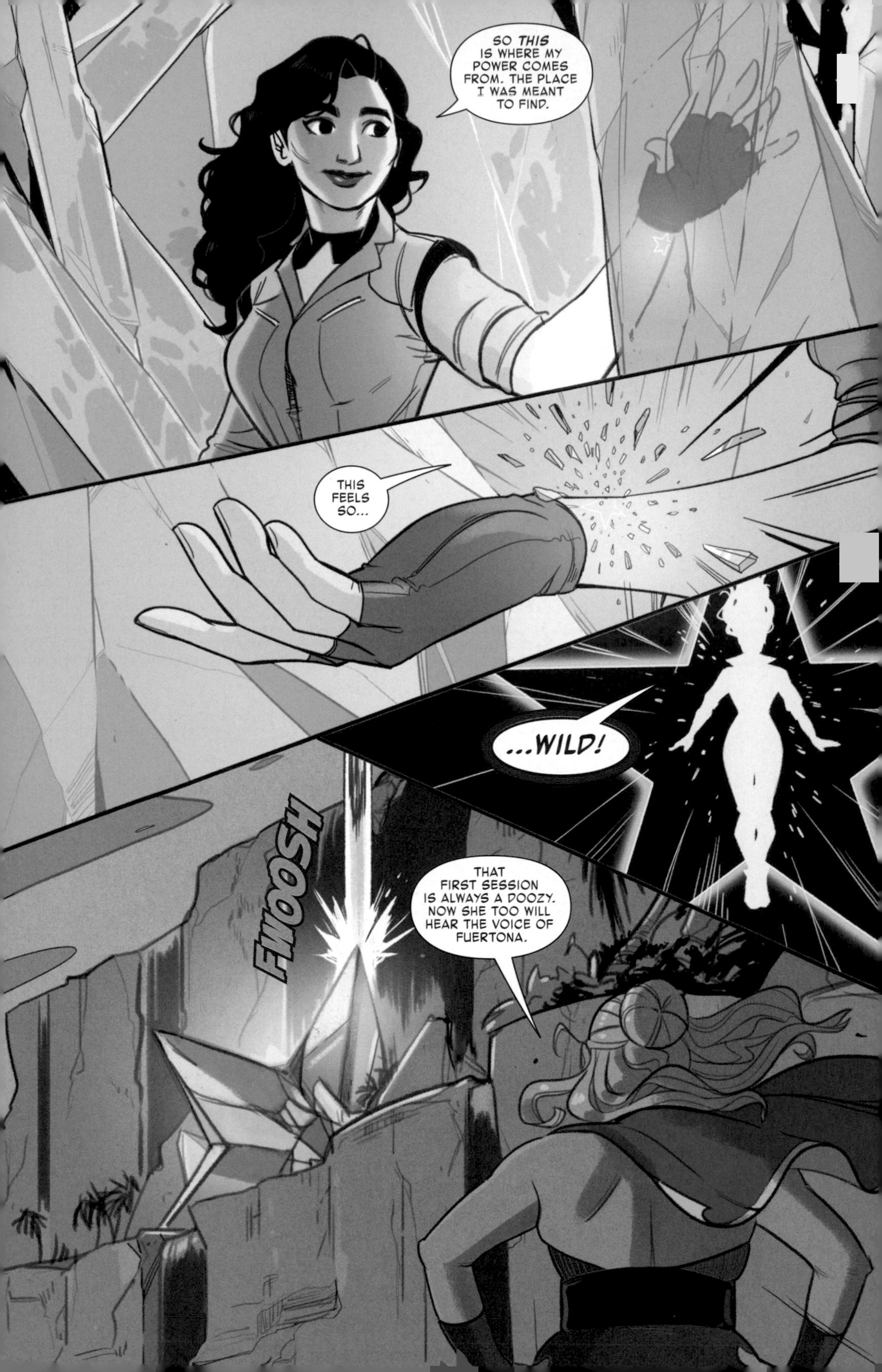
SO THIS IS WHERE MY POWER COMES FROM. THE PLACE I WAS MEANT TO FIND.
THIS FEELS SO...
...WILD!
FWOOSH
THAT FIRST SESSION IS ALWAYS A DOOZY. NOW SHE TOO WILL HEAR THE VOICE OF FUERTONA.

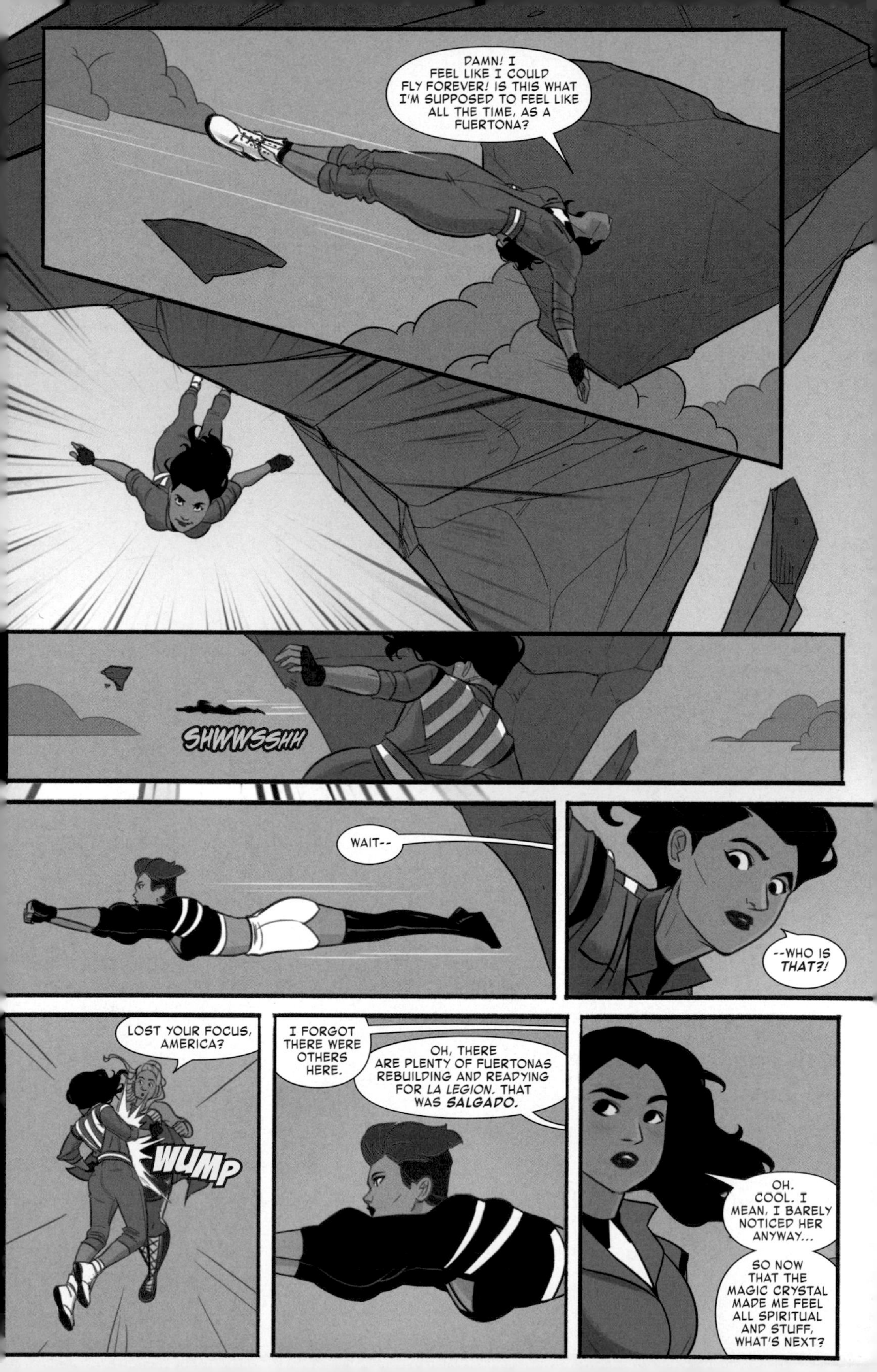
DAMN! I FEEL LIKE I COULD FLY FOREVER! IS THIS WHAT I'M SUPPOSED TO FEEL LIKE ALL THE TIME, AS A FUERTONA?
SHWWSSHH
WAIT--
--WHO IS *THAT?!*
LOST YOUR FOCUS, AMERICA?
WUMP
I FORGOT THERE WERE OTHERS HERE.
OH, THERE ARE PLENTY OF FUERTONAS REBUILDING AND READYING FOR *LA LEGION*. THAT WAS *SALGADO.*
OH. COOL. I MEAN, I BARELY NOTICED HER ANYWAY...
SO NOW THAT THE MAGIC CRYSTAL MADE ME FEEL ALL SPIRITUAL AND STUFF, WHAT'S NEXT?

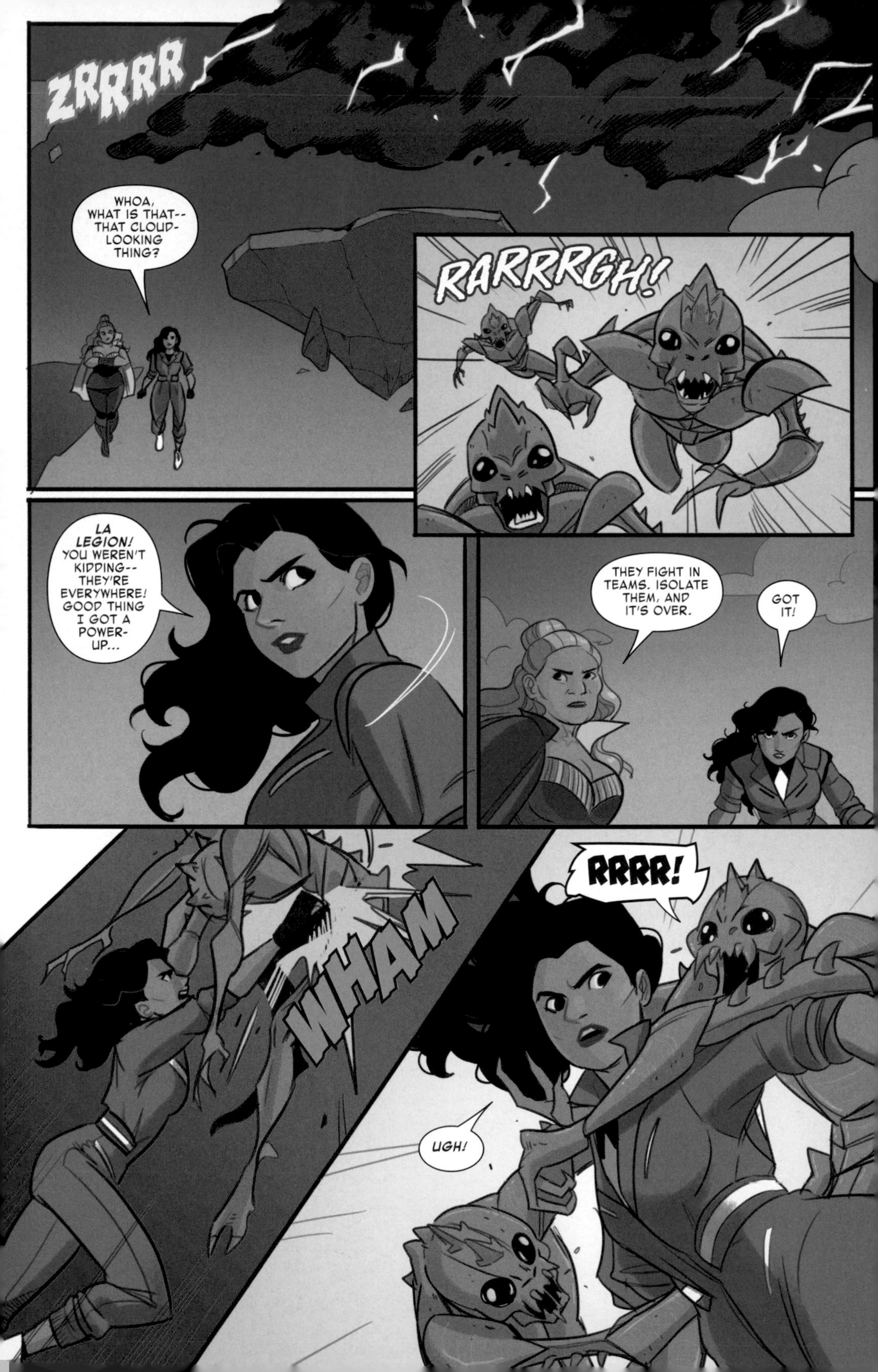
ZRRRR
WHOA, WHAT IS THAT-- THAT CLOUD-LOOKING THING?
RARRRGH!
LA LEGION! YOU WEREN'T KIDDING-- THEY'RE EVERYWHERE! GOOD THING I GOT A POWER-UP...
THEY FIGHT IN TEAMS. ISOLATE THEM, AND IT'S OVER.
GOT IT!
WHAM
RRRR!
UGH!

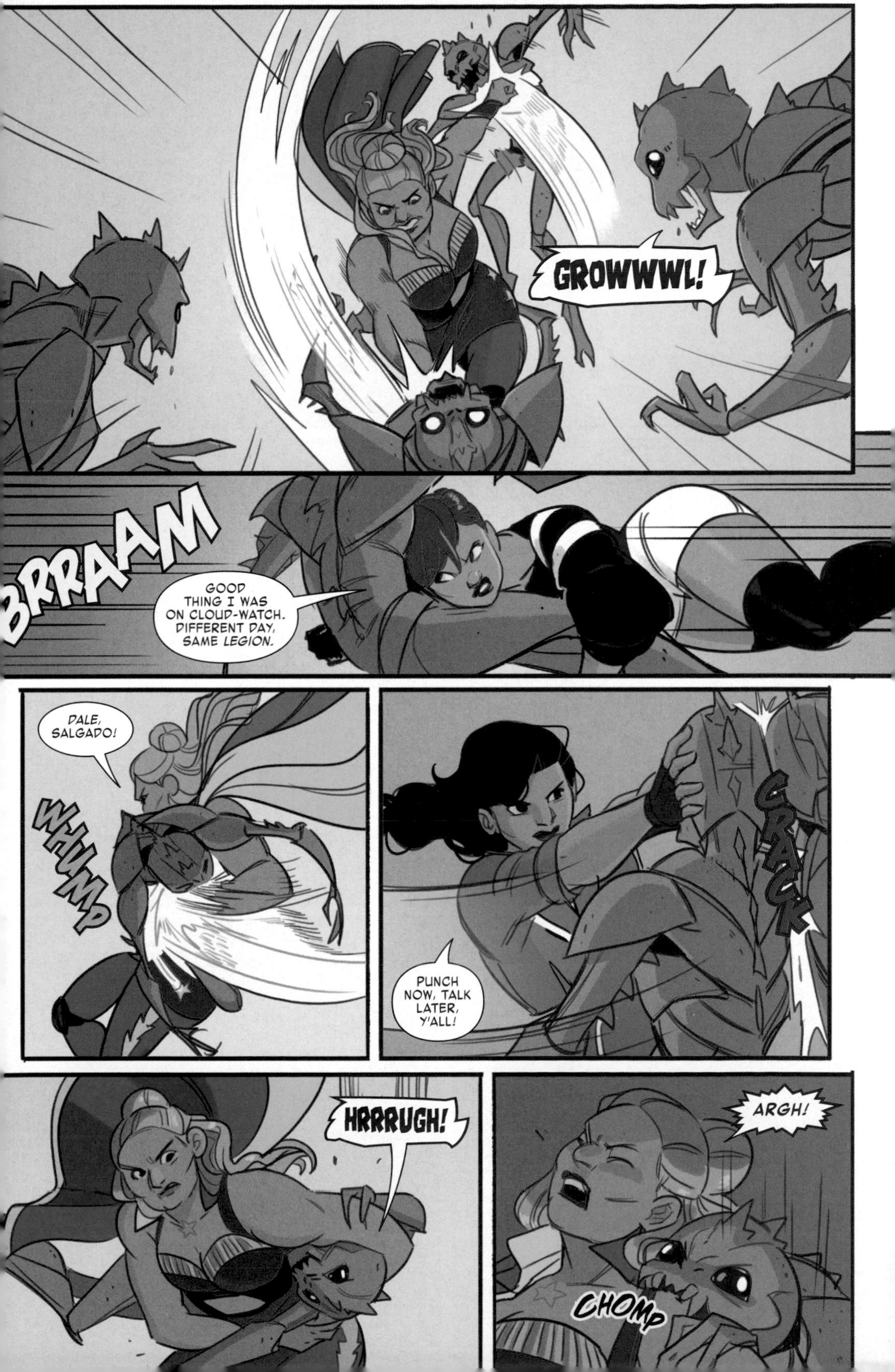
GROWWWL!
BRRAAM
GOOD THING I WAS ON CLOUD-WATCH. DIFFERENT DAY, SAME LEGION.
DALE, SALGADO!
WHUMP
CRACK
PUNCH NOW, TALK LATER, Y'ALL!
HRRRUGH!
ARGH!
CHOMP

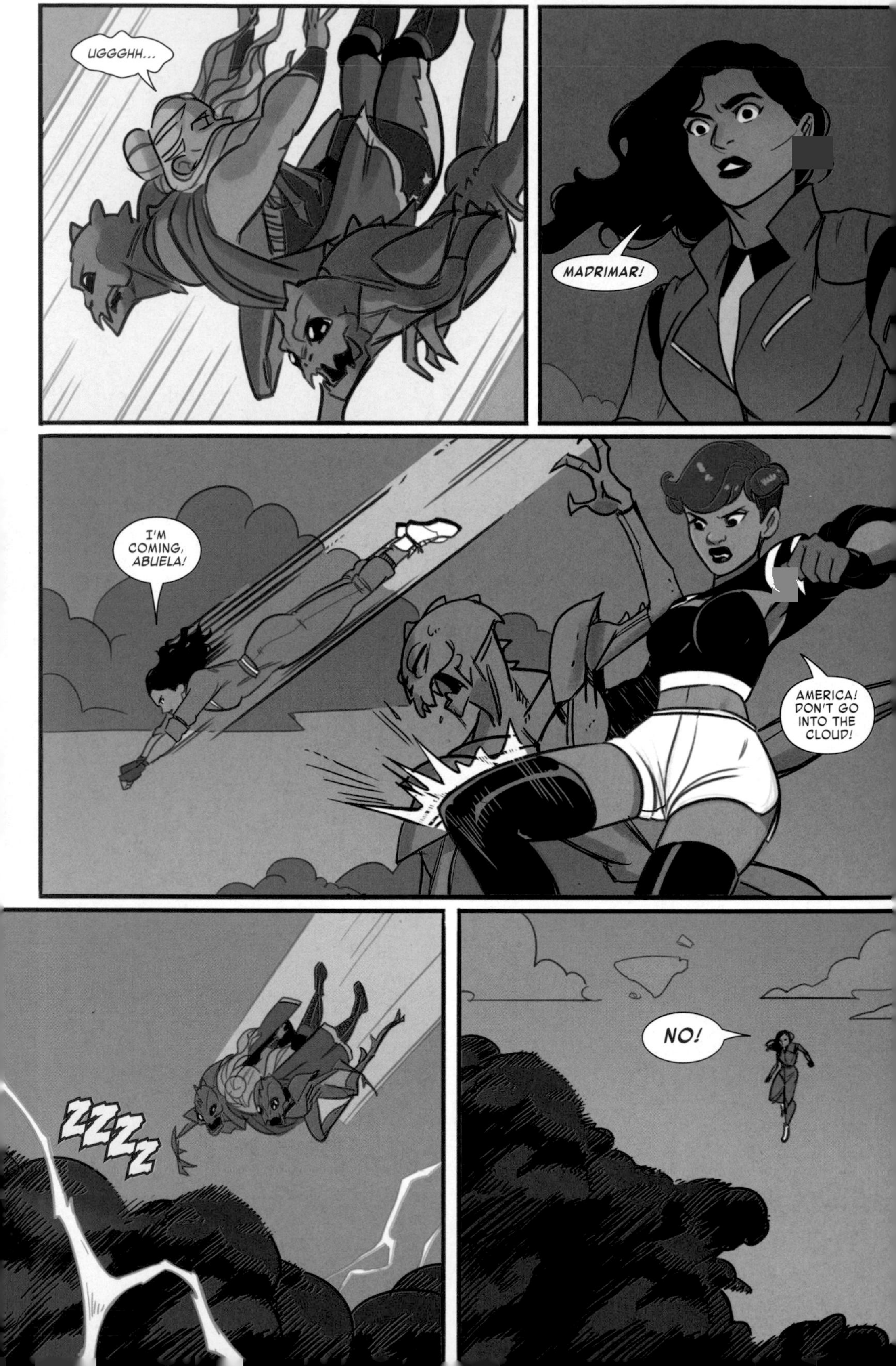
UGGGHH...
MADRIMAR!
I'M COMING, ABUELA!
AMERICA! DON'T GO INTO THE CLOUD!
ZZZZ
NO!

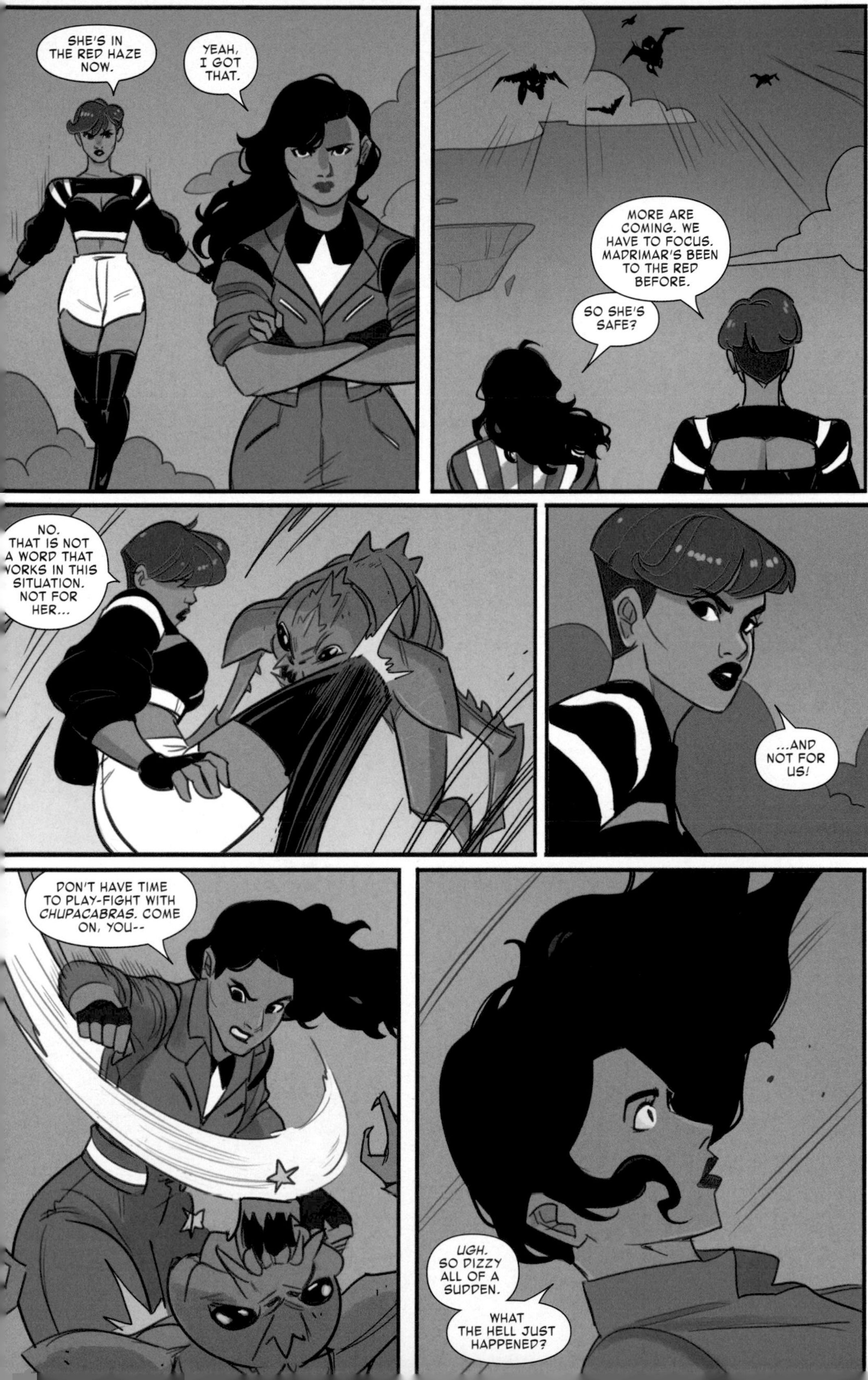
SHE'S IN THE RED HAZE NOW.
YEAH, I GOT THAT.
MORE ARE COMING. WE HAVE TO FOCUS. MADRIMAR'S BEEN TO THE RED BEFORE.
SO SHE'S SAFE?
NO. THAT IS NOT A WORD THAT WORKS IN THIS SITUATION. NOT FOR HER...
...AND NOT FOR US!
DON'T HAVE TIME TO PLAY-FIGHT WITH *CHUPACABRAS*. COME ON, YOU--
UGH. SO DIZZY ALL OF A SUDDEN.
WHAT THE HELL JUST HAPPENED?

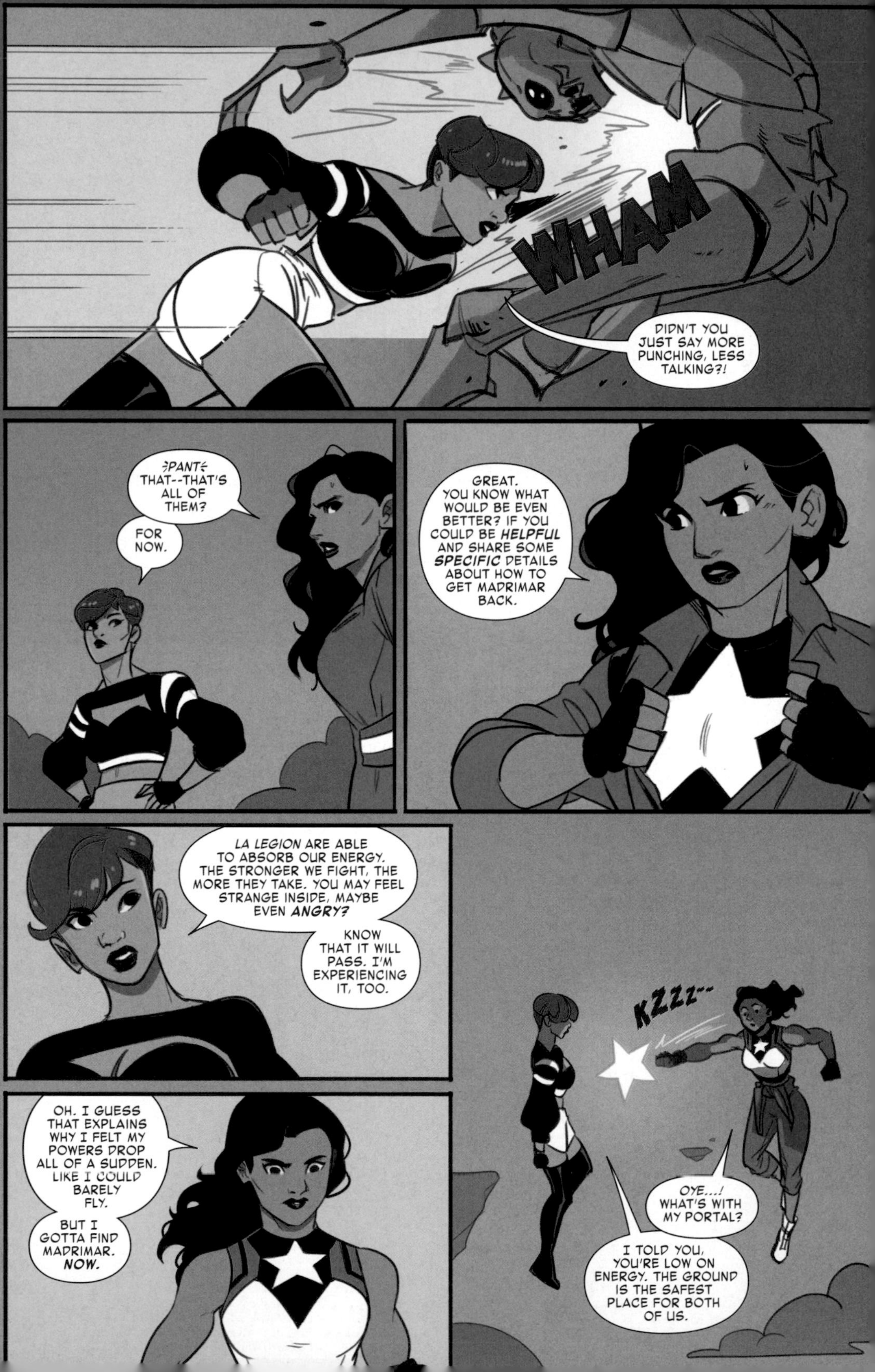
WHAM
DIDN'T YOU JUST SAY MORE PUNCHING, LESS TALKING?!
⋺PANT⋲ THAT--THAT'S ALL OF THEM?
FOR NOW.
GREAT. YOU KNOW WHAT WOULD BE EVEN BETTER? IF YOU COULD BE HELPFUL AND SHARE SOME SPECIFIC DETAILS ABOUT HOW TO GET MADRIMAR BACK.
LA LEGION ARE ABLE TO ABSORB OUR ENERGY. THE STRONGER WE FIGHT, THE MORE THEY TAKE. YOU MAY FEEL STRANGE INSIDE, MAYBE EVEN ANGRY?
KNOW THAT IT WILL PASS. I'M EXPERIENCING IT, TOO.
OH. I GUESS THAT EXPLAINS WHY I FELT MY POWERS DROP ALL OF A SUDDEN. LIKE I COULD BARELY FLY.
BUT I GOTTA FIND MADRIMAR. NOW.
KZZZ--
OYE...! WHAT'S WITH MY PORTAL?
I TOLD YOU, YOU'RE LOW ON ENERGY. THE GROUND IS THE SAFEST PLACE FOR BOTH OF US.

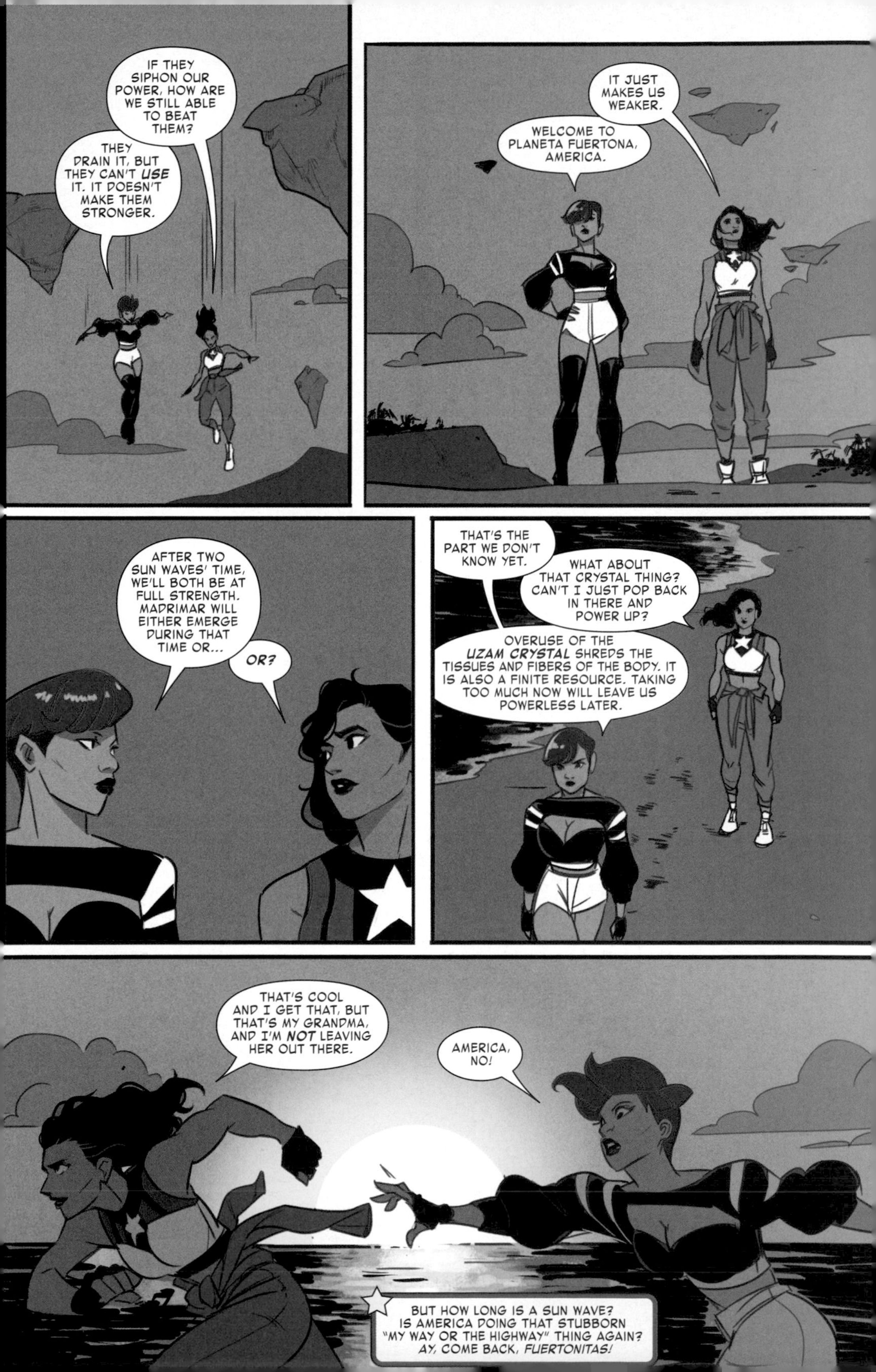
IF THEY SIPHON OUR POWER, HOW ARE WE STILL ABLE TO BEAT THEM?
THEY DRAIN IT, BUT THEY CAN'T USE IT. IT DOESN'T MAKE THEM STRONGER.
IT JUST MAKES US WEAKER.
WELCOME TO PLANETA FUERTONA, AMERICA.
AFTER TWO SUN WAVES' TIME, WE'LL BOTH BE AT FULL STRENGTH. MADRIMAR WILL EITHER EMERGE DURING THAT TIME OR...
OR?
THAT'S THE PART WE DON'T KNOW YET.
WHAT ABOUT THAT CRYSTAL THING? CAN'T I JUST POP BACK IN THERE AND POWER UP?
OVERUSE OF THE UZAM CRYSTAL SHREDS THE TISSUES AND FIBERS OF THE BODY. IT IS ALSO A FINITE RESOURCE. TAKING TOO MUCH NOW WILL LEAVE US POWERLESS LATER.
THAT'S COOL AND I GET THAT, BUT THAT'S MY GRANDMA, AND I'M NOT LEAVING HER OUT THERE.
AMERICA, NO!
BUT HOW LONG IS A SUN WAVE? IS AMERICA DOING THAT STUBBORN "MY WAY OR THE HIGHWAY" THING AGAIN? AY, COME BACK, FUERTONITAS!

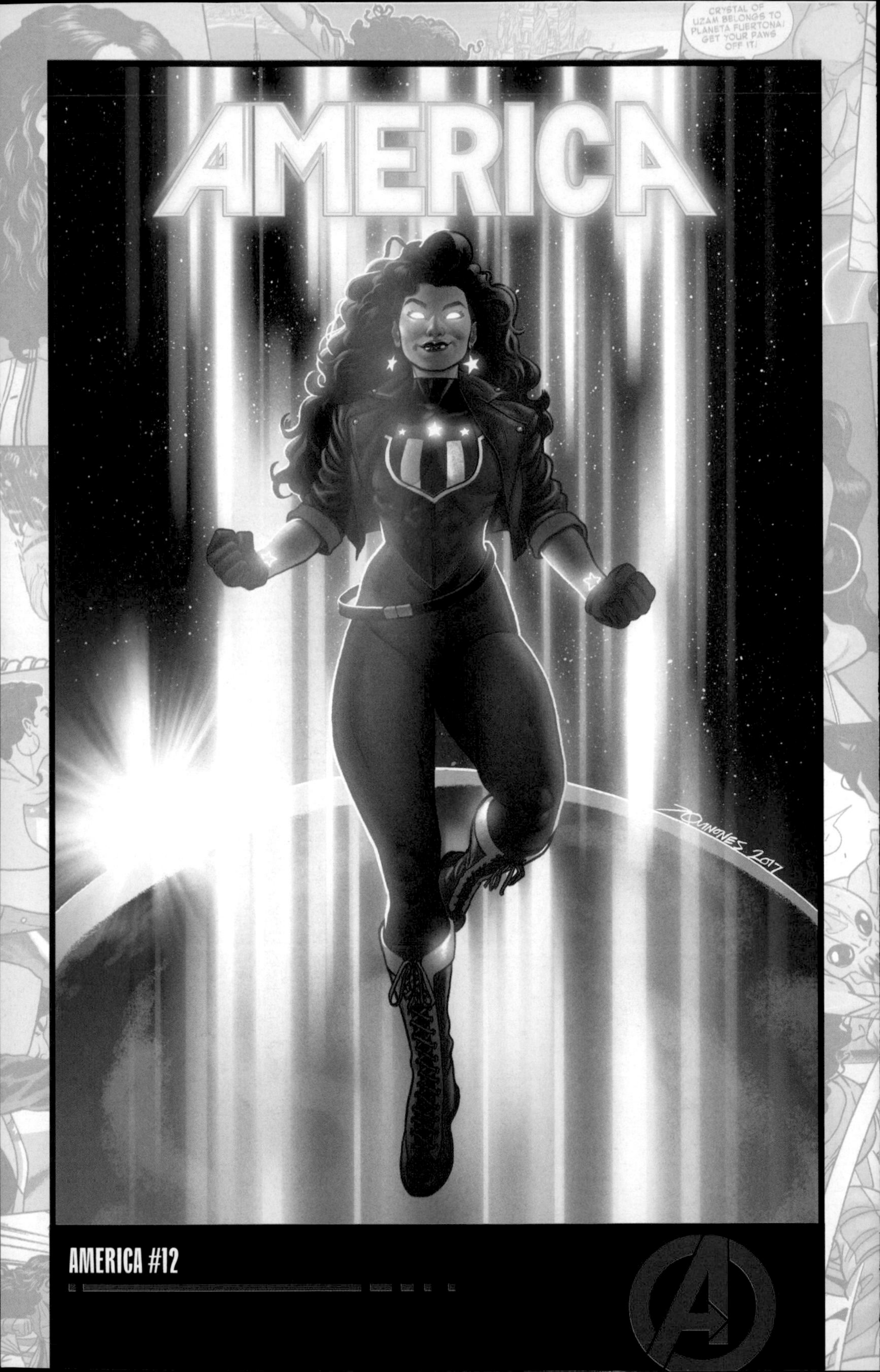
CRYSTAL OF UZAM BELONGS TO PLANETA FUERTONA! GET YOUR PAWS OFF IT!
AMERICA

AMERICA #12

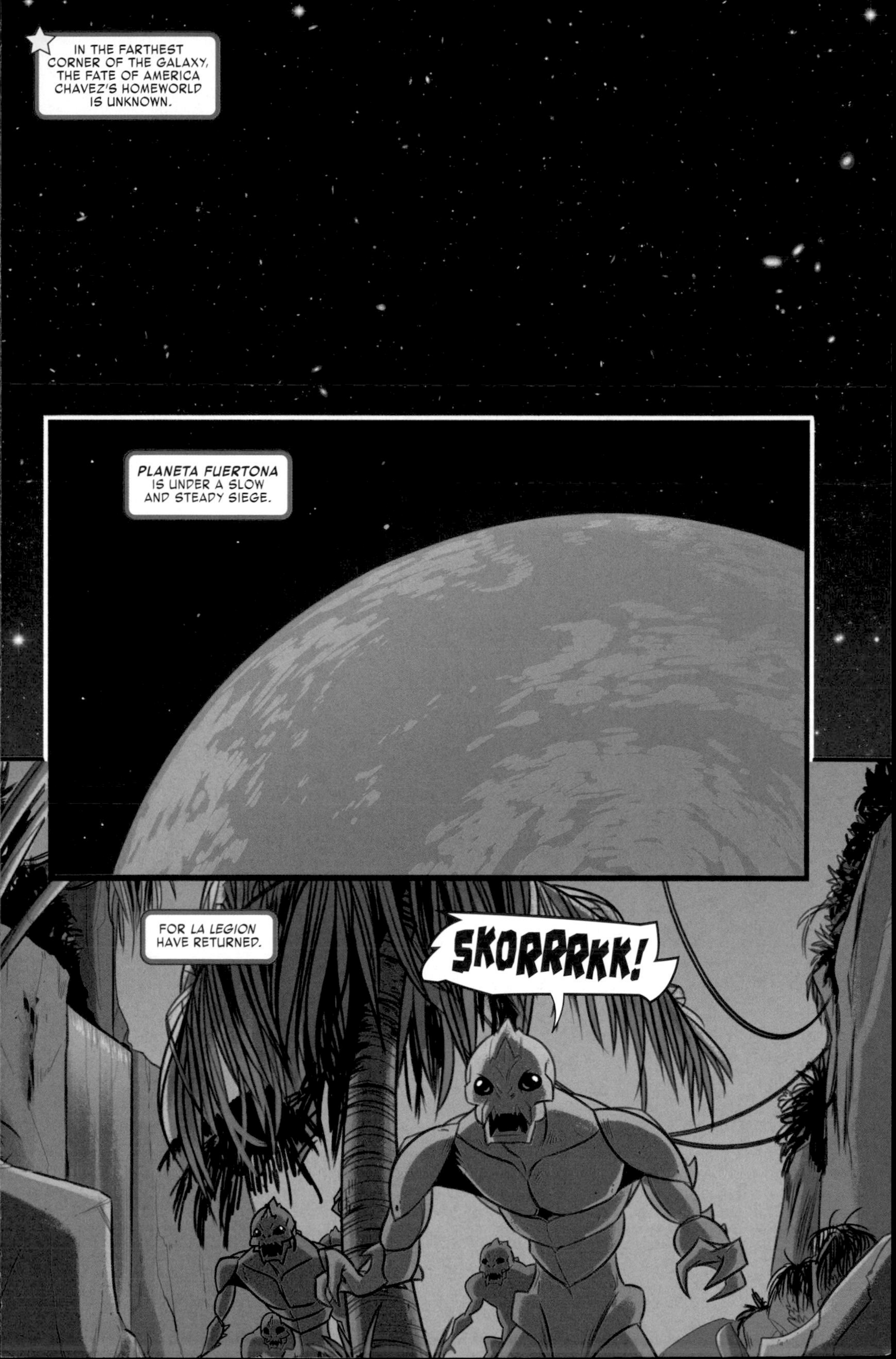
IN THE FARTHEST CORNER OF THE GALAXY, THE FATE OF AMERICA CHAVEZ'S HOMEWORLD IS UNKNOWN.
PLANETA FUERTONA IS UNDER A SLOW AND STEADY SIEGE.
FOR LA LEGION HAVE RETURNED.
SKORRRRKK!

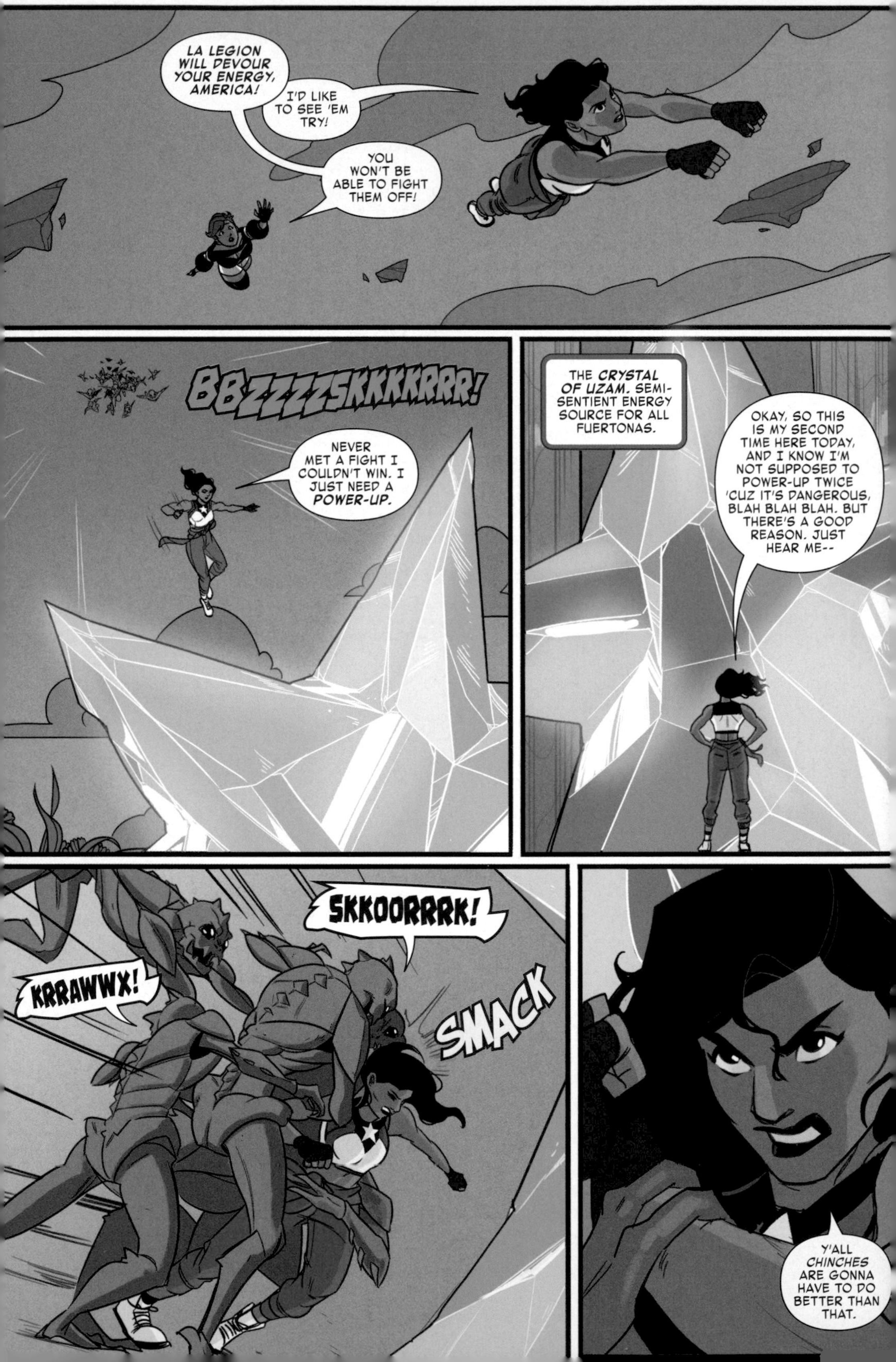
LA LEGION WILL DEVOUR YOUR ENERGY, AMERICA!
I'D LIKE TO SEE 'EM TRY!
YOU WON'T BE ABLE TO FIGHT THEM OFF!
BBZZZZSKKKKRRR!
NEVER MET A FIGHT I COULDN'T WIN. I JUST NEED A POWER-UP.
THE CRYSTAL OF UZAM. SEMI-SENTIENT ENERGY SOURCE FOR ALL FUERTONAS.
OKAY, SO THIS IS MY SECOND TIME HERE TODAY, AND I KNOW I'M NOT SUPPOSED TO POWER-UP TWICE 'CUZ IT'S DANGEROUS, BLAH BLAH BLAH. BUT THERE'S A GOOD REASON. JUST HEAR ME--
SKKOORRRK!
KRRAWWX!
SMACK
Y'ALL CHINCHES ARE GONNA HAVE TO DO BETTER THAN THAT.

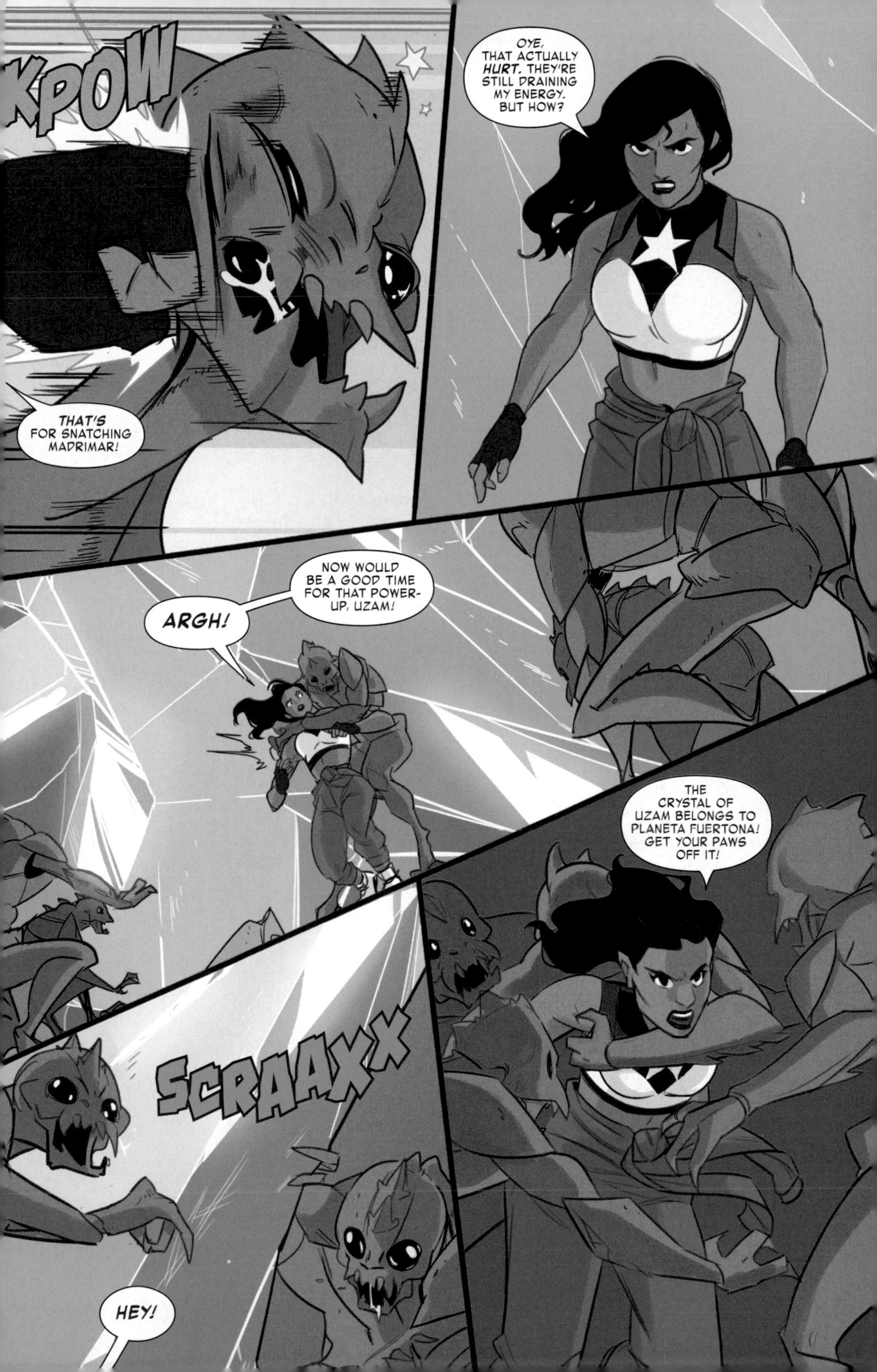
KPOW
THAT'S FOR SNATCHING MADRIMAR!
OYE, THAT ACTUALLY HURT. THEY'RE STILL DRAINING MY ENERGY. BUT HOW?
ARGH!
NOW WOULD BE A GOOD TIME FOR THAT POWER-UP, UZAM!
SCRAAXX
HEY!
THE CRYSTAL OF UZAM BELONGS TO PLANETA FUERTONA! GET YOUR PAWS OFF IT!

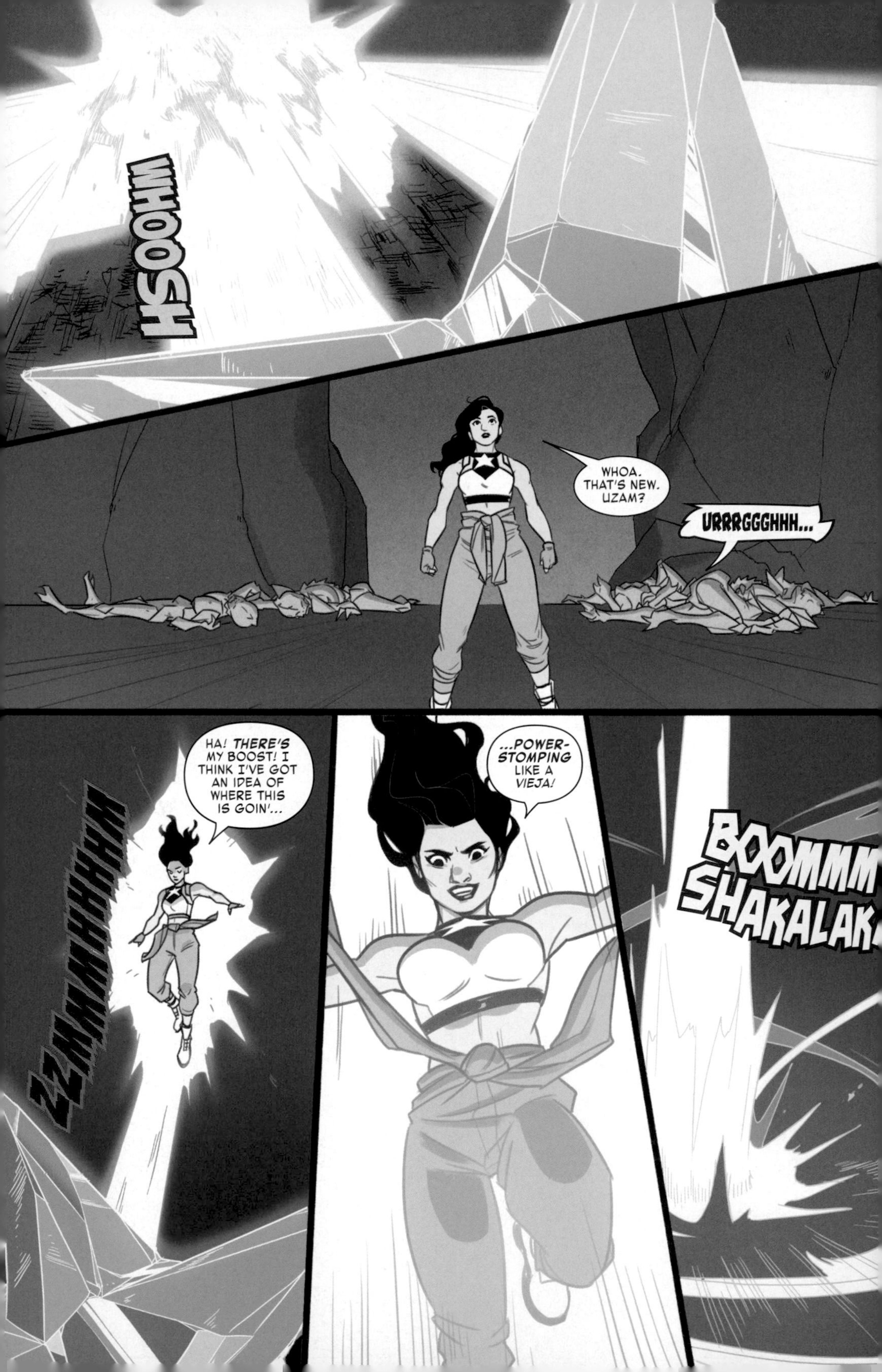
WHOOOSH
WHOA. THAT'S NEW. UZAM?
URRRGGGHHH...
HA! THERE'S MY BOOST! I THINK I'VE GOT AN IDEA OF WHERE THIS IS GOIN'...
...POWER-STOMPING LIKE A VIEJA!
BOOMMM SHAKALAK

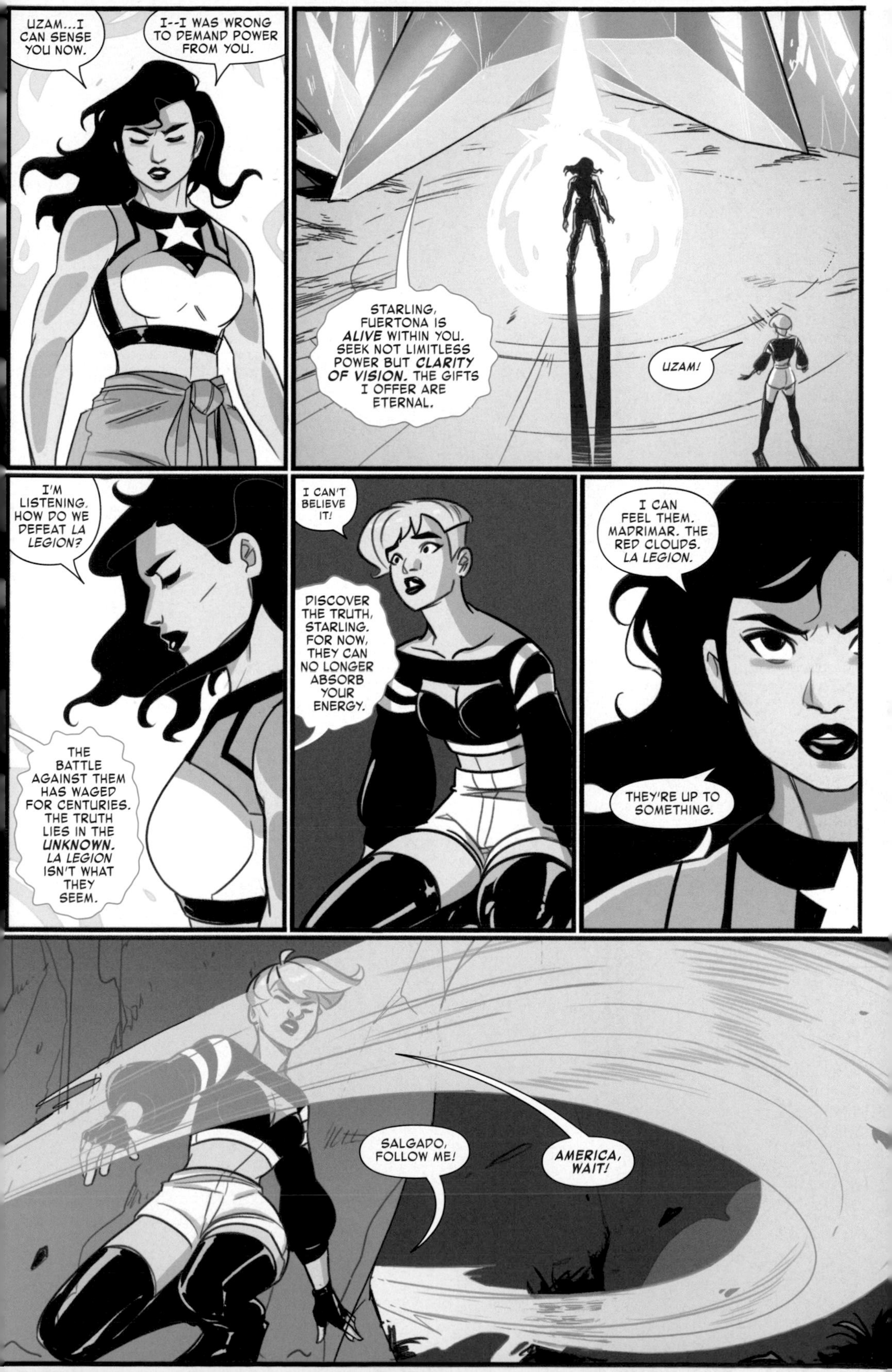
UZAM...I CAN SENSE YOU NOW.
I--I WAS WRONG TO DEMAND POWER FROM YOU.
STARLING, FUERTONA IS *ALIVE* WITHIN YOU. SEEK NOT LIMITLESS POWER BUT *CLARITY OF VISION.* THE GIFTS I OFFER ARE ETERNAL.
UZAM!
I'M LISTENING. HOW DO WE DEFEAT *LA LEGION?*
THE BATTLE AGAINST THEM HAS WAGED FOR CENTURIES. THE TRUTH LIES IN THE ***UNKNOWN.*** *LA LEGION* ISN'T WHAT THEY SEEM.
I CAN'T BELIEVE IT!
DISCOVER THE TRUTH, STARLING. FOR NOW, THEY CAN NO LONGER ABSORB YOUR ENERGY.
I CAN FEEL THEM. MADRIMAR. THE RED CLOUDS. *LA LEGION.*
THEY'RE UP TO SOMETHING.
SALGADO, FOLLOW ME!
AMERICA, WAIT!

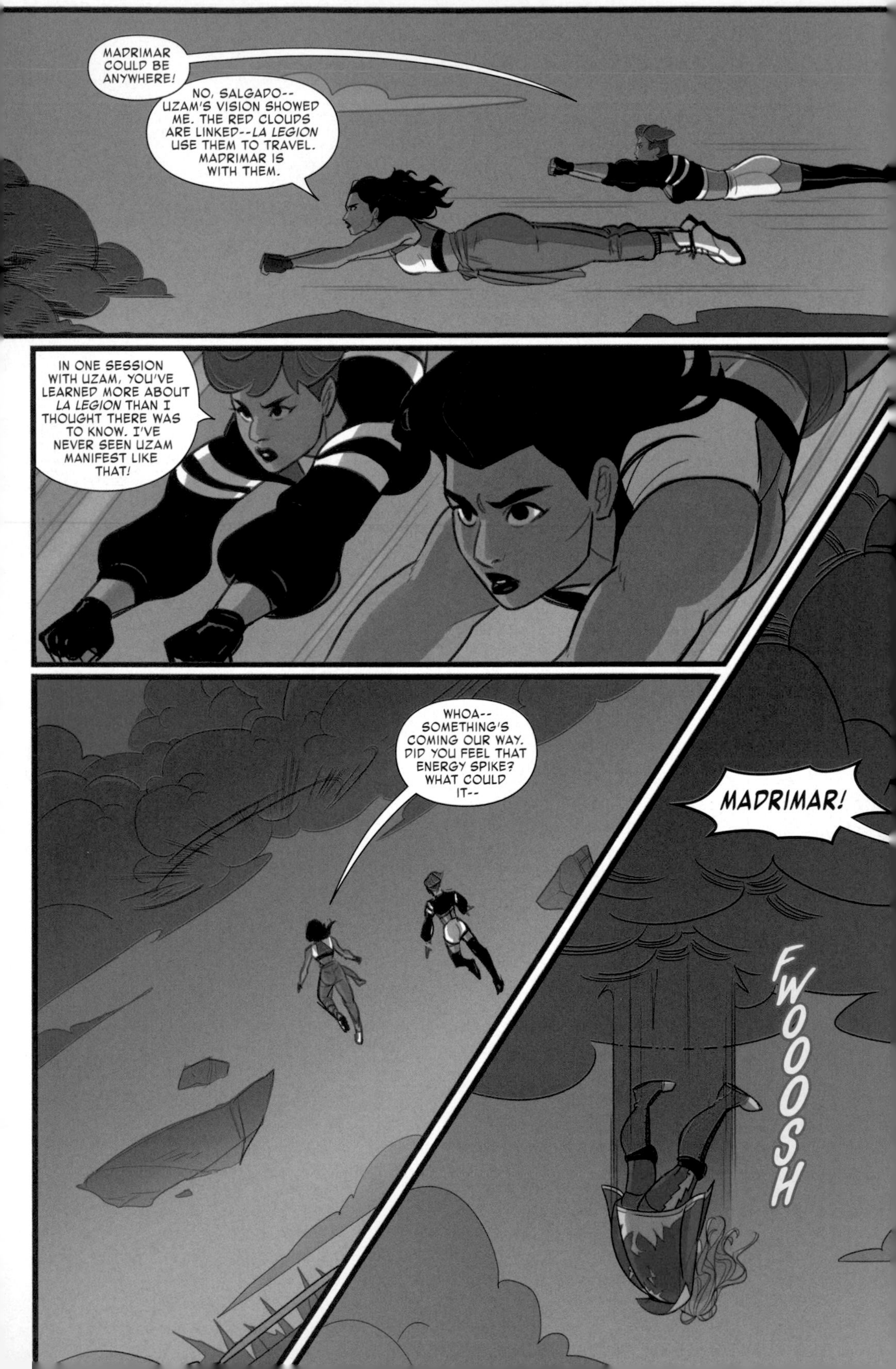

MADRIMAR COULD BE ANYWHERE!
NO, SALGADO-- UZAM'S VISION SHOWED ME. THE RED CLOUDS ARE LINKED--LA LEGION USE THEM TO TRAVEL. MADRIMAR IS WITH THEM.
IN ONE SESSION WITH UZAM, YOU'VE LEARNED MORE ABOUT LA LEGION THAN I THOUGHT THERE WAS TO KNOW. I'VE NEVER SEEN UZAM MANIFEST LIKE THAT!
WHOA-- SOMETHING'S COMING OUR WAY. DID YOU FEEL THAT ENERGY SPIKE? WHAT COULD IT--
MADRIMAR!
FWOOOSH

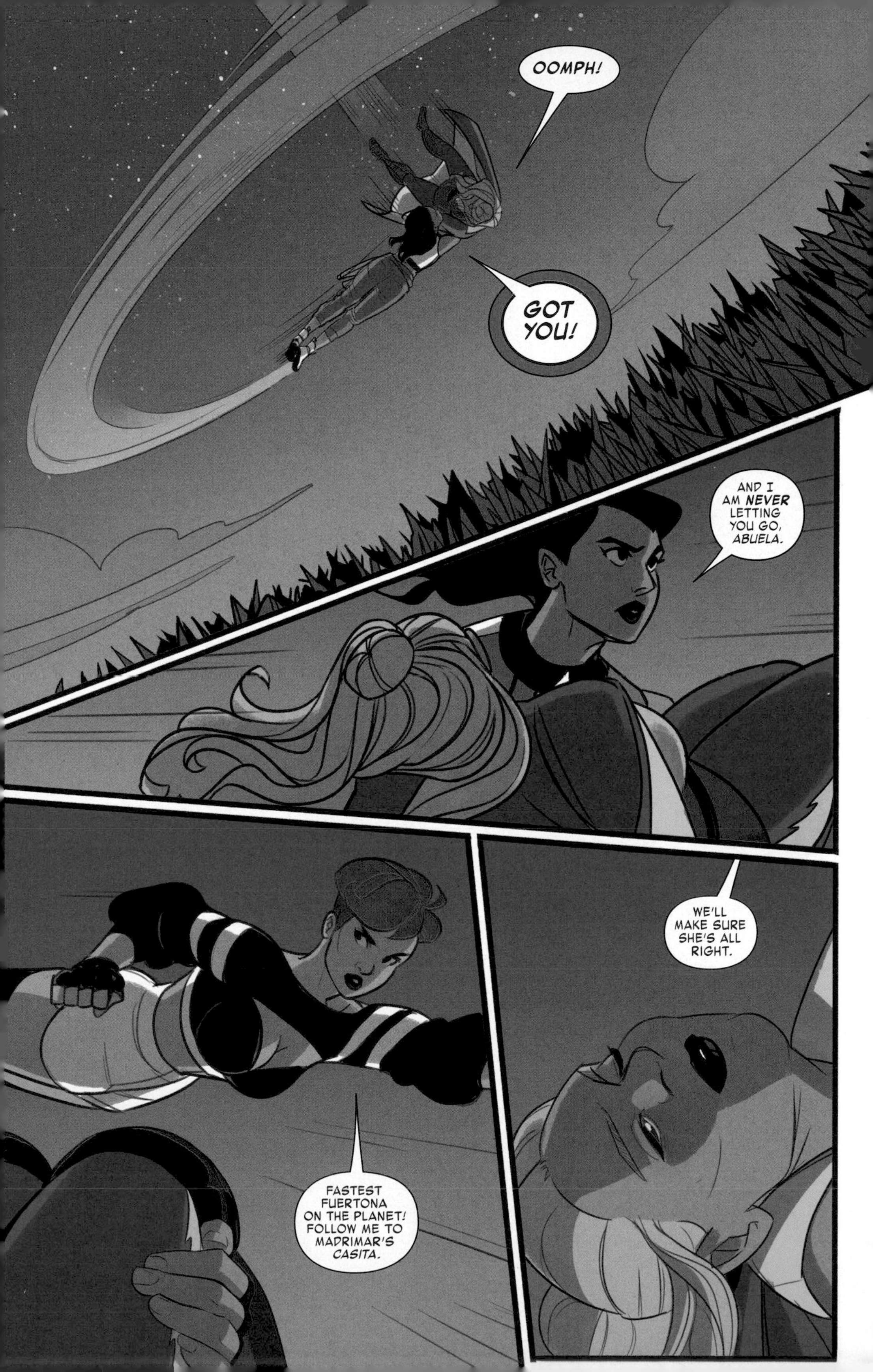
OOMPH!
GOT YOU!
AND I AM **NEVER** LETTING YOU GO, *ABUELA.*
FASTEST FUERTONA ON THE PLANET! FOLLOW ME TO MADRIMAR'S *CASITA.*
WE'LL MAKE SURE SHE'S ALL RIGHT.

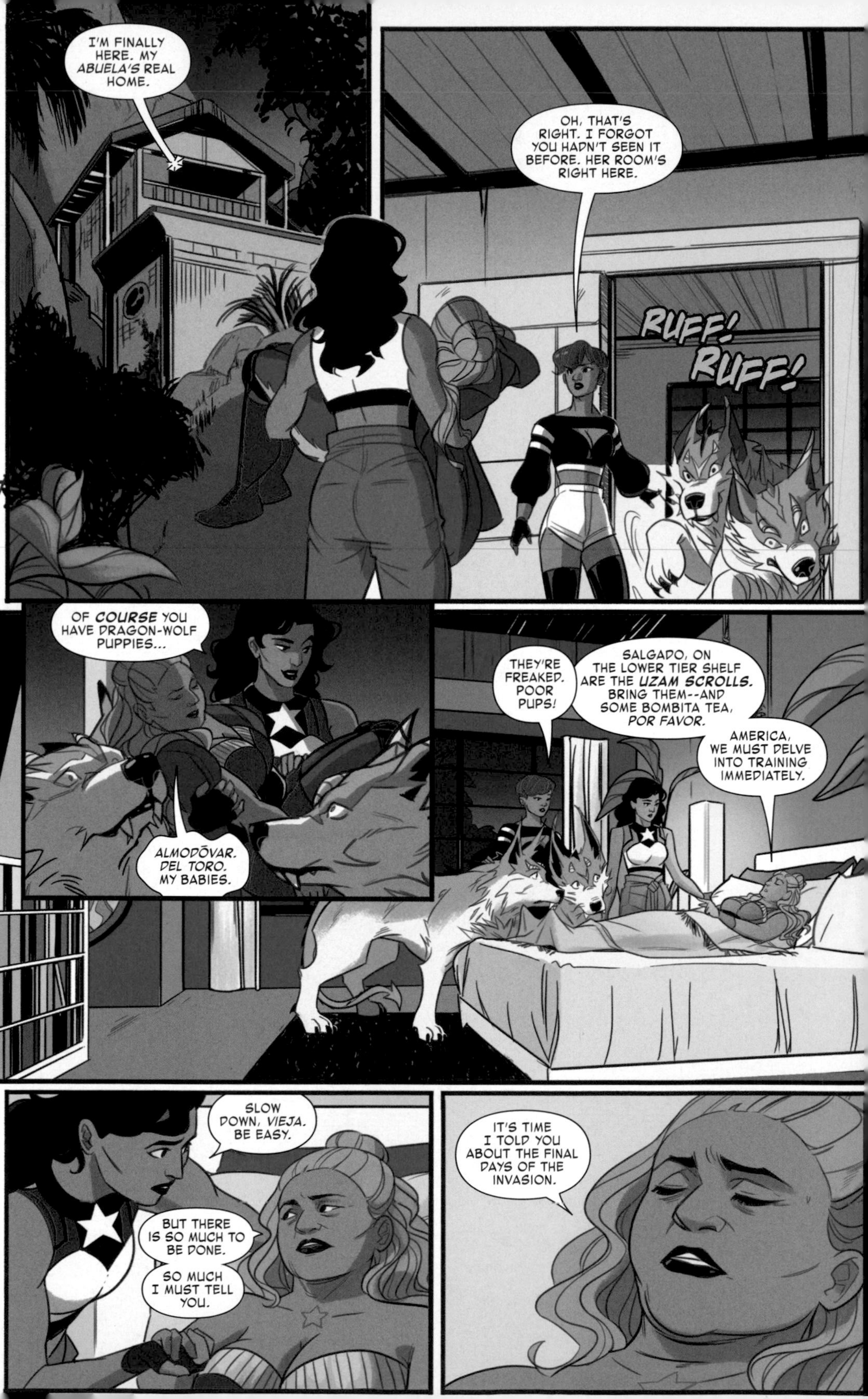
I'M FINALLY HERE. MY *ABUELA'S* REAL HOME.
OH, THAT'S RIGHT. I FORGOT YOU HADN'T SEEN IT BEFORE. HER ROOM'S RIGHT HERE.
RUFF! RUFF!
OF **COURSE** YOU HAVE DRAGON-WOLF PUPPIES...
ALMODÓVAR. DEL TORO. MY BABIES.
THEY'RE FREAKED. POOR PUPS!
SALGADO, ON THE LOWER TIER SHELF ARE THE ***UZAM SCROLLS.*** BRING THEM--AND SOME BOMBITA TEA, *POR FAVOR.*
AMERICA, WE MUST DELVE INTO TRAINING IMMEDIATELY.
SLOW DOWN, *VIEJA.* BE EASY.
BUT THERE IS SO MUCH TO BE DONE.
SO MUCH I MUST TELL YOU.
IT'S TIME I TOLD YOU ABOUT THE FINAL DAYS OF THE INVASION.

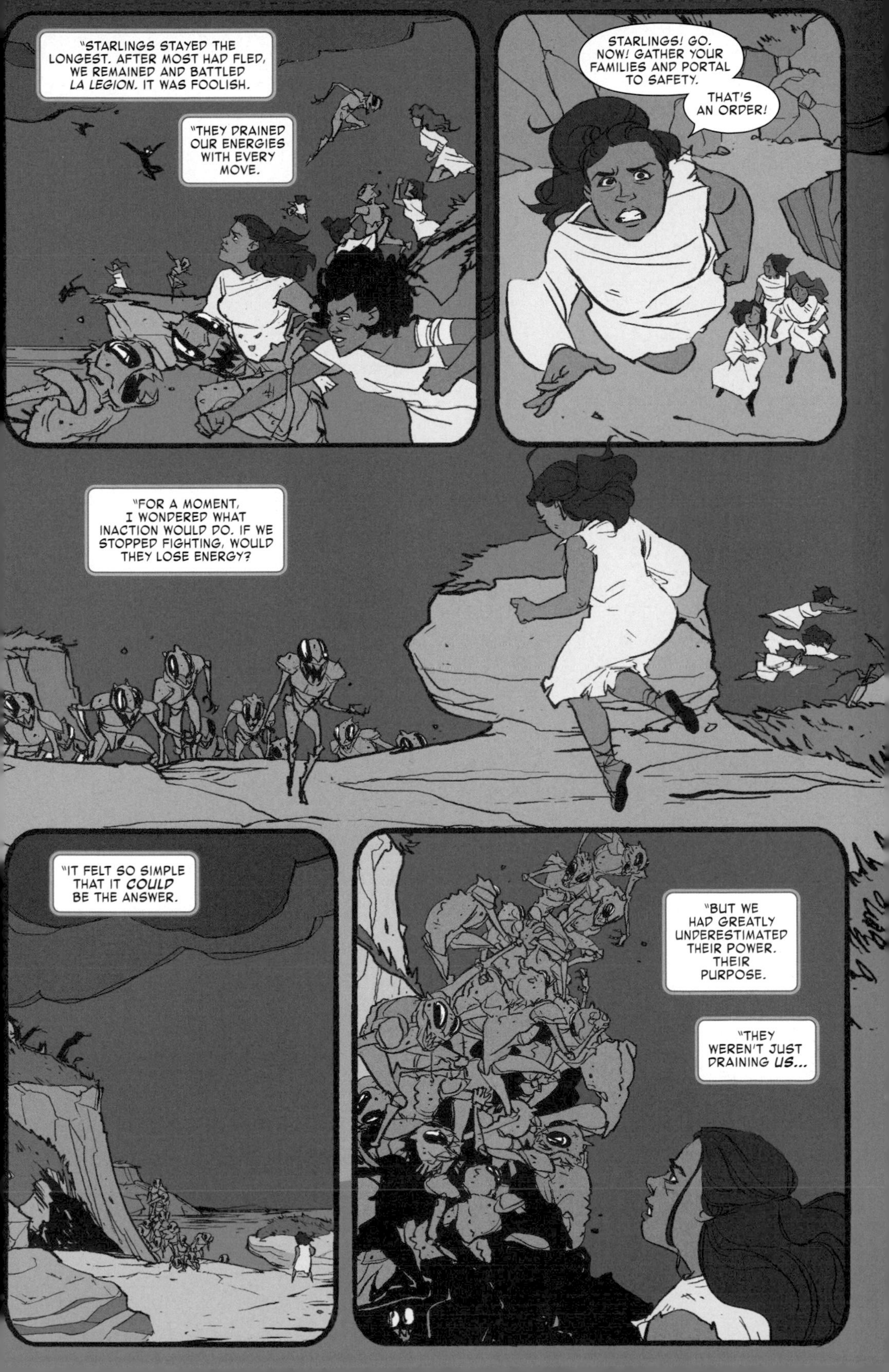
"STARLINGS STAYED THE LONGEST. AFTER MOST HAD FLED, WE REMAINED AND BATTLED LA LEGION. IT WAS FOOLISH.
"THEY DRAINED OUR ENERGIES WITH EVERY MOVE.
STARLINGS! GO. NOW! GATHER YOUR FAMILIES AND PORTAL TO SAFETY.
THAT'S AN ORDER!
"FOR A MOMENT, I WONDERED WHAT INACTION WOULD DO. IF WE STOPPED FIGHTING, WOULD THEY LOSE ENERGY?
"IT FELT SO SIMPLE THAT IT COULD BE THE ANSWER.
"BUT WE HAD GREATLY UNDERESTIMATED THEIR POWER. THEIR PURPOSE.
"THEY WEREN'T JUST DRAINING US...

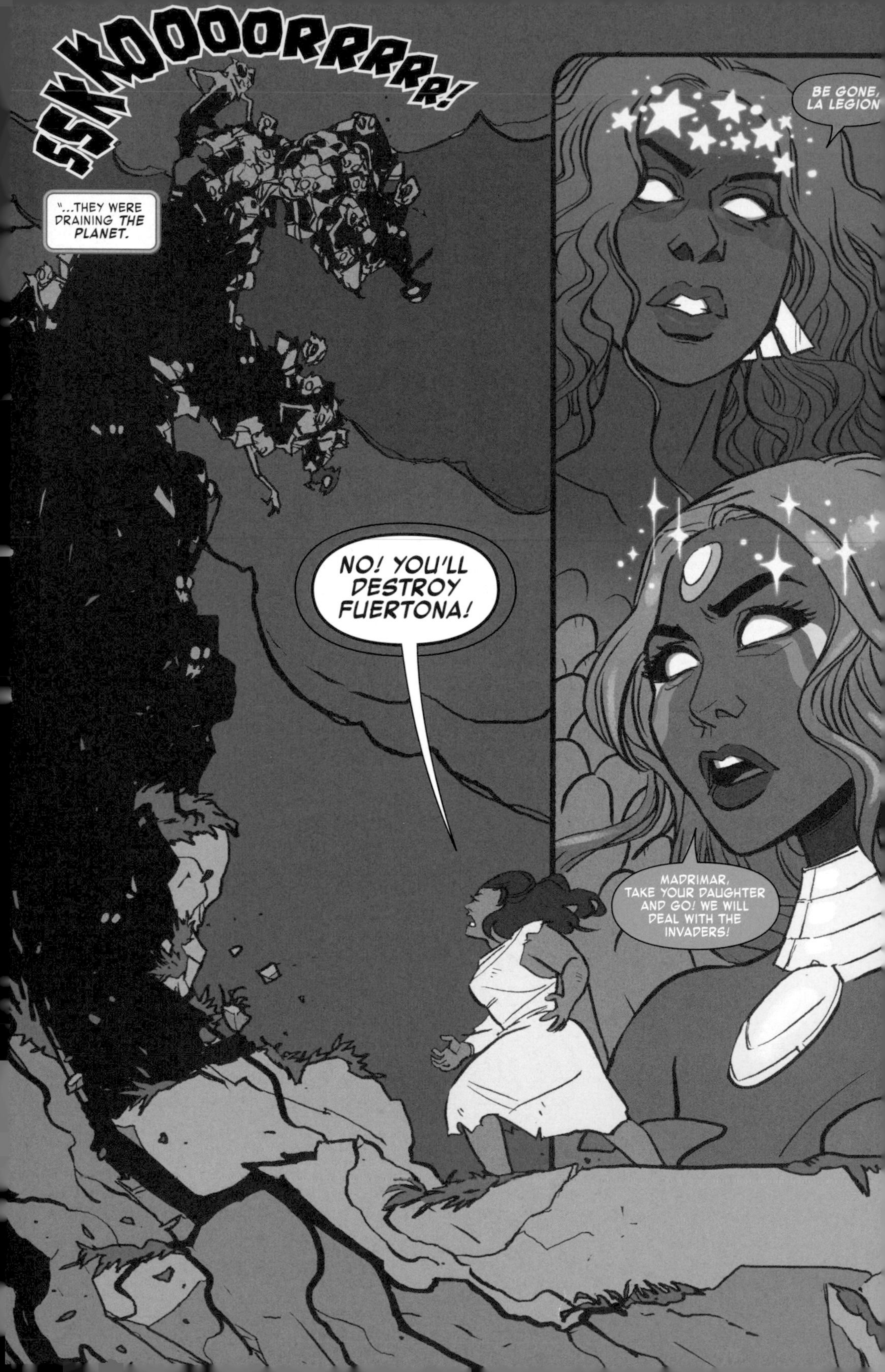
SSKOOOORRRRR!
"...THEY WERE DRAINING THE PLANET.
BE GONE, LA LEGION
NO! YOU'LL DESTROY FUERTONA!
MADRIMAR, TAKE YOUR DAUGHTER AND GO! WE WILL DEAL WITH THE INVADERS!

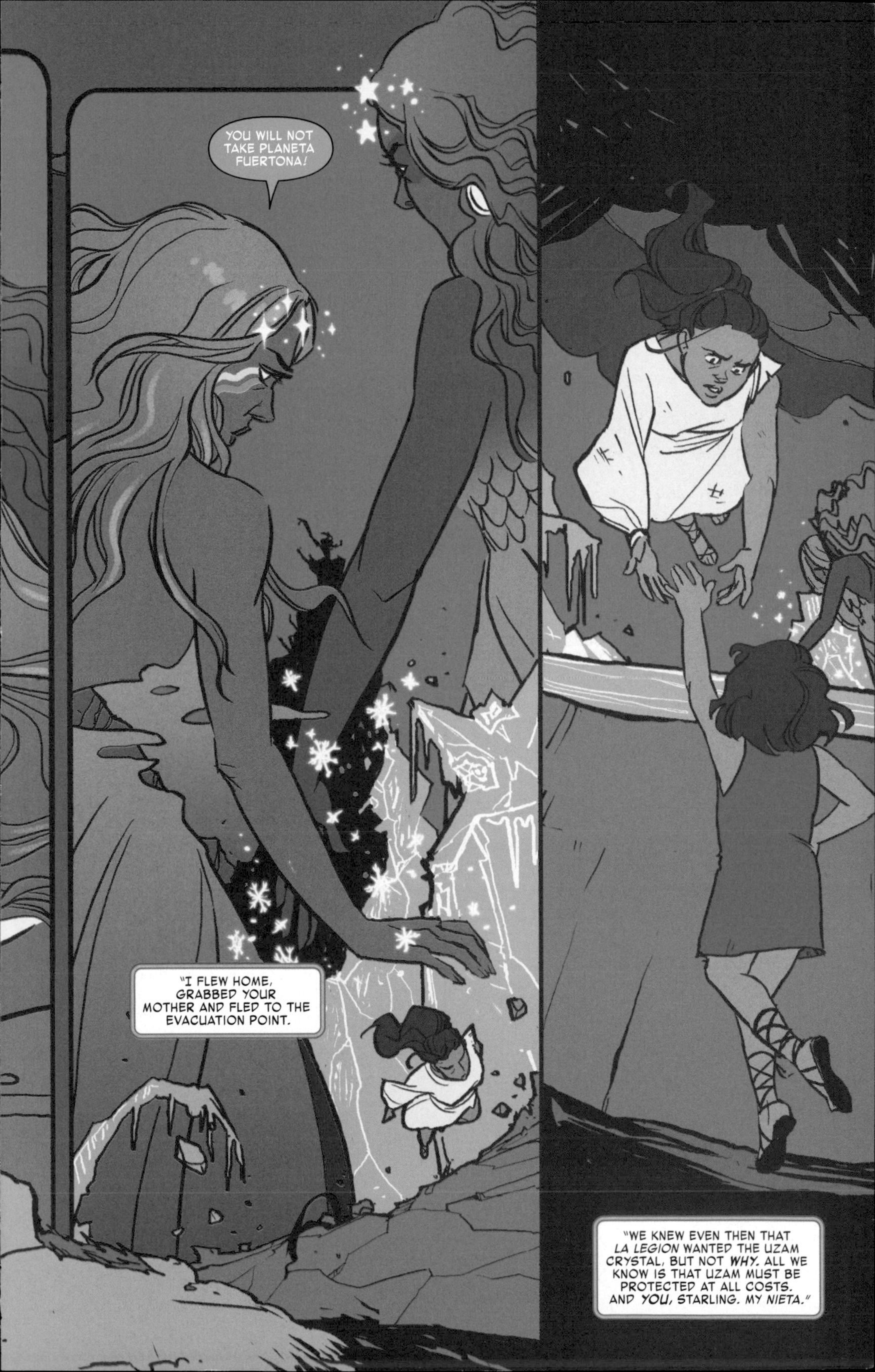
YOU WILL NOT TAKE PLANETA FUERTONA!
"I FLEW HOME, GRABBED YOUR MOTHER AND FLED TO THE EVACUATION POINT.
"WE KNEW EVEN THEN THAT *LA LEGION* WANTED THE UZAM CRYSTAL, BUT NOT *WHY*. ALL WE KNOW IS THAT UZAM MUST BE PROTECTED AT ALL COSTS. AND *YOU*, STARLING. MY *NIETA*."

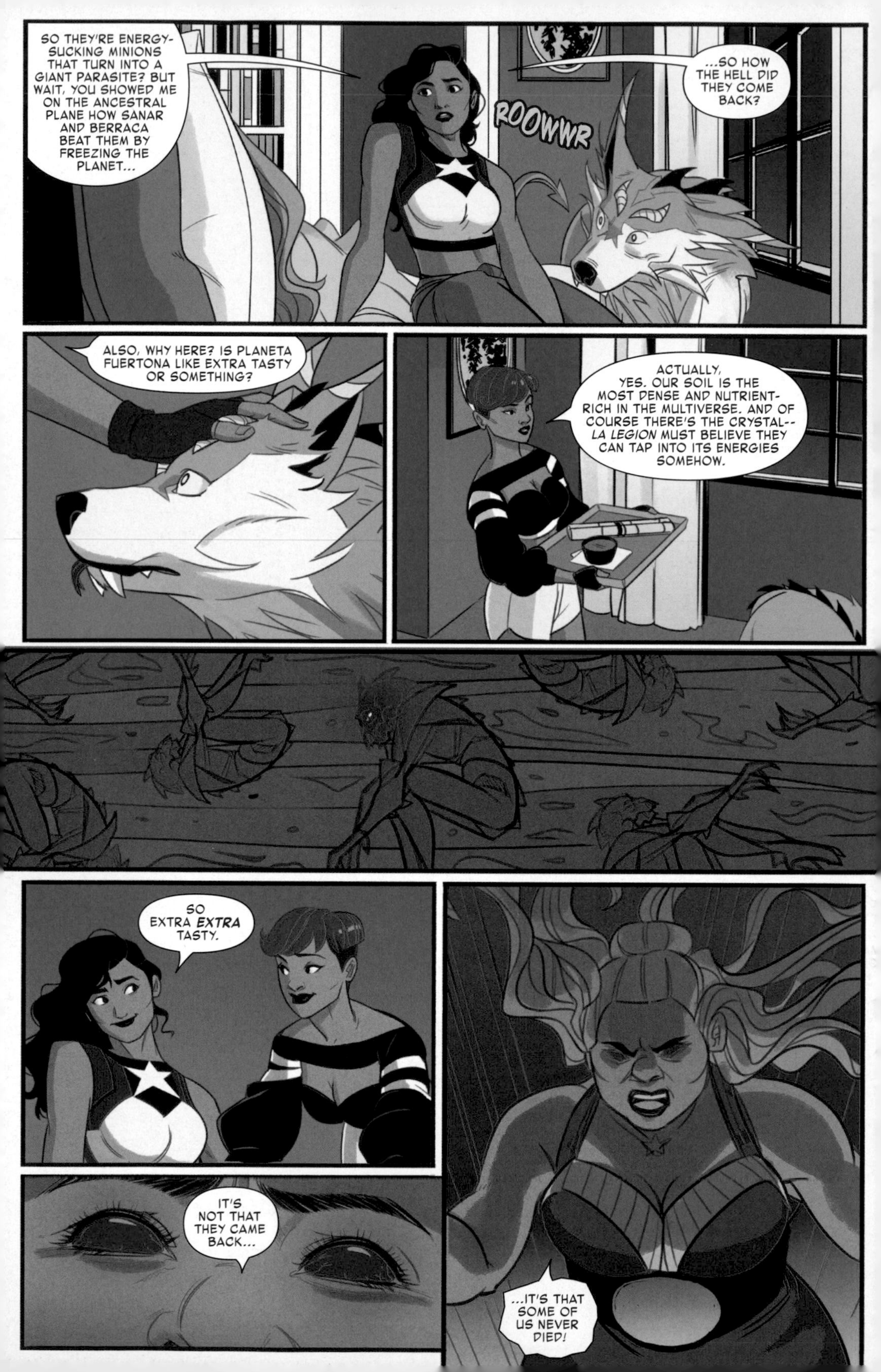
SO THEY'RE ENERGY-SUCKING MINIONS THAT TURN INTO A GIANT PARASITE? BUT WAIT, YOU SHOWED ME ON THE ANCESTRAL PLANE HOW SANAR AND BERRACA BEAT THEM BY FREEZING THE PLANET...
ROOWWR
...SO HOW THE HELL DID THEY COME BACK?
ALSO, WHY HERE? IS PLANETA FUERTONA LIKE EXTRA TASTY OR SOMETHING?
ACTUALLY, YES. OUR SOIL IS THE MOST DENSE AND NUTRIENT-RICH IN THE MULTIVERSE. AND OF COURSE THERE'S THE CRYSTAL-- *LA LEGION* MUST BELIEVE THEY CAN TAP INTO ITS ENERGIES SOMEHOW.
SO EXTRA ***EXTRA*** TASTY.
IT'S NOT THAT THEY CAME BACK...
...IT'S THAT SOME OF US NEVER DIED!

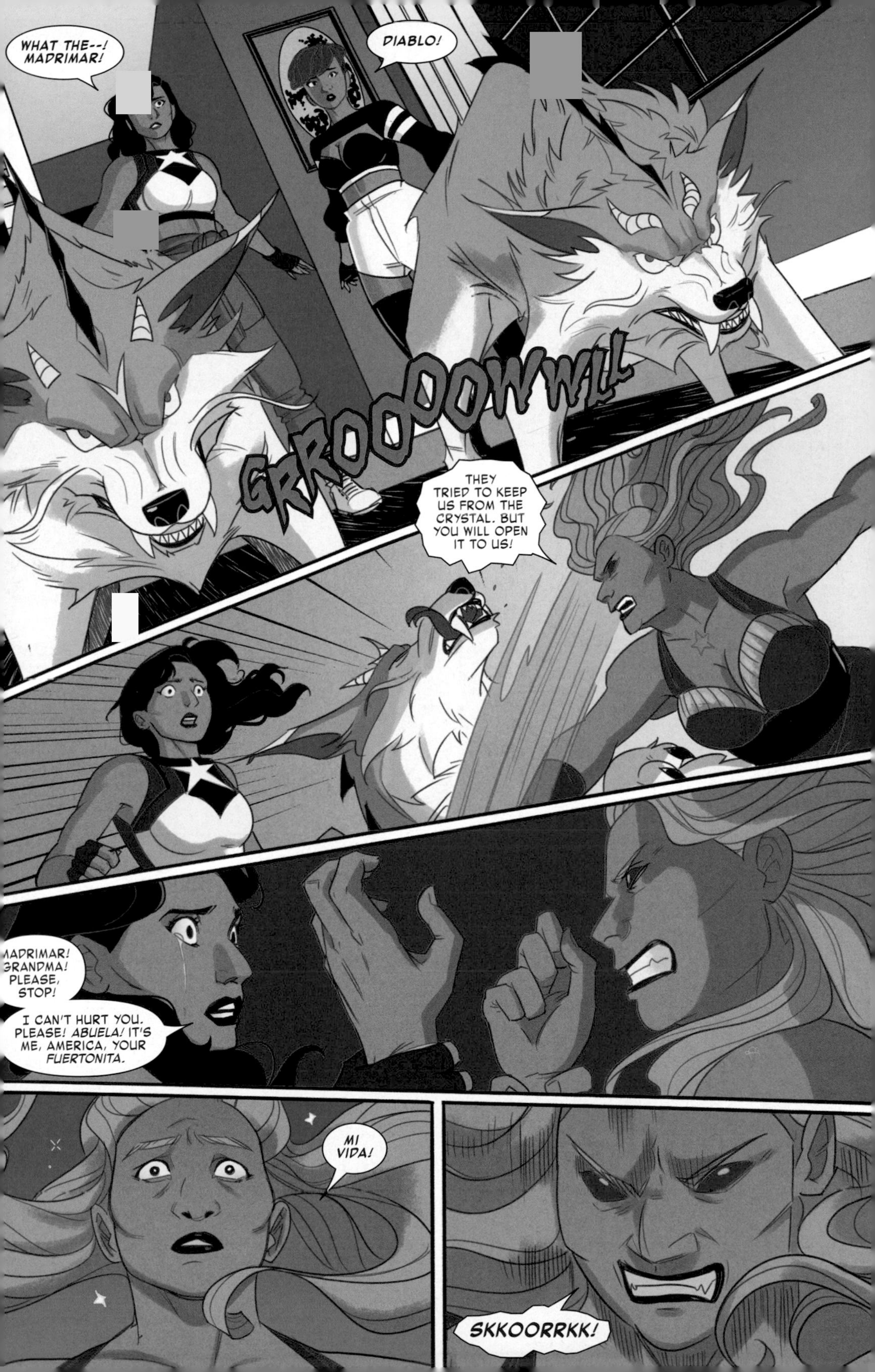
WHAT THE--! MADRIMAR!
DIABLO!
GROOOOWWLL!
THEY TRIED TO KEEP US FROM THE CRYSTAL. BUT YOU WILL OPEN IT TO US!
MADRIMAR! GRANDMA! PLEASE, STOP!
I CAN'T HURT YOU. PLEASE! ABUELA! IT'S ME, AMERICA, YOUR FUERTONITA.
MI VIDA!
SKKOORRKK!

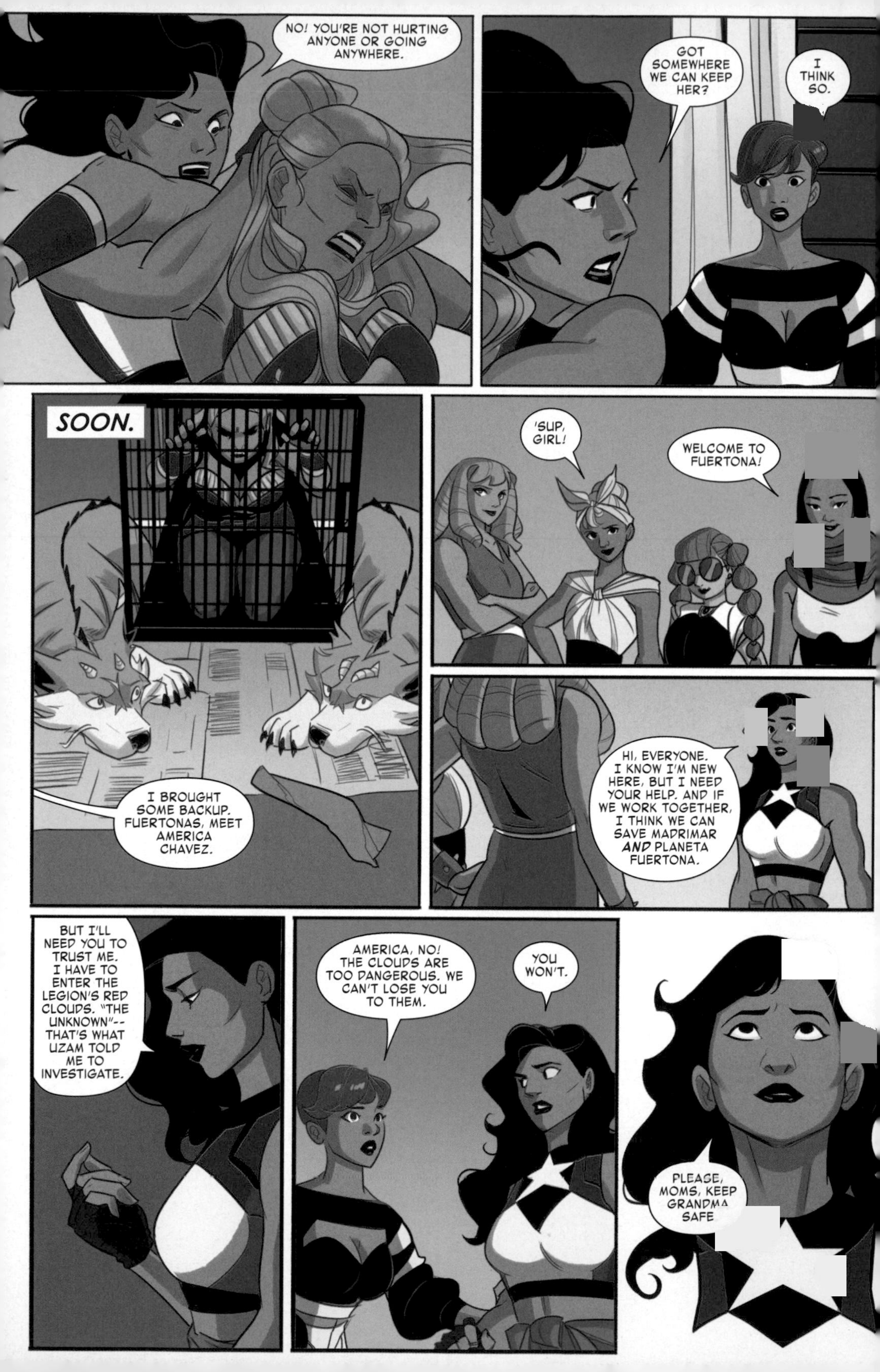
NO! YOU'RE NOT HURTING ANYONE OR GOING ANYWHERE.
GOT SOMEWHERE WE CAN KEEP HER?
I THINK SO.
SOON.
I BROUGHT SOME BACKUP. FUERTONAS, MEET AMERICA CHAVEZ.
'SUP, GIRL!
WELCOME TO FUERTONA!
HI, EVERYONE. I KNOW I'M NEW HERE, BUT I NEED YOUR HELP. AND IF WE WORK TOGETHER, I THINK WE CAN SAVE MADRIMAR AND PLANETA FUERTONA.
BUT I'LL NEED YOU TO TRUST ME. I HAVE TO ENTER THE LEGION'S RED CLOUDS. "THE UNKNOWN"-- THAT'S WHAT UZAM TOLD ME TO INVESTIGATE.
AMERICA, NO! THE CLOUDS ARE TOO DANGEROUS. WE CAN'T LOSE YOU TO THEM.
YOU WON'T.
PLEASE, MOMS, KEEP GRANDMA SAFE

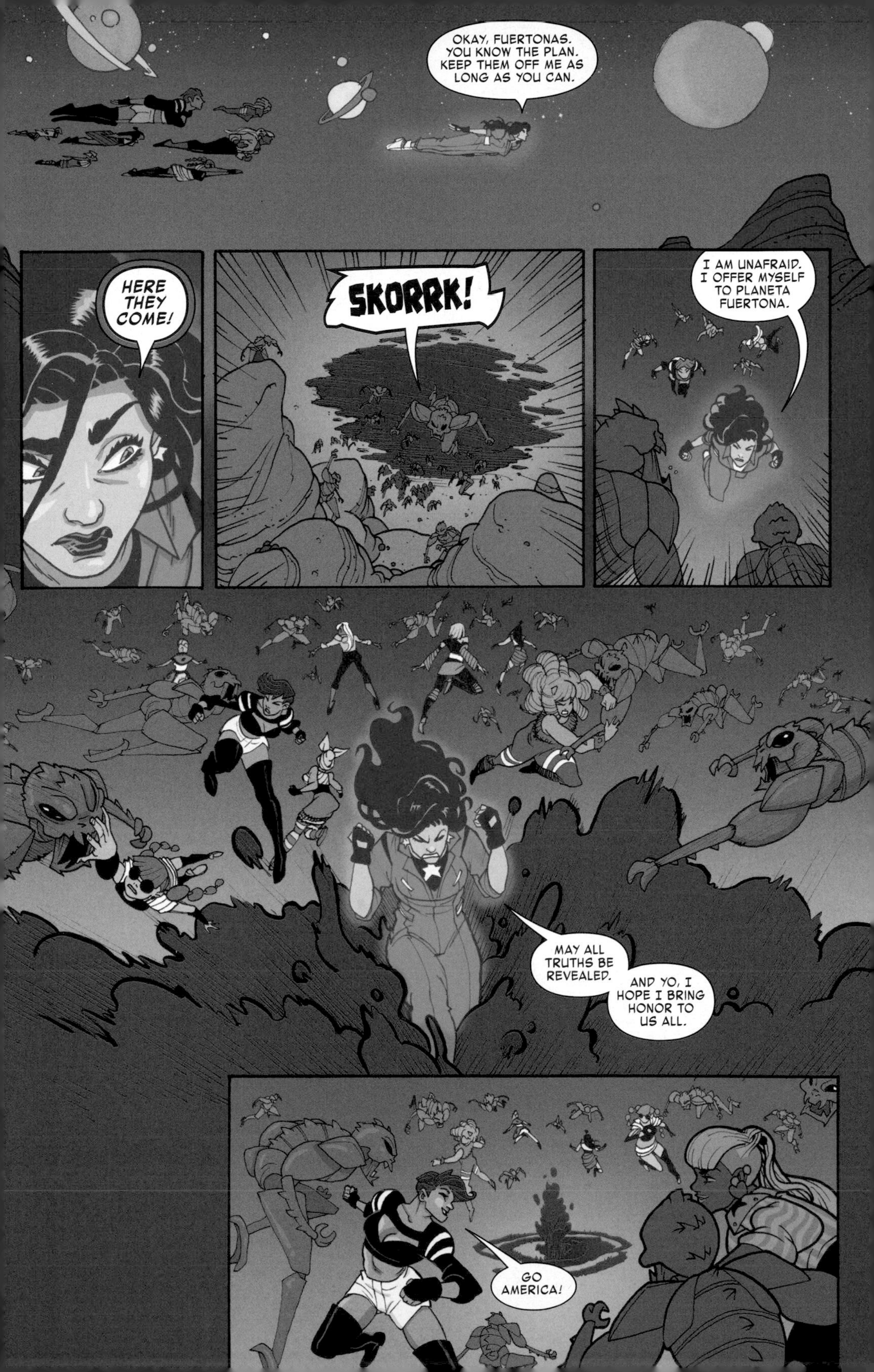

OKAY, FUERTONAS. YOU KNOW THE PLAN. KEEP THEM OFF ME AS LONG AS YOU CAN.
HERE THEY COME!
SKORRK!
I AM UNAFRAID. I OFFER MYSELF TO PLANETA FUERTONA.
MAY ALL TRUTHS BE REVEALED.
AND YO, I HOPE I BRING HONOR TO US ALL.
GO AMERICA!

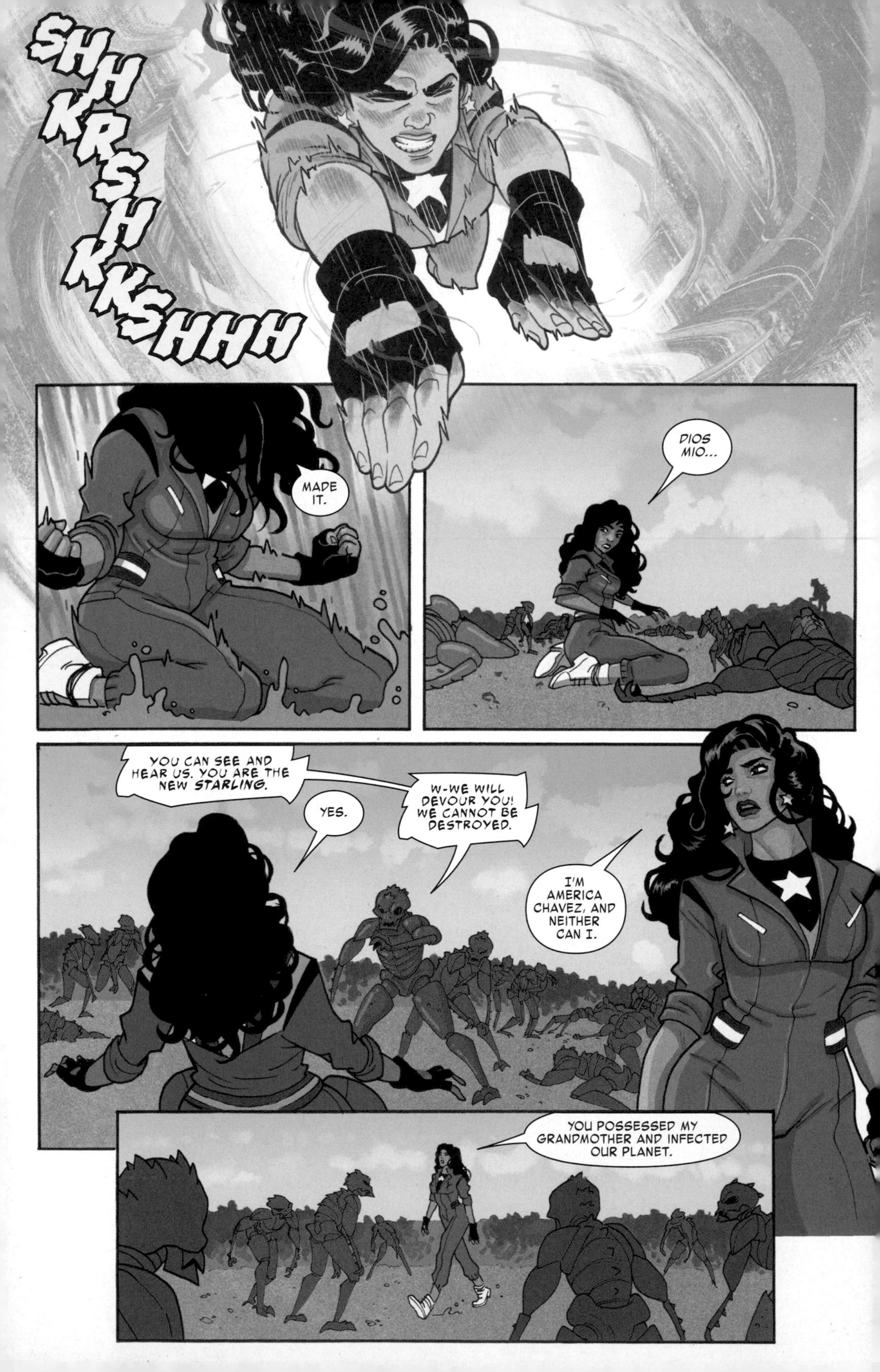
SHHKRSHKKSHHH
MADE IT.
DIOS MIO...
YOU CAN SEE AND HEAR US. YOU ARE THE NEW STARLING.
YES.
W-WE WILL DEVOUR YOU! WE CANNOT BE DESTROYED.
I'M AMERICA CHAVEZ, AND NEITHER CAN I.
YOU POSSESSED MY GRANDMOTHER AND INFECTED OUR PLANET.

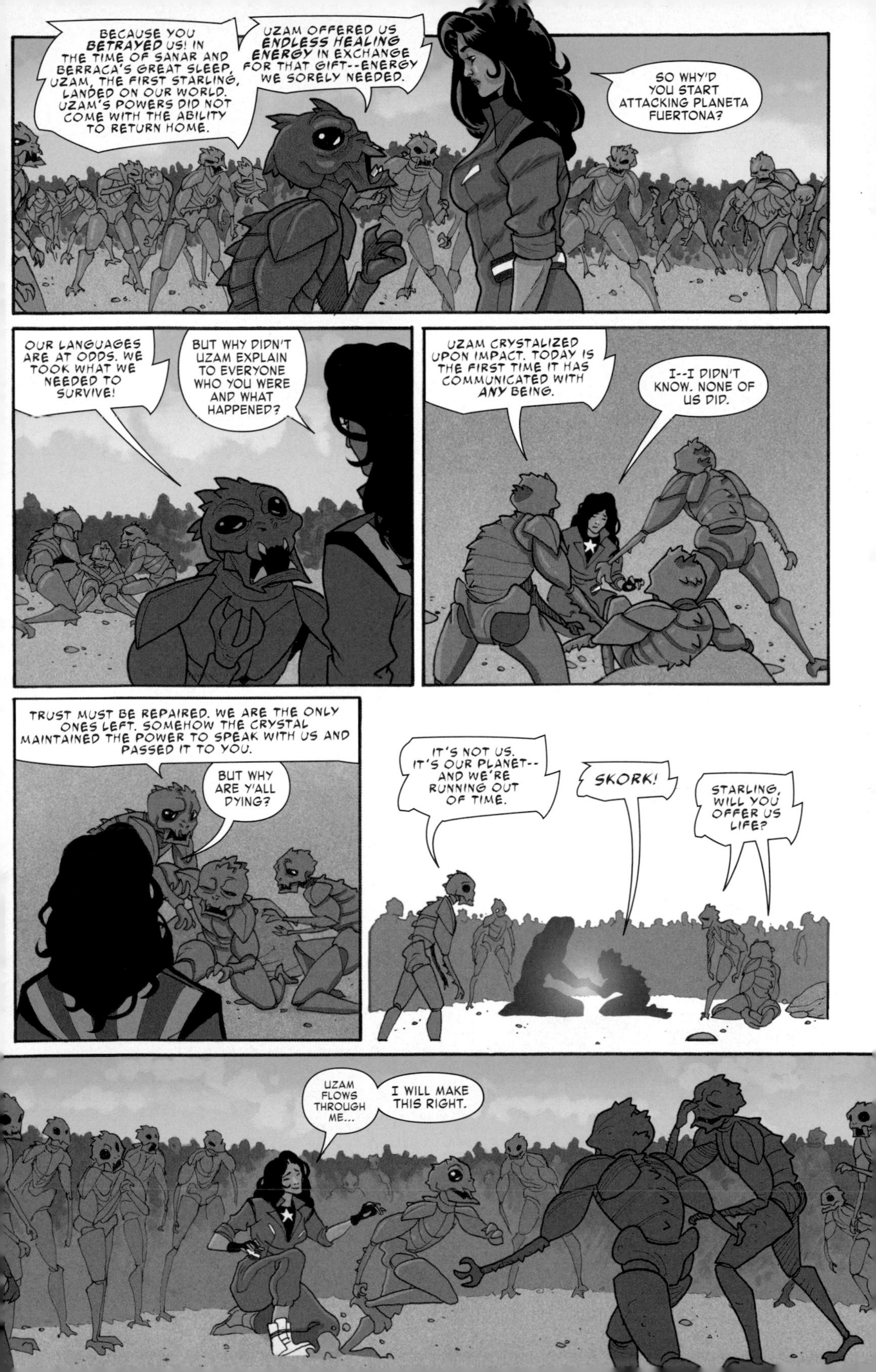
BECAUSE YOU BETRAYED US! IN THE TIME OF SANAR AND BERRACA'S GREAT SLEEP, UZAM, THE FIRST STARLING, LANDED ON OUR WORLD. UZAM'S POWERS DID NOT COME WITH THE ABILITY TO RETURN HOME.
UZAM OFFERED US ENDLESS HEALING ENERGY IN EXCHANGE FOR THAT GIFT--ENERGY WE SORELY NEEDED.
SO WHY'D YOU START ATTACKING PLANETA FUERTONA?
OUR LANGUAGES ARE AT ODDS. WE TOOK WHAT WE NEEDED TO SURVIVE!
BUT WHY DIDN'T UZAM EXPLAIN TO EVERYONE WHO YOU WERE AND WHAT HAPPENED?
UZAM CRYSTALIZED UPON IMPACT. TODAY IS THE FIRST TIME IT HAS COMMUNICATED WITH ANY BEING.
I--I DIDN'T KNOW. NONE OF US DID.
TRUST MUST BE REPAIRED. WE ARE THE ONLY ONES LEFT. SOMEHOW THE CRYSTAL MAINTAINED THE POWER TO SPEAK WITH US AND PASSED IT TO YOU.
BUT WHY ARE Y'ALL DYING?
IT'S NOT US. IT'S OUR PLANET-- AND WE'RE RUNNING OUT OF TIME.
SKORK!
STARLING, WILL YOU OFFER US LIFE?
UZAM FLOWS THROUGH ME...
I WILL MAKE THIS RIGHT.

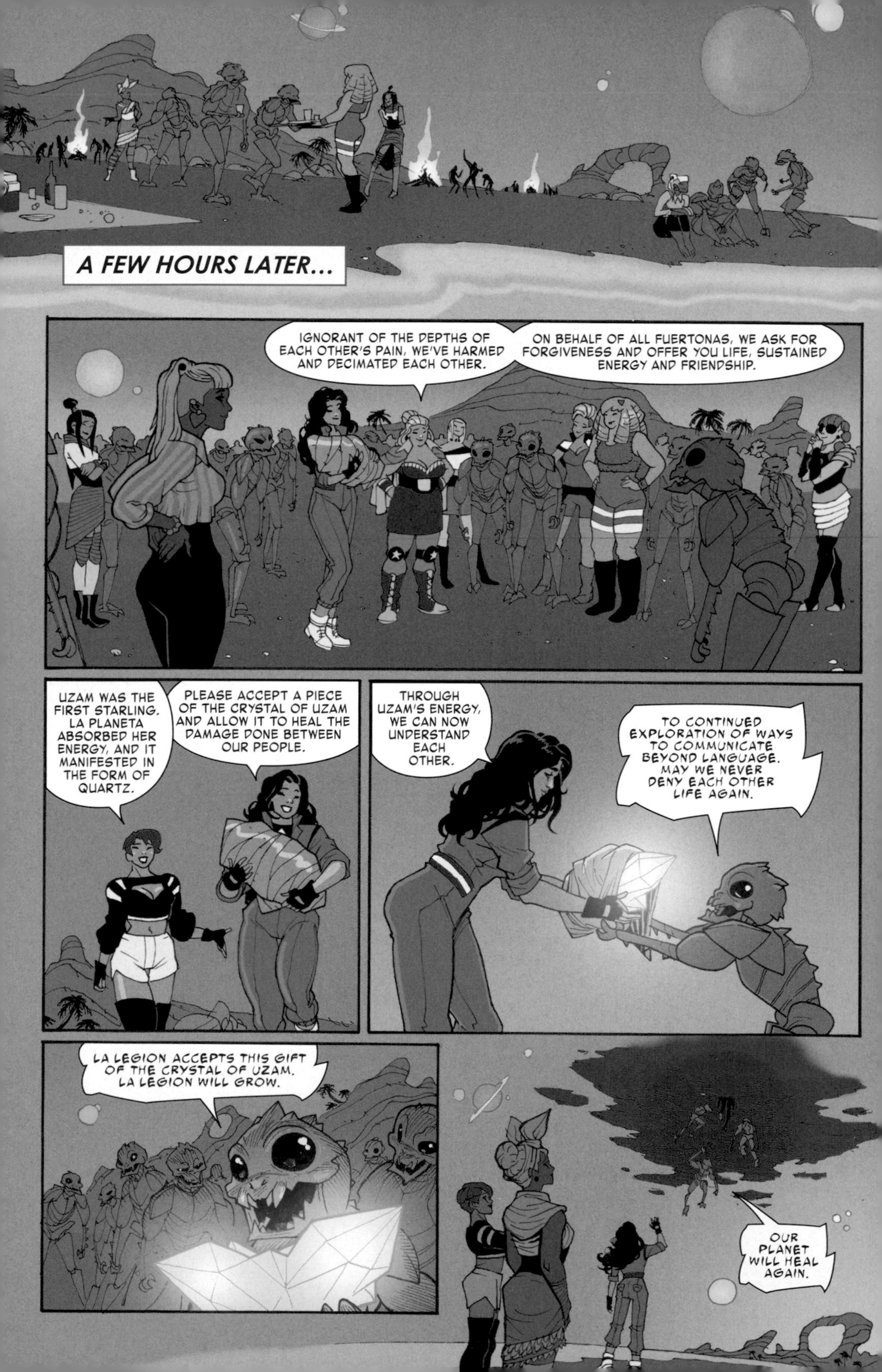
A FEW HOURS LATER...
IGNORANT OF THE DEPTHS OF EACH OTHER'S PAIN, WE'VE HARMED AND DECIMATED EACH OTHER.
ON BEHALF OF ALL FUERTONAS, WE ASK FOR FORGIVENESS AND OFFER YOU LIFE, SUSTAINED ENERGY AND FRIENDSHIP.
UZAM WAS THE FIRST STARLING. LA PLANETA ABSORBED HER ENERGY, AND IT MANIFESTED IN THE FORM OF QUARTZ.
PLEASE ACCEPT A PIECE OF THE CRYSTAL OF UZAM AND ALLOW IT TO HEAL THE DAMAGE DONE BETWEEN OUR PEOPLE.
THROUGH UZAM'S ENERGY, WE CAN NOW UNDERSTAND EACH OTHER.
TO CONTINUED EXPLORATION OF WAYS TO COMMUNICATE BEYOND LANGUAGE. MAY WE NEVER DENY EACH OTHER LIFE AGAIN.
LA LEGION ACCEPTS THIS GIFT OF THE CRYSTAL OF UZAM. LA LEGION WILL GROW.
OUR PLANET WILL HEAL AGAIN.

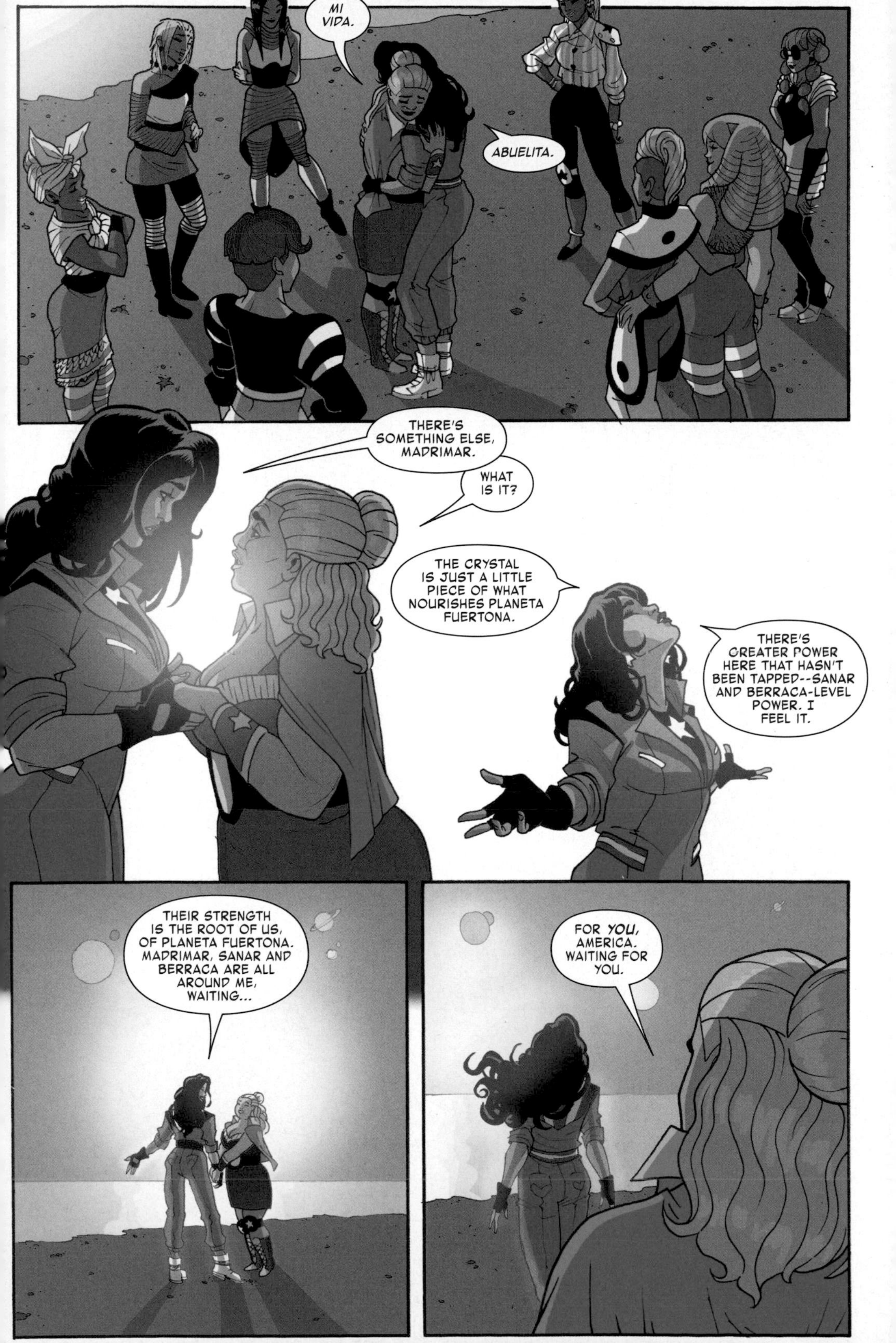
MI VIDA.
ABUELITA.
THERE'S SOMETHING ELSE, MADRIMAR.
WHAT IS IT?
THE CRYSTAL IS JUST A LITTLE PIECE OF WHAT NOURISHES PLANETA FUERTONA.
THERE'S GREATER POWER HERE THAT HASN'T BEEN TAPPED--SANAR AND BERRACA-LEVEL POWER. I FEEL IT.
THEIR STRENGTH IS THE ROOT OF US, OF PLANETA FUERTONA. MADRIMAR, SANAR AND BERRACA ARE ALL AROUND ME, WAITING...
FOR YOU, AMERICA. WAITING FOR YOU.

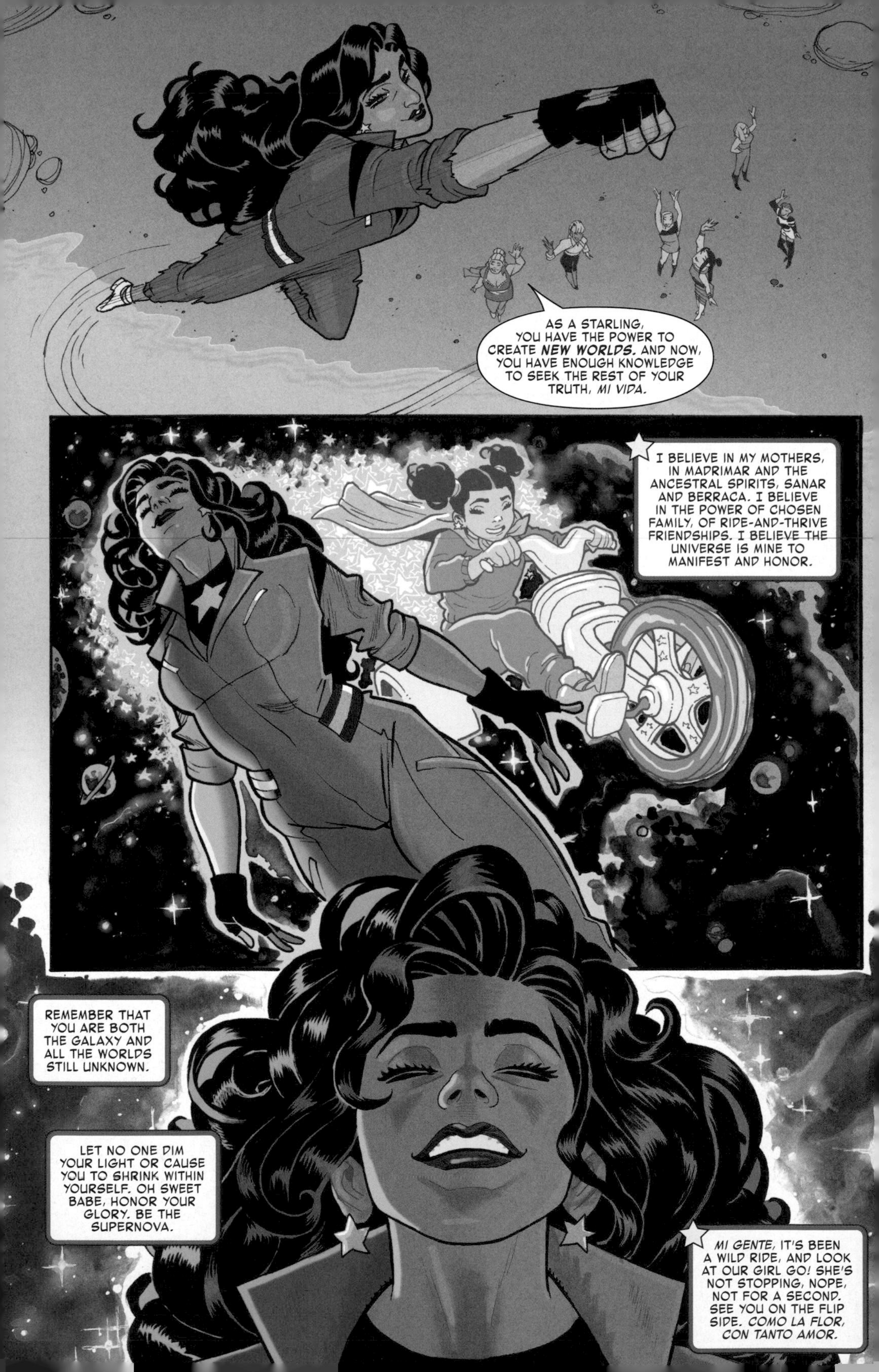
AS A STARLING, YOU HAVE THE POWER TO CREATE *NEW WORLDS.* AND NOW, YOU HAVE ENOUGH KNOWLEDGE TO SEEK THE REST OF YOUR TRUTH, *MI VIDA.*
I BELIEVE IN MY MOTHERS, IN MADRIMAR AND THE ANCESTRAL SPIRITS, SANAR AND BERRACA. I BELIEVE IN THE POWER OF CHOSEN FAMILY, OF RIDE-AND-THRIVE FRIENDSHIPS. I BELIEVE THE UNIVERSE IS MINE TO MANIFEST AND HONOR.
REMEMBER THAT YOU ARE BOTH THE GALAXY AND ALL THE WORLDS STILL UNKNOWN.
LET NO ONE DIM YOUR LIGHT OR CAUSE YOU TO SHRINK WITHIN YOURSELF. OH SWEET BABE, HONOR YOUR GLORY. BE THE SUPERNOVA.
MI GENTE, IT'S BEEN A WILD RIDE, AND LOOK AT OUR GIRL GO! SHE'S NOT STOPPING, NOPE, NOT FOR A SECOND. SEE YOU ON THE FLIP SIDE. *COMO LA FLOR, CON TANTO AMOR.*

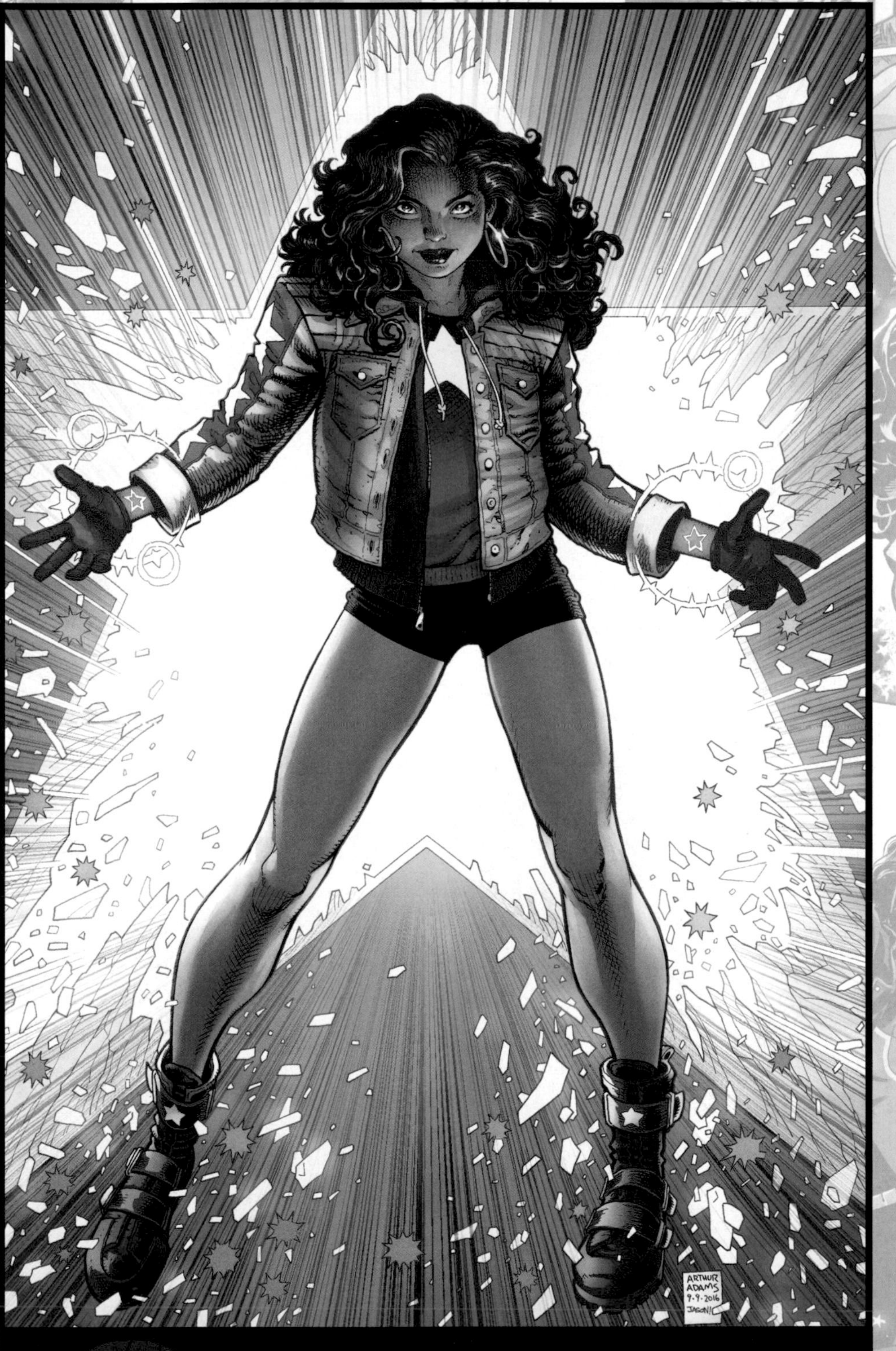

AMERICA #2 VARIANT

BY ARTHUR ADAMS & JASON KEITH

AMERICA #2 VARIANT

BY MARGUERITE SAUVAGE